Book One of the Bellême series

The
**RAVEN**
the
**LION**
and the
**WHITE**
**DRAGON**

by Roy Stedall-Humphrycs

Copyright © 2017  Roy Stedall-Humphryes
ISBN-13: 978-1543225990
ISBN-10: 1543225993

Library of Congress Control Number: 2017902703
CreateSpace Independent Publishing Platform,
North Charleston, SC
U.S.A.

All rights reserved.
No part of this publication
may be reproduced, stored in a retrievable system,
or transmitted, in any form or by any means,
without the prior permission
in writing of the author.

www.roystedallhumphryes.com

Cover,
Maps and illustrations
are the property of the author.

## ACKNOWLEDGEMENTS

I give thanks to the tremendous facilities
of the British Library,
Archives Départementales de L'Orn and
the many historians including,
Ian W. Walker and
the late Professor Frank Barlow whose books
opened up the 11$^{th}$ century medieval world to me.
I also wish to thank
'The Writers' Workshop' and
the author, Julia Hamilton whose detailed analysis and
wise council has been a lesson in itself. The support of my family,
especially my wife Linda
whose judgement, unselfish support and editorial advice
has kept me focused especially in the
final draft of this book.

To my wife
Linda

# CONTENTS

Acknowledgements ................................................................. page 005
Dedication ............................................................................. page 006
Place names and their Anglo Saxon equivalents ................. page 013

### Maps
British Isles and London in the 11th c. ............................... page 008
England and Normandy in the 11th c. ................................. page 009

### Family trees
Wulfnoth and Edric ............................................................. page 010
House of Godwin ................................................................ page 011
Ducal house of William of Normandy ................................ page 012

Prologue .............................................................................. page 019

| | | |
|---|---|---|
| I | Duke William's fortress, Rouen, Normandy ............... | page 021 |
| II | Farndon Bridge a Welsh crossing point ....................... | page 026 |
| III | London, the River Thames ........................................... | page 062 |
| IV | Earl Harold's New Year court ...................................... | page 087 |
| V | On board ship bound for Flanders ............................... | page 097 |
| VI | Rouen, Normandy ......................................................... | page 108 |
| VII | Dover, Kent .................................................................. | page 113 |
| VIII | Bradwell-on-Sea, Essex ............................................... | page 135 |
| IX | Night visitor - Upper Barnstæd ................................... | page 160 |
| X | Easter court, Winchester, Hampshire .......................... | page 174 |
| XI | The training of Wulfnoth and Edric ............................ | page 183 |
| XII | A lightning strike ......................................................... | page 189 |
| XIII | The Royal Palace at West Minster ............................... | page 224 |
| XIV | Upper Barnstæd ............................................................ | page 253 |
| XV | Rouen, Normandy ......................................................... | page 271 |
| XVI | Upper Barnstæd ............................................................ | page 287 |
| XVII | Newgate, London .......................................................... | page 305 |
| XVIII | A meeting at Southwark, London ................................ | page 338 |
| XIX | The King's Palace, West Minster ................................. | page 363 |
| XX | The Vintry .................................................................... | page 382 |
| XXI | Bad news from the south ............................................. | page 419 |

*Anglo Saxon place names prior to 1066*

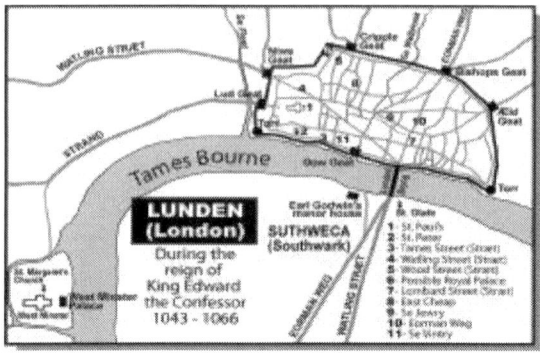

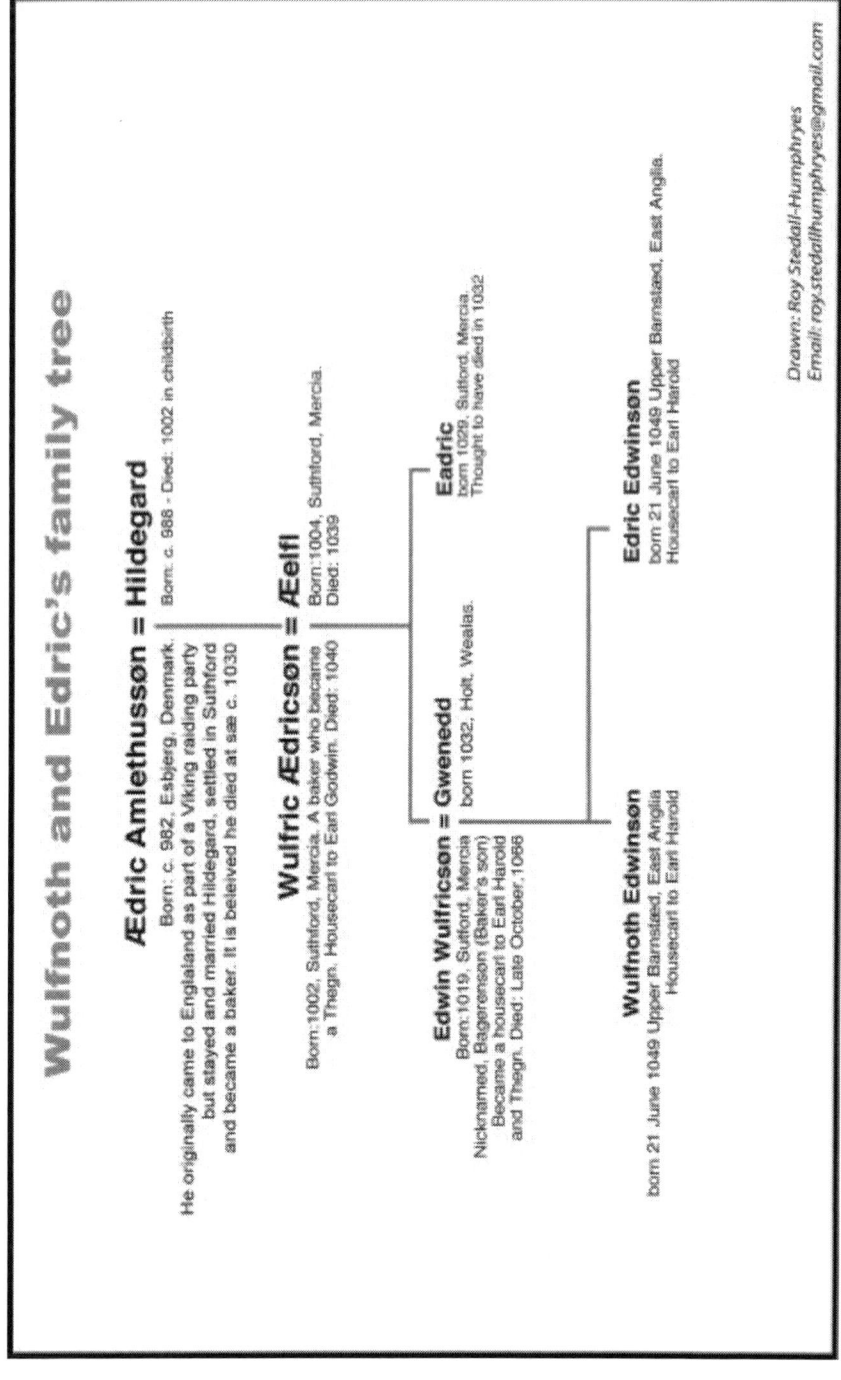

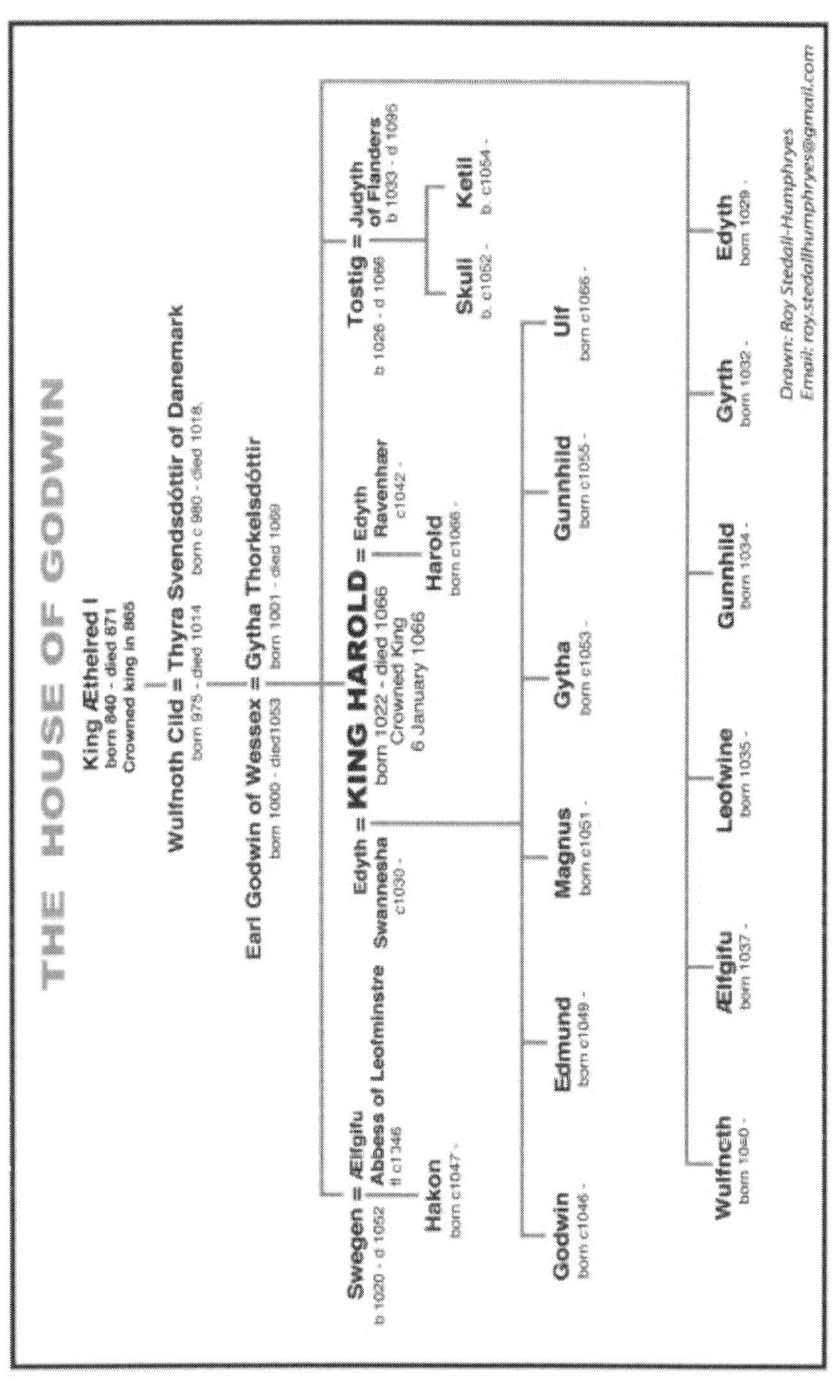

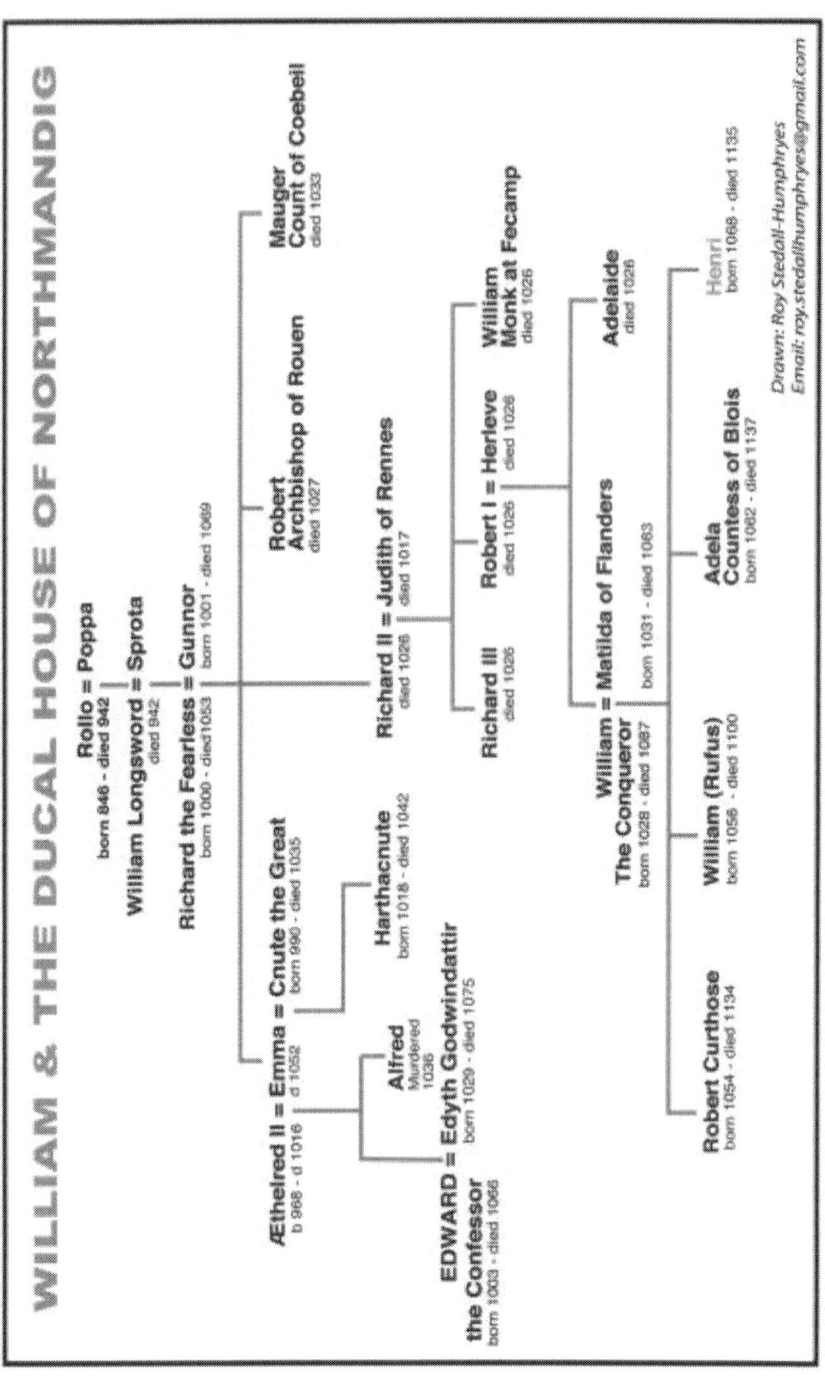

# PLACE NAMES & THEIR ANGLO SAXON EQUIVALENTS ETC.

For the reader to appreciate the different spellings of place names in Anglo Saxon England in the 11c, I have drawn up this list. Of course name spellings themselves at that time showed little consistency also the boundaries of the various Earldoms changed, it seemed from year to year.

Ambleside, Cumbria........................... **Hamel Sætre, Northymbria.**
Badbury, Dorset................................. **Badbyri, Wessex.**
Beverston, Gloucester........................ **Beverstane, Mercia.**
Bradwell-on-Sea, Essex..................... **Ithancester, East Anglia.**
Broxton, Cheshire.............................. **Brocctun, Mercia.**
Bath, Somerset................................... **Bathum, Wessex.**
Bicester, Oxfordshire......................... **Burencestre, Mercia.**
Bosham, West Sussex........................ **Bosham, Wessex.**
Bristol, Bristol................................... **Brycgsstow, Wessex.**
Canterbury, Kent................................ **Cantwareburh, (Cent) Wessex.**
Carmarthen, Wales............................. **Llanteulyddog, Wealh.**
Canvey Island, Essex......................... **Convennon Teg, East Anglia.**
Cardiff, Wales.................................... **Cærtaff, Wealh.**
Carlisle, Northumberland................... **Cærluel, Northymbria.**
Caster, Hertfordshire......................... **Ceaster, Mercia.**
Chester, Cheshire............................... **Legeceaster, Mercia.**
Colchester, Essex............................... **Colne Ceaster, East Anglia.**
Corringham, Essex............................. **Corring Ham, East Anglia.**
Coventry, Warwickshire.................... **Coventre, Mercia.**
Cirencester, Gloucestershire.............. **Cyrescestre, Wessex.**
Doncaster, South Yorkshire............... **Cair Daun, Northymbria.**
Dorchester, Dorset............................. **Dornwaracaster, Wessex.**
Dover, Kent....................................... **Dofras, (Cent) Wessex.**
Dublin, Ireland................................... **Duiblinn, Erinn.**
Dungeness, Kent................................ **Denge Nes, Wessex.**
Ely, Cambridgeshire.......................... **Ellg, East Anglia.**
Exeter, Devon.................................... **Escanceaster, Wessex.**
Farndon Bridge, Cheshire.................. **Fardune brycg, Mercia.**
Fulford Gate, Yorkshire..................... **Fulfordegade, Northymbria.**
Gloucester, Gloucestershire............... **Gleucestre, Mercia.**
Guildford, Surrey............................... **Geldeford, Wessex.**
Hastings, East Sussex........................ **Hæstingas, Wessex.**
Hereford, Herefordshire..................... **Herefordscir, Mercia.**
Ilchester, Devon................................. **Ceaster, Wessex.**

| | |
|---|---|
| Ilkley, West Yorkshire..................... | **Llecan, Northymbria.** |
| Ipswich, Suffolk............................... | **Gippeswic, East Anglia.** |
| Isle of Man...................................... | **Ellan Vannin, Mercia.** |
| Isle of Wight................................... | **Wihtland, Wessex.** |
| Lancaster, Lancashire...................... | **Lune Cæster, Northymbria.** |
| Leominster, Herefordshire................ | **Leofminstre, Mercia.** |
| Lincoln, Lincolnshire...................... | **Lindsey, Northymbria.** |
| Llandovery, Wales.......................... | **Llanymddyfri, Wealh.** |
| Land's End, Cornwall .................... | **Steort** *(tail or end)* **Wessex.** |
| Leicester, Leicestershire.................. | **Legracæster, Mercia.** |
| Lympne, Kent.................................. | **Stutfall, (Cent) Wessex.** |
| Milden Hall, Wiltshire..................... | **Mildanhald, Wessex.** |
| Manchester, Lancashire................... | **Mancæstre, Northymbria.** |
| Monmouth, Wales........................... | **Abermynwy, Wealh.** |
| Neath, Wales................................... | **Nedd, Wealh.** |
| Newcastle, Northumberland........... | **Monkchester, Northymbria.** |
| Norwich, Norfolk............................ | **Norwic, East Anglia.** |
| Northampton, Northamptonshire.... | **Northumtun, Mercia.** |
| Nottinghan, Nottinghamshire.......... | **Snotingaham, Mercia.** |
| Oxford, Oxfordshire........................ | **Oxenaforda, Mercia.** |
| Pangbourne, Hampshire................... | **Pegingaburna, Wessex.** |
| Pevensey, East Sussex..................... | **Pefenesæ, Wessex.** |
| Portchester, Hampshire................... | **Portus Aurni, Wessex.** |
| Porlock, Somerset........................... | **Porteloca, Wessex.** |
| Reculver, Kent................................. | **Reculfcæstre, (Cent) Wessex.** |
| Rendelsham, East Anglia................ | **Rendlæsham, Est Anglia.** |
| Richborough, Kent.......................... | **Rithubi, (Cent) Wessex.** |
| Rochester Kent................................ | **Hrofescester, (Cent) Wessex.** |
| Rye, Kent......................................... | **Rie (Cent) Wessex.** |
| Salisbury (Old Sarum, )Wiltshire.... | **Searoburh, Wessex.** |
| Scilly Isles, Cornwall...................... | **Enesek Syllan, Wessex.** |
| St Albans, Hertfordshire.................. | **Verlamchester, East Anglia.** |
| Silchester, Hampshire..................... | **Ciltestere, Wessex.** |
| Southampton, Hampshire................ | **Hamwic, Wessex.** |
| Stamford Bridge Yorkshire............. | **Stoneford Brycge, Northymbria.** |
| Land's End, Cornwall...................... | **Steort, Wessex.** |
| Southford, Lincolnshire................... | **Suthford, Mercia.** |
| Tadcaster, North Yorkshire............. | **Tades Caester, Northymbria.** |
| Tamworth, Staffordshire................. | **Tamaweord, Mercia.** |
| Thanet, Kent.................................... | **Tanet, (Cent) Wessex.** |
| Thorney Island, London.................. | **Thorney Igland, Lunden.** |

Uttoxeter, Staffordshire..................... **Wuttuceshædde, Mercia.**
Wallingford, Berkshire...................... **Gualhenfforda, Mercia.**
Wanborough, Wiltshire..................... **Wôdnesbeorg, Wessex.**
Weston-on-Trent, Derbyshire........... **Westune, Mercia.**
Wigan, Lancashire............................ **Wibiggin, Northhymbria.**
Winchelsea, Kent.............................. **Winceleseia, (Cent) Wessex.**
Winchester, Hampshire..................... **Wintancaester, Wessex.**
Wroxeter, Shropshire........................ **Cair Guricon, Mercia.**
York, Yorkshire................................ **Eoforwic, Northymbria.**

## The main English Earldoms, Rivers, Seas and Countries:
**East Anglia. Cent.**
**Mercia,** *The Northymbrians called Mercians,* **Suthymbrians.**
**Northymbria, Northymbres, Northymbrian.**
**Wessex.**

*Bourne or an alternative O/E spelling Burne. The place called, Kilburn was originally Cye Bourne – royal stream but has been known, at different times and in different places, as Kelebourne, Kilburn, Bayswater, Bayswater River, Bayswater Rivulet, Serpentine River, The Bourne, Westburn Brook, the Ranelagh River, and the Ranelagh Sewer. It is of similar size to the Fleet.*

River Medway...................................... **Meduma.**
River Itchen......................................... **Ealden Icenan,** *Old Itchen.*
River Severn........................................ **Sabrina.**
River Thames....................................... **Tames Bourne.**
Bristol Channel.................................... **Brycgsstow Sæ.**
English Channel................................... **Englisc Sæ.**
Irish Sea............................................... **Iras Sæ.**
North Sea............................................. **Northerne Sæ.**
Ireland.................................................. **Eriuland or Erinn.**
North= North and **Northerna, Northerne.** South= **Suth**
Southern= **Sutherne. East and West**
Bridge= **brycg.**
Island= **Íegland** or **Igland.**
English................................................. **Englisc**
Englishmen.......................................... **Engliscmen**
Denmark.............................................. **Danemark**

Danish.......................................................... **Danisc**
Normandy..................................................... **Northmandig**
Norman........................................................ **Northman**
Normandish................................................. **Northmandisc**
Norway........................................................ **Norveg**
Norwegian................................................... **Norvegian**
Sweden........................................................ **Swedeland**
Scandinavia................................................. **Scedenig**
Wales........................................................... **Wealh**
Welsh........................................................... **Wealhasc**

## ANGLO SAXON WEAPONS

**Skeggox or Skeggy** = Long handled (Bearded) axe.
**Sweord or Swyrd** *(Battle Sword)* = Double edged Battle Swords could be up to 40" in length x 2.5" wide and kept in a leather sheath.
Edwin calls his battle sword; 'Head Biter' as in the manner of the Vikings who personalised their weapons; their life savers.
**Franzisca** = Small throwing axe.
**Seax** = A deadly Knife, the blade of which could be up to 20" in length.

## Old English WORDS

**Morðor** = Murder
**Myrðrian** = Murdered
**Morðorslaga** = Murderer.
**Gemæd** = Mad, Insane, Crazy
**Bær** = Stretcher

## FOOD

**In Northymbria** a lot of Norwegians still hung onto their old familiar food, such as this dish called: Hangikjöt:- Lamb hung in a smoker, smoked by the burning dried sheep's dung.

# The
# RAVEN
## the
# LION
## and the
# WHITE
# DRAGON

by Roy Stedall-Humphryes

The old order of
King Edward the Confessor's realm
is under threat
from within and without.
From
Norveg
to the east
and
Northmandig
to the suth.
An Anglo Saxon family
become embroiled in the tumultuous
events of eleventh century
Englaland.

# Prologue

*Early morning, April, 1032*

**- Weolud, Mercia, Englaland -**
The River Welland, Lincolnshire, England

An ominous high curved prow gradually emerged out of the swirling mist, revealing a ship bristling with metal helmeted warriors; a recurring spectre of horror along the east coast of Englaland.

"Vikings! Viking raiders!" shouted a shepherd, standing on the bank of the Weolud, his voice cut short by an arrow striking him in the mouth; another thudding into his chest.

"Wake up! Edwin! Wake up! We're on fire! Where is Eadrick? The village is under attack! Vikings!"

"What?" said Edwin rubbing his bleary eyes in the half-light; now hearing the warning church bell.

Suddenly the bell stopped ringing.

"Wake up! Get yourself dressed and find your brother. Move!" His father rushed out of the room.

Edwin dressed rapidly as smoke began to fill the room. Dropping a piece of rag into a bowl of water, he put the stinking wet cloth over his nose and mouth and began a frantic search, shouting for his baby brother.

"EADRICK! EADRICK! EADRICK!"

From the other side of the house he could hear his father also shouting his brother's name. Most of all he could hear his mother's frenzied screams. Screaming for her baby.

Through the ever-increasing heat and smoke the search was becoming impossible. Still he had to carry on and find Eadrick. The ceiling behind him collapsed in flames. Now the whole house began to vibrate and suddenly roof timbers to his left appeared to explode in a ball of fire, falling to the floor in a shower of sparks.

His exposed skin beginning to singe, half blinded by the smoke and fumes Edwin burst out of the main door of the house only to be seized and thrown to the ground.

"Grab ham!" shouted a foreign voice.

Edwin's arms and legs were tied with ropes.

"Han er den siste," shouted another.

Not able see or to wipe his streaming smoke-smarting eyes, he felt every pebble and rock as he was dragged along the road to where others were imprisoned screaming.

He heard his name and felt a cloth dabbing his eyes.

"Father! Where is Eadrick?" whispered Edwin, now able to see.

"He was nowhere to be found." His father was holding his grief stricken wife, momentarily quietening her by hugging her close to him.

Edwin looked back at their house and bakery. It was now nothing more than a raging inferno.

"Poor Eadrick," he closed his eyes as he tried to imagine his brother's pain.

"Flytte ut! Ta denne varen tilbake til skipet!" came the order.

"Father, what are they saying?"

"I think they're taking us to their ship."

# CHAPTER I

*10 May, 1041*
**- Duke William's Fortress, Rouen, Northmandig -**
Rouen, Normandy

"Stop that that noise!" he mouthed to himself through clenched teeth, thumping the stone floor with his fist with each word. Edwin felt like shouting aloud but he couldn't. "I can feel my heart pounding, I'll never get back to sleep. I know it's not their fault." He was fully awake and would have to put up with the grunts, coughs and snores that resonated around the Duke's great hall.

Lying back in the darkness he gradually relaxed, became perfectly still, not moving a muscle, allowing his mind to disconnect from the rest of his body. It was a regime he practiced, from time to time, to clear his mind. After some while he moved his head, glanced over at one of his sleeping companions who, despite his nudging, continued to make popping sounds with each breath expelled from his hairy, unwashed face. Edwin smiled to himself. He turned away allowing his thoughts to drift from the safety of his rock hard bed, which was warmed only by radiated heat from the dying embers in the fire-hearth in the centre of the hall, to his sæ journey the previous day. He was the youngest of a small troop of warriors, a twenty-two year-old housecarl from Upper Barnstæd, who had volunteered to accompany Bishop Ælfwine of Wintancaester to Duke William's palace in Rouen, with the royal warrant requesting Prince Edward's return to Englaland. King Harthacnute and his council of wise men, the Witan, had declared Edward heir to the throne of Englaland.

Edwin coughed to clear his throat and turned onto his side.

He remembered the steersman shouting, "Strike!" and pulling hard on his oar in unison with the rest of the crew, feeling the ship slide silently through the calm waters out of Bosham harbour; the raising of the sail, the harbour, the coastal headland and the Wihtland soon lost from sight to the cold, damp, dawn mist. Though Edwin had much experience at sæ, he always felt a dreaded unease when losing sight of land and he wasn't the only one to experience that same fear; fear of the sæ and of being vulnerable. He remembered, ten or more years ago, as a boy, walking bare foot on the mudflats at low tide off Convennon Teg, which was not far from his home and seeing a wreck of a ship far out on the flats. It had been exposed by the low tide. He had walked towards the wreck, feeling the sandy mud squeezing and oozing between his toes, kicking through the piles of excreted lugworm casts that dotted the surface of the flats. Arriving at the wreck he found it to have been carrying huge blocks of rough-hewn stone and although the bulk of the wreckage had long been washed away, most of the keel was in place, trapped by the stones. The tide had been about to turn and by now the clear waters were up to his ankles. On a whim he had ventured a little further, feeling the hard rippled mud floor under his feet. He had felt the water turn icy cold and had been gripped by fear. Immediately ahead the sæ was black. He had found himself standing at the very the edge of the mud shelf where it dropped suddenly away into the unfathomable deep. Realising the danger he was in he had turned and fled back, panic stricken, towards the beach.

Edwin opened his eyes wide and was relieved to hear the snores and feel the floor of the hall. 'I must have drifted off,' he thought. 'Why do I stick my neck out, volunteering for these damn sæ journeys? To prove to myself that I'm not afraid? If so, I must be stupid because each time I crew or sail out to sæ, I'm gripped by my own intimate terror of the deep and of losing sight of land.'

Changing position he tried sleeping on his stomach but, still feeling uncomfortable, turned onto his right side, pulling the cover over his head, continuing to muse about the journey, the battle against the storm, their ship tossing every which way, plunging into bone juddering waves. He began to grin as he remembered the Bishop draped over the side spewing his guts. 'You would have thought, seeing as he is a bishop, he would have had divine protection, being fortified by the responsibility of representing King Harthacnute, as his royal messenger boy.

'Oh Wodin!' Edwin winced again and thought about the giant wave that had crashed over the bow and nearly washed the Bishop overboard. 'He disappeared from view! We were struck with sheer fucking panic! He had the royal warrant. But there he was, still on board hanging on to the ship's rigging for dear life, his feet kicking wildly in the air. I hate the sæ and the sæ hates me! I was glad to see the Seine, Rouen and dry land. If yesterday is anything to go by, all I can say is this doesn't bode well; in order to get mummy's boy, the precious ætheling back to Englaland.' Edwin winced, 'He's a grown man for fuck's sake, who still jumps when mummy calls.'

He drew back the cover and saw that somebody had lit an oil lamp at the far end of the hall. He took a deep breath and watched the distant flickering flame. 'I almost feel sorry for King Harthacnute, our ill looking monarch. Pity he is such a nasty bastard. Thin and pale as he is and coughing up blood, I doubt if he will last much longer, and he's only twenty three years of age.'

"Wilf! Have you got your stuff packed?" asked Edwin.

"Yep! I just have this small bundle, I'll strap it onto my back."

"Well, we need to find the Prince and see whether he needs any help."

"I suspect he's got more than a large chest to take back. After all he's been over here, what is it, twenty years?"

"More like twenty five," replied Edwin.

Wilf was a year older than Edwin but a head shorter and built like a rock, with arm muscles to crack walnuts. He had been trained by his father as a swordsmith but had become bored with village life, so had left to become a warrior and eventually a housecarl. He said it was for the adventure and travel. Like Edwin, he favoured the battle sword over the skeggy. As someone once said, you're at a disadvantage when swinging that long handled axe. You can't hold a shield at the same time, unless you have tremendous arm muscles to do it.

Approaching Prince Edward's room they could hear him in private conversation with someone.

"Shhh!" whispered Edwin, bringing them both to a halt outside the slightly open door. "There's something odd between Edward and this fourteen-year-old Duke."

They remained outside, listening.

"Thank you for all your advice, Uncle Edward," said William, "I shall feel quite empty and sad when you leave."

"William, don't be sad, just be safe."

"On your journey, as well as your own knights, you will have six of mine for your protection."

"Thank you William. I think you will need them more than me. I know you still miss your father. What is it… six years since his death? It's hard for a young man to lose his father but you have to go on. You must be strong and train hard. I know you have many enemies, but believe me, you have even more friends. Roger de Montgomery and William fitzOsborn for example are risking their lives to protect you."

The thin, pale skinned, thirty-nine year old Edward, put his arms about the youth who, Edwin had observed, had a hard edge to his character which others, he thought, didn't see.

"Will you return soon to see us, Uncle Edward?"

"I don't know. Hold me tighter…yeees, that's better. I have such love for you William. I wish I could stay but my mother says I must obey the King's wishes and return to Englaland, which now seems a strange country to me after living here in Northmandig with you your family and friends, for so long."

"But when you are King you will forget us."

"I could never forget *you,* William…"

There was a long pause. Edwin had to hold Wilfred back from giving their presence away.

"I was thinking… about you and this country of Northmandig. What if, I made you my heir, *my* ætheling?"

"You want *me* to be heir to the Englisc throne, Uncle?"

"Yes! Why not! I have loved you like a son; more than a son."

"But when you are married you will have sons of your own. How could I be your heir?"

"It doesn't mean I will *have* to have any children," Edward closed his eyes, "and you will still be my heir, I guarantee it. Then Englaland and Northmandig will be joined under one kingship. What of that, my young Duke?"

"Have you told anyone else of your plans, Uncle?"

"No! This is between you and me for the time being. Kiss me my boy."

'The old bastard!' Edwin thought and signalled to Wilfred to make a noisy entrance.

# CHAPTER II

*September, 1048*

**- Farndune Brycg, a Wealhasc crossing point,
over the Afon Dyfrdwy -**
Farndon Bridge a Welsh crossing point over the River Dee

A shivering hooded youth, his threadbare cloak wrapped securely about him with rope, trudged across Farndune Brycg and onto Wealhasc soil. Scuttling down the river embankment he crept under the brycg, wedging himself between the timbered supports to find shelter for the night, pulling his bundle of possessions in after him.

They were cast-offs; rags he had collected on his travels. Untying it he wrapped the rags around himself, insulating him from the penetrating, damp, night air. He now felt safe and began munching on bits of cold rabbit meat he had cooked earlier in the day.

He didn't know his real name nor, for that matter, how old he actually was, although he thought he was about sixteen years, counting the winters.

Viking raiders from the Northerne Sæ had invaded the Englisc coastline and had attacked his village, burning it to the ground. A child at the time, not more than two or three years old, he vaguely remembered some sort of dark place he had crawled into, away from the terrifying flames. It was his continuing nightmare; a raging inferno that was about to devour him, not being able to move a muscle to get away and waking petrified, his whole body covered in sweat. His rescuers thought he was the sole survivor. Passing travellers from Legracæster, a day's journey to the west, who had found him days after the raid crawling amidst the charred ruins, had adopted him, calling him 'Ruffous' because of his mop of reddish hair. He often wondered about his parents, thinking he must have been hidden from the raiders by them. Were they alive or dead? Or, like so many others, taken away across the sæ to be sold as slaves.

Three years ago he had returned to Suthford, his place of birth. All that remained of his village was a wilderness, interspersed with moss covered, charred timbers and a ruined baker's brick oven where his parents' house had once stood. One thing he was able to discern from people who lived nearby. He was the son of Wulfric the baker, a churl, a freeman; not a thrall, a slave, someone's property as he had once thought. Yet, having been the son of a freeman, he was still a nobody, a person without property and a proper name. 'I'm an outcast,' he thought. 'I might as well be a thrall.'

In the failing evening light he felt for a comfortable position to lay his head. 'That's better.' He blinked his watery eyes. 'At least I'm warmer down here and safe for the night. I'll be glad when I'm at Elwen's place, she'll have some work for me and some hot food and I'll be able to sleep in her barn.' The thought brought a smile to his grime ridden face. 'I hope she is still alive and if she ain't, I'll go back home, team up with my step-brother Pæda and go suth.'

Early in the morning, when there was barely enough daylight to see, he awoke to shouts and trampling feet on the timbered boards of the brycg above him. Ruffous kept silent and noted they were travelling east into Mercia. 'Who are they,' he wondered. 'Best not to know, ain't my business.'

After a while all was quiet. Packing his few belongings, he moved from under the brycg and looked up at the grey dawn. 'Mmm, it looks as if it might rain, I'd better be going.'

## - A journey to Northhumtun, Mercia -
Northampton, Northamptonshire

Reaching the high ground, Edwin turned in his saddle and cast his eyes suth across the forested roof of the land, towards Lunden.

They were five miles north of King Edward's royal palace at West Minster and Edwin was already feeling uneasy.

"Why have we stopped," queried Osgar.

"I need to think," replied Edwin.

"You could have done that before we left Lunden."

Edwin ignored the remark and continued to turn over in his mind what had been troubling him. He looked towards his friend Osgar, a dark haired, stocky figure, from Norwic, whose father owned a small fleet of ships, exporting goods to the continent. Osgar, being a rich man's son, it seemed to Edwin, had had his position bought for him and now he was, like Edwin, one of the privileged few. A thegn and housecarl to Earl Harold.

'Others,' Edwin reflected, 'say he is a skilled warrior, let's hope they're right. Money can't buy you everything my friend and yet, there is a rumour going around, that you're never satisfied with what you have.' Edwin smiled to himself. 'He does look odd sitting on that horse. I don't know what it is, he sort of sits in the saddle in an odd way, off balance you might say.'

"I'm wondering," said Edwin at last, "why our King is sending us north to Earl Leofric of Mercia, using us as his messengers. Is he expecting just the two of us to help fight a bunch of Wealhasc raiders, Os? What's the real reason I wonder."

Osgar gave a shrug.

Giving his companion a questioning look, Edwin continued, "The Earl is well capable of handling the Wealhasc with his own men, so why get us involved? He may be getting old but he isn't stupid and he has a strong army; Mercian housecarls, some of the toughest anywhere. If you've ever seen them in action you would know what I mean."

"Perhaps the King doesn't trust Earl Leofric and wants us to spy on him?"

"Don't know. Leofric is one of his most loyal supporters, which makes it all the more puzzling. It's just ... I can't rid myself of the feeling we're being, set up. Believe you me Os, we had better tread..." he didn't finish the sentence but sat for a while longer searching the distant, tranquil land before him, hoping an answer would fall into place. His eyes followed the old Roman road north as it descended with a slight sweep to the right, before disappearing from view amidst dense forested land.

A fusion of thoughts, seemingly unconnected memories, flooded into his mind. Edwin had once let his mother, Æelfi measure his height. She had said he stood, a blond haired, statuesque, seven feet. Statuesque? He liked to think he was no different from his companions who were also strong and just as capable as he. As far as his height and reach were concerned, true, it did give him an advantage when in combat. His friends at Earl Harold's court, likened him to Stonehenge; his rock hard muscles, sagacious chiselled head set on thick broad shoulders. His beguiling smile hid his ability to see through people's duplicity. Although these attributes made him formidable, at the same time they made him feel embarrassed.

He had soon been brought to the attention of Harold Godwinson, Earl of East Anglia, but he really didn't like being thought of as different or indeed better than anybody else. He, like the rest of the Earl's troops, was tough and good at what he did; fighting. Everybody had their strengths and weaknesses and he would have to go along with his friends' and Earl Harold's view of him, despite trying to play it down.

He remembered when Wulfric, his father, presented him with his battle-sword, the handle beautifully inlaid with gold, saying to him, "Defend the King, your hearth and your home with honour."

Even though Edwin was a trusted housecarl to Earl Harold, it nevertheless seemed strange to him that the King should have taken a liking to him. The thought made him feel uncomfortable. Was it because he had been one of the chosen few who had sailed from Bosham to Rouen in forty-one with King Harthacnute's writ, summoning Prince Edward to appear at the Englisc court to be made heir? What Edwin couldn't get over was hearing the Prince, before leaving Rouen, promising Duke William the crown of Englaland, when he died.

'Bloody fool!' he had thought at the time. 'Making promises without the Witan's approval, it's never been heard of. Anyway the Duke's a bastard. His only blood connection is a very tenuous one through Edward's mother, William's great aunt, Emma of Northmandig.

"When you bow to His Majesty, make sure your arse is against the wall," he had heard someone shout, followed by howls of laughter, as he left Earl Harold's court. There were many rumours circulating about the King's sexuality. It was on his mind though. Why had King Edward chosen him and Osgar for this, in his opinion, unnecessary mission? Everybody knew of the conflict between Earl Godwin and the King. But now, another possible factor was being thrown into the arena.

'What of Earl Leofric and where do I stand in all this?' Edwin thought. 'Leading Earl Leofric's Mercian troops into battle against the Wealhasc. Is the King hoping it will all go wrong, causing bad blood between Earl Leofric and Godwin? These two Earls are the most powerful families and such discord would cause a tremor throughout the country. The King's a cunning old bastard! I think I know what he's up to! A rift between the two Earls would further weaken Godwin's influence. Edward's bitterness towards Earl Godwin and his sons has been festering for twelve years, unjustly in my view. After all, it was Earl Godwin who championed him at the Witan, gaining him his crown despite the misgivings of some of the other earls. Yet now, he blames Godwin for the death of his brother Alfred. The fact was, the prince had been dragged away into the night, from Earl Godwin's manor, by King Harold Harefoot's men.

The poor sod had had his eyes gouged out and left for dead. As the Earl has said many times, and I believe him, how could he have opposed the King's men? Well, we will continue to Mercia, on behalf of King Edward. I will certainly go with all humility and help the aged Earl, but I will steer us clear of any political trickery he may put in our way and we will bring back intelligence regarding the Earl's loyalty and the strength and purpose of the Wealhasc attacks.'

He felt better now he had a clear plan. He would get to know Leofric and make him his friend, if it was at all possible.

"Let's go," shouted Edwin at last, spurring his horse, "I want to get to Tamaweord by tomorrow night."

"Hey!" called back Osgar, "Look! Pheasants! Let's bag some."

"No! Not here, this is the Bishop of Lunden's hunting preserve. Don't want to cross swords with his foresters."

"Oh well, it was a nice thought. Where are we staying tonight?"

"Northhumtun, if we ride hard enough."

While Osgar stabled their horses Edwin entered the thatch-roofed inn through a small door which faced the main road. Stepping into the vaguely familiar, dimly lit, mud floored hall, he was met by a warm, friendly hubbub of voices. He knew where he wanted to be and that was at the far side of the room, so he began easing his way among the people until he found an empty table to his liking. From the centre of the room smoke from the burning wood drifted, infusing a pungent smell of oak into an atmosphere already thick with the smell of human sweat. He wiped his smarting eyes with a piece of cloth.

"Who's upset yer? Wife kicked yer out into the stræt?" boomed the voice of the innkeeper, standing next to him. He was tall, although not as tall as Edwin, barrel-chested and, as he spoke, his hairy chin moved up and down in a supplementary gesture of inquiry.

"Why don't you do something about that smoking fire of yours? It's making my eyes water."

"Aah! I've seen you before. When was it …don't tell me. Last year. You were with an Earl and a troop of housecarls. What was the Earl's name…? Harold I think it was." He then continued in a whisper, "What are yer doin' here …official business?"

"No! I'm going to a wedding, up near Wuttuceshædde."

"If you say so," said the innkeeper. "Oh yes! I remember you! Edwin!

"You've got a long memory my friend."

"Well, who else is as tall as you and has a mop of blond hair and a braided beard…"

"I know. I stand out in a crowd."

"Yes, in a word, you do."

"Now," continued Edwin, "I need a room for myself and my friend. We'll also want a hot evening meal."

"Hild!" shouted the innkeeper, turning his head slightly towards an open hatch in the wall, "Heat up the stew we've got two more customers for your special." Then in a conspiratorial tone, he continued, "I've got an empty room up there." He pointed to the end of the gallery. "When you're ready I'll show it to yer, but be careful."

"Why?" replied Edwin, stroking his plaited beard. "Are you expecting trouble?"

"Hope not. It's just …I glimpsed the royal satchel, under your cloak."

"You don't miss much do you?" said Edwin, holding the man in a hard stare and tapping the leather satchel with his forefinger. "This is King's business. Let nobody else know of it otherwise it will be the worse for you and your family. Understood?"

"Understood," the innkeeper replied, slowly nodding his head.

"Now! Let's have a look at this room."

As Edwin began following the innkeeper he saw Osgar approaching, carrying their bags.

"Just in time. This way."

A heavily built door stood ajar at the far end of the first floor gallery.

"Well, here's the room," the innkeeper said, pushing the door wide open, "it's the safest in the house."

It was simply laid out with three beds. Two separated by a small table and the other bed, which was slightly smaller, up against the furthest wall. A shuttered window gave out above the stables below, the view half obliterated by the overhanging roof thatch.

"If you want an oil lamp it will cost you extra."

They both nodded. Throwing their bags onto the spare bed, they left with the owner. Edwin had noticed what looked to be a large blood stain on the floor by the side of the bed nearest the door. Although the floor seemed to have been scrubbed congealed blood could still be seen between the floor timbers.

The owner hadn't missed Edwin's glance.

"We had a bit of trouble here last week. Two brothers fighting over a cock fight bet. I had to throw 'em out," he said with a chuckle.

To have made that large a stain, thought Edwin, needed enough blood to drain a body dry. The man was a liar.

There were fewer people now. Seated around the table next to theirs, were a group of soldiers who had taken no notice of them when they first came in and were now in deep conversation.

"Who are they?" Edwin enquired, not wanting to point.

"Northmen! The King's friends. They're from that newly built Pentecost castle, over in the suth-west," replied the innkeeper, his eyes searching Edwin's as if to gauge his reaction.

Edwin knew of Ralf of Mantes, nephew to the King, and of Ralf's timbered castles. What worried him was that this castle was in Wealh, with another further north.

'Surely,' he thought, 'this is what's causing these attacks. Northmen taking Wealhasc land with the full support of the King. To defend themselves against the Wealhasc they are building fortresses with watered moats.'

"Personally, I don't have much to do with Northmen," Edwin

said, appearing unconcerned, "as long as they don't interfere with me."

"While you're here then, don't make any trouble."

"You'll get none from me. We just want a hot meal and to lay our heads down for the night."

"Why take this table then?" the innkeeper asked, with a quizzical look. "I should have thought you would have wanted to be as far away from them as possible."

"We like being amongst people," replied Edwin, with a smile, "not stuck in a corner, out of the way. It makes life interesting."

The innkeeper shook his head as he walked away, not understanding his Saxon clients, and disappeared from view into the kitchen.

Someone banged on the table next to them, followed by raucous laughter, then one of the Northmen glanced at Edwin and began whispering.

Osgar leaned towards Edwin, "I know why you chose to eat at this table," he whispered, "but I feel self-conscious, uncomfortable, you might say, sitting here with them next to us. It won't do my digestion any good either."

Two large bowls of stew landed on the table.

"Call out when you want the lamp," said the innkeeper, walking away.

"I didn't want him," said Edwin, indicating the departing figure, "to know about our business but unfortunately he saw the royal bag. I tried to make him think we were just travelling north to a wedding."

"Alright, but if he does have any idea of our business we had better be away directly and find somewhere else. And another thing, just because you're head and shoulders taller than me and well connected doesn't mean I'm less than you. Your turn to stable the horses next time."

"Alright, alright. I'll stable them next time. But listen, Os, have I ever said you were less than me?"

"No."

"Well then. You and I go back a long way so let's eat and rest up here. Shouldn't have any problems."

"Fine. But I still don't like this place."

As Edwin gathered up another spoonful of mutton stew he was aware of being observed. One of the men on the next table was trying to get his attention. Edwin smiled, slurped up the spoonful of stew and gestured for the man to speak.

"Excusez moi, my Englisc no good."

"Continuer monsieur, my French is no good either, please," Edwin replied, laughing.

"You are going on long journey?"

"Yes. We are going north to my brother's wedding. It's going to take several days and I'm hoping it doesn't rain."

"Be careful, there are Wealhasc bandits prowling ze countryside. Would you like one or two of us help protect you?"

"No thank you," said Edwin, catching Osgar's eye. "It is good of you to offer your service. Innkeeper!" he shouted, "Give these good men a round of beer."

"No, no, no necessary," said the Northman, gesticulating with his hands, unwittingly revealing a long thin bladed dagger tucked in his belt.

"I insist. Innkeeper!" shouted Edwin again, indicating drinks all round. "I am happy, so I want everyone else to be happy too."

Osgar sat staring at his friend who gave him a knowing wink.

"Ready?" said Edwin, getting to his feet. "Let's get to our room."

"You are leaving?"

"Yes. We have a long way to travel tomorrow," said Edwin, with a wave of farewell.

Osgar lay back on his bed, fully dressed, broadsword by his side and nonchalantly moved his feet, wiggling his toes, casting amusing shadows from the light of the lantern, onto the far wall.

"Those Frenchies really wanted to know our business. You bet your life, a little way out of town and...," he drew his finger across his throat.

"Ballocks, Os! They ain't Frenchies, they're Northmen, didn't you hear the innkeeper?"

"They all sound the same to me," replied Osgar.

"There's a big difference, Os. These are mean, cunning bastards and I don't trust them. Help me move this bed over against the door."

Osgar lifted the back end of the bed so that it was wedged against the door. They both picked up their axes and embedded them into the floor against the rear bed legs, to stop the bed from sliding.

"That bed won't shift in a hurry."

"Good," said Edwin. "It'll stop anyone from pushing open the door without us knowing. You had better put your boots back on, just in case. In the meantime, I'll stand guard on the first shift and perhaps tonight we'll be able to get at least some sleep." Stabbing his sword into the blooded timber, he continued, "I'll unwrap the bows and make them ready."

The night was passing peacefully until, a little while into Osgar's shift, a slight noise brought his attention to the door. In the dim light, he could see the latch being lifted and someone pushing against the door.

Osgar shook Edwin awake.

"We have company."

Without speaking further they took up their bows, nocked them and waited.

Craaash! The door suddenly caved in, over the immovable bed. Men in full armour, their swords glinting in the dim lamplight, struggled amid the splintered wreckage of the door and the bed, to get into the room.

Edwin and Osgar shouted their battle call, "ABRECAAAN! OUT! OUT! OUT!

Their shouts were greeted by thrashing swords.

The two housecarls fired their bows, reloaded and fired again.

One figure collapsed dead onto the splintered door, another onto the floor outside while a third was heard crawling away, calling for help. They reloaded and waited for the next attack.

There were sounds of scraping feet as if someone was being dragged along the gallery and down the stairs to the floor below. Several distant voices could be heard, a shriek and then silence. Then the innkeeper called out.

"You up there! King's messenger and your friend. Throw down your weapons. These people are threatening to kill me and my wife. They want the royal satchel and your money. Then you can go on your way without harm."

"Os, those bastards are not laying a hand on this satchel."

Stepping over to the window, Edwin gently slid the shutters to one side and looked out. "All's quiet. No one's about. I think we can get out through this window, hop down to the stables and get away. What do you think?"

"Worth a try. What about the innkeeper and his wife?" replied Osgar.

Edwin hunched his shoulders.

"Too bad. If we step onto that gallery we will be sitting ducks. Of course, if you fancy your chances, you're welcome to try but I'm out of here."

"I thought I would mention it, that's all," replied Osgar, wrenching his axe out of the floor.

"Take my axe as well. You climb out the window first while I get near the doorway and sneak a few more shots down into the hall below."

"Shit! That was close," shouted Osgar, as they galloped out of the town.

"I'm just grateful they weren't waiting for us in the stable. At first I didn't think our bags would go through the window," said Edwin laughing. "I couldn't see a thing but I fired two shots anyway, heard a yell and fired another before leaving."

"That's one place we can't go back to."

Wrapping his cloak tightly around himself, Osgar felt a little warmer. "I need a good night's sleep."

"Me too. At least we got out of there alive," replied Edwin, still laughing. We should be at Tamaweord by mid-day."

Through the grey mist and drizzle they could just make out the raised fortifications of the ancient buhr.

"Even from a distance Tamaweord looks formidable," said Osgar, seeing it for the very first time.

"'Allo, 'allo what's this," muttered Edwin, reading the crudely written sign swinging from a tree. "Would you believe it. Brycg works ahead."

"We're in luck," said Osgar, "we can use this rickety brycg instead to cross the Tama."

"There's another one further on to take us over the Anker."

As they eased their horses across the Anker they could see, up the river, the ruined remains of the main brycg, its central supports smashed and washed away as the result of recent floods.

"This brycg won't last long either by the looks of it. Do you know, Os," said Edwin pointing, "the last time I was here I knew that brycg up there was rotten. Nobody ever wants to spend money on repairs. I told them then it was dangerous and needed repairing. But nobody ever listens."

"Will you stop moaning, Ed! Look on the bright side. See! They've even got a fortified geathouse."

"Of course they have. This place used to be the old royal capital of Mercia but in those days its fortifications were much stronger."

"So, Earl Leofric lives in the old royal palace?"

"No," replied Edwin. "The old palace was burnt down years ago by Viking raiders. His place is in the centre of the town. Let's get a move on. I'm hungry and am getting soaked."

## - Tamaweord, Mercia -
Tamworth, Staffordshire

"Shit! The geat's shut," muttered Edwin.

"You there! What's your business?" shouted a voice from above.

"The King's business. I have message for Earl Leofric," shouted back Edwin.

As the two great doors creaked open they spurred their horses forward through the high lofted, timbered geathouse and along the main stræt, lined both sides with an assortment of large and small thatch-roofed houses.

"If this was once a royal capital, it don't look much now," commented Osgar.

"It's certainly gone down a bit since I was here last."

As they approached the centre of the town the houses were packed closer together, separated only by narrow stinking alleyways.

"Leofric's place is that large building over there," Edwin said pointing.

Like the rest of the buildings, except for the stone church on the opposite side of the crossroads, it was built of timber but was on two floors. The lower containing the main hall for official functions, the upper floor a gallery giving access to the Earl's solar, sleeping quarters and rooms for visiting dignitaries.

"Mmm," Earl Leofric looked up from the King's message, fixed his eyes briefly on Edwin and continued reading.

Edwin observed him. So this was the famous Earl whose troops had saved him, his family and the villagers of Suthford from sæ raiders, sixteen years ago. Edwin put that episode from his mind; he was paying more attention to Earl Leofric's wife, Lady Godfigu. She fascinated him. He looked at her keenly but was careful not to give offence. She was in her thirties he judged, of slight build, average height and together with her long dark hair and fine pale skin, she was every inch a very beautiful, mature woman. He wouldn't have thought she could have been tough enough to rebel against that husband of hers but she had. From the stories he'd heard, she had ridden naked through the town of Coventre, on a bet, to force Leofric to reduce the town's taxes. Yes, but the old bastard had given her - as if she had had a choice in the matter - an armed escort of housecarls, forcing the townspeople inside their houses shuttering their windows, dragging out anyone who peeked at her. One did, the poor bastard, and he was chopped for it. What was his name... Tom? He wondered, if she had also ridden bare back. He couldn't help smiling to himself at the thought of it.

"Do you find something here amusing?" said the Earl, giving Edwin a threatening look. "Because we would like to know what it is."

"My lord, I didn't mean to show any disrespect. I was remembering last night's escape from a trap set by a group of Northmen knights, in Northhumtun. They were after that royal document."

Earl Leofric shook his head and said no more but continued reading.

Edwin gazed at the pennants and the other hangings that adorned the walls of the great hall. All the while his gut was churning with a feeling of foreboding.

'I bet Osgar is pissed, being left outside. What was in the King's message. If only I could have somehow read it. Impossible! That would have meant breaking the royal seal. He is about finished reading, best not to look nervous.'

Earl Leofric put the scrolled message down but continued to stare at it for some time, seemingly perplexed. At last, he looked up at Edwin.

"At first light, you will take some of my mounted troops north towards Westune," he ordered, in what to Edwin was an unusually strange, highly pitched, unsteady voice.

"My lord," asked Edwin, "Where exactly is Westune?"

"The captain of my guard, Hengist, knows the way," replied the

Earl, pointing to a burly man guarding the door, who looked to be in his thirties.

Their eyes met, 'I know that man. I swear I've seen him before,' thought Edwin.

"He'll also be your second in command," continued the Earl, in a louder voice. "Find these Wealhasc bandits and kill them but capture their leader Gruffydd ap Llywelyn alive, if you can, and bring him to me. It'll be a long ride. Make sure you have plenty of rest. Hengist will show you to your quarters."

With a wave of his hand the old Earl dismissed him and departed with his wife through a door, half hidden behind a large decorative curtain, to their apartment. Edwin followed Hengist out of the hall and through the main door.

"So?" asked Osgar, falling in behind Edwin as they followed Hengist towards a small building. "What did he have to say, where are we going and when?"

"We ride north at dawn. Question Hengist here, he knows more than me," replied Edwin, feeling somewhat angry. It wasn't at all what he had been expecting. Leofric hadn't even enquired as to the King's health or even Earl Harold's.

Hengist continued marching as if he hadn't heard them talking.

"Here is where you sleep tonight," he said in a thick Norvegian accent, pointing to a long building, "and over there are your horses."

"Before you go Hengist, haven't we met before?" asked Edwin.

He shook his head. "No! Never! Never seen you before in my life."

"Sorry, my mistake. It's just…your face seems familiar," replied Edwin.

Without more ado Hengist left, disappearing from view as he entered the Earl's residence.

"He doesn't say much," ventured Osgar, throwing his bags into the corner of the room. "Are you sure you know him?"

"I know him from somewhere," replied Edwin, still troubled. "I never make a mistake." He lay on the bed with his arms folded back, cushioning his head, wondering where and when he had seen the man before. He shook it from his mind for the moment.

"He is a surly bastard. He's supposed to know the route to Westune. Know the place?"

"I've heard of it," replied Osgar. "Never been there though."

"By the way, Hengist will be second in command … on the Earl's orders."

"To be expected I suppose," said Osgar, raising an eyebrow, "but we had better keep an eye on him. I don't trust him."

"I agree.

I'm not exactly happy about this assignment," said Edwin, peering out of the door, into the predawn darkness.

"Nor am I," replied Osgar, yawning. "Where's my jerkin? I can't find anything in this place. I already feel we're in enemy territory not to mention the fact I hardly slept last night because of the crashing thunder and pounding rain. What say we forget about the Wealhasc and head back home?"

"You know as well as I," said Edwin, buckling on his belt, "it can't be so. And those Northmen we escaped from were part of the King's privileged few. They belong to his nephew Ralf. The whole business stinks and I don't like it any more than you, but we're here and we must make the best of it."

"I suppose we'll have to," Osgar replied, following Edwin to the stables.

Mounting his horse, Edwin gave Osgar a grin.

"Well my friend, let's join the others and get this over with."

They were greeted by fifty mounted housecarls, each helmeted, chain-mailed, with thick leather capes, appearing like a herd of glinting, mettle tipped tents.

"Forward!" shouted Hengist, as they approached.

### -Brocctun Wuduholt, Mercia –
Brocton Wood, Staffordshire

After a while the thick forested land began to thin out, opening up to cultivated land a few miles from the Wealhasc border. Homesteads were dotted across the landscape, many of which had been left in charred ruins.

"This devastation is only days old. The Wealhasc must be back over the border by now," muttered Edwin, as they passed several more ruined houses. The surviving owners, having hidden from the raiders, were repairing the damage, trying to return their lives to normality, if it were ever possible.

'Why?' thought Edwin. 'Why? Why not move further away from the Wealhasc border and rebuild your lives somewhere else.'

The answer of course was, no! These were churls, freemen living on their precious land, handed down through the generations. They *couldn't* move away and land was expensive.

From the hilltop Edwin could see, between the trees, the lie of the land for miles, much of it forested, stretching far beyond towards the Afon Dyfrdwy and into Wealh. Like the other riders, he sat easily in the saddle, the still air was loud with bird song. Peaceful animals scrambling about gathering food for the coming winter were registered in Edwin's mind and understood. Scanning the distant land below, he saw a momentary glint of metal. He refocused his eyes. Yes. A thin column of smoke, barely discernible against the backdrop of the opposite hillside to the north.

"What's that hill called," asked Edwin.

"Don't know. Why do you ask?" replied Hengist.

"Because the enemy are down there in the valley between it and us," said Edwin, calmly pointing.

Others had also noticed as the fire appeared to be spreading.

"Look! There! More smoke over to the west of it," said another.

Everybody gazed at the distant scene. The impulse was to charge down to investigate, but not Edwin. 'Have we been seen?' he thought. 'If so, it could it be a trap, a killing field.' Edwin knew about the Wealhasc and their tactics with the short bow.

Hengist looked towards Edwin. "Your command friend."

'On my shoulders you mean!' thought Edwin, with an inward grin. He brought his horse forward and faced the Mercians.

"Osgar take one man and reconnoitre the land below. The rest of us will follow but with caution. Any questions?" He looked at Hengist who nodded in agreement. "Let's go."

A movement ahead brought Edwin reaching for his bow, shouting, "Disperse!"

The two riders skidded to a halt, Osgar sweating and obviously excited.

"There's at least thirty of them. We nearly rode into a trap. They were waiting for us."

All eyes were now focussed on Edwin.

"Tell me Hengist, which route would they take to Wealh if we attacked them?"

"There's only one route from where they are," he replied, dismounting and brushing the ground clear of leaves with his feet. He began drawing a map in the earth with the tip of his sword. "This is where we are." He momentarily looked up at Edwin. "They are here, and here is Fardune Brycg which crosses the bourne," he continued, stabbing the earth. "It's the only way across for them."

Edwin looked at Hengist and paused.

"Then it'll be best if we split into two groups. You smoke them out and drive them towards the border and we'll catch them before they cross the brycg."

"Sure you won't get lost?" Hengist said, with a mocking laugh. "We do the work while you two sutherners take it easy."

"Well," replied Edwin, keeping calm. "If I take fifteen of your men, they should know the way and the lie of the land, so we won't get lost! Eh?"

"They also know the way back to Tamaweord! Alric, take *twelve* men and go with these soft sutherners."

Edwin held Hengist's gaze for several moments until Hengist looked away.

"*Fifteen,* I said," he shouted.

"You heard me!" shouted back Hengist.

"*Of course we sutherners,* in polite company, regard *you* northerners as illiterate savages. I shan't reveal what we really think of you but that's by the way. Just give me what you can afford, Hengist. You obviously need the extra troops more than us!" Edwin replied, with a grin.

"I'll see you dead and strung up but for the moment that number is all I can afford. All you've got to do is stop the bastards before they get to the brycg. That is, if you can manage it!"

Edwin couldn't see any point in arguing further. 'He hates my guts and I'll have to live with it but that's the last time I'll give way to him.'

"Let's not waste any more time. Let's go!"

Edwin rode up to Alric, a thin man whose light brown hair hung down his back in a single, thick, untidy braid.

"Will this track take us to the brycg?"

"No! But the road you see over there will," he replied, pointing. "We have to continue up here as we are, keeping the road in sight for as long as we can."

The forest cover, where they had stopped, had thinned out sufficiently to see a fair distance ahead.

"Do you see that hill with an odd shaped tree atop of it?" said Alric. "The road sweeps to the right there and just beyond is the brycg."

"Good," said Edwin. "I feel exposed here. Look! There's a track here which branches off to the left. Let's take it and move further up into the forest.

"A house ahead," whispered Osgar.

Edwin caught a fleeting glance of a young woman, running through waist high bracken only to disappear among the trees. On closer inspection the house was a low timbered construction, easily overlooked. Its overhanging thatched roof was covered with branches and leaves, merging the dwelling almost completely and eerily into its forest surroundings.

An old man came out from a darkened doorway followed by an old woman. They held their hands clasped as if in prayer.

"Don't harm us," the old man pleaded.

Edwin rode forward.

"You and your family are quite safe. Have you seen any other soldiers?"

The old woman shook her head as if frightened to say more.

"There are Wealhasc soldiers attacking villages around here and you haven't seen anything of them?"

The old man stepped forward.

"They keep to the main road below. They don't see us but we see them."

"When was the last time you saw them?"

"Three days ago, going east."

Edwin noticed the woman give the man a severe glance but thought it only natural for her, not wanting trouble.

'I can't see the girl. They're very protective of her,' he thought. 'I would be too.' He was conscious of the fact that Hengist must be attacking the Wealhac by now.

"Keep inside your home. Don't go out unless you have to. Maybe there will be soldiers roaming around here soon. If you're seen you'll be in danger. Do you understand?"

They nodded, went inside and shut the door.

A few moments later he had already lost sight of the house.

Further on they came to a clearing, high enough to afford them a good view. Edwin looked back towards the east. He could just make out distant smoke rising.

"I don't like this one bit. With so few of us, we're vulnerable," said Edwin, as they emerged from the forest.

"It's completely flat arable land. Is that the brycg?" asked Osgar, pointing.

"Yes," replied Alric. "There's a deep embankment, a good place to hide the horses."

"Wait! Things are looking brighter already. See those farm wagons?" shouted Edwin, spurring his horse.

"We can make use of them," replied Alric, following him.

"That's my very thought." Edwin remembered another occasion where he had improvised, using a similar tactic. "If we take those wagons, tip them on their sides, blocking the road on the approach to the brycg and use them as barricades, it will give us an advantage against the returning Wealhasc. With all the produce spilled out onto the road it'll look like a natural accident. Does this brycg have a name?"

"Farndune Brycg," said Alric," and if you want to know, this bourne is the Afon Dyfrdwy."

"With Wealh on the other side?"

"Yes."

"Well then. This is a good place to make our stand," said Edwin.

"And we'll trap them in sight of their homeland," interjected Osgar, with a wicked smile.

Edwin glanced over towards the bourne. 'Good! The horses can't be seen. Alric has a good head on his shoulders, shows initiative but …Ooh no!'

"That's all we need" whispered Osgar, turning and thumping the upturned wagon with his fist.

A gaily coloured, travelling minstrel wagon was making its way across the brycg when it came to a stop mid-way.

"Eh! You there!" shouted the driver, "clear this road!"

Edwin put on his helmet, brought its hinged nose-piece down, raised his battle-sword and together with Osgar and Alric, walked up to the front of the wagon and snatched the reins from the driver.

"Take this painted toy over there onto that track and head north.

Understand?"

By now four others had poked their heads from out of the covered wagon to see what the commotion was about but seeing armed men, said nothing and disappeared from view. A little boy pushed his way out of the covers and jumped down.

"Mister, is that a real battle-sword?" he asked, waving his own small wooden replica in front of the immovable and deadly Edwin.

"Yes. And what's your name, young soldier?" Edwin enquired.

"Sebbi."

"Well now Sebbi," said Edwin, sheathing his sword and throwing the reins back to the petrified driver, "tell this man there is going to be a terrible battle." Lifting the boy, he sat him next to the driver. "Now! Get this wagon out of here, as fast as you can!"

The frightened driver nodded and making sure the brake handle was free, cracked the whip across the backs of the pair of old horses. The wagon began to rumble forward and onto the track.

"Move! Move! You're not going fast enough!" shouted Edwin. "Move!"

The wagon with its rickety covering swaying from side to side, bounced along the rough track and was soon out of sight.

"Look! There's another wagon coming towards us from the east! The Wealhasc are coming," whispered Osgar.

"I bet it's full of prisoners," replied Edwin, shielding his eyes from the intermittent sun glare, focussing his attention on the approaching group. "I count seventeen armed men on foot and a driver." Edwin blinked and rubbed his hand over his eyes again.

"You've got bloody good eyesight," replied Osgar. "Yes! I can see them clearly now."

Unsheathing his battle sword Edwin stabbed it into the ground and took hold of his bow.

"I'll take the one with the whip." He gave a cursory look at his men then turned to Osgar who was crouching next to him. "Os! Glad to see you've got plenty of arrows, I'm thinking we'll need every last one of them. These Mercians haven't got a bow between them."

"My men don't use them!" broke in Alric, tapping his long handled battle axe with pride. "With one stroke I could sever the head of a horse. We housecarls of Mercia are not peasants, hunting rabbits."

Edwin shook his head at the sheer stupidity of the man.

"Give me your skeggy for a moment."

Alric handed him his bearded axe. Lifting it, Edwin swung the weapon, feeling its weight and balance before handing it back.

"That's a nice weapon," said Edwin, "but you'll need both hands to use it and you won't have a shield up front to protect you. I'll stick to my trusty, double edged 'Head Biter', and my shield and bow. I shall only use my skeggy if I have to."

"But a bow is a weapon of the Wealhasc, not for real men, " Alric replied, dismissively.

"And I thought you had promise, how wrong can one be," smiled Edwin. "Listen boyo, as the Wealhasc would say, their arrows are deadly. But for your information, Osgar and I, are thingaliths, housecarls acting for the King. Privileged soldiers to Earl Harold Godwinson. You want to know how we East Anglians fight? Just watch and learn how real men do it!"

Alric said no more but thought, 'Thingalith? What's he talking about. That title went out with old King Offa and that was years ago.' But like the others, he watched the enemy approach and waited for Edwin's command.

"Os! Let's hope we can release those prisoners without harming them. We can fire off a couple of shots each before they have a chance to react, just to even up the numbers," he said smiling.

'Now we wait,' he thought to himself. 'Come on, come to Edwin. Shit! They've stopped! Have they seen us? No, they're on the move again. Perhaps tipping these wagons over was too obvious. Come on, come on my beauties, come to Edwin. The Wealhasc do look a bit ragged. I'll bet they've been mixing it with Hengist. That's a thought, where is that bastard? He and his troop should be chasing this lot from behind.'

Taking careful aim, Edwin and Osgar pulled back their bows and fired, killing the wagon driver. Moments later, two more arrows found their targets.

Emerging from behind their barricades Edwin's men, line abreast with raised axes and drawn battle-swords, with shields held out in front, advanced.

The surprise was total. Few of the enemy were able to retaliate in time. Edwin's men, oblivious of the few missiles being fired at them, struck into the Wealhasc… until there was a deathly silence. It had taken just a few moments.

A lone voice called out, then a chorus began shouting from the wagon, "Help us! Release us!"

Edwin and the others hacked the wagon open. Suddenly, Osgar shouted, "Ed! Look! In the distance! There's more of them?"

"Quick!" ordered Edwin. 'Take these people down to the river and out of sight!"

"They're mounted and approaching fast!"

"Get to the horses!"

"Us men of Mercia stand and fight," shouted Alric, swinging his axe in the air.

"Please yourself," said Edwin, turning to Osgar. "That's one mad bastard but I like his courage."

Scrambling down the embankment they mounted their horses and, half obscured from view by bushes, they waited.

"They've seen Alric's men. Prepare to attack!" Edwin gave the war cry.

"Abrecaaan!"

A horseman, using his spear as a lance, raced towards him. With one swipe Edwin shattered the spear with his sword, turned, spurred his horse again and sliced off his enemy's head, glancing at it as it rolled along the ground.

"Ed! Watch yer back!"

He was already waiting with his battle sword. More Wealhasc blood splashed onto his face, as he swung his sword, severing a man's arm.

"They're making for the brycg," shouted Osgar.

"That was short and sweet," said Edwin. "Well, well, well! We have company." He galloped up to welcome Hengist and his troop.

"Hengist! Nice of you to join us."

"Piss off! We chased them to you and you let them get away."

"Couldn't be helped we were somewhat busy," Edwin hissed. 'The arrogant bastard!' he thought, 'I would like to shove my sword up his jumped up arse!'

"What's that on your face and beard, blackberry juice?" replied Hengist.

"It'll be *your* guts and blood if you don't curb your tongue."

"What do *you* say Alric," Hengist said, turning as Alric approached.

"I'd be careful if I were you. Edwin and his friend are fucking killing machines."

"Mm! Seems my judgement maybe in error. When you're under the command of strangers, unknowns, it's always difficult to gauge their abilities. I don't like taking orders from fools."

"We'll say no more about it," replied Edwin, pointing to the embankment. "We have released a dozen of your people."

"Good. We'll have to leave them, to make their own way back to their homes. In the meantime what do we do now? Cross Farndune Brycg, and go after the Wealhasc?" said Hengist. "Because I say we do! You've done what you had to do. I can take command from here and you can go back to the King."

Edwin looked at Osgar who gave him a wink, as if to say let's chase some more game.

"Joint command. If you're gonna cross that brycg into Wealhasc territory, you'll be needing us. We'll come with you but in two groups, keeping the same men, and we'll meet back here at dusk. That gives us five hours."

"I'm not sure I like being on this track," said Osgar, in a low voice.

"Nor me. Not with trees on either side of us." Edwin was beginning to feel nervous. "You could hide an army in there. I have a nasty feeling we're being watched and I think we … Save yourself Os! Ride!"

Edwin's world was suddenly shattered by the pounding of missiles. Rain upon rain of arrows, their metaled heads clanked and crashed on Edwin's helmet and the shield strapped to his back, most glancing off. He spurred his horse… "Aaah!" A powerful numbing thud in the shoulder whirled Edwin off the horse. The ground seemed to float up at him, in slow motion as if in a dream. Grass and bushes enfolded him. A pulsating pain began to boil up and burst out of his shoulder. Stricken, he lay in the undergrowth. Disoriented and unable to move, he looked up at the spinning trees and drifted into unconsciousness.

Edwin opened his eyes. 'I'm blind!' he screamed to himself in panic. In the blackness, he moved his head from its side position and faced upwards.

"Stars! A bright, white, waning moon!" he mumbled with relief. 'How long have I been lying here?' he thought. 'The Wealhasc! Where are they? Why haven't they found and killed me?' He continued to lie where he was not knowing the extent of his injuries. He could hear the rustling sounds of animals. 'What's this. Shit! It's wet and warm. Blood! Lots of it! Thank God it's not summer, I'd be eaten alive by ants. I must get up, start moving before I bleed to death… Fucking shoulder! It's killing me! Where am I? I don't know. The moon's gone. I must find the track. I can't hear anyone, only the odd animal sniffing around for food. Somehow I've got to get up and find help or I'll die here in this fucking Wealhasc forest.' He felt a branch. 'It feels old, dry and strong. I'll use it to prop myself up. I must walk. It's times like these you don't need the weight of weapons…but I must keep them. They're my life!'

Heaving himself up he felt the hardness of an immoveable,

unseen trunk of a tree. Slowly he managed to stand upright and make his way forward through the undergrowth.

"Aah! Bloody pain. Well so far, so good," he muttered, casting his hands over his weapons; "Sword, bow, knife, axe and thank God for my shield. It must look like a bristling hedgehog. Can't manoeuvre myself to get rid of those fucking spent arrows. Maybe I can make use of them later. I must find help and get that arrow out of my shoulder otherwise I shall be dead in a few days. Right! Let's go. Look at me," he tried to imagine how he would appear. "I'm fully armoured but useless; I can just about manage to walk, barely able to get my dick out to pee never mind unsheathing my sword. Edwin old lad, you shouldn't be here and you shouldn't have ridden into that trap. And that reminds me, where is my horse? Oh well, never mind. I knew it felt wrong from the start! Must find shelter and help. This is taking longer than I thought. God knows what time of night is it, or is it nearly morning? 'Allo! I'm in luck. I can see a light. Let's hope for the best."

The cottage was set apart from the village. Edwin moved closer.

"Well, wish me luck, Woden! ...I can't even turn my head up to the night sky, not that there is much to see. Probably covered in cloud by now. Let's have a look at this house. It's worth taking a chance. I'll shuffle up to that un-shuttered window."

He peered through the window. 'What's this? A young woman eh! Very young. Sixteen I'd say and with long red hair, just my sort. Busying herself with bowls on a table. Is she married I wonder, where's the rest of her family? She's moved out of sight. Where's she gone? Oh yes. She's back, doing something with the fire ...I feel dizzy. Ooh shit!'

The woman inside the cottage froze.

"Who's there?" She quickly took a torch from its stanchion, lit it and opened the door. "Who's there?"

"I need help," groaned Edwin.

"You're lucky the arrow didn't penetrate the bone," said the young woman, putting down the hot iron tongs. "You're brave. You didn't scream when I put the hot iron to your wound. Not a murmur. Mind you, another couple of days and that arrow tip would have corrupted the flesh and then there would have been no hope for you. What are you doing in our country anyway?" Not waiting for an answer she carried on talking as if to herself. "You're a trespasser that's what you are. Getting hurt and wanting me to make you better. Who are you, Engliscman? You should know better than to come here and do mischief. And when you are better, what will you do then? Carry on as before? As if I didn't know what you men get up to."

"Do you mind shutting up," croaked Edwin, "I can't take any more of your mindless chatter. I don't know who you are. You're skilled, I'll give you that, skilled enough to be a physician and you've saved my life. I must be lucky but I do know pain. Years ago, when I was a kid, I escaped from a fire when we were attacked by Viking raiders. I'm very thankful to you but I just can't stand...." He drifted off into a fitful sleep.

He was aware of someone lifting his head. The smell of something pungent met his nostrils, but he couldn't place what it was.

"Drink this! It will help you gain strength."

It was hot and tasted of pond weed but he didn't much care what it was or how it tasted. He was thirsty and would have drunk his own piss if it had been put in front of him. 'That's a point,' he thought. 'No! it ain't that.' He pushed the bowl away from his lips,

"What's your name," he asked.

"Never mind my name, drink the rest of this broth. There's only a little bit left."

"I've been a very good boy," he said smiling, "and have drunk my medicine to the very last drop. Now, what's your name?"

"Gwynedd, and that's all you need to know because I've got

someone else who needs my attention."

"I didn't mean to take your precious time from your husband."

"Nooo, he's not my husband, he's another one of your lot, in a far worse state than you."

Edwin, for the first time, realised he was half naked. His Jerkin, armour and weapons were piled by the bed.

"What do you think you're doing?"

"Trying to see who he is, that's all."

'Sitting up straight is not so bad,' he thought, as he leaned over and grabbed his bow. Then, using it as a prop, he stood up. 'I feel a bit light headed but otherwise I'm alright.' He began to walk slowly over to the other side of the room.

"Well, well, well! I'll be struck down by lightening. The almighty Hengist! What happened to you?"

"Same as you, fart-face. Skewered …but in the groin. This maybe the end of me."

"Don't say that Hengist, you'll get over it."

"As good as she is…and I've *never* before seen her like," Hengist slowly took a painful breath, "the wound is deep and I reckon I'll be dead within a couple of weeks."

"No. That can't be right, me 'ol lad. I won't have anybody to take the piss out of or hate, will I? Many a time I've thought of shoving my sword up your arse but this …You'll get better, I'll personally see to it. Look, I've my reputation to think of. I can't go back to Earl Leofric with his top commander laying cold and dead on a bær can I?"

"Ha fucking ha. Fucking sutherners."

"Language! Mind your mouth!" shouted Gwynedd.

Hengist smiled. "Well I'll make an exception. I suppose you're not *so* bad for a sutherner. By the way, any chance of you showing me how to use that bow of yours? I'd like to get my own back on those bastards?"

"Language!"

Edwin shook his head. "There's no stopping her."

Hengist lifted his arm and taking hold of Edwin's hand, squeezed it hard.

"Get me back to my people. Don't leave me here."

Edwin nodded. "I'll get you back and alive. You have my oath on it."

Hengist closed his eyes. Edwin released his grip but remained watching him. 'I know it!' he said to himself. 'I know I've seen him before somewhere. That twisted nose and slit of a mouth, hardly any lips to speak of…yes, I've seen your hairy face before but when and where?'

"Are you going to stand there all day?" interrupted Gwynedd.

"He's one of my commanders, a right pain in the arse …and now, a friend. A friend I want to save."

"Well come over here and let him rest, and while you're about it, get some rest yourself."

"What's happening?" whispered Edwin.

"I don't know. I think some villagers are passing by. Lie still! Don't make a sound! I'll cover you with these goat skins, just in case."

"Thanks," replied Edwin.

'These goat skins stink!' he thought. 'Still, she's taking a hell of a risk for us. What else could I have said, I suppose thanks is better than saying nothing. I'm not going to lie here for hours, waiting to be spiked. If I can move my good arm, I might be of help.' Edwin felt from under the covers for his sword but only found his seax. 'I suppose this knife is better than nothing.' Propping up the cover he could see his sword. Stretching forward he groaned silently. 'Got it. Good. Now I've two weapons. At least I have a chance of skewering one of them if they come in here. How did I ever get into this mess ….bloody Hengist. It's his fault! How could I have refused to go with him? I would have looked a coward in front of his men, and if that had got back to Leofric …what a right fucking mess. What's that! Someone's banging on the door. If she's caught with us in here, they'll string her up as a traitor for sure, never mind what they'll do to us! Better be ready. I'll use the seax, not enough room under here to swing my sword. Use that later. I'll lie still and listen and then pounce.'

"All right, all right! What do you want here?" Gwynedd shouted.

"Open up! Have you got any Englisc in there?"

Edwin could only hear one voice from outside. 'Perhaps it's a lone villager.'

"Open up, woman!"

"Would I be still alive if the Englisc were in here? Look for yourself. You of all people should know better."

"I know about you and your witchcraft business. The village doesn't trust you and nor do I! You're like your mother and you know how she ended up...in flames," he laughed. "What's that over there?"

"Nothing. Just a pile of goat skins."

"I saw it move...and these. Weapons. Englisc weapons?"

A low groan came from the corner. The Wealhascman spun round. "Who's that?"

"Don't you touch him. He's dying."

"Traitor! Witch! You've got Engliscmen here! You'll pay for this when I tell the rest of 'em. And over there, is that another one of 'em?"

'Shit! That must be me. I'll wait for him to get close.'

Edwin felt the goatskins being moved.

"Leave them alone," shouted Gwynedd.

"Out of my way, Witch, or I'll stick you with this."

"I wouldn't if I were you," gritted Edwin, bringing his long bladed seax close to the man's neck. "One squeak out of you and you're dead."

Gwynedd had already grabbed hold of her skinning knife when another villager entered. The sound brought her spinning around in panic, plunging the knife into the man's stomach. Gwynedd's reaction and phenomenal speed was a complete surprise to Edwin and to Hengist who, lying on his side, was awake and wide eyed. Wrenching the knife out, she flung it away in disgust and watched in utter horror as the man collapsed to the floor.

"What have I done? What have I done?" she whispered.

"You've saved all our lives, that's what you have done," replied Edwin, trying to be conciliatory. Turning to his prisoner, he said, "Are there any more of you outside?"

He shook his head nervously.

"Gwynedd! Get a hold of yourself. We have to move fast! Have you any rope?"

"Yes!" she replied.

"Then get it now before the villagers realise these two are missing."

"That's better, he shouldn't give us any more trouble."

Edwin's prisoner was in his twenties and now had his legs and arms bound and a rag stuffed into his mouth. They dragged him away and propped him up against the wall in the far corner of the room with the dead man.

"Gwynedd, I need to make a bær for Hengist. It's the only way of getting him to the border and into Mercia. Can you find me two long branches and …"

"I know what a bær is and how to make one. I'm not stupid!"

"Well woman! Get to it!"

"Alright, alright! I'm not one of your thrall slaves or whatever you call them."

"I didn't say you were. It's…we need to get out of here and across the border, fast."

"That should do it," Edwin said, dragging the bær over towards Hengist. "By the way, how are you going to deal with them?"

There was a long pause. Gwynedd wrung her hands, momentarily closed her eyes and began rocking herself backwards and forwards.

"I don't know, I don't know! I didn't mean to kill him. I had to shut him up. I don't like hurting anyone but he," pointing at their prisoner, "will tell everyone and then they'll do the same to me as they did to my mother. Burn me on a pyre."

"Why don't you come with us?" said Edwin.

"Where would I go?"

"Gwynedd, saving our lives has destroyed yours. I'm offering you a life in Englaland. I've land in the suth. You could live there. It's up to you. What's it to be? We need to be out of here. Fast!"

"I'll pack my things."

Walking wasn't so bad now for Edwin, most of his armour was on the bær with Hengist but the weight of the bær was something else. Gwynedd had amazed him. Apart from her strength, the speed with which she had knifed the man was frightening. Edwin had barely seen the movement. 'One thing for sure, I can't take any liberties with her.'

Gwynedd could lift and pull as well as any man and Edwin told her as much. She took a last look back at her home disappearing into the distance.

"What was that? Did you hear?" said Gwynedd.

"Yes. Something in the woods, probably an animal…I hope," replied Edwin. The track turned to the right. "I don't remember coming along here or this far. I know it was at night but still I'm surprised how far I did walk before I found your place. Look! There's my horse! I can tell by the saddle"

Edwin hitched the bær to the horse and they went on their way without meeting or seeing anybody else.

Crossing Farndune Brycg, Edwin gave a disappointed sigh. The wagons and food had disappeared. Nothing remained, not even the dead bodies. It was if the battle had never taken place. Which prompted Edwin to think, 'No matter what mark I make, even after a short time, as shown here, I wouldn't be missed. It would be as if I had never existed.'

"Anything wrong," enquired Gwynedd.

He shook his head. "Nothing. We had better get some water and tend to Hengist's wound before moving on."

Gwynedd tugged at Edwin's sleeve, "Mounted troops approaching the brycg!"

"They're ours, Mercians!"

"But they're coming from my country!"

"Where did *you* get to?" said Edwin, addressing Osgar who approached with Alric at the head of the Mercian force. Not waiting for a reply he continued, "A fine companion you turned out to be."

"Have you done?" replied Osgar.

Edwin ignored him while he assisted Gwynedd with the injured Hengist.

"He looks a bit better. At least he's drinking and is cheerful."

Alric had dismounted and was kneeling beside his commander.

"How bad is it?"

"I think I'll survive. After suffering this woman and that fucking sutherner's company, I can survive anything," replied Hengist, who was obviously in pain.

"Thanks!" shouted Edwin, "I knew I should have left you behind, you ungrateful bastard."

"Piss off!" replied Hengist, turning to Alric and smiling. "Take no notice of him. Saving me has given him airs." Waving Alric away he beckoned Edwin to come close.

"What's wrong now?" Edwin asked.

"Nothing! I'm sorry! Sorry about everything." He turned away and closed his eyes.

'Sorry for what?' Edwin thought. 'Strange.' He looked over at Osgar who seemed, to Edwin, to be somewhat distant.

"So," he called, "what happened to you after we were attacked?"

"After you shouted, get out! I did just that, raced like hell out of there. Later, when we came back, it was getting dark and you were gone, couldn't find you. We searched till nightfall. After meeting up with the others, I heard that Hengist was missing too. We rode on just beyond the village and found a bunch of Wealhasc fighters holed up in a barn. We torched it. They won't be bothering Mercia again. We have no idea who their leader was but it certainly wasn't Gruffydd ap Llywelyn …he would have come out pleading for his life. So, what do we do now?"

"As I said. It was a waste of time. A wild goose chase. We'll head back to Tamaweord and home."

"What about her?"

Edwin looked at Gwynedd. "My offer still stands."

She nodded.

# CHAPTER III

*Early October, 1048*
**- Lunden, Tames Bourne -**
London, the River Thames

Edwin strode down the nearest of the five piers that projected out from the northerne bank, just up river from Lunden Brycg. The timbers sounded hollow underfoot. A fleet of docked square rigged, single-masted ships, the life blood of the city, was tied to the piers and to the many wooden mooring posts just visible above the surface of the Tames' high tidal mark. The surface of the bourne was glistening darkly through the bobbing and swaying sæweed.

'This ship seems about to leave,' he thought, 'although there doesn't appear to be anyone on board except him.'

"You there! Are you the captain?" shouted Edwin.

The man, wearing a leather scull shaped cap, looked towards Edwin and laughed. Glancing from side to side he raised his white bearded head.

"As I own this vessel, I suppose I am," he replied with a grin, exposing his two remaining front teeth, like crooked stumps of wood.

'Sarcastic bastard,' Edwin thought.

"You going down or up the Tames?"

"Down."

"When is this ship sailing?"

"When my crew get back."

"How long will that be?"

"Anytime now. There-e-yar, I can see 'em returning now,"

replied the captain.

"Do you know Corring Ham?"

The captain thought for a moment, took his oily looking cap off and scratched his balding head. "Is that, just before Convennon Teg?"

"Yes, that's the place."

"That's a fair ol' way. I was only going as far as Dart."

"I'll make it worth your while," said Edwin.

"Is that all three of you and your horses?" he said, looking towards the bank.

"No. Just me, the woman and two horses," replied Edwin.

"That'll be…"

Edwin could see he was eyeing his sword.

The man began sucking on his remaining teeth.

"Are you a housecarl?" he asked at last, squinting his beady eyes at Edwin.

"What does that have to do with the tide and the river," Edwin retorted, ridding himself of his smile and looking straight into the man's dark brown eyes. "If you're thinking of over charging me, the King will hear of it!"

"Oh!...I see! You're one of those…specials… Thingaliths, that's it, royal guards or something?"

Edwin didn't reply, satisfied only to let the man think what he liked.

"Well, that's different. If you're a King's man I'll only charge you twa silver pennies."

Edwin, kept his gaze firmly fixed on the man.

"A penny then. Will that be alright sur?"

Edwin slowly nodded in agreement, then turned and walked back to rejoin the others.

While Gwynedd was leading her horse onto the ship, Edwin spoke softly to Osgar.

"So, the King wants you to join his guards here in Lunden. What about Earl Harold. Don't you owe him your loyalty?"

"Fuck loyalty, Ed!" replied Osgar, "I'm looking out for me! The number one boss-man here is the King and if he wants me, so be it. I'm his man. Let the Earl sort it out with the King. Anyway, the pay's better and I get to see the country in luxury... and why not?"

"Soft living won't do you much good."

"You're just jealous. Don't tell me you wouldn't appreciate a bit of the good life as well."

"I'm happy as I am. My family owes a great deal to the Godwins." He didn't elaborate, but gave Osgar a smile, shook his calloused hand and then led his own horse onto the ship. 'So, the bastard has gone over to the King. Perhaps I can make use of him.' Even so Edwin felt slightly crushed. 'I thought he was my friend, someone I could trust with my life. Instead, he's revealed his true self for the first time. Shit! And I didn't know. Maybe I didn't want to know. I should have asked him outright about the trap he led me into. Or was it my mistake? He didn't get a scratch! It really depresses me not knowing. If I ever met him again, could I trust him? Tread cautiously Edwin my boy. But the more I think about it, the more certain I am he had a hand in leading me into that trap and I think he knows I know it. Couldn't find my horse? Bollocks! He never even tried. He'll be messing with Leofric next and if he does, he'll find himself playing a very dangerous game. Hengist would see through him. Why! Why have I still got Hengist on my mind?'

"Alright captain, ready when you are," he shouted, not looking back.

With the ship untied from its moorings, the ebb tide forced the vessel away from the pier. The captain, manning the steering arm, navigated the vessel into midstream, the square sail raised and flapping in the light breeze.

"Is anything the matter?" asked Gwynedd.

"Why do you ask?"

"When you returned from saying good-bye to your friend, you looked troubled."

"Nothing you need to worry about," said Edwin.

'How can I tell her I don't trust my King or Osgar, the man who I thought had been my friend for years…I can't. Thank god Earl Harold was at court. He too was mystified as to why I had been sent north. Come to think of it, he looked edgy. Must be some smelly politics going on. At least I'm not involved. Decent of him to let me take some time off, to allow my shoulder to heal …I'll wait for his call. Call for what? Who knows. In the meantime, I'll settle in and enjoy this trip down river and home.'

"That's an old and odd looking brycg," said Gwynedd, watching it retreating into the distance.

"Yes, Lunden Brycg is a real lash-up," replied Edwin. "There's been a brycg there for hundreds of years but that one has been there since…well before my father's time, which reminds me of a story he once told me. Thirty-four years ago, during Cnute's reign, after he had kicked out King Æthelred, the old King tried to come back and regain his crown but, in those days, Cnute's viking army occupied Lunden. Æthelred made a deal, with a friend of a friend, by the name of Óláfr. Well, to cut a long story short, Æthelred financed a small fleet of ships, with Óláfr leading them. He sailed up the Tames, mooring upstream and, would you believe it, ripped the roofs off some houses, fixing them to their ships, then rowed up to that very same brycg. They hooked grappling irons and ropes to the main supports and waited for the ebb tide. Then they rowed like bats out hell, pulling the brycg supports away. With half the brycg wrecked, nobody could cross the river, isolating Cnute's men to the north of it. The local boatmen made fortunes ferrying goods and people across. Even today people sing about, Lunden Brycg falling down!"

"I can believe it," said Gwynedd, fascinated by the story.

"Well, that's why that selfsame brycg looks so odd, because the rebuild and patchwork was done on the cheap, which is typical of today! No spare money in the royal coffers. Yet this country is one of the wealthiest; certainly better off than Northmandig, or even Danemark and Norveg, combined."

"Mm." Gwynedd thought for a few moments. "But tell me, why

did they put the roofs from the houses onto the ships?"

"To protect them from the missiles being thrown down on them from the brycg above."

"What happened to Æthelred. Did he get his crown back?"

"Not then, but he did regain it some months later."

Leaving Gwynedd to rest amidships, Edwin went forward to the bow, grabbing at each of the two crutch-posts in turn to keep his balance. The ship was moving faster than a horse could gallop. Together with the tide and breeze no rowing was needed. The crew, apart from adjusting the sail and trimming the rigging, spent most of the journey talking and laughing among themselves, away from the passengers.

They had just past Dart. Edwin thought that they must be planning to dock there when they returned on the incoming tide. It was mid-afternoon, the sun was quite low and beginning to cast an ochre glow over the landscape. A cold sharpness in the air made Edwin shudder. He would be glad to be back home in his familiar surroundings. But what of Gwynedd he thought. How would she fare, being uprooted and living in an unfamiliar land and environment. He had saved her life by taking her away from her village but would she be happy here? And what would she do?

"Corring Ham's coming into view," shouted the captain.

"Is this where you live?" enquired Gwynedd, looking around her as she led her horse off the long jetty and onto dry land.

"No, not here. A little further inland," replied Edwin.

### - Upper Barnstæd, East Anglia -

Gwynedd had already dressed and gone out by the time Edwin emerged from his own room and entered the main hall the following morning. He felt strangely alone.

'Why?' he thought. 'How could she have this effect on me.' He was angry. No woman had ever moved him like this before. He poured himself some mead, gulped it down, slamming the jug back onto the table and watched some spilt liquid spread and disappear down into the dark spaces of the timbered joints.

"Bitch!" he hissed through his teeth. 'Why am I angry?' He drew a deep breath and looked around the hall. The only other person there, beside himself, was a serving woman who had just entered to place some logs on the central hearth.

"Have you seen Gwynedd?" he shouted.

She nervously returned a blank expression.

"Gwynedd did you say?"

"Yes," replied Edwin, in a calmer voice. "The woman I brought here last evening."

"I don't rightly know of any woman by that name, sur. But I did see a woman earlier, wearing a grey cloak."

"That has to be her. Where did she go?"

"I think she was walking towards the village but I've never seen her before. Perhaps Egbert might know. He was talking to the smithy as she passed him by."

Edwin thanked her. He thought about pouring himself another drink but decided not to. Leaving the hall he made his way to the stables.

"Egbert! Have you seen a woman wearing a grey cloak?"

"Yes, I did. Says her name is Gwynedd. Is she a friend of yours?"

"Sort of. Did she say where she was going?"

"She said she was going to the village."

"Good." Somehow he felt relieved. "What's happened since I've been away?"

"The usual trouble. Bloody Viking raiders! A fleet of them, twenty-five ships in all, landed on the coast over yonder. They then sailed suth to Tanet and got a real thrashing. The local Thegn got his men together and made 'em run like rabbits back to their ships."

"Has anyone asked for me?"

"No. But the royal fleet has put to sæ, so I hear."

"Thanks. If anybody wants me, I shall be over by the fishery."

Egbert was in his early fifties a studious man who managed

Edwin's estate. A man who he could rely on, who had been his father's friend and was part of the family. Egbert's son, Edmund, was coming up to fifteen and showed real promise in his military training. Edwin felt sure he would eventually take over Egbert's position, when the time came.

His mind kept going back to Gwynedd. 'Why am I so drawn to her, fascinated by what she does and protective of where she goes?' Deep down he knew the answer. This was new to him. He had a powerful yearning to be near her. He shook her from his mind, saddled his horse and rode off.

The easterly breeze had a cold edge which made him shiver. Edwin rode past the fishery to a favourite grassy knoll overlooking the Tames. Sitting on the hillock, he looked out across the water, towards the estuary. A flock of sæ birds reared up into the sky, momentarily suspended in the air before diving, skimming the surface of the water, rising up and repeating the performance, then breaking away and flying northwards as if alarmed by an unseen disturbance. 'I should have worn a cape,' he thought. The rising sun cast his elongated shadow across the uneven ground, resembling no particular shape, merely a dark smudge. He sat motionless, taking in all that was around him.

Edwin had inherited two hundred acres of prime grazing land, enough to keep three hundred head of sheep and forty cows, plus a fishery, tucked away to the west of the creek, close to Convennon Teg.

His father, Wulfric, had been a self-made man and had left all this land to him. Edwin felt proud and secure but he missed his parents, especially his father. He couldn't help but reflect on the past weeks and the suspicion of betrayal by his friend, Osgar. 'Time will tell,' he thought. 'What really happened? Certainly Earl Leofric seemed surprised at my return to Tamaweord and the King didn't seem that interested in what I had to report when I arrived back at West Minster. The King's a mystery, I don't seem to be able to read his mind at all or am I losing my touch?'

His father had once said to him; "Be self-contained, believe in yourself, trust no one and don't believe half of what you hear."

Wise words indeed Edwin thought, smiling to himself. His father had been a hard man but a bloody hero, a force to be reckoned with. He had started out as a baker in the north of the country. Edwin again remembered their village being attacked and fired by Viking raiders in the early morning darkness; the warning bells, his father waking him, his mother's frantic screams at not finding his little brother Eadric who had crawled away and died in the flames. His parent's utter distress. Their frantic attempts to break free from their captors but most of all his mother's screams! Those he could never forget. And being helpless when they were being bound and dragged away by force from their fired and wrecked home, to be sold as slaves across the Northerne Sæ. But they had been saved before they boarded the raider's ships by a miracle; the arrival of Earl Leofric's men. It was ironic he thought, being rescued all those years ago by the same man who was now planning trouble against the Godwins. A strange twist of fate.

With only the rags they were wearing, they had travelled to Lunden, away from the death of his brother. His father would shout! "I am a freeman and yet I have nothing!" Of course it hadn't been true. He had his wife and son and he never gave up hope for their future. He had striven to rebuild their lives. Edwin took a deep breath at the thought of those days. At the age of thirteen it hadn't seemed so bad. For his mother and father it had been devastating. His father had taken whatever work he could and, being a baker, he was never out of work.

One day Edwin's father decided to have a broadsword custom made. He had taken him to a smithy in Lunden. Most housecarls had their swords forged to their particular specifications. Edwin remembered the smithy summing up his father's height, reach and great strength for this specially long bladed sword. The biggest surprise to him was that it was to have a gold filigree inlay. Where had his father found that sort of money? Not many could afford a battlesword and fewer still could afford to have one made. As it turned out, it was the best investment ever. His father had already mastered the weapon; as if he had been wielding such a weapon since birth. Now with this sword, no one could touch him for he was the master of it; one stroke could chop a man in half. In those early days, news travelled fast and it soon came to the notice of a thegn on the suth side of the Tames, who introduced his father to Earl Godwin. Realising his father's potential, the Earl had employed him as one of his bodyguard and in so doing had given his father land and a great house in Upper Barnstæd.

"Hengist!" he shouted aloud. "It was Hengist." He suddenly remembered the face of the young Viking raider who had laughed at his mother's screams! "It was him! That strutting bastard! He was no more than three years older than me. Oh yes, I remember you now alright, Hengist! You must have been recruited by Earl Leofric soon after. And I saved your fucking scrawny neck." He shook his head and gave a hollow laugh. "Life's queer that's for sure."

Edwin strode into the hall early the next morning, poured himself a mug of weak beer from the pitcher on the table and looked around before sitting down. Pulling a bowl of pork fat towards him he broke off a piece of freshly baked bread, scooped out a knifeful of the fat, spread it on the bread and took a bite. "Mm… could do with a bit more salt," he said, taking a pinch and grinding the crystals, between his thumb and forefinger, over the rest of the bread. Partially raising his left arm, he gave a silent groan. How long would his shoulder take to heal he wondered?

"You should have your arm in a sling," said Gwynedd, joining him at the table.

"This is the first I've seen of you, since we arrived. Where have you been?" Edwin took a swig of beer.

"Ah! Is the Englisc Thegn missing me?"

"I meant it! Don't you think it unusual *not* to see one's guest? By the way can I get you a drink?"

"As I don't often get a chance to sleep in a *nobleman's* house, I'll have some of your nice mead," she replied with a smile.

Edwin sent a servant for some mead.

"I've been looking around your village and land."

"Oh! What did you find out?" he said, pouring some of the mead that had been brought, sparingly into a small mug, pushing it towards her.

"Everybody likes you," she replied, picking up the mug and giving it a strange look. "Are you sure you can afford this?" she added sarcastically.

"It's expensive and I have only one barrel left."

"Well that's alright then. One barrel is all I need."

'Why is she trying to annoy me?' he wondered.

"I'm glad somebody likes me," Edwin replied, ignoring the barbed comments. He decided to change the subject. "As it's a sunny day, would you like to go for a ride?"

She looked at him for a moment as though undecided.

He thought he would decide for her. "Well, I'm going. Drink up and follow me," he said getting up and making his way to the stables.

Gwynedd shouted to his departing back, "I'm going to collect my cloak first."

Reaching high ground before the creek and Convennon Teg they could see the plains, which at high tide would be flooded, and beyond that the mouth of the Tames and the open sæ.

Gwynedd, sitting astride her horse, peeked out from the warmth of her hooded cloak and seemed fascinated by a group of figures, far off on the mud flats.

"It's so featureless and bleak. What are those people doing over there?"

"Some are collecting cockles, others are digging for bait," replied Edwin.

"What sort of bait?"

"Lug and ragworm mostly."

He felt his answer had satisfied her curiosity. Gazing ahead towards a far distant shape on the horizon, he waited for her to continue the conversation but she said nothing. He had decided to gently distance himself from her until she wanted him, made some demand of him. But he could not deny she had disturbed him.

"I'm feeling chilled to the bone and the sky is looking threatening," she said finally, nudging her horse close to his.

He looked up and felt a few spots of rain on his face.

"Let's head back before it pours…too late! Make for that barn," he shouted.

"What are you smiling about," said Gwynedd, angry at being trapped in a storm.

"Nothing," lied Edwin, trying to sum up the woman by his side. He had decided against riding for home in this torrential rain, preferring to wait it out in the shelter of the building. The notion of spending some time with her in this rundown place amused him.

"You're smiling again!"

"You've become very spiky. It's difficult to get a civil word out of you," he said, dismounting and looking out of the shelter.

"I don't know what you're up to but I'm staying where I am on this horse and will leave the moment this rain stops."

"Well, that might be some while," he said, looking up at the sky. "For god's sake woman! I'm not going to rape you! I don't see this rain stopping. If anything it's coming down harder and will probably carry on like this for the rest of the day."

"What do you think we should do then?"

"Well, I don't intend to get soaked. There's a pile of dry hay in the corner, I intend to lie on it and rest up until this," he pointed to the still darkening sky, "blows over."

"Help me down then," said Gwynedd, having changed her mind.

"My God! The woman trusts me," he said aloud, holding her under the arms and setting her on the ground.

Gwynedd removed her wet cloak.

He was all too aware of the hard nipples showing through her dress.

Conscious of her body's reaction to him, Gwynedd became embarrassed, took hold of the cloak again and wrapped it tightly around herself.

He could see she was nervous and he pointed to more hay in the opposite corner.

"You can rest over there if you still don't trust me."

She gave him a cold look through half closed eyes, that he would come to know well.

Edwin lay down, folded his arms behind his head and stretched out his legs while she sat against the opposite wall, her arms clasped around her knees.

"What were we saying?"

"We were talking about the rain," she replied, not looking at him.

"No! Before then…Oh I know, about you saving my life. Don't forget, I saved yours."

"I *risked* my life in order to save yours," she replied. "I could have kept my door shut tight instead of letting you in!"

"It wasn't only me. Why did you put your neck out to save us both?" Edwin said, turning towards her, leaning on his elbow.

"I don't know …perhaps it was your baby blue eyes," she retorted, with a mocking laugh.

"It was too dark to see my eyes. And Hengist?" he queried.

"Well! I couldn't let the two of you die, could I? Put it down to a weakness of mine…men."

"You're as good as most physicians I have met. How did you come by that knowledge?"

"From my mother."

"I think I heard you say she was burnt alive." He beckoned to her. "Come over next to me and explain what really happened?"

She rose reluctantly and sat down an arm's length from him.

"The church hated my mother because of her power to heal."

"The church? Why?"

"Don't tell me you've never heard of the church demonising women like us. Calling us witches."

"Of course I have but I've never met a witch or anyone like you before, never thought about it until now."

"Well, that's what they do to us."

"Why?"

"Because they're frightened of losing control of their flock, at least that's what my mother used to say and she was right. So they called her a heretic. Of course she believed in God or at least in a God like most others, but perhaps a little differently. When people were ill they would knock on our door instead of the priest's."

"I see."

"In the old days, people like my mother were venerated. They were called the 'Wise Ones.'"

"Sort of physicians," replied Edwin.

"Yes. I was only a young girl when she was killed. She understood so much; plants and their properties. She used them for good, to cure people's ills. For that, they burnt her alive!"

Sadness swept over her.

Edwin wanted to hold her, to make her feel safe and secure but he couldn't. He couldn't move his hand or his arm, it was if he were paralysed. 'She would think I was only wanting her for sex.'

"Do you still miss her?"

"Of course." Her eyes began to fill with tears.

"Do you know, you are the second woman to save me."

"Who was the first?"

"My mother."

He told her about the attacked, his brother and their escape to Lunden.

Gwynedd thought for a while. "Your brother might still be alive?"

"That would be impossible. He couldn't possibly have survived. The place was ablaze!"

She gazed at him. "He looks just like you but with reddish hair."

"What are you talking about," he said, shaking his head, "my brother is dead. He couldn't possibly have escaped that fire!"

"I'm telling you. I saw this young man about a week before you came. He stopped by my door. I gave him some food. He's about seventeen and he told me he had been born in Suthford and his father was a baker."

His mind went back to that blazing inferno, the chaos, screams and being dragged away. "If he's alive, I'll find him," said Edwin, unable to fully take in what she had just said.

"Where are your parents now?" she enquired.

"They're both dead."

"I'm sorry."

"It happens," he said. "My father was tall, strong as an ox. He was never ill and nothing could defeat him. It seemed that he would go on forever. Then one day, he dropped dead and six months later my mother died of a fever."

"That's terrible to lose both parents in so short a time."

Edwin looked up at the roof as the sound of the rain increased. Looking out of the open doorway, he watched the rain pounding the ground with such force it splashed ankle high before flowing into a gully surrounding the barn and running away.

"I have some bad news and some good news. Which do you want to hear first?"

"Give me the good news," she replied.

"The roof doesn't leak. The bad news, we may have to bed down here for the night."

Gwynedd remained silent.

Edwin awoke to a loud clap of thunder; it was night. He put a protective arm over Gwynedd, who was now lying next to him.

"Don't paw me!" she blurted suddenly, awakened from a troubled sleep. "I'm not one of your whores from the town."

"Paw you?" Edwin shouted. "Paw you! It was just a protective arm, nothing more! I didn't paw you! I don't paw women!"

He got up and went to his horse. "Paw you!" he muttered. Mounting his horse he turned towards Gwynedd, "I don't paw, grab or force any woman. I'm getting out of here. Fuck the rain, fuck the thunder and fuck you too. You can make your own way to wherever you damn well like!"

"Stop!" shouted Gwynedd, running towards him. "You can't leave me here!"

"No such word as can't! I'm leaving, just watch me," he retorted.

"I'm sorry!" she shouted back, grabbing hold of the reins and Edwin's leg. "I really am, truly sorry."

In the darkness he could just make out her face, her eyes wide open and glistening.

"You need me!" she shouted. "Your shoulder. It hasn't healed yet."

"I don't understand you! You insult me and now you want to care for me. What am I to do with you?"

"A powerful man like *you*, doesn't know what to do? Asking *me*, a mere woman? You'll have to put up with me while your shoulder heals. Then I'll leave and make my own way in the world. Who needs men?"

He looked down at her for a moment, then dismounted. Still gazing at her as if transfixed, he began speaking, half to himself.

"One moment I can't bear the sight of you, the next, I can't bear not seeing you. How can that be?"

"I don't know," she shrugged, "It's a mystery."

He took her hands in his.

"I swear to you, I don't take advantage of women, least of all you. You saved my life. Now! Shall we start again without the insults and wait for this storm to stop."

She raised her head and nodded.

"You shouldn't be so bloody sensitive."

He thought he detected a wry smile on her face. She looked away.

'Who has won here,' he thought, as he unbuckled his sword belt, carefully laying his sword and seax by his side, between them.

'Gwynedd or me? I'll have to out-think her… but how can I? Day and night she's always in my thoughts. I've got to keep ahead of her.'

Gwynedd remained nervously awake. Not that she was worried about Edwin, asleep by her side. She looked at him. He was gently snoring. His lips, occasionally, would pout forward and flutter on a breath.

She smiled. 'Bloody big softy! I've got you around my little finger, boyo.' But she too was unsettled, yes she was frightened. Ever since her mother's death, she had been alone and had had to protect herself. She remembered with horror, the priest shouting, "Look! See! She doesn't scream, she must be *a witch*! She's with the devil!" She had crawled away and hidden behind their house and cried and cried. Then they had chased her out of the village to live in a rundown cottage; to live alone. 'I should be grateful they didn't burn *me* as well. What was it the priest said, "We can't burn her child, that would be a sin." Hypocrite! I had no one to turn to. Mother never spoke about my father; her dark secret. But she had been a good woman and helped people with their problems. She had cures for most ailments and was mid-wife to many mothers of the village. Then they killed her. Why? Why? If mindless, easily lead people could do that…' she closed her eyes. 'Then what of me? I'm now a woman without a home and in a foreign land. What does Edwin see in me? What does he want me for? He says he likes me and thinks of me all the time. Ooh, he's turned over.'

Her eyes, having got used to the darkness, could just make out the horses standing inside the half open doorway. She stared at Edwin for some time. 'I must say, he would be a fine catch. He's not bad looking and he's intelligent, at least for a man. And he has property, powerful friends and is kind. Yes, I suppose he's not bad really.' She continued looking at him. 'I want him and I want him to protect me.' She felt an unusual warm glow all over and moved closer to him.

Edwin awoke in an instant and made a grab for his sword.

"Shush! It's only me. I'm cold," she lied, putting her arm around him, snuggling up close.

"What this?" she said, picking up the sword and knife which had separated their bodies.

"Let me take those. I thought you were…a phantom grabber!"

"Shush! Don't speak," she whispered.

'She's giving me orders!' he thought. He was now fully awake and grinning. 'It's alright for her to grab but not me it seems.'

Her hand burrowed its way under his tunic and began gently massaging his back. He closed his eyes and relaxed, letting himself feel the tips of her fingers stroke the skin between his shoulder blades, before firmly pressing down the length of his spine. He let his imagination run uncontrolled.

He rose up above her and lightly kissed her forehead, her nose, the soft lips that slowly parted. Suddenly she thrust her tongue against his, he gripped hers with his lips. Then they were wrestling, like two crossing swords, twisting, turning, their mouths becoming a tireless brawl. Arms, hands, clothes torn, legs entwined, bodies naked… he sank deep down into her warm, moist deliciousness. Her body stiffened as she gave a wild scream! He stopped!

"Don't stop!" she yelled.

He pinned her down by her shoulders. "*Woman!*" he muttered, "*you're, .. still, .. giving, .. me, .. fucking orders. Don't, .. you, .. ever, .. stop?*" He felt the inner heat of her body. A calmness swept over him which changed gradually to an increasing, pulsating, powerful urgency. Nails tore into bodies, blood! Pain! Inner muscles gripped him. He repeatedly plunged ever deeper, then rearing up at last, he collapsed at her side, as to a spent, hapless, beached ship.

The following morning Edwin awoke to sunlight streaming in through the open doorway of the barn. His shoulder throbbed, the dull pain made him wince. Gwynedd was tending his shoulder and humming. She smiled and kissed him.

"I think we should be getting back," he sighed. "I'm really

hungry."

"It's far too early and besides, I want to know more of your sensitive nature."

*Christmas Day, 1048*
**- Upper Barnstæd -**

All had been prepared for the day's festivities but Edwin had other thoughts on his mind. He looked up and walked over to Egbert.

"Are all the plans for today complete?"

"All done, as you can see. Tables and seats are laid out, fire lit. As it's a small gathering, I think one lamb should be enough to go around."

"Put another lamb on to roast. If we have anything left over, give it to the villagers."

Egbert agreed.

"About the sword for your son," said Edwin. "Do *you* want to present it or do you want to leave it to me. I don't mind which. Your choice."

"We would much prefer for you to do the honours," said Egbert.

"Thank you. By the way, have you seen Gwynedd?"

"I think she's over by the stables."

He left the building and began trudging through the mud. 'I'm always losing her. She's never… am I being possessive? Yes I am.' He scanned the outbuildings, half lost in the morning gloom. 'Aah! Here she is.'

"Gwynedd, there's something important I want to say to you."

"I have something to say too."

He passed over her reply, his mind so absorbed by what he wanted to say.

"Well, let's saddle up and go for a ride."

"In this weather?"

"Yes."

Edwin, gripping hold of the pommel of his saddle, hunched forward and looked at the distant misty skyline, across the field of grazing sheep. It seemed to symbolise the uncertainty of what he was about to say. He was nervous. His horse fidgeted as if it was as tense as he.

"Well, you've brought me out here on this damp, cold day. It must be bad news," she said, brushing aside loose strands of hair that had blown across her face. "Tell me what's bothering you."

Edwin hesitated. He knew in his mind what he wanted to say but now… 'Suppose she refuses me,' he thought, 'what then?' All night he had gone over and over his speech and had forgotten most of it. 'Oh shit! The worst she can do, is to say no.'

"Gwynedd, you are a strong, unusual kind of woman who knows her own mind. I've never met a woman such as you before and possibly never will again. I suspect, if I gave you a sword you would weald it as well as any man. But since bringing you here, to Upper Barnstæd, I've come to know and rely on you and have grown very fond of you and I hope you have grown fond of me."

"Of course I am fond of you…"

"Our children would need a father!" he blurted out.

"Who says I'm pregnant?"

"I'm just saying, if you were …after all, we did have more than two bites of the cherry!"

"Thanks! I'm now a cherry!" replied Gwynedd, looking towards the sheep, which were slowly edging closer.

"You're in my country, a foreign country and perhaps you think you're at my mercy."

"I'm at no one's mercy!"

"Gwynedd, I didn't mean it to sound like a threat. You know you are at liberty to leave and go back at any time. Damn it! What I want to say…is…will you marry me!" he almost shouted.

Gwynedd turned towards him. "Marry?"

"Yes! Marry!" he said. 'It's all a bloody disaster,' he thought.

"I can see by the look on your face, the answer is no! God in heaven, I'm as nervous as a rabbit, sitting here feeling like a blabbering half-wit. Help me out Gwynedd, yes or no! Will you marry me?"

"I'm waiting for you to say something before I answer you."

"What?"

"One word has four letters in it, and is very important," she replied, now beginning to feel the cold west wind.

His stomach was starting to rebel. He imagined knives were churning about his insides. 'This is slow torture. Of course I know what the words are, damn it! And she knows I know. I'll have to give in. But only this time! Why does she always have to try to be in control! It's unsettling. Perhaps she can read my mind. That's a thought. After all, she is one of those …'wise ones' Scary! But she makes love like a dream. Who could ask for a better woman for a wife. A wife who could also protect your back in a fight?'

"I'm still waiting," she said, holding the reins and looking ready to gallop off.

'I'm going to make her wait…at least for a few more moments.'

"I Love You! Now will you marry me?"

"I want you to mean it! Then I'll give you my answer."

'She does want to marry me,' he thought. 'But it's like squeezing blood out of a stone?' He dismounted and knelt on one knee.

"Gwynedd! Please… I love you… I truly love you… now will you marry me?"

Pulling at the reins she made her horse rear.

"YES, I'll marry you," she shouted. "I'll race you back to the stables."

"Bloody woman! I'll get the better of you yet!" he shouted after her.

Getting up from the wet, muddy ground, he leapt onto his horse and galloped after her.

After the Christmas Day church service, the gathering, led by Edwin and Gwynedd, entered the main hall. At first, Edwin hadn't noticed the shadowy figure standing apart, just inside the door. Alarmed when the figure moved, he drew his sword in an instant, pushing Gwynedd behind him.

"Osgar! What are you doing here?"

"I mean no harm!" Osgar held his arms out-stretched, away from his sword belt. "I need your help."

Edwin gave him a hard penetrating look.

"I mean it Ed, I'm in trouble."

Edwin turned to Gwynedd.

"We need one more at our the table. Osgar, go with Gwynedd, I'll join you later."

Edwin stepped into the centre of the hall to join his old friend Egbert who was waiting with his son, Edmund. Taking a newly forged broadsword and a shield from Egbert, Edwin held the sword up, turning around for all to see. He then called Edmund to stand in front of him.

It was if he were seeing the young man for the very first time. Edwin hesitated. He involuntarily compared Edmund's face to that of a young woman. There was no hint of hair. He shook the notion from his mind.

"Before we celebrate further on this Christmas Day, I would like to present Edmund, son of Egbert, with this sword. As you all know, the skeggox, the long handled bearded axe, has always been the favourite weapon of a housecarl but this young man has a long and powerful reach. With this sword, together with this shield he will be well equipped for battle." Edwin handed Edmund the weapons. "You have trained well and are strong. May these weapons protect you, your hearth and your home, with honour."

"Thank you sir," replied Edmund.

Edwin and Egbert watched with pride as the young man walked away.

"I'll notify Earl Harold that he has another good man to call on," said Edwin.

"When are you seeing the Earl next?" enquired Egbert.

"On the fourth of January, his first court of the New Year."

"I hope he doesn't call on my son too soon. His mother dotes on him, it will break her heart to lose him."

Edwin smiled.

"He'll be alright, there are no great battles to fight. Go and enjoy the rest of the day with your family."

"Thank you for your gifts. We could never have afforded that marvellous sword and shield without your help."

"My father always said, possessing a sword and knowing how to use it makes a man of you. Without it, you're only half a man, unable to protect your family."

"True! I have fond memories of him, and of him saying those very words to *me* when he gave me my sword."

Edwin signalled for the meat to be cut and mead to be poured. Passing by the spit, he breathed in the succulent aroma of roasted lamb.

"I don't like the church and its liturgy. Never have," whispered Gwynedd, seated next to Edwin at the top table.

"I'm not saying you have to like it," he whispered back, their heads almost touching. "This is my village. It's a heavy responsibility and I have to be seen following the duties of a responsible Thegn, a representative of Earl Harold and the King and I have to keep the church on my side. These people look to me for direction and leadership, they need to believe in something greater than themselves and to have enough food to live on. That's what keeps them going. They're not like us. I believe in… a sort of God as you do, but I'm not sure about the church's ritual. It's not so long ago my forbears believed in the old religion. Now, I'm at a crossroads and not sure. Let me say, I'm thinking about it."

"Well, I don't like being organised; controlled as if I were a ewe, part of a flock," she replied.

"We're so similar you and I. My mother and father taught me to read. So I don't need priests to give me their version of things or tell me how to behave. But they, the villagers," he indicated the people seated about them, "except for Egbert over there and his son, can't read …and they don't want to."

A steward served them their trenchers of steaming meat.

"I'm as hungry as a horse," he said, picking up his knife, stabbing a piece of meat and stuffing it into his mouth.

"I'm not so sure I want to be your wife now," she said, with a wink.

"You'll be fine," he replied, taking another piece of meat. "With your knowledge …you can help the people of the village with their maladies."

"Or I could train to be a soldier, like yourself," she took a sip of mead, "I'm quite strong and agile."

"I'm all for you being able to wield a sword, but a soldier you couldn't be. Takes years of training and muscle building …look at these muscles," he said, holding up his arm, before putting it around her.

"I want to be more than just a wife."

"You will be, I promise you."

Osgar, who had been talking to the elderly woman next to him, leaned over.

"No harm in learning how to wield a sword or fire a bow."

"Absolutely," said Edwin to Gwynedd, with a smile. "I'll get Egbert to train you."

Most of the people had left by mid-afternoon. Gwynedd organized the servants who were clearing the tables, leaving Edwin and Osgar on their own.

"What's happened at the West Minster court? Why do you need *my* help?"

"I've had enough of it, that's what! I want to come back into the Earl's favour."

Edwin didn't answer straight away but got up, walked about, then stopped and leant against one of the four great timbered central pillars of the hall. Tracing his finger over the carvings on the pillar, he said, "What makes you think we can trust you!"

"If that's your answer, I'll go to him myself!"

"You're forgetting something," Edwin retorted.

"What's that?"

"As one of the Earl's commanders, I'll see to it you can't! So, you had better tell me everything."

"Look! I'm no spy…what I have to say could get me killed!"

Edwin, looked about. "Nobody is within hearing. Whatever you have to tell Earl Harold you had better tell me first and I'll be the judge as to whether you can see him or not. After all, I haven't forgotten your involvement in that Wealhasc trap!"

Osgar shook his head, "No, no! You're wrong! I could have been shot as easily as you. When you said go I turned and rode like the wind. There were so many arrows in the air, it's a wonder I wasn't shot full of them… not one hit me. Not a scratch. But my horse was like a pin cushion and paid the price. I got clear and was found by the others. By the time I had a new horse, it was dark. And that's the God's honest truth. If you don't fucking believe me, tough, I'll get my own help!"

"Well, someone was trying to kill me, beside the Wealhasc," said Edwin.

"Now we're getting to the meat of it!" Osgar moved closer. "Like you, I'm sure the King and Earl Leofric are up to something. Whatever it is, it won't be to Earl Godwin's betterment, if you see what I mean."

"Can't you be more specific?" asked Edwin.

"You know that Northman…what's his name… Robert something or other, who became Bishop of Lunden four or five years-ago?"

"Robert of Jumièges, yes! What about him?"

"He's got the ear of the King…I know… I heard them talking. He's trying to get the King to divorce Harold's sister."

"What! Why?"

"He knows the King hates Earl Godwin. That he only married

Edyth to keep the Earl quiet because he needed him. He blames Godwin for his brother's murder."

"Yes I know all about that. Are you sure about the Bishop wanting King Edward to divorce Edyth?"

"Absolutely."

Edwin's mind was racing, trying to plan his next move.

"Now will you take me back and be my friend? My life's on the line."

"I'm taking Gwynedd to Harold's court in a few days, you can come along and take your case to him then."

# CHAPTER IV

*4 January, 1049*

### - Rendlæsham, East Anglia, Earl Harold's New Year Court -
Rendelsham, Suffolk

"How far is it?" moaned Gwynedd, who was sitting awkwardly on her horse, her face hidden within the hood of her heavy fur cloak. "I'm sore, where you wouldn't want to know. After travelling all day yesterday and most of today, I am frozen stiff!"

"You told me you were tough," replied Edwin, who wasn't going to give in to her. 'If she wants to be my wife as I want her to be, she'll have to get used to travelling the country in all weathers.' He was also feeling the icy weather; his gloved hands were hurting with the cold. 'I'm glad I made her wear extra clothing.'

Edwin glanced behind. Osgar was an old campaigner and didn't complain. The only things that were keeping them from freezing were their heavy fur cloaks and the warmth from the bodies of their horses. He often asked himself how horses managed to keep going in this cold weather.

"It won't be long," he shouted. "With Gippeswic behind us… we'll probably be there very soon, certainly long before the sun goes down."

"Soon can't be soon enough for me and what sun? Are you joking! I haven't seen the sun all day, never mind yesterday! This weather is far worse than it is in Wealh. Look at it! Ever since we left it's been pelting down with sleet and now this snow."

"Look on the bright side Gwynedd, the landscape is beautiful and… Look!" he shouted, "see that dark smudge over there?"

"Yes!"

"That's Rendlæsham."

"All this and a sore arse as well, just to be wedded by the Earl!" She spurred her horse to a gallop. It didn't matter to her to be half blinded by the snow, she just wanted to get there, get off her horse, put on dry clothes and have a hot meal.

"Where's your spirit of adventure?" he shouted to her receding back. "You should be glad to be marrying me?"

"Did I hear you right? You're marrying her?" asked Osgar.

"Yes I am! Why?"

"Just asking."


Earl Harold's hall was a large building on two floors. The lower was for supplies, the upper his main hall and living quarters.

Edwin and Osgar had caught up with Gwynedd who was waiting for them. Taking hold of her hand, Edwin escorted her up the steps to the main entrance. Two servants followed with their luggage, which had been removed from their packhorse.

Coming in from the cold deadened world outside, made silent by the snow, they were immediately swamped and embraced by warm air and the noise of laughter and music. The sudden temperature contrast made Gwynedd giddy and forced her to hold onto Edwin to prevent herself from falling.

"Are you unwell? It's not the baby is it?" queried Edwin, with concern.

"I'll be alright," she replied. "The heat in here has made me a bit unsteady. I'm alright now."

"You going to change your clothes?" inquired Edwin, of Osgar.

"What clothes. I'm alright as I am, I'll soon dry out in this warmth."

Edwin turned to Gwynedd. "Let's get into that room where they took our luggage."

When Gwynedd reappeared on the arm of Edwin, they were greeted with hushed comments of surprise and admiration. Edwin was wearing his finery and strapped to his side was his prized broadsword. Gwynedd had changed out of her damp travelling clothes and into her wedding dress, a simple cream coloured linen gown, edged with silver embroidery with a matching silver cord loosely tied at her waist. On her head, a cream frilled veil.

A steward showed them to their seats, near the top table. Osgar had managed to get a seat on the opposite side of the hall.

"So this is how the Englisc nobility live," said Gwynedd, feeling much better now, confident that she looked beautiful. She smiled at Edwin and squeezed his arm. "You look very handsome."

"I'm trying to compete with you! I think I've just lost! You're a joy to behold…a rival to the Earl's wife," he said.

"Nonsense!" she replied, looking around the hall.

Two individual spits by the central fire hearth were being turned continually, by attendants. A group of musicians were playing but because of the noise she could only clearly hear the beating of the drum.

Gwynedd pulled at Edwin's sleeve.

"The smell of that delicious roast meat is getting to me; and those poor musicians over there are playing their hearts out. Nobody is listening to them."

"Why should that concern you? These are leading Thegns of Harold's earldom, they have a lot to talk about. Some of them have travelled from the other side of the country and most haven't seen each other for months."

"Well, I play the harp and when I play, I like to be heard. I know what it's like not to be taken notice of."

"I didn't know you played the harp," said Edwin, in surprise. "You never told me. So, you have hidden talents. Any more surprises?"

"I may have," she said, with a smile.

"All this time, I didn't know."

Just then Edwin caught the attention of Earl Harold. "I must leave you, I'll be back soon."

"Where's my wedding crown? It's fallen off." she whispered frantically.

"Here!" he said, handing the delicate crown of leaves to her, "I must go."

Gwynedd took the crown and placed it on the table beside her. She followed his movements to the top table then shifted her focus of attention around the hall, observing the different characters; some showing off, obviously acting a part.

'I don't feel out of place at all,' she thought. 'Illustrious people they may be but listening to them, we have a lot in common. Yes, I look forward to making some new friends here.' Gwynedd watched Edwin talking and laughing with the Earl. 'They could be brothers. So that's Earl Harold. Um, quite a handsome man.' She noted his tanned, weathered face. The same type of pickled face she remembered of seaman who had brazened the salt wind gales, although his, she thought, wasn't pickled exactly, maybe a bit more weathered than most. 'He's meticulous,' she thought, also noting his neatly trimmed moustache and beard. 'His blond hair is almost the same colour as his wife's but perhaps with a tinge of red. What's his wife's name... Swannesha, Eadgyth Swannesha, lovely name. Yes, she does have a beautiful neck but I wouldn't have thought it was anything like a swan's. A beautiful looking woman though.' She noticed Eadgyth's hair was in a single braid that stretched down below her waist, interwoven with a gold cord. 'I wonder how old she is? Can't be more than...twenty four. She's very rich, so Edwin tells me, daughter of Alfgar whoever he is. She's pregnant! Yes, I swear she is. How long have they been married, three years, and now about to drop her second child. Well, she looks very good on it that's all I can say. When I told Edwin I was with child, he was so happy he cried, cried like a baby. Do I look pregnant? I don't think so... maybe a little bump, not enough to notice though. What's he doing? Both he and Earl Harold are walking around the top table, into the centre, in front of the dais.'

From behind her, a steward whispered, "Lady Gwynedd." He took hold of her crown of leaves and held it above her.

"Yes," she said in surprise.

The steward placed the crown on her head. "Follow me." He led her into the centre of the hall to join Edwin and Earl Harold.

A loud, reverberating sound from a ram's horn blew, signalling silence. The Earl held up his hands.

"My lords, friends, ladies. Edwin of Upper Barnstæd, is to be married this day, to the beautiful Gwynedd of Holt."

A roar went up. A few voices shouted, "Don't do it Edwin, stay free and single! You haven't got it in you!"

Gwynedd, to the left of Edwin, stood before the Earl.

The steward came forward and whispered, "My lord, I can't find any twine."

"No? There should be plenty. Well, never mind the string." Earl Harold turned to Edwin.

"Unbuckle your sword belt," he said in Edwin's ear. "It's only symbolic anyway, I'll use the belt instead."

Raising his voice he continued, "Give me your right hands and I'll join them with this belt."

Edwin could feel Gwynedd shaking with nerves. He squeezed her hand and smiled.

Earl Harold cleared his throat…"Repeat after me. I Edwin……"

"I Edwin, Thegn of Upper Barnstæd take Gwynedd of Holt as my wife, as the King's law of East Anglia and Englaland permits, and thereto I pledge my troth and all that I have promised her before."

Earl Harold now held both their bound hands in his and turned towards Gwynedd. "I Gwynedd….."

"I Gwynedd of Holt take you Edwin, Thegn of Upper Barnstæd to be my husband, as the King's law of East Anglia and Englaland permits, thereto I pledge my troth."

A steward proffered a silver goblet of mead, the Earl offered it in turn to the newlyweds.

"Now Edwin you may kiss your bride!"

A tumultuous sound went up from the crowd. The belt falling to the ground, Edwin took hold of his wife in a bear hug, swung her around and kissed her again.

"We're married!" he whispered to her, "but I'm not so sure I'm going to like the next part!"

"What do you mean! Next part!" she anxiously whispered in reply.

"The Earl's commanded me to do the Sword Dance!"

"The what?"

"You'll see!"

"I don't know it but I don't mind playing the harp," she replied laughing.

"You don't know our music!"

"You hum it and I'll play it," Gwynedd replied, finding it hard to stand upright for laughing.

Amidst the noise of the hall, the prelude to the sword dance began. The group of musicians gathered around the two men who were to dance. After a few moments they moved away revealing two naked combatants. Edwin faced his adversary in the centre of the hall, both were armed with shields, broadswords held low, sword points touching.

At the end of a long bellowing sound from the horn, a loud single beat from the drum brought everyone in the hall to an expectant silence.

Edwin wondered how good this young Æfa was. He had seen him before and knew he was agile but that was all.

'Let's hope,' he thought, 'with his shoulder length hair, he isn't another biblical Samson.'

Edwin put his hopes on his superior strength and hard won fighting experience.

The drum beat increased in speed to a roll, signalling for them to leap back. Then as the beat continued rhythmically, they moved around each other, poised to attack. A short sharp blast from the horn, joined by an hypnotic rhythm from two pipers, underscored by a low drone from a chanter, accompanied the attack. The horn sounded again. They banged their shields together, stepping back to beat their swords against the shields in time to the rhythm of the drum. Edwin wielded his sword and brought it down hard on the other's shield, which clearly shook his opponent who returned a sword blow of his own.

Gwynedd could see that Edwin's shoulder scar was weeping and hoped that his opponent couldn't see it. She was astonished and fearful at the same time because of the near reality of the fight, even though it was just a stylized dance. She couldn't help grinning, finding it difficult not to laugh when the dancers' penises flapped and flopped this and that way with every prancing movement.

More blows crashed down on shields as they circled each other. Edwin feigned by dropping his shield only to bring it up in time to take a blow from his opponent. They continued to circle each other. Waiting for the next attack, Edwin withdrew a few steps. Arching his body, he suddenly performed a backward roll. With his shield for support, he sprang back up onto his feet, using the momentum in one fluid movement to bring an extra jarring blow crashing against Æfa's shield. As if in answer, to prove his youth and suppleness, Æfa made a back-flip, to the cheers of the audience. Edwin, anticipating the move, had his sword point at the young man's abdomen as he sprang back onto his feet.

As Æfa accepted defeat with a bow, pandemonium erupted. The noise was so great it drowned the sounds of the horns and drum.

Earl Harold led Gwynedd into the centre of the hall once more and handed her the winner's prize; a beautifully decorated, long bladed seax.

Standing before her husband, trying hard not to let her eyes wander suth, she presented him with the prize and a crown of leaves as winner of the dance.

"I wasn't too flashy, was I?" asked Edwin, as they made their way out of the hall towards the changing room.

"No but you were a bit floppy," she grinned. "How did you know he was going to do that…whatever he did?"

"Back flip?"

She nodded.

"After my back roll I gambled he would try to outdo me, following it with an advance and there he was at the end of my sword and there you have it."

"Just like that?"

"Just like that," he answered.

Back in their seats she observed Osgar exiting through a side door.

Earl Harold was no longer in the hall.

*21 June, 1049*
### - A surprise at Upper Barnstæd -

"Get me Hilda!" shouted Gwynedd, "my waters have burst!"

A messenger went running to the village to fetch the midwife, while Edwin helped Gwynedd to bed.

"I knew something was wrong."

"What's wrong!" Edwin was worried, he didn't know what to do. "Hilda should be here soon."

"I've had a back ache for the last couple of days. That should have told me."

"Told you what?"

"The birth was imminent! It shouldn't be now! It's not due for another three or four weeks!"

"Gwynedd, is there anything I can do?"

"Nothing! No, not at the moment. Ah! I can feel the contractions. Come on Hilda! Where is that woman?"

"Here! Here I am, Gwynedd. I came as quickly as I could, and I've brought my sister, Sexburg."

"Sexburg! There won't be much sex around here for a little while," replied Gwynedd, easing herself into a better position.

"Well, at least you haven't lost you sense of humour, my lady. Now! You sir! Out! Out if you don't mind. This is women's work," commanded Hilda, ushering Edwin out of the bed chamber.

"Ah, Egbert, you've heard!"

"I thought I'd better keep you company. Sometimes birthing can take a long time. Thought of any names?"

"No, not really…well, yes I have. If it's a boy we'll call him Wulfnoth for my father and if it's a girl, Eadgyth, after Earl Harold's wife."

"What's that," asked Egbert.

Edwin's cloak was draped over a large object by the side of the door."

"A gift for Gwynedd. I'll sho…"

The cry of a baby made Edwin look up. He was expecting to go in but Sexburg came out barring his way.

"Not yet, sur," she said, disappearing back into the chamber.

After a second cry, she returned.

"You have twins!"

"What!" shouted Edwin, "What sex?"

"Two healthy boys!"

Edwin pushed her aside and ran in.

Gwynedd was lying back, looking pale. In her arms were their babies. Gently touching their hands with the tips of his fingers, he couldn't help marvelling at their smallness. Falling on his knees, he took one of Gwynedd's hands and kissed it.

"Thank you, darling, for making me the happiest of men."

"Stop getting all emotional," she whispered, through her own tears.

Edwin taking a cloth from his pocket, held it to Gwynedd's nose, "Now blow!"

"Have you thought of any names?" asked Hilda.

Edwin looked to Gwynedd. "Wulfnoth…and… Edric?"

Gwynedd propped up on puffed up pillows smiled and nodded.

"One more thing," said Edwin, giving Hilda a knowing nod.

Hilda brought into the room the shrouded object.

Pulling his cloak away, Edwin revealed Gwynedd's present.

"A harp! she blurted. "It's so beautiful," she continued with moist eyes. "Where did you get it?"

"It's a long story," he said smiling. "I'll tell you about it later."

Gwynedd closed her eyes and drifted into a deep wonderful sleep.

# CHAPTER V

*September, 1049*

### - On board ship bound for Flanders -

Brihtric Meaw, a Thegn and aid to King Edward, like so many Engliscmen, including Earl Harold and Edwin and many others of Scandinavian origin, had fair hair. It was not uncommon in Englaland.

'His is white,' thought Edwin, 'that's why Brihtric has been singled out and nicknamed, Snowy I suppose.' Edwin had never been given a nickname, at least not in his hearing. Never! Not once. True Brihtric, as a career diplomat, travelled to the continent a great deal and over there his long white hair would probably be somewhat unusual. Perhaps that was the reason? At least that was Edwin's conclusion.

'Is he handsome? Yes, I suppose he is. Wealthy? Yes and, from what I hear, has a way with women. A career soldier who never swung an axe in battle in his life! God save us. And I'm supposed to accompany him to Flanders and keep him out of trouble while he brokers a peace between Henry, the Holy Roman Emperor, Count Baldwin of Flanders and King Swegen of Danemark? Best of Englisc luck, that's all I can say. Although, Brihtric does have a smooth tongue, I'll give him that.'

To Edwin the man was not a professional soldier at all, not in the normal sense of the word, though he professed to be. Certainly he was no housecarl, although he would have liked to be. To begin with, he was not fit or strong enough and was too... soft. The man was being laughed at and didn't know it. In Edwin's opinion, he spent too much time dictating. Ear bashing scribbling clerks; and charming women even though he had a wife and two kids at home near Gleucestre.

Edwin could see from the look on Brihtric's face he was not enjoying the sæ crossing and, in a way, felt sorry for him. He would be pleasant enough and look after him as best he could. He would also carry out Earl Godwin's instructions; bring back his eldest son, Earl Swegen, to King Edward's court to beg for the King's forgiveness.

Swegen Godwinson's younger brother Harold didn't like him and Edwin could see why; Swegen had not only taken a shine to Ælfgifu Abbess of Leominster, but had kept her his prisoner, some say, and made her pregnant! Edwin shook his head. He tried thinking about the Abbess as a sex slave.

'Ah well,' he thought, 'it takes all sorts. And as if Swegen wasn't in deep enough trouble, he goes and murders his cousin, Beorn, then flees to Count Baldwin's court for protection! Now his father has persuaded the King, against his better judgement, to take him back once more. That is, if he promises to be good boy.' Edwin drew a lungful of sæ air. 'God knows what's going on because I'm damned if I do.' He looked up at the sky, blinked and turned away as the sun came out from behind a cloud.

### - Lodging house, Bruges, Flanders -

A rapid knock on his door brought Edwin leaping out of bed, grabbing for his sword.

"Who is it?"

"Brihtric! Open up! I need your help!" an anxious voice whispered at the door.

Edwin quickly pulled Brihtric inside, looking to see if anyone else was about.

"What's the problem?"

"I'm in real trouble. Matilda wants to marry me!"

"Matilda? You mean the Count's daughter?"

"Yes, who else?"

"What have you done?" asked Edwin, lighting a candle and trying to control his anger at being woken from a deep sleep.

"The Count asked me to accompany his daughter around their palace gardens."

"So, what's so difficult about that?"

"Wait! She said I was the most handsome of Engliscmen, loved my hair and complexion and hadn't met anyone like me before."

"I see!" said Edwin, realising where this was leading.

"She was fed up with being chaperoned and wanted to be free. Free to see the world and get away from her domineering father."

"So, what happened next?"

"In the evening, she invited me to her room."

"And of course, naturally, you went."

"Well yes! She called me, her snowy Anglo Saxon. It all seemed so innocent, leastways at first." The nervous Brihtric was beginning to perspire. "She started to strip off!"

"We *are* talking about Lady Matilda?" asked Edwin, who was now feeling somewhat nervous of his charge.

"Of course. She was obviously waiting for me to make a move but I just stood there not knowing what to do. Then suddenly she makes a dive for me! Her hands were all over me. If you see what I mean!"

Edwin went to the door and locked it. If it wasn't for the fact Brihtric was talking about Matilda, he would have thought it amusing. But this! This was something else. Both their lives were now at risk.

Brihtric continued, "I couldn't believe what was happening! She demanded I make love to her. Edwin, don't look at me like that!"

"I'm stunned, and am not doing or saying anything for the moment."

"You don't have to. I can see it in your eyes. She demanded I make love to her, otherwise she would call her father."

"What... did you do next?" As if he didn't know what was coming.

"We had sex or to be more correct, she mounted, and *made love to me!*"

"And, of course, you let her?"

"What would you have done in my place?"

'What would I have done indeed,' Edwin thought. 'God help us. A horny Matilda running after her adored Thegn who I'm supposed to be keeping out of trouble! Also I'm supposed to be bringing back to Englaland a repentant, horny Earl Swegen Godwinson.'

As much as he disliked the man standing in front of him, so Edwin couldn't help but like Swegen, even though he had killed his cousin Beorn in a fight. Edwin didn't have an explanation as to why. 'Perhaps it is because, in those days, he was so full of fun, almost a child and I can easily see why his father, Earl Godwin, loves him. He is his first child; his love child. But nevertheless, he is a hot head who can't keep his cock in his pocket.'

"What else could I do?" Brihtric continued to bleat, "I have just helped her father make peace with Emperor Henry and persuaded Earl Swegen to return to Englaland and now this. Lady Matilda may only be four-foot tall but she's all animal; appetite of a lion. When I got out of her bed, I could hardly stand. Look, I'm still shaking; I gave her my all and she still wanted more."

Edwin couldn't help smiling to himself. This was too bizarre for words and yet he was scared. All Matilda had had to do was scream rape and the whole palace would have been at their throats. He sat down on his bed in deep thought, oblivious of the cold night air.

"You realise," said Edwin, in a lowered voice, "Duke William of Northmandig is seeking her hand in marriage."

"I've heard the rumour but I don't know whether it's true or not."

"Oh yes, it's true alright and you don't want to get on the wrong side of that bastard. He'll string you up by your balls, hack you to pieces, and *then* he'll kill you. Especially if you've made her pregnant!"

Brihtric began rubbing his forehead feverishly.

"Pregnant! I hope not! What can I do? Help me Edwin, help me!"

"You've done what the King sent you here to do… and more! I suggest you leave now, quietly, while it's still dark. Take the first ship out. I'll say, I don't know where you are. I have to stay here until tomorrow to conclude my business with Earl Swegen and make sure he comes back with me to Englaland. So go! Get you gear and go!"

"Right now?"

"Yes! Right now! Go! Get out of here! Fast!"

*December, 1049*
**- Lunden -**
London

Lunden was in the middle of a blizzard. Snow flakes the size of pennies were falling thick and fast. Edwin stumbled along with Osgar through the knee-deep drifts. The usually packed stræts were mainly empty, but for hardy adventurers, as the two men made their way along Tames Stræt to the 'Grape Vine', a wine shop situated in the Vintry along the north bank of the Tames. What sounds could be heard were muffled into insignificance.

"Osgar! Get in here quick,' said Edwin, whose feet were cold and wet.

They were met by a blanket of warm, stifling air and the jarring noise of laughter. Raucous voices were trying to talk over everybody else. It seemed the entire population of Lunden was here. Edwin marvelled at the atmosphere, quite opposite from the dead silence of the white world outside.

"Move yourself, Os!" he shouted.

"I'm doing my best, Ed. There's so many in here, it's like battling against a shield wall."

"Follow me then," shouted Edwin, as he elbowed himself forward, Osgar tucked in close behind. Cupping his hands to his mouth, Edwin shouted, "Mind yer backs!"

As if by magic, bodies moved aside giving them passage through to a table on the far side of the room.

"Well, that was easy enough," grinned Edwin, "I wonder why these tables are empty?"

"I suppose, most want to stand or move about."

"'Allo, 'allo, what brings you here, lads?" said Alf, the owner.

"Give us two cups of your finest mead. And mind, Alf," said Edwin, "don't give us the rubbish we had last time. We want the strong stuff, cos we're frozen stiff and need thawing out."

"Right you are, lads," replied Alf, disappearing amongst the crowd.

"Keep yer head down, Os'," said Edwin. "Brihtric's here and I don't want him to see me…Shit! Too fucking late!"

"Edwin, just the person I want to see," greeted Brihtric.

"Really?" he said, trying to look surprised. As far as Edwin was concerned, Brihtric was bad news and he didn't want to be part of any scheme he was into. He looked to Osgar.

"We should be leaving. Mustn't keep Osbert waiting."

"Please Edwin, I must talk to you!"

Edwin feeling helplessly trapped, shook his head. "What do you want to see me about?"

"I can't talk here. There's a private room, over there," he replied indicating a closed door at the back of the room.

"Allo! Another one," said Alf, putting down the mugs. "And what's your poison, if you don't mind me asking?"

"The same as them. Can we use your private room?"

"Well, I suppose so, go ahead."

Brihtric gave Edwin a nervous look, "I need to speak to you. Alone!"

Edwin turned to Osgar, "Sorry Os, it's a private matter, it will only take a moment or two."

"Not to worry Ed. I'll make my way back over to the table. But give us a yell when you're ready."

Edwin watched Osgar push his way through and disappear among the crowd, then followed Brihtric into the room.

Closing the door, Edwin was surprised to see Brihtric collapse onto the nearest chair, sobbing.

"Hey up Brihtric, what's amiss?"

"What am I going to do? She's written to me!"

"Who has?"

"Matilda of course! The Count's daughter! She's pregnant and demands I go back to her. She wants to marry *me* and not the bastard northman, Duke William!"

A bang on the door brought a momentary relief to Edwin.

"Here we are lads," said Alf, putting mugs on the only table in the room. "I've brought another one for you Edwin and for this you can thank your friend Osgar who's looking all alone and bored."

"Thanks, Alf, I'll see him in a bit. Tell him I won't be long," replied Edwin, closing the door.

"What does all this have to do with me?" asked Edwin, who didn't want any part of it and anyway he was hardly a friend. He had never met Brihtric prior to meeting him on board ship to Flanders. If he had had a choice, knowing what a liability the man was, he would have made some excuse not to have gone to Flanders at all.

'If only I had the gift of foresight,' he thought.

"I don't know what to advise, seeing you're already married. Then again, the Pope could always annul your marriage and you could marry Matilda, then you'd be set up for life and probably be the next Count of Flanders."

"You jest. It's alright for you, you're not at court advising the King! I'm married with two children! You know what our pompous, pious King would do!"

"What would the pious King do? You're the one who is nice and snug with him," replied Edwin, beginning to get angry.

"What would he do? He would make me his enemy. Throw me out of his court. Dispossess me of my title, lands, everything. Do the very same as he has done to Earl Swegen. Edwin! What am I to do?"

"First of all, you're not Earl Swegen Godwinson. You haven't kidnapped and raped an Abbess and you certainly haven't killed your cousin. Look on the bright side, Lady Matilda loves you."

"You're not taking any of this seriously. You're my only friend!" he pleaded.

"I do take all this very seriously!" Edwin replied, trying to keep his anger in check and speaking quietly and deliberately. "You have implicated me in this affair by the very fact you have spoken to me about it. You ensnared yourself in this potentially dangerous situation, when you should have kept your cock buttoned up! Didn't you see the danger? Listen, you fucking half-wit, didn't you realise getting your leg over Count Baldwin's daughter would get you in real trouble? It doesn't matter if she was the seducer. You just don't get yourself into those kinds of situations unless you are free do so!" Edwin took hold of the mugs and handed one to Brihtric. "Drink up, you need it more than I."

Brihtric swallowed the entire contents in one gulp. "Well! I still don't know what to do."

"I'm trying to think, man!" said Edwin, wiping his mouth and beard with the back of his hand. "The best advice I can give you is, if you are not prepared to dump your wife and kids and marry Matilda... then don't say a word. Not to anyone and certainly do not reply to her letter. I don't know what else to suggest. What she will tell her father is any one's guess. I hope for your sake she doesn't sail over here, demanding an audience with the King. Although I doubt that, knowing the King's dislike for Count Baldwin."

"Do you think not replying to her will work?"

"I don't know," said Edwin, forcing an end to the conversation by moving towards the door. "Just don't say anything to anyone and don't... reply... to that letter."

He left the room, slamming the door after him.

"Where's your friend, Brihtric?" asked Osgar.

"Don't ask! I don't want to know any more. The man's a disaster waiting to happen," replied Edwin. "Let's get out of here.

Osbert's smithy was much larger than one would have imagined from the outside, until you opened the thick wooden door and stepped inside the cavernous dark interior.

"Let's get near that brazier," said Edwin, rubbing his hands. "I haven't seen your father in a while, how is he?"

"He is a broken man. Can't do the work he loves because he can't use his fingers especially his right hand. All the joints are swollen and painful. An old crone around the corner calls it, artetic… sciatic or something and gave my father some stuff that smelled of vinegar. I threw it out… it was giving him ulcers."

"I'm sorry to hear that. Next time, I'll bring Gwynedd with me. She might be able to help."

"Thanks all the same Ed, but I don't think anyone can help."

"You know old friend, you should bring him in here, into the place he loves, to watch you work, rather than be miserable and alone."

Edwin found it hard to see his friend in such a mood, a far cry from his normally jolly self. He looked intently at the unmarked pale skin, shock of dark brown curly hair and manicured beard and moustache. Although they were both of the same great height, Osbert looked taller because of his powerful build. It was as though he had invented arm muscles. He could lift an iron anvil in each of his oversized leathery hands. Yet, he was a cultured man who could turn his dark brown eyes and nose, in an instant, from the metal work and brazier, to gaze at a fine wine, sniff its aroma and tell you its quality.

"You've come about your hauberk," said Osbert, unhooking the heavy metalled coat of mail from above, with a long pole. "Don't bother trying it on, it'll fit."

"I'll take your word for it. Phew! It weighs as much as Osgar here!"

"A big feller like you shouldn't have a problem wearing it!" replied Osbert.

"I'll let you know when the time comes…if I survive!"

*February, 1050*
## - Upper Barnstæd -

"Edwin, are you awake? whispered Gwynedd.
"Yes."
"What's on your mind."
"Brihtric Meaw! That's what's on my mind."
"Then you should put him out of your head and go back to sleep."
"Easy for you to say. The man spells trouble!"
"Go and see our babies. I'll come with you."
The twins were sleeping peacefully. Edwin wanted to take them out of their cradles and hold them. They're two little miracles,' he thought. 'How could it be, a simple act of love and passion could bring about such a marvel?'
"I know what you're thinking. Let them sleep."
"But they've grown so much in eight months."
"It's the Wealhasc milk," giggled Gwynedd.
"I still find your emotional attachment for Wealh, difficult to understand," said Edwin.
"I don't understand it myself" she sighed, "but I was born there. It's a beautiful country and language."
"That it is," replied Edwin. "Let's go outside, I need some fresh air."

"I can hardly see where I'm treading, said Gwynedd as they stepped out into the cold moonless night. "Well, what do we do now?"
"Hold onto me Gwyn, I know the ground," he said leading her towards the stable.
"What's that," she whispered, pulling on Edwin's arm. "It's coming from inside. The door's open."
"It's no place for us, " he whispered, shutting the stable door

quietly and leading her away,

"Who's in there?"

"I think it's Edmund," he said, laughing softly. "I think he's showing one of the village girls how to break in a horse"

"You men! You're just like children," she said scornfully. "More likely, the girl's showing him a thing or two."

Crash!

"What was that!" whispered Gwynedd, in alarm.

A young girl ran out, stopped momentarily, looked towards Edwin and Gwynedd as if she wanted to say something but thought better of it, turned on her heels and hurried off, sobbing.

"Is anything amiss?" asked Edwin, as Edmund appeared at the doorway.

"No! Nothing," he replied, walking off into the darkness.

"Who was she?" asked Gwynedd.

"I don't know. Too dark to see her properly."

"Let's go back inside," she said, tugging at Edwin's sleeve. "I'm getting cold."

# CHAPTER VI

*January, 1050*
- **Rouen, Northmandig** -
Normandy

William, Duke of Normandy, threw Matilda's letter to the floor. The hardened, burly, russet haired twenty seven year-old, looked at his companion, Roger de Montgomery. They were of similar age. Roger, being ten months older and taller by a hand, stood an athletic six feet. He had dark brown hair with a hint of red, bushy eyebrows and a prominent nose and chin. He had been one of the young Duke's staunchest supporters since their teens, aiding him in his struggle to survive and reinforce his control over the duchy. With his great victory at the battle of Val-ès-Dunes, three years before, the barons' rebellion had been broken. William had consolidated his power over the entire duchy and now he could relax. It was time for marriage and to build a dynasty.

"What do I do about this Flemish bitch?"

Roger didn't reply, just hunched his shoulders.

"Count Baldwin is supposed to be a friend. He agreed to my marrying his daughter! And this business with Pope Leo has been hanging over my head for the last twelve months, forbidding me to marry her on the grounds of 'consanguinity in the fifth degree'. Now, she dares send me that fucking letter written on *pig's skin*. On *pig's skin!* I can read that little bitch's mind. I know she's alluding to my mother! She's reminding me that my grandfather was steeped in piss, to cure leather. And she has the gall to send this, this letter, saying she won't marry me because I'm not good enough …because of my low birth!" William's expression changed to an evil grin, "You remember when we laid siege to Alençon and catapulted pieces of our prisoners over the town walls?"

"Surely, my lord, you don't intend chop *her* up into bits?"

"No! But I will have her. Come on Roger, you're my councillor, give me good council!"

"Well, my lord," replied Roger, "why don't you ride to Flanders and take possession of her before one of King Edward's favourite thegns takes her from under your nose."

"What!" William shouted. "From under my nose! Who's been sniffing around?"

"Brihtric Meaw, a blond haired Engliscman, she calls Snowy."

"Snowy! She calls him Snowy?" he shouted, "Snowy! How do you know all this?"

"I have my contacts."

"Why didn't you tell me about this earlier?"

"I've only just heard about it," replied Roger.

"Steward! Get my horse! Snowy, a fucking Engliscman!" he continued muttering, through clenched teeth, "Roger, get a company of men together. We have no time to lose."

"Where, are we going exactly?" replied Roger, as if he didn't know.

"I don't know man!" he replied "... Bruges! We'll make for Bruges."

### - Bruges, Flanders –

"I think we're in luck, my lord," said Roger, pointing to Matilda. "She's the one with a group of attendants, riding to church."

"I know what she looks like, man! I've got eyes, I can see her!"

One could tell at a glance the high standard of Lady Matilda's horsemanship. Though she was diminutive in size and quite easily mistaken for a child, she rode astride the animal with confidence, carrying herself with an elegance which complimented her beauty.

She wore a dove coloured cape secured at the neck by a gold clasp, the hood flung back to reveal her hair, the colour of gold ochre, which hung down to her waist in two braids entwined with gold thread.

"Right, I'll have her, she can't get away from me now!"

"My lord!" said Roger, grabbing the Duke's reins. "you can't go charging ahead and take her by force!"

"Really!" rounded William. "You ever take hold of my horse again, I'll… get out of my way, man!"

"You're coming with me!" stormed Duke William, grabbing hold of Lady Matilda's plaits.

"Who the devil are *you*, to come here on the day of worship, armed, helmeted and in mail tunic as if for war! Get away from me!" she shouted, outraged.

William attempted to pull her off her horse but lost his grip. The horse reared, Matilda in the struggle fell to the ground and ran into the nearby church.

"Stay here!" William shouted to his men. He leapt off his horse and ran after her.

The door of the church slammed shut, its echo resounding throughout the lofty building. The sound of the Duke's footsteps came heavily down the central isle towards the small figure kneeling in front of the altar, the holy cross hanging above, giving her futile protection.

"You're mine!" hissed William, as he calmly took hold of her long plaits again, dragging her kicking and screaming out of the church.

The abrupt attack stunned the crowds and Matilda's attendants, into silence.

Flinging her onto the bed in her chamber, the Duke called to his men. "Stay on guard and let no one in. Keep this door shut and barred until I order otherwise!"

"You're an animal," she screamed. "What my father sees in you I can only guess at; titles, land and power but I know what you really are; a lowly bred bastard! The seed of a Duke, contaminated by the daughter of a piss ridden tanner and grave digger!"

He stood, half amused by her vitriol.

'She's fiery!" he thought. 'I like her. I like her a lot! Right now she's in my power with the door barred and nowhere to go. Well, her father consented to my marriage proposal, despite the Pope, so here goes. Let's make it absolute!'

"How dare you treat me like this. I'm a Lady, descendant of Charlemagne and I am a Capet; a direct descendant of King Robert the second of Francia. I order you to open that door and take me to my father!"

"Oh, shut up girl! I've heard it all before. You may be a lady and pretty too, but you fart and piss just like everyone else."

"What are you doing?"

"I said, *shut up!*"

Matilda made an attempt to get to the door.

William grabbed her arms, slapped her face and flung her back onto the bed then pinned her down with the weight of his body.

"*Now*, you're mine!"

He dressed slowly and deliberately, occasionally glancing at her. Matilda remained silent on the bed, curled up, her knees touching her chin.

'I won't sob in front of that bastard, like a weak child!' she thought. 'What's happening to me? I should feel horror. I should feel humiliated. But I don't.' Questions raced through her mind; her out of control sexual desires. How could she explain those to anyone? She knew she couldn't even explain these things to her mother who, on the very onset of her daughter wanting to talk about anything intimate, turned a deaf ear, entreating Matilda with her usual reply; "Go to confession."

'Who then can I talk to? No one. Am I going mad? I remember

the uncontrollable joy I felt when Brihtric first touched me and came inside me. Now, I hate him! I offered him everything and he treated me like a whore! I'm having his bastard child. Now this. Fucked by a tanner's bastard grandson. But he did show tenderness and I do like the smell of his body. If I marry him I'll have no shame. After all being a Duchess is not so bad. He was gentle, which was quite surprising and I think I was more violent than he. And the look of surprise on his face when I dug my nails into his back and screamed to be fucked harder! Oh God! That's a thought. Perhaps he won't want to marry me after all, leaving me to have Brihtric's bastard and be shamed in front of mother and father… and the Court.'

Now, she couldn't even remember the sound of Brihtric's voice, just the Duke's.

'Could I fool him into thinking it is his? Yes. Why not. He did rape me. How would he know it wasn't his? So it will be a little early. It happens.'

She smiled.

# CHAPTER VII

*July, 1051*

**- Dofras, Wessex (Cent) -**
Dover, Kent

Eustace, Count of Boulogne, and his mounted troop of warriors, were already dressed in full armour, as if for battle, as they descended on the coastal town of Dofras. The Count sought out the nearest inn to the port, demanding free board and lodging.

"No my lord Count. I refuse! It is not fair to me and the other innkeepers!" pleaded the landlord, following him outside, looking across the road towards the townspeople who were gathering, wondering what the commotion was about.

"Listen well, innkeeper," shouted the Count "I'm here on your King's business. You have refused me and my men, hospitality."

He knew very well the Count's reputation and his family connection with the King but still he wasn't about to be intimidated.

"That's a lie!" shouted the innkeeper. "Just because you're on the King's business doesn't give you the right to threaten and demand from the King's peace loving citizens free board and lodging. This is Earl Godwin's earldom and we have rights as do every other innkeeper in the kingdom. We have the right to see the colour of yer money. We're fed up with you fucking Normans, throwing your weight around!"

"Rights! Rights!" shouted the Count, raising his voice ever louder as he looked around at the gathered townspeople. "Piss on your Earl!" Count Eustace spat the words out into the innkeeper's face. "*You* and every other innkeeper in this decrepit village have *no* rights! And certainly, no right to question my authority!"

The Count turned to one of his knights, "Kill him!"

The innkeeper was quicker than the Count's man and plunged his seax into the knight, rapidly withdrawing the blade.

"You lot were already dressed for trouble and you came here looking for it. Clear out! Earl Godwin will hear of this!"

Two arrows, fired from the crowd as if to make the point, struck down a second knight, his neck and jaw exploding in a spray of blood. There was a tumultuous cry from the crowd, the men waving their swords high in the air.

Leaping onto his horse, the Count and half his warriors raced off, back towards Lunden, fighting their way clear, but not before losing more of their number. The rest of his knights, to the sound of crashing doors and swords, struggled to fight their way out of another inn.

"I dare say there'll be trouble from the King in a few days," moaned the innkeeper.

"You had no other choice. He was going to cut you down," said his friend, walking forward.

"He thought we were a bunch of useless peasants," he grinned. "Every last one of us are the Earl's men and we know how to use a blade as well as the axe. By the way, what's the damage?"

"I don't know let's walk through the town and find out."

After burying their own dead, the townspeople put the other bodies in the back of a cart, to dump them at sæ.

"What was the final score, Wilf," asked the innkeeper

"Twenty of ours and nineteen of theirs."

*August, 1051*
## - A meeting at Gualhenfforda, Mercia–
Wallingford, Berkshire

"Twenty five, twenty six, twenty seven, twenty ...."

"Sir," interrupted a messenger. "Are you Edwin, Thegn of this place?"

"Yes! Who wants to know?"

"I come from Earl Harold. You are to meet him at Gualhenfforda, urgently. He says to keep it secret."

The messenger glanced nervously at Edmund, who had been watching Edwin exercise.

"What's it about?" enquired Edwin, as he lay prone, his arms locked straight, holding up a heavy oak beam.

"I can't tell you. Just... that you have to be there," replied the messenger, obviously impressed by Edwin's strength. "And you have to be well armed."

Edwin continued with his press exercises.

"Twenty eight, twenty nine, thirty." Then he lifted the beam into its rack. "Mmm!... I'd better get dressed. What's your name?"

"Swein," replied the messenger.

"Well Swein, have you eaten?"

"No, Sir."

Edwin turned towards Edmund. "You're coming with me!"

"Where?"

"You heard the man, Gualhenfforda; fully armed, with byrnie and helmet. And by the way, nobody else is to know where we're going except your father."

Having passed through Lunden's Niwe Geat by late morning they were heading west.

"My lord," asked Edmund, "how long will it take us, to get to Gualhenfforda?"

"We'll be there by this evening. We're taking the old roman road to Ciltestere, then before you know it, we'll be in Gualhenfforda."

Edmund was about to say something, thought better of it, reined his horse and dropped back behind Swein, the messenger.

"So," said Edwin, turning to Swein, "what's news from the great wide world."

"The King has pardoned Swegen Godwinson."

"That I know," said Edwin, raising eyebrows. He was still surprised that King Edward had given way to Earl Godwin.

"You seem to be well informed, sir!"

"I hear bits of news. I like to know what's going on. What else?"

"I meant to tell you earlier. Earl Harold has had no news from Earl Leofric, concerning the whereabouts of your brother."

'I didn't expect Leofric to put himself out for me,' Edwin thought. 'Why would he do that anyway. At the first opportunity I'll search Mercia myself. But where would I look? I'll make contact with Hengist, he owes me. He has contacts all over Mercia.'

"Anything else?" he asked.

"Duke William of Normandy has married Matilda of Flanders and they already have a son."

"Really! I'm not surprised! I mean, I'm not surprised he married her," Edwin said with a wry smile. "What else?"

"Let me think…oh yes! The King has made the Northman bishop, Robert of Jumièges, Archbishop of Cantwareburh."

"Yes! I heard that as well. That won't be popular. Nor will this fiasco in Dofras with the King's friend and brother-in-law, Eustace of Boulogne, which is, if I'm not mistaken, what this meeting is all about. Are you hearing all this young Edmund?"

"Hearing what exactly?" Edmund replied.

Edwin smiled to himself. 'Good man! A bright answer, he'll go far.'

"What is that round looking ruin?" asked Edmund, pointing.

"That was where the ancient Romans held games and festivals or something. I believe they called it a coliseum."

Passing through what used to be a stone built geathouse, they rode along in silence. It was a ghost town of crumbling buildings, surrounded by ruined town walls.

Leaving the place far behind, Edmund rode up to Edwin.

"It gave me the creeps, there wasn't a soul there. Why has it been deserted and left in ruins?"

"Don't know. Maybe it's because it's too far away from the sæ. On the other hand, Wintancaester to the suth is more convenient; situated by a navigable bourne."

"What bourne?"

"Icenan," replied Edwin "and it has easy access to the sæ. Can't tell you more than that."

Edmund was not totally convinced.

"But Ciltestere still has stone and brick, defendable town walls and good roads. It doesn't make any sense."

Edwin laughed. "You take it all too seriously. Who knows why people choose one place over another. Perhaps they don't like being reminded of the ancient Romans or maybe it has bad spirits."

"But that was hundreds of years ago, yet we still use their old roads."

"That's because they're still the quickest way between one place and the next," replied Edwin.

He remembered meeting an old priest who had stopped by his home for food and rest. The priest had told him about the Romans and their armoured cohorts. The way they went into battle in square formations; their weapons and machines of fire and destruction. It was the second time he had been to Ciltestere. Remembering the priest, the place from then on always gave him a chilling experience, expecting to see roman legions rising up from the ruins and descending on him with their short swords.

"You've gone very quiet, my lord Edwin," said Swein.

"Nothing. Just thinking."

They were approaching the town of Pegingaburna. Edwin could

see Edmund was clearly uncomfortable. "What's up Edmund?"

"My arse is sore and that water to the right of us, looks very inviting."

Edwin began laughing and drew up beside him.

"You would like to dive in that bourne to cool your arse?"

"Something like that."

"Stay in the saddle lad. If you want to be a professional soldier and earn the respect of others, you'll have to be prepared to put up with discomfort and travel long distances. This is nothing. Just ignore it lad, the pain will ease off. Aye up! We're almost there."

They had past a clump of trees, Gualhenfforda could be easily seen. It was all the more noticeable in the evening sunlight from the glint of metal from Earl Harold's mounted forces.

"Are they *all* of the Earl's housecarls?" asked Edmund in surprise.

"No. There looks to be only about a hundred. Let's get a move on before we come across the King's men."


"It's about time Ed," shouted Osgar, riding forward to meet them. "Good to see yer."

"Are we waiting for anybody else?" enquired Edwin.

"No! You're the last."

"Move out!" came the command.

"Where are we off to now?" said Edwin.

"The King's palace at Gleucestre. He has called a Witenagamot."

"And we're going to pick up Earl Godwin and the rest of his sons at his manor house at Beverstane, yes?" said Edwin.

"That's about it."

*1 September, 1051*
## - Earl Godwin's manor house, Beverstane, Wessex -
Beverston, Gloucestershire

Edwin, moving around the camp, met an old friend he hadn't seen for some years. Hendric had been a smithy who had worked for Osbert in his Lunden workshop until he became bored, when he fancied a change, a more adventurous type of life. Now he was one of Earl Swegen's men. He was tall, ruddy faced with a strong muscular build. He strode with confidence, always with his round shield slung at his back and like Edwin himself, preferred the broadsword to the skeggy.

"How's life?" greeted Edwin.

Hendric came close, speaking in a whisper.

"One day at a time Ed, one day at a time. Between you, me and the brazier, Swegen's a bit of a liability but he has a good heart."

"Tell me about it!" Edwin said laughing.

"Who's this young lad?" enquired Hendric.

"Edmund. He also craves the army life and excitement. His father was an old campaigner and now manages my estate."

"Well, you've got the build alright, lad. What news from the east?"

"Apart from that business in Dofras, not much going on at the moment," replied Edwin.

"Well, for your information, that Northmandisc Archbishop and his ilk are favourites with the King and are stirring things up, against your lot, the Godwins."

"You mean, Archbishop Jumièges."

Hendric nodded.

"I thought as much."

"I'd better get back to my lot. Keep well and watch your back, Ed."

"You too."

"Wouldn't you like to be in there," said Edmund, indicating

towards Earl's Godwin's grand looking manor house.

"Absolutely not," replied Edwin. "It concerns the Godwins and the King, in other words, politics. To be honest, I don't like getting mixed up with politics."

"Then why are we here?"

"To protect the Earl's family at the Witan. Old man Godwin has upset the King, which is not difficult to do these days. In the meantime, look for a place for us to bed down. Wait! I think I heard my name. I'll see you later."

"You're wanted inside," said Osgar.

"Now what!"

"Mount up!" said Edwin the following morning, slapping Edmund on the back. We're leaving immediately."

"Where are we going?"

"The King's royal court at Gleucestre."

"How far is that?"

Edwin rubbed his chin, "Not far, should be there mid-morning."

"Do you mind if I don't join you, cos my arse is still sore."

"Get on your horse and stop moaning."

On their way out of the camp and onto the road north, Edwin thought perhaps he should have left the lad behind with the others. He certainly didn't need anybody with him and yet, why not. Edmund needed experience and what better way than to travel the country and meet new people. He felt he owed it to Edmund's father. If the youngster had stayed behind mixing with the others, sure he would learn soldiering but he knew they were a tough lot and Edmund still needed his guidance.

Edwin didn't pay much attention to the beauty of the landscape, he was more concerned with the possibility of the King's troop movements and traps. A little way back, when the trail had been on high ground, they had had a clear view of the Sabrina, a tidal bourne that flowed from the Wealhasc mountains, down through Gleucestre and out into the Brycgstow Sæ to the west. They had encountered nobody of note, but had kept their armour hidden beneath their capes to avoid interest.

They passed through the sutherne geat and into the fortified city of Gleucestre. Troops were everywhere. Obviously the King was expecting trouble. Nobody stopped them, not even a vacant stare, which pleased Edwin and yet at the same time disturbed him. They rode through the city and out of the north geat, towards the royal palace at King's Holm.

At the fortified geatway entrance to the palace compound, they were ordered to stop. All around were hundreds of troops and, from what Edwin could hear, most seem to have come from the north of the country.

"Identify yourselves," ordered one of the five guards, who confronted them with spears at the ready.

"Edwin, Thegn of Upper Barnstæd and my steward, Edmund. I have a message for the King from Earl Godwin."

"Give me your message," ordered a man with a heavy Northmandisc accent, who appeared to be sergeant of the guard, although he gave no indication as to his rank. "Nobody comes any further."

Edwin opened his satchel and handed him the sealed message.

"Stay here!"

Edwin and Edmund, without dismounting and without being offered refreshment, watched the Northman march away with a swagger.

'Jumped up bastard,' Edwin thought. 'If he was under my command I'd either make his life hell on earth or throw him back from whence he came, or perhaps both.' He smiled to himself as he watched the man disappearing through the palace entrance.

Being in the saddle was beginning to feel uncomfortable. He thought of all the places he would rather be than here.

'We should be safe here, after all he is our King,' he thought.

Edwin felt a tug on his leg. It was Hengist.

"What's a sutherner doing here?"

Edwin, forgetting momentarily about his young steward who was yawning from boredom, sat up with a start. For a brief moment Edwin didn't recognise him.

"Oh, it's you! I've just brought a message for the King from Earl Godwin."

Hengist raised his eyebrows. "That'll be interesting," he said with a smile.

"Quite a crowd you have here," said Edwin, looking around.

"A whole load more arriving from the north and east," he replied, leaning forward out of hearing of others. "The King knows about your massed army, he's getting panicky."

"What massed army? We haven't got that many," Edwin lied, with a smile.

"You've met Willy the Northman?"

Edwin bent low from the saddle and whispered.

"You mean the arrogant bastard?"

"That's the one."

"His accent didn't go unnoticed. What's he doing here anyway?"

"The King has commandeered him from Earl Ralf."

"Then I'd better play dumb, cos I came upon a crowd of them a while back."

"That was you?" he said, with a grin from ear to ear. "You caused quite a stir. Oh! Before that bunch get too close and nosey, I've come across someone who claims to be your little brother."

"My brother? Is he here?"

"No. He's not here. I've got him working his arse off back in Tamaweord. He wasn't in too good a shape when presented himself at the town geat; he was half starved. I'm trying to making a soldier of him."

"Have you told him about me?"

He nodded. "His story seems good enough."

Edwin still couldn't shake the memory of that day from his mind. 'I can't believe it. He couldn't have survived that fire, nobody could have, I was there!'

"Are you alright Ed?"

Shaking his head, "Yes. Just something I was remembering."

Edwin now noticed the Northman emerging from the palace and marching towards them.

Pushing Hengist aside, he barked, "You! Take this."

"Fuck off Willy! He's my friend," said Hengist, holding his axe blade to the man's throat. "You ever try knocking me out of the way again and insulting my friends, I'll chop yer dick off." Elbowing the Northman out of the way, he turned to Edwin. "Watch yer back, Ed."

He nodded. 'Why does everybody keep telling me to watch my back. I always do,' he thought, patting his broadsword, "They'd better not make 'Head Biter' angry," he said, grinning at Hengist.

Hengist gave Edwin a wink and walked away.

The Northman came closer.

"You should choose your friends more carefully," he hissed, this time thrusting the King's reply into Edwin's hand. "Take this back to your Earl."

The other guards, who had now joined the Northman, were laughing as they slapped the rumps of Edwin and Edmund's horses, sending them off at an almost uncontrollable gallop.

*Early October, 1051*
## - Upper Barnstæd -

Outside the village Edwin brought their horses to a stop. He sat for a moment, bathed in the late autumn evening light, observing the distant birds gathering in their thousands, swirling around, hither and thither in ever alternating shaped clouds, as if directed by an invisible artist, impatient to desert the Englisc landscape; to escape the coming winter and fly suth across the Englisc Sæ.

"Don't you love this time of year, Edmund?"

"Not really sir. It looks as if everything is about to die."

"Mmm. With the Godwins thrown out of the country, anything can happen. Go you ahead, your mother and father will be pleased to see you back."

After Edwin had watched him gallop off, he nudged his horse forward and for the first time since his youth, he felt unprotected, vulnerable.

Gwynedd had seen him approaching and was standing just inside the hall, her hands on her hips.

"The master of all that surrounds us has arrived home at long last."

Edwin slid off his horse. An eager stable boy, without saying a word, took the reins and led it away.

"I may not be the master for long. The news is bad!" announced Edwin, as he approached his wife.

"How bad?"

He shook his head. "Very."

She put her arms about him, then suddenly stepped back wrinkling her nose.

"Yuck! You're disgusting. You smell of rancid horse sweat."

"Not surprising. We've been riding hard for a long time and I'm dead tired."

"I'll get some hot water. You need a wash my lad."

"Don't go to sleep in the tub," said Gwynedd, shaking him. She held up a sponge and was about to squeeze water over his head. "So what happened?"

"Slow down woman, I'm tired!" Edwin closed his eyes for a few moments, leant forward, cupped some water in his hands and drenched his face. He did this several times until his thoughts began to take some sort of order.

"We eventually arrived at the royal palace in Gleucestre but the King was already prepared; armed with thousands of troops. The northerne Earls, Siward, Leofric and the Northman Ralf were there in force. All we had were just under two thousand and we wouldn't have had that, had I not warned Earl Godwin."

"It seems a lot to me."

"In war two thousand troops ain't much to speak of."

"Well, what happened?"

"Bloody mayhem that's what. The King began accusing Earl Godwin of defying his authority and fomenting rebellion. Godwin denied it of course. He was innocent and claimed he had the right to be outraged at the King's order to unjustly punish the people of Dofras, who were only defending themselves against the unprovoked attack by Count Eustace and his troop of knights. Then Earl Godwin pointed out Count Eustace and asked the King why that foreigner was at the Witan. The King had stood up in a rage.

"The Count has every right to be here!" he had shouted. "He is family! My former brother-in-law! Show him the respect he deserves!"

"With that, Earl Godwin spat on the ground. The King's fury was embarrassing to watch, he went totally berserk and accused the Earl of murdering his brother Edmund. Then all hell broke loose. Earl Swegen lost his temper, which didn't take much doing, accusing the King of allowing foreigners to undermine the Witan. While all this was going on, that cunning bastard, Robert of Jumièges, the newly installed, Archbishop of Cantwareburh, was bending low, whispering in the King's ear. I don't like him, he's dead evil! He's a snake in the grass if ever there was one. The whole scene was then made all the more diabolical by the King's half crazed mother Emma, who was whispering in the King's other ear."

"Surely the rest of the Earls can see what the King's mother and the Archbishop are up to," said Gwynedd.

"It didn't look like it from where I was standing. Edward is a weak King. Those two are making the most of it, especially Jumièges. They're like a plague, spreading poison wherever they go and the King has caught the decease."

"What can be done then?" asked Gwynedd.

"To be honest, I don't know. I've never seen or heard a Witan in such uproar. Thank the Gods, Bishop Stigand was there otherwise there might have been war. He was able to calm everybody down.

Earl Godwin was forced to give his youngest son, Wulfnoth and Swegen's five-year-old son Hakon as hostages to the King. Then the meeting broke up, arranging to meet again in Lunden a couple of weeks later. On the way to Earl Godwin's place at Suthweca, a lot of the Thegns became scared and started to drift away, leaving no more than five hundred of us."

"What do you mean, scared?"

"They're basically loyal to the King and were frightened of starting a civil war; Godwin versus the King."

"Would it come to that?" asked Gwynedd, nervously.

"I really don't think so. I know Earl Godwin wouldn't want it. But just prior to this second meeting in Lunden, the Earl tried a final plea to the King. He wanted safe conduct so that he could be heard before the Witan, to prove that he was innocent of the King's brother's murder but the King refused and with his massive army to back him was now more confident than ever. He turned a deaf ear to the Earl. Jumièges and the old bat Emma, have at last got their way. Godwin and his sons have been declared, 'Nithing'; losing all their possessions and titles and given five days to get out of the country, never, never to come back."

"Everything? Banished for ever?" Gwynedd said in amazement.

"Yes!"

"There's no possible way for Earl Godwin to get any sort of justice for himself or his sons?"

"No!" replied Edwin. "The King declared he would only give him and his sons peace when his murdered brother Alfred was restored to him alive, together with his men and possessions."

Gwynedd gave a short mocking laugh.

"The King's brother has been dead for years. How could he? King Edward has really lost it! He is insane."

"Very likely!"

"Likely! Of course he's insane!" Gwynedd said, raising her voice.

"Gemæde or not, after fifteen long years Edward still blames Godwin for his brother's death. He won't believe otherwise. As it was told to me, Cnut's son, that ol' devious sod, King Harold, *Harefoh,* him of the nimble feet, sent to Godwin's manor house in Geldeford, in the middle of the night, a large troop of fully armed housecarls, demanding possession of Prince Alfred and his attendants, to take them to the King. How could Godwin refuse in the face of the King's armed men?"

"How could he indeed," replied Gwynedd.

"Anyway, to cut a long story short, it transpires, the Prince's attendants were killed and he was tied to the underside of a horse and had his eyes dug out. He was left to bleed to death, somewhere near Elig. As I said, all Earl Godwin wanted to do, was to prove his innocence to the King and the Witan, and to seek justice for the men of Dofras. On top of all this, the King has gone back on his word, also declaring Godwin's eldest son, Earl Swegen an outlaw. Poor ol' Swegen broke down and cried like a baby. It was terrible to see one of Godwin's sons in such a broken state.

"Fearing for their lives and the lives of his supporters, and that includes us, Earl Godwin and his family made the decision to immediately ride out of Lunden. Harold and Leofwine have made for Brycgstow and thence to Eriuland and Godwin and his sons, Tostig and Gyrth with their wives, to Bosham to take ship to Flanders.

"Before Earl Harold left, he advised me to get out of Lunden fast, to ride for home. Otherwise the King would be wanting my sword, probably accusing me of treason. Or he might even make me one of his precious inner guards, they call, 'thingalith.' Either way it was not for this boyo, so here I am, your brave Edwin. Now! How are you and how are the children?"

"Wonderful. Our little boys are into everything, like normal two and half year-olds. Wulfnoth is the terror. He leads Edric into all sorts of mischief. Edwin, Edwin!"

He had fallen asleep.

*November, 1051*
## - An early morning visitor -

Edwin nudged Gwynedd awake.

"Get dressed! I heard a noise."

"Noise? It's not even dawn, it's still dark," replied Gwynedd, rubbing the sleep from her eyes, "What can it be?"

"I don't know! It could be the King's men. Get dressed!"

On hearing a knock on their bedroom door, Edwin took hold of his broadsword and stood poised.

"Who is it?"

"It's Edmund. I have somebody here, calling himself your brother, sir."

"My brother? Take him to the main hall," replied Edwin, looking at his wife, who was already dressed.

"If he's the same person I saw passing through my village, I'm sure I'll recognise him," she said.

"Right! Let's go," replied Edwin. Making sure his knife and sword were securely sheathed in his belt, he unbarred the door but stopping short of opening it, he turned to his wife, "I feel nervous. What if he's not Eadrick and if he is, will he hate me?"

"Why should he? You and your parents couldn't find him in that fire, besides, you were all captured and couldn't do anything about it."

"Perhaps you're right," he answered. For a brief moment his mind went to the fire and the panic and grief. "If he is Eadrick, it'll be a bloody miracle."

"What are we waiting for," said Gwynedd, putting her hand gently on his. "It could be a wonderful reunion."

Edwin nodded and opened the door.

A tall sandy haired man, who looked to be in his twenties was standing by the top table drinking from a cup. He turned towards Edwin smiling.

"Nice stuff," he said waving the cup at Edwin.

Edwin didn't reply. His whole being clenched. 'It's not him, I know it.' He took in the man's appearance and the sound of his voice to see if there was any family resemblance. There was none, other than his general appearance, likening him to many of the people he knew.

"Haven't I seen you before?" asked Gwynedd.

"I'm not sure," he said deliberately, squinted his eyes. "No, not as far as I know."

"You used to pass through my village, odd jobbing for the widow, Elwin."

"Not odd jobbing any more," he replied, refilling his cup without asking.

'He's dodged the question,' thought Gwynedd.

"I'm soldiering for Earl Leofric now."

"I know you are," said Edwin, giving a slight nod.

"Well!" continued the man, casting his eyes around the hall. "A fine welcome this is for your long lost brother, Eadrick."

"So! You know your name?" replied Edwin, regretting having said it.

"What is this? Of course I know my name!" he said suddenly slamming down the cup on the table, spilling the mead which flowed across the uneven surface, dripping onto the floor. "Am I being interrogated as if I were a foreigner? I've come all this way from Tamaweord and this is all the greeting I get from the brother who left me to die?"

"Well, I can see you're alive now and making yourself at home," answered Edwin, keeping his anger in check. "If you *are* my brother Eadric you are more than welcome but I need proof."

"What type of proof do you need, big brother?...Even your wife recognised me!"

"She only recognised the similarity to a man who passed through her village."

"Well for someone who left me to burn to a crisp in Suthford, you don't seem all that pleased to see me."

"Not true! We searched the house but couldn't find you. I can still hear my mother screaming, as the raiders dragged us away. You think we didn't care and gave up looking? We had no choice. If it hadn't been for Leofric's troops, I wouldn't be here talking to you!"

"But you continue to disbelieve I'm your brother, right?" he replied, his voice beginning to slur from the quantity of mead he had drunk.

"I want to believe. But I don't see how you could have survived. Our house was a fireball when we left."

"Well, I did survive! I was found crawling among the smouldering ruins, picked up by passing strangers and taken to Legracæster where I was brought up. And now," his voice was becoming louder, "I'm standing in front of you and you can't even bring yourself to believe I'm your brother."

"How did you learn of your name and that I was looking for you?" enquired Edwin, in a calm voice.

"It was Hengist. He put the word out, that you were looking for me."

"Yes. I am or was. These are strange times and we have to be certain." Edwin stepped forward with a smile and put his arms about his brother. "Welcome home and now you can pour us *all* a drink."

'Umm,' he thought, pouring the mead and looking around the hall, 'not bad, not bad at all. Than cunt Hengist, if he didn't know it, has given me a leg up. I don't have to go back there and work my bollocks off or to that pigsty back in Legrecæster. I can make a good and easy life here.'

"Gwynedd, is he really the person you saw?"

She thought for several moments, "I don't know. Having only met him briefly that one time. But he didn't know the village I was talking about. He evaded the answer. My instinct says no. They're about the same age, both have reddish hair although this person's more towards light brown but the same sort of build and height. Come to think of it, his voice is different, low and guttural whereas I think the other had a softer and higher tone. But that was some time ago. Now he's cleaned up and obviously well fed and dressed it makes it difficult to judge but my answer is probably not."

"Well, like you, I'm not entirely convinced. I think he's playing the part, so let's play along with him for the time being," said Edwin.

"When you hugged him did you feel anything? A connection or warmth from him?" asked Gwynedd.

"No! I felt absolutely nothing. I pride myself on being able to read beneath the surface of people's minds but this, I just don't know. My gut feeling tells me he's *not* Eadrick."

"If he's not your brother, then who is he and why is he here?"

"Want of a better life than the one he has? Who knows? When he was first admitted into the hall, Edmund said he began pouring himself cupful after cupful of mead and carried on pouring and drinking as if there was no tomorrow. When we left him he had another two. That's strong stuff. If I had drunk the same amount I'd be under the table!"

"Never mind his drinking, the question is, what do we do with him?"

Edwin went over to the bedroom window, opening the shutter he turned his faced towards Gwynedd and gave a half smile. "We'll play for time."

The muted chorus of winter birds had passed. Dawn was beginning to break, revealing a grey patchy sky. He didn't have a complete answer but he knew the man's true identity would reveal itself.

"Did your brother have any distinguishing marks on his body? Or would he have worn a charm to ward off evil spirits?"

"Not to my knowledge. That's what makes it so difficult," replied Edwin. "He mentioned Legracæster, a town to the suth west of Suthford where he was taken, apparently. All I can remember of that place is that it was quite big. If I had the time, I could probably find out more but I haven't, at least not yet."

"Why not?"

Edwin came close to Gwynedd and whispered.

"I heard a rumour. A rumour that Earl Godwin and his sons are about to return."

"Do you think the King will let them back into the country?"

"Not willingly." Edwin tilted his head to one side and paused. "Don't you think it strange that he, this man who calls himself Eadrick, should come here at this particular time?"

"I don't think he has anything to do with the other. Who told you the Godwins are about to come back?"

"One of our fishermen. He had been casting his nets off the coast of Flanders and met up with someone he knew on one of the Godwin ships. If the information is correct, they won't be coming back on their own, begging! Which gives me hope."

"Being hopeful is one thing but aren't you being somewhat overly suspicious about our guest?" queried Gwynedd.

"Possibly! But you have suspicions too. There is so much going on at the moment. There has been no word from the royal court in Lunden nor from Ælfgar, our newly appointed Earl of Anglia. The King must know I'm a Godwin supporter and certainly Earl Leofric and his son Ælfgar know, which does make me nervous. I feel the very ground we stand on is shifting and I can't do anything about it. Nobody has contacted me not even Osgar and now this … this person turns up from Leofric's stronghold claiming kinship without any proof…yes! I'm on edge."

"What do you intend to do then?"

"At the moment I don't know… we'll wait and see. I do not wish to throw him out, at least not yet, …he could *be* my brother but then again, not. We'll keep an eye on him, taking note of what he does and were he goes. In the meantime I'll speak to Edmund and his father. They'll keep us informed."

Edwin looked up at the sky, collecting his thoughts. He lent back on Egbert's garden seat, linking his hands behind his head.

"What do you make of this man?"

"He has animal cunning, undisciplined and he is a drunk. The man's here in your home with no proof of being your brother or being *any* kind of kinsman. Probably got himself thrown out of Mercia."

Edwin listened to his old friend, who he respected for his honesty, in the secure knowledge that whatever they discussed would go no further.

"Long ago, I knew a man, in fact we trained together back in the old days. What was it, twenty years ago, anyway before the present lot took over."

"You mean our present King?"

Egbert sucked on his lips and nodded.

"Yes. As I was saying, I think his name was Æthelred…yes that's right Æthelred. He was bloody good. A more talented man it would be hard to find anywhere. He was hard to equal, stronger than most, as I said, there wasn't a man to touch him. When he came at you with his skeggy, you had better move fast or run for it! That man could have risen to the top, beyond a 'Thingalith', even to Earl or, at the very least, a wealthy landed Thegn. I say he could have, if he hadn't been a pissing drunk. Show him a barrel of mead or beer, didn't matter which, he would go through the whole fucking lot and disappear for days, then reappear not remembering a damn thing. In fact, even after only two or three mugfuls he would have total memory loss. A real shame! When he was sober he was a ruthless, brilliant fighter. I wouldn't have liked to been up against him but when he was drunk, a child could outsmart him and hammer him to the ground. A total waste of an incredible talent."

"What happen to him?"

"I saw him a few years later begging in Gualhenfforda of all places. He could hardly walk. His legs were like brown knurled sticks. On top of which, he complained of terrible pains in his stomach. Since then I've seen several men, men I grew up with, becoming drunkards like him and in the same condition and situation. Helpless and aimless, staggering towards their own total destruction."

"As much as I always like listening to you, what has this got to do with this... brother of mine?"

"As in all these cases, none of them could be trusted. That drunkard who says he is your brother, be very careful. I wouldn't trust him! Not even as far as I could throw him."

"Thanks for the sermon," laughed Edwin, "I appreciated it."

# CHAPTER VIII

*Early December, 1051*
**- Ithancester, East Anglia -**
Bradwell-on-Sea, Essex

On approaching Ithancester, a small East Anglian fishing village, situated on a promontory facing the rich fishing grounds of the Northerne Sæ, Edwin felt a penetrating chill and a twinge of vulnerability as he looked about the snow sprinkled landscape. Trees and bushes were bent double, wizened like old men and women of the field, shaped by the biting, prevailing easterly winds. He felt thankful there were no cutting winter winds today, just a light westerly. But the land did make him feel uneasy. The whole exposed area was low lying flatland, and thus prone to the vagaries of the weather, especially to spring floods.

Edwin had taken the man calling himself, Eadric, east into the countryside, in the hope that time spent together would somehow reveal his true identity.

The small harbour before them boasted ten fishing boats and, in pride of place, three longships which had been captured the previous year from Viking raiders; now moored for swift departure for battle.

"By the way, shouldn't you be reporting back to Hengist?" asked Edwin, as they rode into the village.

Eadrick thought for a moment.

"It's more important I spend as much time with you to make up for all those lost years. It's not everyone who discovers their family, thought lost for ever."

"Yes I can understand that," answered Edwin, uncomfortably.

Suddenly Eadrick shouted, "Look! Two ships. They're heading this way!"

"They're longships! Let's hope they're not raiders!"

"What'll we do?" replied Eadrick, who was looking scared.

"Protect the people of the village, that's what!" replied Edwin, dismounting, banging on the half opened door of the large house they were passing.

"Longships approaching!" shouted Edwin, as two men emerged from the darkened interior.

"Who are you? You're not one of us," said the taller of the two.

"Does it matter? You'd better be ready, they could be raiders," replied Edwin. Not waiting for a reply he turned away and remounted his horse.

He heard one of men shout, "Get armed and ready to sail and tell the ol' man!"

Edwin turned to Eadrick.

"Go over to that church and ring its bell to warn everybody!"

"What will you be doing?"

"Organising a welcoming party."

The captured longships had already departed. Edwin was amazed at their rapid deployment. One moment they were lazily moored side by side, the next they were manned, under full sail and accelerating out to sæ.

At the sound of the church bell, men from the village, fields and other places nearby flooded into the village, marching to the quayside. The fishing boats, their haul of fish offloaded, were now spread out to block entry to the harbour.

"Not counting the crews already at sæ, there has to be over sixty of us. I wouldn't have thought there were this many men in a village of this size," said Eadrick.

"That bell you rang could be heard a long way away. They're used to warding off sæ-raiders."

They waited, their eyes focused on the slow moving warships.

Edwin was now becoming curious.

'I can't quite make out what our ship's captains are doing,' he thought, 'unless those others are friendly. Now our ships have turned about and are sailing back towards harbour with the other two following.' He turned to say something to Eadrick, but he wasn't there and couldn't be seen anywhere.

Edwin eyed an old man. "Have you seen the man who was here with me a moment ago?"

"You mean that scrawny sod with sandy hair?" replied the old man, through a toothless mouth.

"That sounds like him."

The old man nodded in the direction of an inn.

"Over there! He's gone for some liquid courage." He cleared his throat and spat in the dirt.

Most of the men had their skeggies at the ready. Others like Edwin, had broadswords drawn and were cursing or bragging about what they would do.

The old man had manoeuvred himself close to Edwin's side. As far as Edwin could judge, he was in his late fifties with long greying curly hair and stood about three hands shorter than himself. He had apparently seen off many a raider with his sharp edged, long handled axe, which rested for the moment on his shoulder. He elbowed Edwin in the ribs.

"I bags the big one, standing on the leading foreign longship."

"You've got bloody good eyes for an old man!" replied Edwin.

"Listen stranger! To be ahead of the game, you need a regular diet, a man's diet; a woman a-night, eat plenty of fish and it'll make yer strong and improve yer eyesight!"

"I'll bear that in mind old'un when I get back home but between you and me, I think you'll find those ships are friendly," Edwin replied, with a smile.

A great cheer went up, in and around the harbour as the two foreign longships raised the Red Dragon pennants of Wessex.

Edwin moved forward to greet Earl Godwin.

"My lord, welcome home."

"Whether I'm still welcome here or not remains to be seen. You are Edwin of Upper Barnstæd?"

"Yes my lord!"

"I thought so. I've seen you at my son's Harold's court. I knew your father, Wulfric."

"My lord, I heard a rumour the royal fleet is about. It could be dangerous here!"

Earl Godwin scanned the men on the quay until his eyes settled on Eadrick who had emerged unsteadily from the inn.

Beckoning Edwin to come close, he asked, "Who's that man?"

"I've only known him only a short time. He claims he's Eadrick, my long lost brother."

The Earl raised his eyebrows.

He whispered, "I'm only here to test the waters so to speak and then we're back to Flanders."

Addressing the men on the quayside, Earl Godwin called, "Is there a Hensen here? Thegn of this village?"

"That's me!" replied the fish eating, woman a-night, old'un.

Edwin was utterly surprised. If ever there was an unlikely looking Thegn it was this old'un.

"I need to talk to you," said the Earl.

Earl Godwin led Hensen away. As he was passing Edwin, the old'un, gave Edwin a huge smile, clenched his fist and made a pumping action with his arm, before stepping on board the Earl's ship.

"Whoever would have thought it," said Eadrick, who had quietly returned to Edwin's side.

"Why not!" answered Edwin.

"I don't know!" said Eadrick. "He looks decrepit and he stinks."

"So do you…and you're drunk again!"

"I went for a piss and had a quick drink, that's all." He brought his head close to Edwin's, "I don't like the way you speak to me."

He spat the words out into Edwin's face through the acrid smell of alcohol. He then turned towards Earl Godwin's ship.

"I wonder what they're talking about."

Edwin shrugged his shoulders. "Who knows."

Shortly after the old'un had stepped back ashore, the Earl's two ships turned about and put to sæ.

The old'un beckoned to Edwin.

"What does he want with us?" said Eadric.

"Not you, Eadric. He wants me!" replied Edwin.

The old'un led Edwin away from the crowded quayside and spoke in a whisper.

"Earl Godwin is returning to Flanders but you're not to breath a word of this to anyone. I mean anyone. Come July or August of next year, be prepared. The Earl's family will be returning in force."

"He will have a fleet?" replied Edwin.

"Just be prepared." He tapped his nose. "Tell no one. That's what he said."

*July, 1052*
## - Return from exile in Eriuland –
Ireland

It took Earl Harold a short time to get his sæ legs back again. He patted the steersman on the shoulder before taking a firm grip on the ship's sternpost. Steadying himself, he looked towards the disappearing landscape with a mixture of emotions; sadness at leaving Diublinn and gratitude for the fact that he and his younger brother Leofwine had spent ten good months at King Diarmait's court. In fact, he couldn't remember ever having spent so much time, precious time, in the company of his younger brother.

The arrival of the messenger with news from their father had both puzzled and excited him and Leofwine. What had changed? The very thought of being reunited with their father and the rest of the family had given them renewed hope for the future. The scrawled message, obviously written in great haste had only said:

*Dated this, 2nd June 1052*
*My dearest sons,*
*Gather what forces you can and sail to Wihtland with all urgency.*
*Your loving father,*
*Godwin, Earl of Wessex.*

Harold reread the message, put it back in his pocket, smiled to himself and turned to the steersman.
"Did you enjoy last night's celebrations?"
The steersman nodded and gave a wink.
"That Iras King knows how to give a party."
"What do they call that stuff we drank last night, water of life or something?"
"I think it's called, Uisge beatha or something like that. Anyway that's what I was told," replied the steersman.
"Whatever…more like gut rot and it's messed up my head," replied Harold, looking back at the ever retreating Diublinn, trying to focus his eyes on his brother's ship and the rest of their small fleet.

The distant Celtic hills to the suthwest, rising from the green flat lands were now diminishing gradually to merge into a single, long dark smudge on the horizon.

"Eric," said Harold to the steersman, "just keep to the same course as before but this time we're making for Porteloca on the north Wessex coast."

The sæ weathered steersman paused before answering, looking about, breathing in the early morning air.

"I know where it is, my lord. But before we get there, there's Skalmey to think on. That's one dangerous íegland and has some nasty neighbours. Sheer black granite, ship killers. It'll be night when we get there and they'll be lurking and sticking out of the sæ like devils!"

"It'll be fine. You're just an old worrier," replied Harold with a smile. "We'll have a full moon."

"If you say so."

"I know it," said Harold. "With a clear night we'll steer a safe course between the Skalmey and Grassholm. We haven't got much time and that's quickest route to Porteloca."

"Agreed! But if it's overcast I'll steer well clear to the west of Grasholm before changing course for Porteloca."

"Alright!" They had to return, no matter what the risks.

'Father has tested the support for our cause,' he mused, 'and now is the time to strike. What is it I feel? Nervous? Yes. It will be fraught with danger. Excited? Definitely. It'll be good, returning home at last from exile. What was it someone once said; King Diarmait has always been a friend to those in need. Certainly he has been a good and supportive friend, helping to recruit nine captains plus their crews for this venture. We couldn't have ask for more. I suppose he feels indebted because we helped him get rid of that pig, Eachmargach who was calling himself Diublinn's rightful, Irish King. Bollocks! He was a Norvegian freebooter.' Harold gave a wry smile. 'It's made Diermait happy though, and afforded him the opportunity to make his son Murchad, King of Diublinn. Yes, he's a useful friend.'

The steersman shook Harold awake. "Look over there."

Harold blinked, stood up, cleared his head and yawned.

"Where did you say?" he yawned again.

The steersman pointed to a dark shape to port.

"Weird shape. That's Skamey, isn't it?" said Harold. "It reminds me of a mouse with a lump at the end of its tail."

"I suppose you could say that," said the steersman, with a laugh.

Harold looked up at the pock-marked heavens, focussing his eyes on the near full moon.

"Bright enough for you?" he asked with a smile.

"It'll do," replied Eric.

He took note of Eric's dour response but was thankful the man was a careful mariner.

He pointed to the moon. "Have you ever wondered what that incredible beacon is, which aids us in the blackness of the night?"

"Can't say I have," replied the steersman, scratching his beard. "Give it a few days and it'll be gone."

"I know, but it reappears and keeps on reappearing..." Harold could see he wasn't getting anywhere. The look of puzzlement on the steersman's face said it all and so he changed the subject. "All we have to do now, is look out for that other rock; Skokholm on the port side."

"Aye,"

He could just make out their other nine ships in line. Feeling satisfied he turned to the steersman.

"Wake me at daybreak."

August, 1052<br>
- Upper Barnstæd -

"Come back it's dangerous," shouted Gwynedd. Edwin ignoring her pleading, struck out into the cold salt water of the Tames, with their son Edric on his back. Three year-old Edric holding onto his father's shoulder with one hand, shouted with joy as he splashed the water with his other.

Edwin, was fully aware of the dangers of swimming in the tidal waters but it was high tide and would be so for a little while longer before it turned, and quite safe to swim. He didn't attempt to stand on the muddy bottom, he knew the water would be too deep. Anyway it wouldn't be safe for his son. Turning around Edwin swam gently back to the shore.

"I wish you wouldn't do that," said Gwynedd.

Edwin's brother, who was sitting close to Gwynedd agreed.

"If they were my kids I wouldn't take 'em out, the tides and currents here are too strong."

Edwin stood for a moment considering.

'How would you know,' he thought. He couldn't make up his mind whether pull the man to his feet and hurl him into the Tames or land a blow into his intrusive face. He decided to do neither but just looked at him. When their eyes met, Edwin held their gaze for some moments. His brother was the first to look away.

"Why did you do that?" said Gwynedd testily, ignoring the friction between the two men. "That water can be treacherous and I don't want you to take the children out in it again."

"It's high tide and it will be safe for a little while longer and anyway, Wulf will be upset if I don't take him out as well."

"Well, I don't like it!"

"You don't like it because you can't swim. He'll be alright, believe me. Look at him. He's covered in mud, so he needs a good wash. To put your mind at rest, I'll only take him a little way, just to get him clean."

"Alright. But don't go too far, I know you!"

Edwin returned with Wulfnoth still hanging on tightly.

"You see, nothing to be frightened about, he's happy and he is clean."

"Your brother has gone back to the village."

"Good!"

"Is anything wrong?" enquired Gwynedd.

"Could be something or nothing," replied Edwin.

After putting the boys in the back of the cart, Edwin took the reins of the horse and led it away from the Tames and its muddy bank to a patch of grass. He was deep in thought.

"Why have we stopped? And why have you gone quiet on me?" she said.

He didn't reply.

"Is there anything really worrying you?"

"Yes," he replied, after some moments. "Father Oswald called me into his private room earlier today."

"Why!" asked Gwynedd, heaving herself up and making herself comfortable on the tailgate of the cart.

"A woman was found very dead early this morning."

"Very dead. What do you mean, *very dead?*" asked Gwynedd.

"Brutally murdered!"

"Murdered? So we have a crazed woman hater, on the loose in our village?"

"Yes!" Edwin momentarily closed his eyes, "I've seen some horrible sights in my time but when a young woman is murdered it's something else!"

"Who was she?"

"A local girl. She lived on her own at the far side of the village towards the river. Her named was Fran."

"Isn't she the one who helped to crew with the fishermen last week?"

"That's her."

"I remember her now. She was a strong, pretty girl," replied Gwynedd slowly. "Who would want to kill her?"

"We haven't a clue but clearly someone with considerable strength. As Thegn of the village I'm supposed to find out who the bastard is and mete out justice."

"Now, I really feel scared for myself and the children."

"We'll have to make sure the doors are properly closed and barred and all the window shutters are secured at night, until this is over. This and everything else is weighing heavily on my mind. With the Godwins gone, Leofric's two faced son Ælfgar, who has control of East Anglia, won't think twice about throwing us out at any moment. I am surprised we're still here untouched as it is. Then, the King invited that bastard William to court. Rumour has it, he has made him his heir. On top of that, Earl Ralf and the other Northmen have been given even more lands and… and now Edward is said to be divorcing the Queen. It doesn't take much to imagine what Earl Godwin thinks about all of this! His daughter being disgraced, divorced and thrown to the Northman wolves."

"Can he do that?"

"For all I know… that's probably another reason Earl Godwin is planning to come back. I need a drink," Edwin said, leaning over for the flask. "The boys! Where have they gone? They're not here!"

"I don't know!" Gwynedd grew pale.

Edwin slid off the cart and looked underneath.

"They're not here!" He began scanning the immediate vicinity. "They're nowhere to be seen! I'm going back to the Tames and then work my way back from there."

"I'm coming with you. This is all flat land, there's nowhere to hide. They couldn't have gone far. There's only the bourne. Oh God!"

They stood on the highest point of the bank, shielding their eyes, scanning the area.

"Where can they be?" said Edwin. "There are no tracks to here and they couldn't have gone far. We would have seen them if they were trying to make their way towards the Tames." He could feel and hear the panic in Gwynedd's voice as she was calling their names. But the children were nowhere to be seen.

Edwin put his arm around her.

"They couldn't possibly have walked to the bourne in such a short space of time and there are certainly no foot prints to here or along the bank. Wait! I think our two imps are playing a game of their own."

"What do you mean?"

"Look carefully back towards the cart and then a bit to the right of it. That bush! Watch it move."

Grabbing each by their collars and throwing them into the back of the cart, Edwin shouted, "Right you two, stay!"

He held his wife's shaking body.

Between her sobs, Gwynedd said, "I was so scarred. I thought... I thought we had lost them."

Edwin shook his head, "They couldn't have gone as far as the Tames without us seeing them. Let me dry your eyes."

"No! Leave me alone. I feel stupid enough as it is."

"Woman! You're not stupid," he said holding her face close to his. "With you by my side, we can survive anything!"

"Now *you're* being stupid." She smiled, drawing a long, shuddering breath.

"We'll have to keep those two on a tight rein."

"Let's go home."

"Sir!" called Edmund from the doorway. "Earl Harold is approaching."

"Earl Harold!" Edwin shouted, in surprise.

"Yes, sir, he's just a few steps behind me."

"My lord," greeted Edwin, as the Earl entered the hall, "I can't believe my eyes. Welcome."

"My lady, Gwynedd"

"You have taken us by surprise, my lord. Can I offer you some refreshment," said Gwynedd.

"No thank you, lady. I need your husband urgently." he turned to Edwin. "Arm up and come with me."

"Yes, my lord," returned Edwin, giving Gwynedd a sidelong glance.

"Sir," said Edmund, "your brother has ridden off in the direction of Lunden."

"Brother or no brother, he's one of Leofric's men I'm sure of it."

"I wouldn't worry about him," said the Earl. "By the time he gets to Lunden it'll all be over."

Edwin was staggered. He had never seen so many longships. He estimated there were between seventy to a hundred lying at anchor, all in a straight line as far as the eye could see; the lead ship flying the Wessex pennant.

"My lord, I've never seen such a fleet, and all bristling with arms."

"Yes, it's a wondrous sight to see. Men and ships have flocked to us from Eriuland, Flanders, Wessex, Cent and East Anglia. From all over. The King will have to listen to us now."

Edwin embraced his wife and boarded. He didn't want to leave her right now but had no alternative, he had to obey and follow the Earl. Their small boat moved away from the pier, as Gwynedd stood waving.

"Don't forget!" shouted Edwin, "Bar the doors and windows and keep our two tearaways out of trouble."

"I'll keep my seax handy and the boys drunk until you get back," she laughed.

"Then, I'll have to bring back a cartload of mead, won't I?"

They continued to gaze fixedly at each other as the boat moved further away from the pier. Gwynedd's figure became smaller and smaller until she was no more than a tiny dot on the shoreline.

"What's that about barring the doors?" asked the Earl.

"We have a crazed sex killer on the loose."

"Can your wife protect herself?"

"Oh yes!" replied Edwin, pointing toward Edmund. "His father is taking charge of our hall while I'm away. She'll be alright."

As the boat softly bumped against the hull of the lead ship Edwin, following the Earl, clambered up on deck with Edmund close behind him.

"Weigh anchor!"

Edwin turned towards Edmund.

"Did you tell your father where we were going?"

"Yes!" he replied smiling, adjusting his sword belt. "He wished he could have come."

Edwin looked around the ship. It was pressed full of armoured men, many of them housecarls. The rest were the fyrd; men of the field, craftsmen and retired soldiers, who had taken up their old weapons to give support. Like all the other ships in Earl Godwin's fleet, it was full of glinting helmets.

Amidships, gathered about the mast, were orderly stacks of spare weapons; spears, shields and helmets, upon which sat an ever growing number of fighting men who had been boarding at various places along the fleet's route up the Tames.

He could see Earl Godwin with Harold at the prow and was half expecting Osgar to appear out of crowd and tap him on the shoulder but he was nowhere to be seen. There were a few faces he knew, but only vaguely. Edwin kept to himself and wondered what would happen when they eventually reached Lunden.

'Will it be war? And which side will my so called brother be on?' he thought. 'I can't see the King and his Northman friends backing down and handing everything back to the Godwins.'

Edwin had been surprised when Earls Leofric and Siward had acted against the Godwins the previous year. 'Let's hope they've now seen the King for what he is, a weakling! Bending to every lie his mother... I forgot, his mother, nasty Emma, died earlier this year. So there's only Jumièges to whisper in his ear.'

He had lost count of the bends in the Tames but now the bourne was getting narrower and soon would reach Lunden. They had passed Dart some way back, where the ships had picked up more men from the sutherne shore. They must be getting close to Lunden Brycg now but with the crowd in front of him it was difficult to see ahead. A sudden cheer went up, most raised their spears. He could see Godwin's land army just beyond the suth bank, making its way towards Suthweca, Godwin's old Manor.

It was difficult to get information from anyone, only the Godwins knew what they were going to do.

Edwin felt a hand on his shoulder. Someone was trying to push past him.

"Out of my way friend."

"Sure!" replied Edwin. He was trying to make his way aft.

"Before you go friend, besides us in the fleet, who else is with us?"

"Difficult to judge. 'Ere! Arn't you Edwin of Upper Barnstæd?"

"Yes."

"I thought I'd seen you before. Earl Harold went personally to see you."

"That's right."

"We've been sending out riders all over Wessex and to other parts in the west country." The man came closer, spreading his arms out as if he were encompassing the whole of the countryside. "Thousands have joined us and the way things are going, we could be six thousand strong by the time we get to Lunden and the King's palace at West Minster. The plain fact is, none of us want those Northmen here. We know they're in the pay of the bastard from over the other side of the sæ. Did you know that he was here a few months ago?"

"I had heard it rumoured," replied Edwin.

"Well, it was more than a rumour! He was! We certainly don't want him turning us Englisc Thegns and churls into thralls. Freedom is what we have here mate and freedom is what we'll hang on to, to the last drop of our blood."

"Thanks for the information," said Edwin, but the man was already out of hearing and making his way towards the bow,

"Shit! I didn't think to ask him his name."

### - Palace of West Minster -

"Sire," beseeched Robert of Jumièges, "The Godwins have gathered together an enormous fleet and their supporters are coming in from all over the suth. They'll be here soon! Surely you must make a stand! This is insurrection, Sire! They mean to attack you, their sovereign lord! Please, Sire, before they get here, while there is still time. Duke William can help you. I know it! I don't ask it for myself but for your safety and the safety of your realm!"

"Oh, shut up Archbishop!" King Edward rubbed the sleep from his eyes. "You wake me, this early in the morning and now you give me no time to think!"

"But Sire!" pleaded Jumièges. "There *is* no time to think!"

"What! What did you say!"

"Sire! I am truly sorry, I didn't mean that... it's... you must act now!"

"I have told you already Archbishop! I must have time to think!

And stop pacing about my bedroom like a demented monk, I can't stand it!"

Jumièges was too distraught to hear and continued nervously pacing about the room, all the while rubbing his hands together and mumbling, "We're losing time! We're losing time, we have to do something." He knew very well that if old man Godwin ever managed to regain his Earldom he, as Archbishop of Cantwareburh, would be finished and the same fate would befall the Bishops of Lunden, Dornwaracaster and the rest of their Northman compatriots throughout the country.

"Keep still and shut up!" shouted Edward. "You're giving me a headache!"

He thought about Duke William of Northmandig's brief visit five months before. He had noted how much William had changed in the intervening eleven years since they had last been together. From an amiable fourteen-year-old, he had become a steely, cunning, belligerent twenty-five year-old, a formidable adversary for anyone. 'But he still had that, how should I say, longing to be loved by a father, a father he didn't have. Someone close to guide him? Perhaps that is the reason I warmed to him. I sensed beneath his cold exterior, his vulnerability, his need. He could well have been the son I never had and now he is gone, back to his own land.'

"Oh Sire, I am so sorry. It is for the love of you that I am so worried. You need to be surrounded by subjects who you can trust! Your northerne Earls Leofric and Siward are here, but I ask myself, where are their forces to protect you? They are nowhere to be seen! You have only Earl Odda and my countryman Earl Ralf and their men, who are already manning your ships, to protect you. None of these Englisc love you, certainly not the way Bishop Ulf and I love you. Hasn't it been proven beyond doubt the Godwin's are criminals in the sight of God!" Jumièges moved closer to the King, almost whispering in his ear. "As I've mentioned before, I can arrange the annulment of your marriage. Pope Leo won't mind, especially when he hears the truth about your wife's family; her father, old Godwin, who connived in the murder of your brother Alfred. Sire, I can sail to Northmandig this very day and persuade Duke William to come in force. Then we can rid the country of the Godwins for ever and your realm will be safe!"

"Don't be a bloody fool, Archbishop. Godwin may be all you say he is but he is not stupid! As much as I would like William here, it would take him months to get a fleet and troops together strong enough to oppose Godwin." replied the King, combing his fingers through the long greying hair that hung down to his shoulders. "You are wrong! So very wrong Archbishop. Godwin's plans for the moment remain a mystery to me but of this I am certain. He won't attack his King. He's too wary of Earl Leofric and Siward's armed strength."

"But Sire, if that were so, where are their forces? There are hardly enough troops to protect you here in your palace!"

The King swung his thin legs out from beneath the fur covers and sat on the edge of the bed. His loose fitted, creased nightgown, partly open, revealed his chest, the skin of which was blotched and pale. He was a man who looked far older than his forty-nine years. Leaning forward he put his head in his hands.

"Please Sire, What.. do.. you.. want.. me.. to.. do..?"

"I keep telling you! I need time to think! For the moment… I do… not… know… Archbishop! If only my mother were here."

"Sire, you are still surrounded by friends, friends who love you! You have to move on, Sire. You must think like a King!"

"What!" shouted Edward, leaping to his feet, his face reddening with anger. "What did you say Archbishop!" He stood for a moment, shoulders stooped, his head seeming to sink forward into his body. In this bowed headed posture, the King glanced murderously at Jumièges before moving towards the door of a small room: his inner sanctum, his private world.

"Think like a King!" Edward repeated bitterly, "I *am* the fucking King! Archbishop! Know your place!" Slamming the sanctum door shut, blotting out the world, he fell on his knees in front of an altar.

Holding up his clasped hands in desperation, he began silently praying; not to his God but to his dead mother.

*September, 1052*
**- Confrontation –**

With sails furled, the rowers of Earl Godwin's ships maintained a steady progress in a three abreast formation moving ever closer towards West Minster. The fleet had taken this configuration after passing under Lunden Brycg.

The King's force of forty ships were retreating. His two commanders, Odda and Ralph, knew they had nowhere else to go. They had to withdraw or make a meaningless fight of it. Drawing back to just beyond West Minster Palace, the crews were ordered to heave to and stow their oars. Godwin's fleet had boxed them in.

"Where are you going," shouted Odda.

Ralph after leaping from ship to ship, gained the shore.

"You make your own peace with the King and the Godwins," he shouted back, "I'm out of here."

From his position in the stern, Edwin looked on as Earl Godwin shouted orders to the captains of his nearest ships, while Harold stood by his steersman.

There was a complete change from the previous year, when the northerne Earls had backed the King in force. Now their numbers were missing. It seemed to Edwin, that Godwin had planned it beautifully, taking advantage of the Englisc Earls' and Thegns' disillusionment with their monarch who, it seemed, was ever influenced by the growing numbers of Northmandisc Barons and advisors.

Edward had failed his people!

"Heave to," shouted Godwin.

A small boat pulled up alongside. Earl Harold helped the aged Bishop Stigand aboard.

"Bishop, I didn't expect to see you again," greeted Earl Godwin.

"My lord Godwin, I've been hanging on to my bishopric by the skin of my few remaining teeth. But this is a sorry state of affairs and I don't know where to begin."

"That's easy, why not start from the beginning," replied Godwin, with all his considerable charm.

"I haven't been able to advise the King on anything these past months, especially since the death of his mother. Now here I am again… acting as messenger. Archbishop Jumièges has fled the palace and is making for Lunden in the company of Bishops Ulf and William. Also, Earl Ralph has abandoned the King's fleet for his fortress in Herefordscir." He paused to catch his breath. "What can I say, other than they're like rats abandoning a sinking ship and here I am expected to advise the King. So, my lord, you see me here before you once more. The King has commanded a Witenagemot be called for tomorrow morning."

"Bishop, what of my youngest son Wulfnoth and my grandson, Swegen's son, Hakon?"

"They are held under guard but are safe and well at the Royal Hall in Lunden." He suddenly brought his hand to his mouth, "Oh my lord! Jumièges!"

Earl Godwin looked hard at the Bishop. "Bishop! They shouldn't be still held. We must get them released now!"

"My lord Godwin! It was all in good faith," stammered Stigand. "This should not be happening!"

"Father, let me send some of my men," said Harold.

Edwin stepped forward.

"Give me twelve men and horses and we'll have a chance of finding the boys before Jumièges does."

### - The King's Hall, Lunden –

"Pull your cart over here," she said softly. Lady Ælfgifu had just arrived having been given permission, by the King, to see her five-year old son, Hakon, against the advice of Archbishop Jumièges. She had brought two gifts for him; a wooden sword and a cart.

The little boy, hesitating as if frightened, looked up towards his French tutor who smiled and nodded.

"First I have to put my new sword in my belt and load my cart with these magic stones I found under my bed."

"What magic stones are they?"

"They fell out of the sky in the night. My tutor says they are stars, brought down here by an angel from heaven."

"Then you will have to guard and handle your magic stones very carefully so that they will not lose their magic."

Sitting impatiently on his bed, was Earl Godwin's youngest son Wulfnoth. The twelve-year old looked towards Lady Ælfgifu who, as any mother in her position would, was giving her full attention to her son.

"My lady, what news of my father and mother and my aunt the Queen? We hear nothing of the outside world in here," he said, timidly.

Ælfgifu looked at the clerk, but he was reading quietly in the corner seemingly unconcerned.

"The Queen has been sent to Wherwell Nunnery to be looked after by the abbess, the King's sister." She lowered her voice so as not to be heard by the clerk. "Your father is rumoured to have gathered together a fleet somewhere off the Wessex coast."

The clerk glanced up briefly but returned to his book.

Wulfnoth moved over to Lady Ælfgifu, kneeling on the floor at her side and whispered, "But what of my brothers?"

"I don't know perhaps they have joined your father and his fleet."

"My father and my brothers…" Wulfnoth whispered into lady Ælfgifu's ear, "will they defeat the King and set us free?"

"I know nothing of such things," she whispered in reply. "I must obey the King. It has taken me these twelve months to arrange this visit and perhaps, with prayer, our situation will now improve." She glanced towards the clerk who, getting up from his seat, walked across to the door and left the room.

"Thank you," said Wulfnoth, rising from his position on the floor, also moving towards the door. Trying the latch he found it to be unsecured.

While Lady Ælfgifu's attention returned to her son, who was gingerly pulling his cart full of stones over to his mother, Wulfnoth quietly opened the door and slipped out.

"These must be very magical," said Ælfgifu, picking the largest stone out of the cart. "See here, this big one, how it shines. See the delicate light and dark patterns." Holding her son's right index finger she began lightly tracing the ball of his finger over the surface of the stone. "See how smooth it is." She put the stone back in the cart.

"Do you know how to count, my darling?"

Very slowly Hakon replied, "Un, deux, trois, quatre…"

The clerk who had returned un-noticed, was smiling at the boy's pronunciation.

"No," said his mother, "in Englisc."

Hakon gave his mother a big grin and said in a loud voice, "An, twa, prie, feower, fif, siex, seofon…"

"My lady!" interrupted the clerk, "I'm trying to teach the boy the alphabet of the noble class and that of Latin.."

"Enough of this nonsense!" remonstrated Lady Ælfgifu. "He is *my* child and he must learn his mother tongue first! Then he can learn Latin. How dare you, a Normandish clerk, infer that Englisc is *base!* Our culture is a bright shining beacon for all of Europe!"

"Forgive me my lady but I am not a Northman, I am from Francia."

"I do not much care where you come from!"

"It is not my fault, my lady, I was instructed to teach the boys the ways of our church by Archbishop Jumièges." He looked around for Wulfnoth.

"That man…" At the sound of the door opening, Lady Ælfgifu held her son close to her. She was relieved to see Wulfnoth return.

"The guards have left," said Wulfnoth, jubilantly. "There's panic everywhere."

"What news of your father?"

"I'm not sure! I thought I heard voices shouting that father's fleet, bristling with warriors, had past under Lunden Brycg."

Ælfgifu smiled, "Thank the Lord. Now my children, you shall be free. What's that noise and shouting?"

"I don't know my lady," replied Wulfnoth. "Perhaps Father is already here!"

"Where are they?" shouted a voice from below their room.

"I know that voice," whispered Ælfgifu. "Hurry, let's get out of here." They moved towards the door.

"Not so fast, Lady Ælfgifu!" said Archbishop Jumièges, blocking the doorway. "Bishop William and you others grab the Godwin brat and I'll deal with the boy child!"

"No! No!" screamed the mother.

"You there!" ordered the Archbishop. "Tutor or whatever your name is, don't stand there senseless, get out of here!"

"No! Don't touch my baby, you evil swine!" screamed Ælfgifu, her arms ever tighter around her son. "You are not taking my child from me again!"

"Stand aside woman! You there, Bishop Ulf, stop gawping and give me a hand with this whore!"

"But my Lord Archbishop, she's an abbess, you can't treat her like this!"

"A fallen abbess... a whore!" snarled the Archbishop.

"But Archbishop," continued Bishop Ulf, "you can't drag the child away from his mother, this is against everything our mother church stands for!"

"These are our hostages and our only lifeline, you idiot! Move yourself! Grab the child and I'll deal with the woman!"

The Archbishop prised Ælfgifu's arms apart and flung her into the far corner of the room. She immediately got to her feet and charged back towards him, clawing at his face, screaming all the while for her son. A torrent of punches from Jumièges sent her senseless and bloody to the ground.

"Move! Move!" he shouted, "otherwise we'll never get away!"

"But what of his mother, you shouldn't have done that. You can't leave her in that state, bleeding," pleaded the Bishop of Lunden.

"Not you as well William! Leave her where she is. She's a whore, isn't she? Let's get out!"

'Thank God for Bishop Stigand,' Edwin thought, as he and the other riders pounded along the Strand towards the Lud Geat. 'What with the time spent looking for horses, let's hope we aren't too late?' They crossed the Fleet Brycg but found the Lud Geat shut and barred.

"Open up! We're the King's messengers."

"Who says you are," shouted a voice above, from the geathouse.

"Does it look as if we're anyone else, pig. Get this geat open we're in a hurry!"

A small barred window in the geat opened. "Who are you calling…"

"If you don't open up right now, I will personally climb over this geat of yours, drag you out, cut your balls off and feed them to the dogs. Then I'll kill yer! We haven't time to play silly games! Open up!"

"All right, all right, keep yer hair on. I've been up and down these fucking stairs all fucking morning, what with the Archbishop and now you lot."

With the bolts drawn back and the doors swung open, Edwin and the others charged forward.

"Make for the old palace."

Passing to the left of St Paul's church they took the first right turn up Wood Stræt. Edwin, leading his twelve warriors, felt alive.

Crashing through the palace entrance, he shouted at the frightened clerk, "Where's the Archbishop of Cantwareburh."

"He left a while ago."

"Did he have two boys with him?"

"Yes!"

"Where are they taking them?"

"I think they mentioned the Æld Geat because it was the quickest route to the coastal port of Næss."

"You only think?" shouted Edwin.

"By the Æld Geat and Næss…definitely Næss, my lord and… Lady Ælfgifu lies injured upstairs."

"Where upstairs?"

"There, the door to the left."

Edwin bent down cradling the injured woman in his arms.

"My lady! Wake up! My lady!"

She opened her eyes.

"They've taken my baby." Lady Ælfgifu began shaking and crying.

Edwin lifted her to a bed.

"Lie there my lady, I'll get someone to assist you but I must leave immediately and find your son and Wulfnoth."

Edwin led his men outside but not before instructing the lone clerk to attend Lady Ælfgifu.

"One more thing, clerk. Are you certain they didn't leave from the Cripple Geat?

"No, no! I definitely heard them say the Æld Geat."

"Then see to the lady and make sure she doesn't come to any more harm," yelled Edwin. Turning to his men, he ordered, "Make for the Æld Geat! We still have a chance."

A large, angry crowd were milling around the geat and at the sound of Edwin and his mounted troops approaching, turned to face them with their weapons drawn.

A tall helmeted housecarl came forward, "Who are you?"

"We're Earl Godwin's men. We're chasing the Archbishop!" answered Edwin.

"They went through here some time ago, killing three of my men."

Edwin shook his head, "That doesn't surprise me. Who has he got with him?"

"A couple of priests an armed guard of five, all foreigners, and two kids."

"Right! Open the geat. They're Earl Godwin's kids."

"Open up lads, let them through."

"Thanks." shouted Edwin, galloping through the geatway. "Those damn priests are taking them to Northmandig!"


Edwin kicked at the nearest mooring post. In the far distance he could see the ship carrying the fugitives and the children. He felt sick to the stomach after failing to find another ship that could possibly catch them.

'If only we could have ridden faster,' he thought to himself.

"No point in hanging about lads. Let's get out of here and back to Lunden!

# CHAPTER IX

### - Night visitor - Upper Barnstæd –

'What's that? Oh no, they're fighting again,' Gwynedd thought. 'Ever since Edwin's brother returned, the children have been continually disruptive. He's a bad influence. Not that he's done anything out of line…it's just, I don't know, I can't put my finger on it. His story seems solid enough.' She lit a candle. 'Why wouldn't it be, what is there to disprove, he was three years-old when their home was raided.'

She brought her legs out from under the covers and sat up, rubbed her eyes, put on her woollen shawl, took the candle and went to the far end of the room. The children's bed was behind a screen.

"What's the matter now?"

Edric was crying and couldn't be pacified but as soon as she lifted him up Wulfnoth began to cry too.

"I'll get you a little drop of sweet mead."

Gwynedd unbarred the bedroom door and quietly made her way into the hall, took a flask of mead from the table and carried it back to the bedroom.

Dipping her finger in the mead, she wetted the boys' lips until they had gone to sleep, only then did she return to her bed and blow out the candle.

She had just fallen into a light sleep when a noise woke her. Gwynedd's instincts took over. She lay perfectly still. She had been dreading this moment and somehow thought it would never happen. She waited and planned. Like a fool she had forgotten to bar the door again.

"I know you're awake Gwynedd," whispered Eadrick, "I've been standing here admiring your body in the moon glow."

"Get out!" hissed Gwynedd, not wanting to wake the children.

"You're a joy to behold. The rhythmic movement of your tits at your every breath," he moved closer. "You look so inviting."

Not moving a muscle, Gwynedd thought, 'Here is one woman you're not going to touch.'

He moved closer to the bottom of the bed. The moonlight shone through the open window, high up on the wall, illuminating him. She could see he had no knife nor any other weapon as he continued to gaze on her. Gwynedd remained rigid.

"I said get out! This is *my* bedroom where I and my children sleep. Get out!"

He knelt on the bed, tracing his finger over her left breast, then brought his head close to hers and began forcing his tongue into her mouth.

With her right arm she reached out and grabbed the brass candle holder, and swung it down hard on the back of his head at the same time biting down on his tongue.

Apart from a very brief cry of pain, he collapsed without uttering another sound.

Pushing his dead weight off her and onto the floor she spat out his blood and a piece of his tongue. Turning to her boys, Gwynedd was relieved to see they were still asleep.

She dragged the unconscious body out of the bedroom and out of the building, leaving it face down in the dirt outside. Returning, this time she barred both the hall and the bedroom doors. Finding her seax she withdrew it from its leather sheath and kept it close by her.

"Serves me right! I should've barred the door. I should've made sure no one could get in!"

*20 September, 1052*
## - Edwin's return -

"Edwin!" cried Gwynedd, bursting out of the hall and running towards him. "You have to get rid of your brother!"

"What's happened? Where are the boys?"

Alarmed at seeing his wife distraught, he slid off his horse and caught her in his arms. He could feel her whole body shaking.

"Your brother or whoever he is, has to go, right now!" Burying her head into Edwin's shoulder, she whispered, "He tried to rape me! He has to go, otherwise *I* shall kill him!"

While he held her in his arms to calm her, he could see beyond towards the doorway of their home. Eadrick was leaning against the door post, an axe in his hand and a grin on his face.

"Tell me exactly what has happened."

"Two nights ago I accidently left the bedroom door unbarred. Eddy was crying and then Wulf started. I got some mead to help them sleep and had just returned to bed, the next thing I knew, he was standing over me. He tried to rape me, he stuck his tongue in my mouth. I managed to grab the candle holder and bashed him unconscious then I dragged him out of the house. He's a wild animal! *He is evil!*"

Without taking his eyes off his brother, Edwin handed the reins to a servant and walked towards him.

"I want you out of here! Now! Before I kill you!"

"Wha' ever she 'old yer, she's 'ellin yer a 'ack of fackin' 'ies," he said with difficulty.

"What's the matter with your mouth?"

"Ad an acciernt'.. mit mi 'ongue," he replied protruding his lips and exposing his damaged tongue, managing to slowly lick his lower lip, causing long globules of spittle to drip as he began a provocative sucking motion as if he had just eaten and enjoyed a ripe peach.

They stood staring at one another.

"Pack your things and get out of here," ordered Edwin.

"It wasn my iea!" he replied trying to smile, "she a lier. She was on her 'ed all nai ed an wa-ing for it, wiv her 'oor un'ocke. She was, she was askin fo it, she knew I was ere."

Edwin had already unsheathed his sword and began flexing it with wide sweeps in the air. A delicious urge swept over him to slice this man in two, brother or not. He eyed Eadric's fingers as they flexed around the top of the long handled axe.

'If he thinks that skeggy will scare me he had better think again.' Edwin felt the soft nudge of Gwynedd standing beside him. He brought his sword to rest on his shoulder and waited for an excuse to strike.

"You tried to rape me!" shouted Gwynedd. "Bastard! I may have forgotten to lock the door but that room's private and is our bedroom. Why should I have to lock myself in my own bedroom? You're not my husband's brother! You're a liar! A fucking beast! And you know it!"

Eadrick continued provocatively licking his protruding lips again and spat.

"She can say wha she ikes. Awl I un wa make ure she were afe ecause her oor was un ocked."

"Get out!" shouted Edwin, feeling rage rising within. What a fool he had been not to have kicked him out before now!

"Look Edwin! She ain't worf it. She's just a Wealhasc ore and is …..Aaaaah!

Eadrick collapsed to the ground holding his stomach. Gwynedd standing over him, slowly withdrew her long bladed seax and spat on him.

"Burn in hell!"

With lightning speed, she had plunged the knife into him. Edwin had only seen the briefest of movements.

"Get the priest!" he shouted, "get the priest!"

"Is this dying man your brother?" asked Father Oswald.

"That's who he says he is," replied Edwin.

"There is nothing," said the priest finally, "nothing I can do for him except take his confession."

"Father, I'll leave him to you." Edwin walked away to join Gwynedd, who now looked calm as if a great load had been lifted from her shoulders.

"What did you do with your seax?"

"It's here, sheathed in the folds of my skirt."

"I wondered because I couldn't see it."

"You're not supposed to see it," she replied in a cold voice.

"You're deadly! I barely saw a movement."

"Are you surprised? It was you who taught me!"

"I love you Gwynedd and next time I go away, I'll have you close by me to protect my back. Now, let's return to the priest. He should be done by now and ready to leave."

"Wait! He's coming to us," said Gwynedd.

"Did he say... anything?"

"Edwin, you should know as well as I, I can't divulge a dying man's confession."

"But was he my brother Eadrick? If not who was he and what was he doing here?"

"He came from Lagracæster in the earldom of Mercia and his name was Pæda. No relation of yours, I hasten to add, but he did know your brother Eadrick."

"Then my brother maybe alive?"

"I can't tell you that, my son. This poor dying man....."

"Poor my arse, father! That man tried to rape my wife!"

"I understand how you feel Edwin but he has made his confession to God. He was a poor wretch in great fear and in need of God's forgiveness. Try to show some compassion for him. He's out of your reach now and will not cause any more pain or harm."

"Fear! He's lucky I didn't slice him in two! Because of him..." Edwin found it difficult to speak, fighting back his tears. "And you want me to forgive him? No father! That is an impossibility. We opened our hearts to that... *imposter*. I am a man of peace but a man of *this* world and I have to protect my village and my family from scum like him. May his soul be damned for ever more!"

The priest shook his head turned and walked quickly away, his feet hidden under the long cassock which brushed the ground, giving him the illusion of floating in any direction without visible sign of moving legs.

"Father Oswald didn't ask any questions about the dead man's injury," said Gwynedd. "He is dead isn't he?"

Edwin nodded. "Oh yes, he's dead alright," he watched the priest until he had disappeared from view.

Turning slowly he looked at his wife. "Let's get that body to the church and out of the way, the priest can do the rest. He said, my brother survived the fire, and now we know where he was brought up. I must go north to find him. I'm leaving early tomorrow morning. I'll take Edmund."

"I'm coming with you this time."

*22 September, 1052*
**- Legracæster, Mercia –**
Leicester, Leicestershire

As they approached the town of Legracæster, in the late morning, Edwin brought their horses to a stop.

"This is not the place I remember as a boy."

"Are you sure," said Gwynedd, moving her horse in front of Edmund's.

"I just don't remember it being such a shambles. Look at those crumbling walls and towers. Totally neglected. Anybody could walk in. The town's only protection is the wide slow running Legra, at least on one side."

"So!"

"Don't you see? Years ago this town was a Roman encampment, with ready built fortifications but nobody has bothered to repair them. Look. Its ancient buildings have either been quarried for building churches or left empty, leaving the town a defenceless mess."

"You let yourself get too upset over these things, things that don't concern you now," she said.

"But this does concern me. If there should be an attack and Leofric can't contain it, I will be involved, we will all be involved!"

"It is what it is…you can't change things."

Edmund interrupted.

"Why did we give Pæda, or whatever his name was, a church burial? He didn't deserve it. I would have axed him down the middle, thrown him into a hole and forgotten about him."

"I suppose that's one way of looking at it but, on reflection, that would have been going down to his level. If there is a God, he will have to answer to Him. Listen! If we meet his family, don't mention his death. We don't know anything about it."

The three of them rode on into Legracæster.

"Where in this crumbling town are we going?" asked Gwynedd.

"I don't know, we'll just have to ask. See that large, arched building partly made of stone, with horses tethered outside?"

She nodded, "You can't miss it."

"We'll try there. I use to know a Thegn from this place but he died some years ago. Sighard I think his name was. He was very close to Earl Leofric. Probably one of Sighard's sons has taken over."

Edwin put his finger to his lips.

"Quiet!" He gently pushed open the door. Music could be heard over hushed chatter.

"Who are you lot?" asked a armed guard, pushing them back outside.

"I know you," replied Edwin, you're with Hengist. Tell him Edwin of Upper Barnstæd and his lady are outside." He moved closer to the guard. "And tell him, he still owes me a favour."

The guard looked Edwin up and down and retreated inside, shutting the door after him.

A few moments later Hengist appeared, grinning from ear to ear. Clapping his arms about Gwynedd, he said, "What's this favour I owe you and what are you doing here?"

"I said that, to get the guard's attention."

Hengist looked at Edmund.

"Who's this young man?"

"This is Edmund. I'm training him. So, what's going on here?" asked Edwin, looking past Hengist, trying to get his eyes used to the dim light.

"Follow me." Hengist lead them to the rear of a hall.

"Yffi is giving his friends a bit of culture," he said, accentuating the word 'culture'. "He's just arrived back from Francia. See the big girl sitting next to him," he pointed her out with a shaky finger. "That's his new wife and he has also fallen in love with music. This," he said, his arms swivelling about, "happens every Friday afternoon. He's gone culture mad and searches country-wide for different minstrels."

"Is this Yffi the son of Sighard?"

"It is!"

"He doesn't look a bit like his old dad."

"His mother was left alone a lot," replied Hengist, with even bigger grin, "but never you mind that. Sit you and Gwynedd down here and your friend over there. I'll see you afterwards."

Hengist moved away to rejoin his friends on the other side of the room.

"I preferred the group before this one," said Gwynedd, after some thought.

Edmund, who had joined them, didn't say much until Edwin urged him.

"I didn't like the Frencisc stuff either. Didn't understand a word…it was…"

"Un-manly?" ventured Edwin.

"Yes…I'm trying to remember the word my father used to

describe somebody…I know, effete! That's it! Like a woman."

"Otherwise you liked the rest of the music?"

"Yes. I also found our own poems and songs very moving, especially when accompanied by the lyre and drum."

"You think we should have more music at Upper Barnstæd?" asked Edwin.

Before Edmund had a chance to answer, Hengist had rejoined them.

"You're here for a reason. What is it Ed?" he asked somewhat bluntly.

"I need to find where a young man named Pæda lived."

"Why? Who is he?"

"He's the moron you sent to me pretending he was my brother Eadrick!" replied Edwin.

Hengist thought for a moment, "He said he *was* your brother."

Edwin shook his head. " No! But I do need to know where he lived and to find out what has happened to my real brother."

"Mmm. First I'll introduce you to Yffi."

Yffi was a tall, thin, stick of a man. Edwin would have assessed him as being no relation at all to his father who had been thick set, every portion sheer muscle, as opposed to this sinewy overdressed excuse for a man. Yffi's face was also gaunt, as if he had the troubles of all Mercia heaped upon his head.

His Frencisc wife, Beregarda, an obscenely large, over dressed, over perfumed and overly proud woman, gave the impression that to be allowed to speak to her was indeed a blessing from the Almighty.

Looking on with distain, Beregarda said nothing, allowing her husband to speak.

Edwin, giving Gwynedd a vague smile, wasn't having any of this performance and asked Yffi directly if he knew of the person, Pæda.

Yffi beckoned to a steward and enquired of the man.

"Yes sur," he said. "He's a thrall. I haven't seen him for ages but his family live on the outskirts to the north of the town close to the bourne."

"There you are Edwin," said Yffi.

Edwin was caught off balance. 'Why is he addressing me in the familiar,' he thought. 'I've never laid eyes on this dick-head before. Maybe Hengist has said something.'

"What do you want with him?" continued Yffi.

"He may know the whereabouts of my brother who has been lost to me, these past twenty years."

Yffi pulled a face as if affected by a foul smell and turned away to assist his wife, who was struggling to stand upright.

"Best of luck, Edwin," he said not bothering to turn his head, his remaining words lost in the general hubbub as he and his wife left the hall; disappearing into their private quarters.

The whole experience had made Edwin angry. He had stepped into a ridiculous fantasy and paid court to a couple of insignificant, frivolous dabblers, made worse because Yffi was the son of the once proud and respected Thegn, Sighard.

He turned to Hengist who was by his side.

"Is all this for real?"

"What do you mean."

"The play acting!" said Edwin.

"Yes. He's been like this ever since he married the Frencisc woman." Hengist moved closer and whispered, "He won't last long. He can't even shit without someone wiping his arse."

"Well, that's his problem. Right now I need to find Pæda's family."

"Do you need any help?" asked Hengist.

"No. They shouldn't be too difficult to find."

"If you're right," said Hengist, "that bastard certainly fooled me. By the way what happened to him?"

"I believe he met with an nasty accident," replied Edwin, keeping eye contact with Hengist, saying no more than was necessary.

"People like that can be accident prone!" Hengist said with a grin. "But be careful Ed. They're woodland people and are very, very cunning."

"I will bear that in mind my old friend," said Edwin shaking Hengist's arm.

"I feel hungry," said Edmund, sniffing the smell of cooking in the early afternoon air.
"Here, have some of this," replied Edwin, handing him some dried meat. "As soon as we've found these people, we'll look for an inn."
"I'm not hungry at all," said Gwynedd. "I just want to know the answer to your brother's whereabouts."
"We'll soon see," replied Edwin, looking up into the grey sky. "At least it's not raining."
They made their way out of the north geat and then along a narrow track, just wide enough for a cart, keeping close to the bourne on their left, then skirting a birch wood.
On the far side of the wood, stood a ramshackle hut with a thatched roof. The hut was partly built around a birch tree. From a crude roof-vent, thick smoke tumbled out drifting and shrouding the whole place in an acrid fog.
"By the smell they must cooking a stew of rats with a few slugs dropped in for good measure," said Edwin, wrinkling his nose in disgust.
First one face and then another peered out at them from a partly opened doorway. The only occupants seemed to be an aged couple who spoke with a strong local dialect, made problematical by the fact that neither had any teeth.
"What do yer want," they said, almost in unison.
"Do you have a son?" enquired Edwin.
The wizened old man reacted by first squinting. He then closed and opened his unusually huge round eyes. His sallow cheeks had sunken as if the sides of his face had collapsed. As far as Edwin could make out, the man was ready for the bone yard. His round eyes stared menacingly, first at Gwynedd then at Edmund and finally they settled on Edwin. His strange facial expression was as if he was

perpetually seeing ghosts. After what seemed an eternity he nodded.

"He left 'ere over a year ago and we 'aven't seen him since. We've 'ad to manage on our own."

"What do you do?" asked Gwynedd, showing concern.

"We collect birch bark for the local monastewy to make manuscwips," replied the old man, while his wife looked on nervously.

Edwin dismounted smiling, moving closer to the man in order to make him feel at ease.

"Are you the people who rescued a young boy years ago?" asked Edwin, not wanting to give out too much information.

"Boy?" replied the old man. "Do you mean the tot we found at Suthford?"

"Yes," replied Edwin.

"He was 'ardly three years old and covewed in dirt an' charcoal and stuff."

Once the old man had started talking he couldn't stop. Whatever it was, it was as if this had been building up inside him for years, and the great dam of his knowledge wanted to break loose. Now it had. He was going to tell his story and no one was going to stop him.

"He was the only cweature left alive in the village. It was…Suthford, that's swight, Suthford. The place was burnt t' cinders, nuffin left standing. It's a wonder he surwived. He was the same age as our boy Pæda… could av' been his twin bruver."

"What happened to the boy?"

"You mean the one we found?"

"Yes!"

"We bwought him up best we could, as our own you might say. But he got sick and died."

"Died? When? When was that?" enquired Edwin, urgently.

"Let me fink," he said turning to his wife. "It was just before Pæda left wasn't it?"

She nodded.

"Yes! That's wight, just over a year ago when some soldier feller came looking for a long lost kid."

"Do you know what the kid's name was?"

"Err…t' feller said it was Eadwic! Yes, Eadwic it was."

"You buried him?"

"Yer."

Where did you bury him?"

"In the wood, over there," he said, pointing to a large tree that was growing apart from the rest.

"Can you show me exactly where?" said Edwin.

The old man looked uncertain but, at Edwin's urging him with a coin, he showed him the way, not a stone's throw from the hut. He pointed out the grave site. The mound, now overgrown, was partly obscured by brambles.

"Can you tell me anything more about him?" asked Edwin, trying not to show his emotion.

"You seem vewy affected by all this, is anyfing wong?" asked the old man, staring at Edwin.

"Eadrick was my brother. We were separated when our village was attacked. We couldn't find him. We thought he was dead."

"Aah! As I said, he could have been our boy's twin. We loved him and he loved us back but he always wanted to twavel. Doing odd jobs for people, twavelling all over t' place, even into Wealh. He was no 'arm t' anyone and nobody 'armed 'im. He always came back to us. Then he got sick. Funny that was, when he got sick."

"Why! What was funny about it?" urged Edwin.

"'E was wight as wain, strong as an ox, then suddenly ee got sick and died. Now, my poor Eabæ an me are all on our own 'cos our son has taken himself off somewheres and I don't know when he'll be back."

"But how did my brother get sick?"

The old man scratched his head and looked at Edwin.

"Dunnow, just got sick an started vomiting an then ee went all pawalyzed an' dead. Broke our 'earts it did."

Edwin couldn't bring himself to tell them what their son had obviously done, nor how he had died. He shook his head in sympathy and looked at Gwynedd, who he knew was thinking the same as he.

Handing the old man a purse, he said, " Here is a little something more for your troubles."

"What's this for?"

"For rescuing and looking after my brother."

From the corner of his eye he watched the old couple amble off towards their home.

Gwynedd took Edmund aside but kept within sound. Edwin remained by the graveside and said a short prayer. He wanted to say something meaningful. 'What else can I say? That I'm sorry? That I should have made a bigger effort to find you? We did try! We honestly did try, Eadrick. And I looked everywhere even when the flames were raging and spreading through the house! I was scared. We were all scared. Then we were dragged off.' Edwin closed his eyes. 'Why couldn't you have cried out, made a noise, anything? Then we would have found you. Then you would have had a life. A life with us, your family, instead of …this! We could have done so many things together. I still hear mother's screams as we were dragged off, all the while looking back at the fire thinking you were being burnt alive! We missed you little brother, more than words could say. We could have been a complete family and I would have known what it was to have loved you and to have grown up with you.'

# CHAPTER X

*April, 1053*

**- Easter court, Wintancæster, Wessex -**
Winchester, Hampshire

"It's cleaner than Lunden and not so many people," said Gwynedd.

"Yes I agree. Let's move on and find a room and somewhere to stable the horses," replied Edwin.

"Look! Over there," said Gwynedd, "on the right. I can see Edmund."

Not far from the western geat of the city Edmund led them to a tall building set slightly back from the main stræt. A small, almost insignificant, wooden sign hung above the door with the words, Stables & Rooms, painted in white on a black background. Although the main part of the inn was on two floors, it had a single storied extension built to the rear with a corral. Set to one side was a further building, which acted as a covered stable. The main building itself was unusual in as much as it was the tallest in the city; apart from the Minster, two churches and the Great Hall, which dominated the suth west of the city.

"Your man here says you'll be wanting a room too and to stable your horses. For the whole of the Easter period?" queried the man in charge from behind the bar, which he polished continuously as he spoke.

"No. Just a couple of nights," replied Edwin.

"Right. Oh, by the way," the innkeeper continued, giving Edwin and Gwynedd a questioning glance. "You two *are* married?"

"Of course we are, man!" replied Edwin.

"No offence intended. The Earl and the Church are very strict about these matters. Now, is there anything else I can help you with?" He beckoned a boy over. "Take their bags to number three."

Edwin was surprised at the strength of the boy as he took hold of two of the bags.

Edmund stepped forward.

"I'll help the boy and rest in my room a while."

"If that is what you want to do." Edwin leaned close to Edmund, "Have you been having a good time?"

"A couple of days here and you see a whole different life. Yes it's good."

Edwin turned to the innkeeper, "Can you give us directions to Ægbert the baker,"

"Why sure I can. Follow the main stræt. When you get to the second stræt, turn right and the building is on your left. You'll see his sign, it's a large loaf of bread and on the sign it says, 'Ægbert's bread keeps you fed, fit and hard,' the innkeeper said, with a chuckle.

"Head Biter!" shouted a familiar voice, "Head Biter, over here!"

Edwin looked around but didn't recognise anyone.

"Head Biter! Over here!"

Then Edwin saw him. He could just make out Hengist, waving his hand on the other side of the main stræt. He was standing between a collection of carriages and mounted soldiers.

"Head Biter?" giggled Gwynedd. "Just as well you haven't told him about my seax, otherwise he'll be shouting out, 'Stomach Tickler'," she carried on giggling.

"Well, don't tickle my stomach with that thing," he replied, catching a glimpse of it hanging from her belt.

She shook her head.

"We'd better see what your friend wants."

"We're supposed to be meeting him at the baker's, not here."

"I saw you standing over there," said Hengist taking hold of

Gwynedd's hands. "How is the miraculous life saver these days?"

"Happy, safe and the mother of two boys."

"That's wonderful. What are their names."

"Wulfnoth and Edric."

"I'm jealous already." replied Hengist, "putting his hand on Edwin's shoulder.

"Sorry I didn't get a chance to talk to you properly before about your brother. What I wanted to say is you have fallen well and truly on your feet mi ol' lad. The fact is, I'm jealous of yer. Ah, here we are, Ægbert's."

"Why here?" queried Edwin. "Why a bread shop?"

"Wasn't your father a baker? Look, come inside and see for yourself."

The familiar smell took him back to his childhood. Edwin looked around the small room, which was so like his father's shop. To one side a door led to a separate room of long tables with bench seats affixed.

"Sit yourselves down," said Hengist. "About that other business. I heard something but not all. Who was that turd I found pretending to be your brother?"

After Edwin had told him the full story, a stillness descended on the room disturbed only by muffled thudding noises coming from the backroom and Hengist tapping the table-top with his forefinger.

"Well," said Hengist at last. "That bastard certainly fooled me."

"That creature half fooled us as well. I can't help but feel partly to blame for my brother's death and I will take that guilt to my grave!"

"Not your fault man,"

"It is my fault! As soon as Gwynedd told me years ago about the young man she had seen, I should have gone to Mercia myself to find him. Then, Eadrick would be alive today but I didn't!" The memory briefly flashed before him. "Our home and bakery was a blazing inferno. I was convinced that nobody could possibly have survived it"

"Look Ed, you were not to know. If anyone was to blame, it was my people."

"But I should have made more of an effort to find him!"

"Ed, look on the bright side. You're alive and well."

A large woman, dressed in white, put a covered platter onto the table and with one deft movement pulled the cloth away revealing steaming bowls of bread pudding and oatmeal and milk pudding with honey.

"Thanks Torta," said Hengist licking his lips, "Look! My favourites. This here is from her very own recipes. Tuck in and enjoy."

"I didn't know you had such a sweet tooth," said Edwin, recovering from his gloom.

"Tooth…that's about the size of it, Ed. I lost half-a-dozen last year. Give it another two years, I'll be down to just this one," Hengist said, pointing to an upper front tooth. "But I *do* like my puddings and my sister-in-law bakes wonderful bread and sweet puddings and in the summer her…"

"Hold on! She's your…?"

He nodded. "Sadly my brother Yorik fell and drowned in a frozen pond and was never seen again. It was January and the ice gave way."

"I'm sorry to hear that, Hengist," said Edwin, who was by now spooning through his second helping of bread pudding.

Hengist hunched his shoulders, "He was a stupid sod at the best of times, never listened but Torta here has already found a boyfriend who she's training up in more ways than one, if you get my meaning. He's a slip of a lad, only seventeen. Come on Gwynedd have some more of this oatmeal pudding."

"Thanks all the same, but I'm full up."

"Bit of a business going on here yesterday morning." said Hengist.

"Really! What business is that?" replied Edwin.

"A young woman was found dead, strangled and hacked to pieces!"

*Monday, second day of Easter, 12 April, 1053*
## - The Great Hall, Wintancæster, Wessex –
Winchester, Hampshire

"Look at you!" said Gwynedd, standing back and viewing her husband. "You Englisc are supposed to take pride in your appearance. Edwin, we're going to look our best for the King and Earl Godwin… but you're letting yourself go and you have such beautiful hair… come here let me show you!"

Edwin sat down obediently on a stool while Gwynedd sat herself on the bed behind him and patiently arranged his hair. She made a three-stranded braid which hung down his back and four thin braids, two at each side of his face with a further two braids in his beard, one each side of his chin.

"There! Oooooh you look good enough to eat" she said at last. "Now! I must get myself ready."

It was the first time Edwin and Gwynedd had attended a Royal Easter Court celebration together, indeed any royal court gathering. Although Edwin, in the service of Earl Harold, had attended the royal court at West Minster, he had never been present at a royal feast the like of which was being put on here by Earl Godwin. It was much like the celebration when they were married at Harold's court at Rendlæsham, but on a truly lavish scale.

In the centre of the hall, by a huge pile of glowing embers, an ox was being turned slowly on a spit; it had been roasting many, many hours. The spit was as tall as a man.

Amid the pall of smoke, music and general din, Edwin couldn't help but notice the serious politicking that was going on at the top table. King Edward nodding, as if in agreement. The pale and delicate looking Earl Godwin was to his right and Queen Edyth sat on his left.

'Oh shit!' Edwin thought. 'She's spilt her drink. Now both she and her sister-in-law Lady Gytha are laughing. They're obviously making light of the mishap.' He moved his attention to Earl Godwin's right. 'I wonder what Archbishop Stigand is saying to Earl Harold. They are not laughing that's for sure. Wonder if they are talking about the dead woman who was found this morning? I can't help feeling by the look on Harold face, he's worried. He's obviously telling the Archbishop something important.'

Tostig, Gyrth and Leofwine with their heads huddled together suddenly bursting out laughing, 'Tostig is probably telling another of his dirty jokes.'

Although Gwynedd had grown up as a humble country girl, living for the most part on her own, this grand royal occasion didn't fluster her. She was taking it all in her stride. Edwin never stopped being surprised at her ability to mix and communicate on any level. He gripped her arm.

"Earl Godwin doesn't look so good."

"I know, I've been watching him. It's probably the strain over the past twelve months." She leaned closer to Edwin. "He's sick! I mean very sick." Gwynedd moved away, talking to a man who Edwin had seen before but couldn't put a name to.

His eyes took in the whole room.

'The most powerful people in Englaland are here. Leofric, my God he must be the oldest Earl alive. Got to be in his eighties at least by the look of him. Certainly he is in better shape than Godwin. And there's Siward. I've never had much to do with him. What was it someone once said of him, Norvegian by birth and tough as old boots. Yes, he is a hard looking bastard. Been Earl of Northymbria for the past twelve years. Must have got something right otherwise he would have been out on his arse years ago. He's big too! Got to be at least three hands taller than me and just as broad. You couldn't miss him in a crowd, but he does look much older than Earl Godwin.'

"You're very quiet, husband."

"Just looking around and sizing people up. It's not every day you see the power of the country sitting together enjoying themselves.

Just like one big happy family."

"Edwin! Look! Something has happened to Earl Godwin! He's collapsed to the floor!"

"Excuse me, Sire," said Edwin, trying to make a space next to the King. He helped Harold, Tostig, Gyrth and Leofwine to carry their father into the royal chamber.

"Is he dead? He's not moving!" said Leofwine, his eyes searching his father's face for some reaction.

"He's alive," replied Harold, who had his ear to his father's chest. "Tosti! Stop! Where are you going?"

"To see if I can find a physician."

"Good idea!" said Harold, half to himself. "Not that it will do Father any good. I've seen this happen before."

"When," asked Edwin.

"He was ill like this a little while ago but recovered. This week he was back to his normal self. He was talking to the King, the next moment he seemed to go limp and collapse to the floor. No, wait…just before it happened he complained about a headache and feeling nauseous. Then it seemed to pass… and now this."

"This is the second attack in two weeks," said their mother, Gytha, pushing past Edwin and her son Gyrth. "I told him to postpone these festivities, I knew it would be too much for him." She sat on the edge of her husband's bed and began gently brushing his cheek and brow with her hand as if to smooth away his troubles. "Get me a bowl of water and a cloth!" she ordered. She turned towards Harold, her tearful eyes betraying her helplessness. "Harold, I told him to rest but no, he wouldn't listen to me. Wanted to put on a show for the King. He would have been better off resting in the tranquillity of Bosham. Oh God!"

"Are you sure he hasn't just fainted," said Gyrth, looking around as if hoping for conformation. "It *was* hot in there."

"No! Look, at Father's face, it says everything," replied Harold.

"I'm the King's physician," said a loud voice. "Let me pass. Only family here!" he ordered.

Edwin returned to the hall. Apart from the obvious absences from the top table, everything was as normal except he couldn't see Gwynedd. She wasn't in the hall. He approached the man who had been sitting next to her.

"Do you know where my wife has gone?" he asked.

"You mean the woman who was sitting here?"

"Yes."

"Mmm..." he thought for a moment. "I believe she went through that side door," he said, pointing with his knife.

Thanking him, Edwin made his way to the door. It opened out into a passageway which ran left and right. 'Gwynedd, which way did you go?' Following his instincts he turned right and walked until he came to another door. 'No! That's the royal chamber.' Continuing to the end of the passageway, Edwin came to a small door and, pushing it gently open, saw Gwynedd sitting as if in a trance mumbling words he couldn't quite make out. At first he hesitated, trying not to disturb her, then decided to kneel next to her, waiting until she had finished.

She turned slowly towards him.

"I don't know whether it has done any good but, with all the powers I have, I was willing the Earl to recover."

"How can you do that?" Edwin said, not quite believing her although he knew she is had extraordinary gifts.

"I don't know but sometimes it works. I could see immediately he was very ill."

"How could you know from where we were sitting?"

"It's just...I can. I followed you. I could see then it was apoplexy."

"Apoplexy?" he replied. "How could you tell he was that ill?"

"As I said! Because I can! Believe me, I can!"

"How?"

She shook her head. My mother knew of this malady. It's what happens to some people when they get old. They collapse into a state of unconsciousness. Some die soon after. Others wake up, their speech impaired and not able to walk properly but the truth is, they will never be the same."

"But he isn't that old!" Edwin pounded his fist against the wall. "He is only fifty-four. When I sailed up the Tames with him he was fitter than most! I just don't understand it. Do you think he will die?"

"It's possible but if he does regain consciousness, as I said, he won't be the same man."

"What a load of bad luck. First he loses his son Swegen, then he is exiled. Then reinstated; makes it up with the King and now this happens."

"That's why I'm trying to do something. I know it can be done, I've seen it done with my own eyes. Willing him to recover by the power of the mind. Promise me you won't tell anybody that I can do this, because they will accuse me of being a witch!"

Edwin gathered her up in his arms.

"I promise. I won't tell a soul. God in heaven how did I have the good fortune and nerve to take you as my bride?"

"Because I willed it."

Three days later Earl Godwin was dead. At his lying in state, crowds packed the Minster to the doors. More were queuing in the nearby stræts wanting to pay their last respects to the man who had risked everything in defending his people of Dofras. The people of Wessex thought of him as their father, a father to the whole of the earldom, a man who had had more influence over his people than the King himself.

# CHAPTER XI

*Early morning, November, 1055*
- **The training of Wulfnoth and Edric** –

"Come on Wulfnoth, you too, Edric! Keep up with me," shouted their father.

The six-year olds were trailing behind him in the fine drizzle. They had reached a mark, half way to the Tames pier, turned and were on their way back home. Wulfnoth stopped, sat down and refused to run any further. Edric looked at his brother and he also sat down.

Edwin stopped and ambled back to where the two boys were. They both had their arms folded, sitting defiantly in the mud. Their russet hair, made darker by the soaking rain, draped down their faces in tangled strands.

"You can sit here all day and all night if you like. You'll only get colder and wetter. And in the middle of the night rats will come out of their holes and eat you alive and all that will be left in the morning will be the shoes you're wearing, because they don't like eating leather. What do you say to that!"

"I don't believe you," replied Wulfnoth.

"I'll tell you what. If you hold my hands, we'll walk slowly back home and be in time for your favourites; your mother's thick slices of buttered bread, newly baked, warm from the oven."

Edric was the first to stand up. As the three of them walked slowly back to the hall in the rain, he asked, "Would rats really come out and eat us alive, Papa?"

"If you trained hard and were tough like me…..they would be

terrified to come anywhere near you!"

"They're too young to be training in the rain," argued Gwynedd, drying them with a cloth. "Let them have a childhood."

"I know what I'm doing, I'm a professional soldier. I need to build them up, to make them strong before their real training begins. By the time they are sixteen they will have to be strong and professional enough to be wielding a sword and axe in the front line of a battle formation. This is what I am! A professional soldier! Our job is to protect hearth and home. If this village were attacked, with Egbert and his son Edmund, myself and a few others nearby, we'd have a good chance of defending ourselves. I and our sons are not artisans or farmers. They are important too, but they can only function if we protect them and the country."

"How about women and children?"

"That's my point, we're here to protect everyone."

"You should have been the King's political advisor at court," laughed Osgar, who was standing in the doorway, applauding Edwin's speech.

"When did you breeze in?" said Edwin.

"Just moments ago and I hope you don't mind, I left my wet cloak in your main hall. By the way, you have a very astute young man outside."

"You mean Edmund?"

"That's his name. He was about to try and chop me in two."

"He would have done. We protect each other here."

"Well,…I'd better be on my best behaviour then." Osgar stood smartly erect as if a royal mantle had descended on him. "Actually I'm on the King's business. You are summoned to the Palace of West Minster where you will be directly under the command of Earl Harold of Wessex, who will give you further instructions," he said, delivering himself of the message.

Edwin was about to reply.

"I especially like the, Earl Harold of Wessex bit. It sort of... rolls off the tongue nicely," Osgar said smiling. "Oh by the way, Earl Harold wants to see *you* especially."

"Why?"

"Don't ask me, I'm just the messenger. I've got a whole list of Thegns to see."

"What can I say," replied Edwin, as they walked outside into the cold damp air, "other than I'll be there. But what's with the full armour; helmet, chainmail, skeggy, bow and battle sword?"

"Now I'm the King's official messenger, I never know who I might meet on the road."

Edwin noticed some blood on the axe handle.

"Had any trouble lately?"

"Oh that. Just a bit, nothing to shout about," Osgar replied, casually.

"Need to keep your weapons oiled and clean my friend!"

"The trouble with you Ed, you're always the professional soldier and teacher... just concern yourself with your own gear." Mounting his horse, he said, "Don't forget. Day after tomorrow, West Minster Palace. Early!"

"Os! Not so fast," said Edwin holding onto the horse's reins. "What's really happening? More trouble with the Wealhasc or is Earl Ælfgar making trouble for Tostig?"

"Keep this to yourself, Ed. The Northman, Earl Ralf has got himself into trouble with the Wealhasc."

"You mean when Earl Ælfgar was thrown out the country for treason he joined forces with Gruffydd ap Llewellyn and his Wealhasc troops and they have smacked the Northman's arse. Now the King wants us to march up to the border country and look after his Northman friend, Earl Ralf."

"That's about it."

"I'm not surprised Os. Ælfgar, like most of us, doesn't like the Northmen in any shape or size. Poor ol' Ælfgar ever the mouthy bastard."

"Must go Ed."

Edwin nodded and watched his friend ride out of the village until he was no longer in sight.

*Late November, 1055*
### - Herefordscir -
Hereford, Herefordshire

"Never mind the Wealhasc! If I knew I was actually going to be spending my time digging fucking ditches for the Northman Ralf to defend this town, I would have disappeared; gone to the fen country," grumbled Osgar.

"Look at it this way," grinned Edwin, giving Edmund a wink. "You weren't cut out to be a king's messenger, prancing about the King's court. Never mind the Northman, we're here to rebuild the town and protect these good people from more Wealhasc attacks; to keep you out of trouble and turn you into a nice strong lad!"

"Piss off! I was beginning to like mincing around the palace in my nice clean tunic. Anyway, you've changed your tune."

"No! I don't like the Northman but these Englisc townspeople I do like. Big difference."

Coming closer to Edwin, Osgar whispered, "Did you hear about Earl Ralf and his fancy horse soldiers?"

"Tell me."

Osgar, looked around to see who was listening. "Anyway they went chasing after the Wealhasc on horse with lowered spears but..," Osgar broke into a spasm of laughter, "the Wealhasc were waiting for them. The Northmen rode straight into a Wealhasc trap of bowmen. The Earl was lucky to get out alive." Osgar, still laughing, began digging again.

"Their bowmen are lethal and don't I know it," replied Edwin, "but that's not what I was about to ask. Have you heard about that woman in Wintancaester who was strangled and sliced?"

"Mmm. Yer mean chopped by the randy axe-man," replied Osgar, without looking up from his digging.

"Let me know if you hear of any similar killings," said Edwin, climbing out of the ditch and making his way to the wagon closest to them. "I'm going to pour myself some beer. Do you two want some?"

Osgar and Edmund threw their shovels out of the trench and followed,

"Yeh!" said Osgar, "I need a break. Let these 'good' townspeople finish the job. Why are you so interested in these killings?"

"Because it happened in Upper Barnstæd too. The point is, Os, it's the way the women were hacked. Both of us have seen death before… but this is something else. I've got a theory."

"What's that then?" replied Osgar, draining his mug dry and smacking his lips. "Thirsty work this, I could swallow another two mugful's, easy."

"Whoever he is, either he's trying to prove something or he can only get a hard on after he kills and that's why he hacks them the way he does."

"I don't get it Ed," Osgar said shaking his head. "No! I don't buy that at all!"

"I don't mean that, not exactly. It's a power thing! He strangles them, then has sex. Then he's so disgusted with himself and the woman, he goes and destroys her body."

"You know what, Ed? You're way over my head. I always knew you were too brainy for me," said Osgar, laughing again.

"Look at it this way, Os. Who doesn't get a hard on when he's killing in battle?"

"Yes I know, Ed but this is the cold blooded murder of girls. He has to be a weirdo!"

"I agree and while he's at large I fear for my Gwynedd."

"I wouldn't worry about her, Ed, she's more than capable of looking after herself from what I hear. Oy there! You've gone all very quiet, young Edmund."

"Not much to say," Edmund replied, fingering his beer mug.

"What if it's a woman?"

"Don't think so," said Osgar. "She'll have to be one hell of a strong woman to wield an axe like that. Don't let yourself get rattled by this, Ed."

"I'm not rattled. Listen, I'll be back soon, somebody is waving to me."

Edwin walked to where one of Harold's men was waiting. After a short time, he returned.

"Just got news," he said, "we're finished here. We're going back home." He squinted into the setting sun, watching the retreating messenger walking towards the rebuilt west geat.

"Going back? T' think we came all this way and my new skeggy hasn't even been blooded," moaned Osgar, fingering the sharp edge of its blade.

"What's worse," replied Edwin, loading his gear onto his horse, "Æfgar's been let off the hook, even after he made a pact with Gruffydd to help lead a Wealhasc army against us, his own countrymen. Surely that's high treason! Now he's going to get the Earldom of Anglia. Where's the justice in that?"

# CHAPTER XII

*Early April, 1062*

## - A lightning Strike -

"Both of you! Come for me!" shouted Edwin. His broadsword an extension of his muscled arm, he shifted his weight from one foot to the other creating a slight rocking movement from a semi crouched position.

Wulfnoth suddenly lunged at his father, twirling the long handled axe above his head.

Crash! Crunch!

Their father in one movement had countered by chopping through the axe handle, pivoting around to take the next blow from Edric's sword on his shield, forcing him to the ground.

"That hurt my arm!" complained Edric.

"Mine too!" shouted Wulfnoth.

"Think yourselves lucky you're only suffering from the vibration. If I had been going for the arm or body you two would now have been lying there in bits!"

The thirteen year-old boys looked at each other and pulled a face.

"You had better listen to your father," said Edgar, sternly.

Edwin picked up two shields and threw them at his sons.

"Now, we'll begin again with the tactics of shield wall defence."

"No! Not that again. We did that yesterday," grumbled Edric.

"Well! We'll do it again today."

Edgar moved forward and corrected the way Wulfnoth was holding his shield so that it overlapped Edric's by a hand.

"That should do it. Remember! If you let the enemy see any gaps they'll rain arrows down at you."

"And don't forget, the shield wall will shy off any mounted horse," added their father. "Edgar! Where's Edmund?"

"I don't know, Ed. He should have been here early this morning. He's getting lazy of late. I don't know what to make of him," replied Edgar.

Edwin shook his head.

"He's your son my old friend, and you know I only want the best for your lad but he has changed and not for the better, doesn't seem to want to be part of the family. If he's going through some sort of crisis… you know me, I'll help as much as I can."

"Leave him to me. I'll go and find him." Edgar walk away, troubled. Picking up a stick he wacked the nearest obstacle, a tree by the side of the road, before disappearing from view.

"Once again boys!"

Edwin shifted his legs out of the bed, sat still for an uneasy moment before rubbing his eyes. He waved an unsteady hand towards Edgar, who had woken him with the news that Osgar had come with a message from the King.

"Give me a few moments and I'll be with you."

Still emerging from sleep, the world at this moment in time seemed something of a muddle. He knew he shouldn't have drunk so much the night before but he had been so pleased with the boys.

'Boys!' he thought, 'boys! They're not boys, what am I thinking of, they're young men. Give them another two years and they'll be fully fledged warriors, strong and developed enough to fight with the best of us.' He knew Gwynedd wasn't happy about her boys becoming part of the warrior class. 'I suppose it's hard for a mother to see them grow up so quickly. Before you know it they'll riding off and into danger. Where have the years gone? The older I get, so the years pass ever more rapidly. In a blink of an eye our youth's gone but at least I'm still strong and healthy and both Wulfnoth and Edric are healthy too. I am so very proud of them. As I said to Gwynedd last night, I've decided we should celebrate. Celebrate! she had replied, Celebrate what? Life! I had said. Afterwards we sat outside and watched the sun go down, our heaped trenchers on our knees and our mugs full. I knew I shouldn't have drunk so much but when you are happy, you do, don't you?'

"Why are you awake so early, it's before dawn?" murmured Gwynedd, from under the bed cover.

Edwin turned his sleepy head towards the bulge in the bed.

"Edgar says Osgar is outside. I'm wanted at court."

"Where's Edmund? Isn't he supposed to be your steward?"

"Edgar doesn't know where Edmund is and anyway, I'm not awake enough to worry about him," replied Edwin.

Edwin shivered in the dawn's dank mist, his horse thankfully was keeping his arse and legs warm.

"Why does the King want me so urgently that I have to get out of my nice warm bed this bloody early in the morning? Now, you say Earl Harold wants to see me as well," shouted Edwin, looking back to see whether Edmund was still with them.

"What was it someone once said?" replied Osgar. "When the King's off his arse everybody else has to be too."

Edwin wasn't well pleased with Edmund. After being out all night, his father had found him at home, wet through, fully dressed and fast asleep.

"What's with the blood?" asked Edwin.

"Where!" responded Edmund, searching his clothes. "Err... I was in a fight."

"While you are my steward you do not go missing. Where was this fight?"

"Stanford," replied Edmund.

"What happened."

"As I said, I got into a fight. We're not going near Stanford are we?"

"We are. Our route takes us straight through the village."

"No!" blurted out Edmund, "I don't want to go anywhere near that place."

"Well, we're going there whether you like or not."

"Don't worry," said Osgar, "if there's a problem, we're here to protect you and you can't get better protection than from us ol' warriors."

"Can we go a little faster," said Edmund, looking nervous.

"No-one in this village will harm you, just mark your pace," replied Edwin.

"There he is!" came a shout.

"Stop him!" shouted another.

"Who are you?" returned Osgar, bringing his horse to a stop.

"We're on King's business," said Edwin, drawing his sword.

"Just because you're the King's men doesn't mean you can protect the likes of him," said a man coming forward to Edwin.

"Protect him, what's he supposed to have done?" Edwin replied.

"He put the blade of his axe to the neck of my son and was going cut his head off, that's what!" the man replied.

"Is the boy dead?"

"No!"

"Then count yourself lucky he still has a head on his shoulders," laughed Edwin. "You've said your piece now let us pass."

The crowd moved away to let them ride on and out of the village.

"So what was the fight about? It was obviously serious to them," shouted Edwin.

"Oh, it was nothing," replied Edmund.

"Whoa there!" Edwin reined his horse to a stop. " Now tell me what happened."

"I told you. It was about a woman and then I got into a fight."

"A woman eh?"

"They were going to beat me up, until I showed them my axe!"

"We'll talk about this later," Edwin kicked his horse back into action, the other two following. Osgar dropped back a little way to make sure they were not being followed.

## - Upper Barnstæd -

"Hold the axe this way with your left hand and swing it thus!" Edgar said, easing the axe blade out of the suspended tree trunk that was hanging from the rafters. He was in charge of the boys' training while their father was away.

"I hate having to swing this axe that way when I'm naturally right handed, it's hard!" complained Wulfnoth.

"Listen you two! If you were fighting, for instance, against the battle sword of a Northman, he would inevitably hold the sword in his right hand, his unprotected side. Therefore wielding the skeggy in your left hand gives you a distinct advantage, not only of reach but as I have just pointed out, his right side would be unprotected, his shield being held in his left hand. So you two, would be young warriors, you have to be ambidextrous and use your intelligence."

"Ambi what?" mocked Edric.

"Be proficient with both hands, at least that's what Dad said," replied Wulfnoth.

"Correct! So let's be serious because I haven't hauled this heavy tree trunk up for my own amusement. And use your whole body when you swing the axe."

Wulfnoth feeling the weight and balance, gripped the handle and attacked the trunk with all his might!

"Better! Much better! Now again Wulfnoth, put more effort into the swing, don't forget, use your whole body in one fluid movement."

"How are my boys doing?" enquired their mother.

"Doing well. They're strong. I have to keep them on their toes though. I know it's hard training, but the discipline has to be second nature to them. That's why our Englisc housecarls are feared. Feared as much as the Scedenig warriors of Swedeland.

"Your wife, Eabæ, tells me you are going away for a few days."

"Yes. I have some business to attend to," replied Edgar, suddenly looking troubled.

"Oh! Is there anything I can do to help?"

"No. Just something I need to follow up. I'll only be away for a couple of days." He turned to the boys. "You know the regime I've worked out for you?" he said, looking at each in turn.

Wulfnoth and Edric nodded.

"Good! I'll soon be back so I want to see an improvement."

As Edgar ambled away the boys looked at each other and grinned.

"And *I* shall be here to make sure you do. Come into the house and get those sweaty clothes off and wash yourselves. You reek of the cow shed," said Gwynedd.

"Where is Edgar going?" asked Wulfnoth.

"I don't really know," replied his mother. "A stranger from out of town visited him yesterday but that's all I know."

"Is it anything to do with Father?" asked Edric.

"No! According to Edgar, it's purely a personal matter."

"Where is the King sending Father?" asked Wulfnoth.

"I don't know that either, so you'll have to put it out of your mind."

Gwynedd had a pretty good idea. Should she tell the boys? The thought troubled her. She didn't like keeping things from them. If Edwin had wanted them to know he would have told them. She felt sure he was going to Wealh and felt grieved for the people of that country and frightened for her husband. She had no particular love for the people of the village of her birth but if it was Wealh it was going to be a bloody affair. She would put on a brave face and pretend nothing untoward was happening. 'Oh Edwin my love, wherever you are, may you be protected from harm.'

Gwynedd left her boys in the hall and walked outside, towards the river. She didn't know why, just that she wanted to be alone with her thoughts.

*26 may, 1063*
## - Brycgstow, Wessex -
Bristol

Harold's twenty long-ships sped away under cover of darkness from Brycgstow harbour and on towards the Wealhasc coast.

"Doesn't it give you a thrill to be in these ships?" gritted Edwin, his face blasted by the wind and spray. "We're cutting through the sæ and our sails are full to breaking point. Don't yer feel it? The might of these vessels?"

"No!" returned Osgar, unmoved. "Sooner we land the better."

"But don't you feel anything at all, doesn't it get your heart racing?"

"Oh sure! Racing to get off this fucking ship because I feel sick already, that's what! Look Ed, to you, these ships are great and built especially long, to hold a hundred of us, I get that but they're still just fucking ships and they make me sick, alright?"

"Well! We've a long way to go yet."

"I hope not! Ed, the way you talk you should have been a Buscarl not a Housecarl. You're a born sæman, I'm not."

"Well for your information," whispered Edwin in Osgar's ear, "The sæ scares the shit out of me but it excites me at the same time. Makes me feel alive."

"I don't understand you, Ed. You're insane," he laughed.

"Insane or not, we're going to land at Nedd and then continue on foot. How does that sound," returned Edwin.

"Music to my ears."

## - Nedd, Wealh -
Neath, Wales

"Where's Edmund?" shouted Edwin.

"Dunno!" replied Osgar. "All I know is, soon as we landed he was gone. Must be 'ere somewhere."

They scanned the area.

"'Ere, Ed, I don't like this town, the place looks almost deserted, the Wealhasc must 'ave seen us comin' and run for it."

"We're marching inland. Jump to it!" shouted a commander.

Edwin was still looking beyond the quayside but couldn't see Edmund anywhere.

"I know who you're looking for," said a man at Edwin's side, "it's that young 'un, isn't it?"

"Yes," Edwin answered, still scanning the troops, unable to see him. "I haven't caught sight of him since we landed. Have any of you lot seen my steward, Edmund?"

"Yea, I seen 'im, goin' over there." A trooper pointed towards a building, set apart from the others, at the end of the village.

"Come on, Os, let's get him and bring him back here before he's thinking of deserting."

"He wouldn't do that …would he? He's a grown man, a twenty year-old, he's not scared of a real battle, is he?"

"Hope not for his father's sake."

On the banks of the bourne, raised well above the ground and tidal water, standing on blocks of tree trunks to the height of a man's shoulders, stood a run-down building.

"This must be it," said Edwin.

"Looks to be a derelict storehouse," replied Osgar and pointing, "there, in front of that opening on the top floor is the lifting gear."

"I think you're right Os. Let's make for those steps and onto that gallery."

"Can't hear any movement."

"Edmund! Are you there!" called out Edwin through the half open doorway but there was no reply.

They waited for a few more moments with swords raised and on the nod from Edwin, they crashed in expecting to be attacked from all sides but the room was empty, everything was still. After a short while their eyes became accustomed to the dim interior. What used to be a place to store provisions for export up the bourne or to the sæ by ship, was now empty apart from the odd piles of gathered rubbish. A thick layer of undisturbed dust was everywhere except for long irregular scrape marks along the floor.

"Well somebody's been here recently, look at this," said Osgar tracing the drag marks to a set of stairs leading to the floor above.

"Os, you stand guard down here while I go on up."

"Are you sure?" whispered Osgar.

"Just keep guard here. I'll shout if I need you."

As though trapped in time, Edmund stood at the end of the top floor room with axe raised. A petrified, bound and gagged girl lay naked on the floor before him.

"Put that axe down and come with me," ordered Edwin.

Edmund smiled. "Piss off! There's something I have to do first," he replied slowly.

'I wish I had my bow,' Edwin thought, 'I could easily take him out. "Edmund! Put that axe down and let the girl go!"

"You'll have to get past me first."

Edwin, lunged forward, his sword crashing against the Edmund's axe handle, withdrawing out of reach as Edmund brought his seax around.

"You're insane! A Morthorslaga! Murderer! Edwin shouted. In a calmer voice he continued, "Edmund, just drop your weapons otherwise I'll have to kill you and I don't wish to have tell your father what you are and what you've done."

"You don't know what I've done. Do you know what? I don't fucking care." The look on Edmund's face had changed as he half turned his head away giving Edwin a sickly leer. "This bitch deserves to die. They're all filth! Step aside and let me finish it."

"You're Gemæd... totally insane," gritted Edwin.

Edmund began raising his axe...

Crunch!

Osbert's short-handled axe had flashed past Edwin ear, imbedding itself into Edmund's face, the impact bursting the man's eyeballs out of their sockets.

Edwin turned. "Why? I have to tell this to his father!"

Osgar hunched his shoulders, tugged out his throwing axe.

"I hate long arguments!"

"One thing knowing who our sex killer is but another telling his father. Oooh Woden!"

They cut the girl free, hardly noticing her grab her clothes and scamper away.

Looking down at the dead body of Edmund, Osgar spoke in almost a whisper.

"The Earl has to be told."

"You go and bring the Earl here and I'll stay with this… thing."

Osgar, left the room to fetch Earl Harold.

"Why?" shouted Edwin, sheathing his sword. "Why morthor all those poor innocent women, young women in the flower of youth. How many did you butcher? You have dishonoured everything we stand for." He spat on the body. It was no longer the son of the man he respected and loved. It was a thing, a thing of repugnance. He thought of the boy's father again and tried to imagine how he was going to tell him.

"My lord!"

"What's happened here?" shouted Earl Harold.

"I just found out that my steward was gamæd, insane and was about to butcher another girl."

After Edwin had told Harold everything, he ended by taking the blame for Edmund's death on himself.

"I put an end to him for his father's sake."

"You should have waited for me to give judgement!"

"My lord, I am sorry! His father is a close friend. If this man's crime were known, it would bring shame on his family and on our village."

"Listen and listen well!" said the Earl, gripping hold of Edwin's tunic. "If you ever take the law into your own hands again, I will kill you. Is that understood?"

"Yes, my lord!"

"Get rid of the body. And clean this place up! We march in an hour!"

8 June, 1063

## - Off the north-west coast of Wealh -
North-west coast of Wales

"I must be close to getting my sæ legs," shouted Osgar.

"I knew you would," replied Edwin.

"With the wind and crashing waves, I've now puked up the entire contents of my stomach."

"Put it down to experience."

"Ballocks to you Ed. There I was back in Nedd hoping for some action. Then their local chiefs come out of the woodwork suing for peace. It's not very funny! I feel cheated!"

"Looks as if we're almost there."

"Big deal!" replied Osgar.

They were now heading into a large natural bay of calm water the far side of the Afon Dwyryd, a fast running bourne which meandered for miles into a valley of agricultural land to the suth, where forested hills led to mountains in the north, known to the Englisc as Snowy Hills.

As they beached on the soft white sands at the mouth of the Dwyryd, an arrow crashed into the upper edge of the ship's side. A hand higher, Edwin would have been skewered.

"Disembark!" came the order.

"Let's see where that came from," said Edwin, half to himself. Crouching down, taking careful note of the arrow's angle he had a good idea of its trajectory. "Don't go Os!"

"Tell me," replied Osgar, crouching down next to his friend.

"There!" said Edwin, taking an arrow and pointing to a protruding part of the weald that stretched back along the north side of the river and up into the hills beyond.

Nocking their bow strings, they fired together, reloaded and fired again.

"I think that should scare them," said Osgar. "Let's get out of here and take cover."

No sooner had they clambered over the side of the ship and formed up in battle order, arrows came raining in.

"Shields up!"

"Just as well it's early morning and no mist, at least we'll have a chance to see the bastards," whispered Edwin.

"Advance!"

Turning to Osgar, Edwin said, "We're not the only ones who know where the Wealhasc are."

Earl Harold ordered his men to form an arc and advance through the undergrowth towards the immediate forested area to find and destroy the enemy.

"Edwin!"

"Yes, my lord."

"Take a detachment of men, choose your own, and cut them off."

He chose thirty men and, with Osgar acting as his second in command, they made their way rapidly, hidden by the high banks, along the hard sands of the winding Dwyryd.

Edwin glanced back momentarily to see their ships heading out to sæ.

"This is going to work well, Os. Lucky for us the level of the bourne is low, we'll get behind the Wealhasc in no time."

After a mile the hills to their left fell back opening up to more agriculture land. The bourne meandered on into the Wealhasc heartland.

Edwin brought his men to a stop. The banking by this time was low and gave them little or no cover.

"We'll have to make for that range of bushes and then a short dash into the weald."

"Let's hope there's no Wealhasc about because from here to those bushes is, I reckon, about a hundred paces with no protection, except for ducking down behind every blade of grass or dandelion," responded Osgar.

"Ha fucking ha! We'll have get there as fast as we can then, won't we?"

"I'll tell yer what," replied Osgar, "You make it to the weald, I'll stay here behind this grassy sand bank until you give me the all clear."

"Piss off, dick head," grinned Edwin.

"Well, you give the signal then!"

"Go! Go! Go!"


Edwin looked across to Osgar.

"All accounted for?"

They moved slowly, shields forward, weapons drawn. After advancing a hundred paces into the weald, Edwin brought them to a halt and signalled for all to crouch down and stay silent.

He was quite aware of the Wealhasc tactic of luring their enemies into killing zones where their short bows were the ultimate weapon. He wasn't going to fall into any more Wealhasc traps. Instead he and his troop would be the springer of their own trap. Now all they had to do was wait and listen.

Osgar moved closer to Edwin. Nudging his arm, he whispered, "They're coming!"

Edwin nodded. From among the natural forest noises a distant echo of something didn't seem right. A little while later there was the crack of a twig, then a flitter of shadows amid the foliage. Not moving a muscle, hidden by the undergrowth, he strained his eyes and ears. A rustle of leaves; scraping of branch against wavering branch. 'No birds,' he thought. 'They're here and close!' He strained his senses. Crack! 'There it is again.' He looked over at his men, putting his finger to his lips. Turning his head, he could see Osgar partially standing.

"What are you doing, Os?" he whispered.

"Fucking cramp! Aaah! In me left leg. Got to get up!"

"No! They're too close!"

"I'll be alright, I'll press myself up against this tree for cover."

Edwin briefly looked around. 'If I could see the Wealhasc a little while ago,' he thought, 'I'll bet my boots they know where we are. They can't be far away.'

"Os! Get down on the ground and back here!"

"I think the pain's gone," Osgar replied, beginning to crouch down... "Aaaaahh!"

"Nooo!" hissed Edwin catching his friend in his arms.

An arrow had pierced his neck, the metal point poking out the other side.

Os gave a half smile.

"I told yer."

Edwin broke off the tail of the arrow and very gently pulled the rest of it through.

Osgar tried to speak.

"I can't understand you," said Edwin, putting his ear close to his friend's mouth.

"I... can't... feel... my... arm... or... legs... I can't... feel anything!"

Edwin felt for and squeezed his friend's testicles.

"Can you feel that?"

Os gave a slight shake of his head, "No."

Edwin turned to the man next to him, "Find Cearl, the physician."

"Don't move from here," whispered Edwin.

Os gave a sickly half smile and moved his mouth.

Edwin came close, "What did you say mi ol' mate?".

"Don't be funny. How can I fucking well move!"

"I'm going to leave you here with Cearl," he said, as the physician arrived. "We'll be back for you."

On Edwin's nod the rest positioned their shields affront...

"Abrecaaan!"

There had been more Wealhasc fighters than Edwin had first

thought but it didn't matter. He had caught them off guard, totally surprising them by the sudden attack. In the initial rush their archers had briefly stood to fire but Edwin's men had scythed through them like wielding machines of axes and sword blades, before they could ready their bows. Nothing stood in their way. Edwin the reaper, oblivious of what was before him twirled his broadsword like a whirlwind. It seemed to him the Wealhasc were also surprised by the ferocity of the attack; forcing them to run in retreat rather than be obliterated by the onslaught.

Edwin had been so focused on the killing that the sudden disappearance of the enemy had caught him by surprise. He raised his battle sword to stop the advance of his men.

A sound from Earl Harold's horn, brought a cheer from the men.

Edwin signalled for them to stand, shields affront and weapons ready.

By that evening Edwin could see his friend was in no shape to continue any further. He had to be shipped back to Englaland, that is if he could stay alive that long. Osgar had been carried on a bær into their camp and made as comfortable as could be. It had been a long haul from the depth of the weald.

Edwin sat close to him. He tried feeding him, but it proved useless. Although his neck wound had stopped bleeding, Osgar could not swallow any food or drink. His arms and legs lay limp and helpless.

"I'm finding it," he whispered in gasps, "hard to breath Ed. I'm finished!... This is… the end for me! I can't… even piss for myself."

"Can you feel this?" said Edwin and he began to pinch the skin on Osgar's arms and legs.

"Nothing Ed,… absolutely nothing below… my shoulders and… I can't move… anything,… not even my… fingers." He took another gasp of air. "It's a wonder I'm still alive and breathing. I'm finished. Ed,… that physician has… seen it before… and said,… mine was… the worst… he's come across… and that… I'll never… get the use…

of my arms and… legs again." By now his breathing was becoming much more difficult. "I know Cearl… I've seen him… work before… he's a good physician."

"Rest my friend, don't talk anymore," said Edwin.

"Got to… tell… you… Ed. I don't… want to… be… just a… talking, useless head. Listen! Can you… do something… for me.

"What's that, my ol' mate."

"Give me a good death…"

"Listen here lad, when we get you back home, never mind what Cearl said, I'll let Gwynedd apply her magic on you and with time, you'll be back to your old self again."

Os gave a slight shake of his head. "It's not… going to happen… my friend … not ever… not this time…. Ed, about those women."

"You mean the ones Edmund murdered?"

Osgar nodded. "You thought… it was me… didn't you… you ol' bastard," he gasped.

"For a moment it did cross my mind, but only for a moment. I knew it couldn't be you."

"You… and your second sight… thought you could… read… people's minds… got that one wrong… didn't yer!"

"Yes," he replied hesitantly, tears trickling down his face.

"That other bastard… from Mercia… you thought… he was your brother… you stupid… soft sod."

"There was a brief moment back then, when I half thought he could have been my brother."

"Look Ed… you have… to do it… unsheathe your seax… and… give me… a quick death…. I can't do it myself… there's… a good friend."

"I'll have to speak to Harold."

"The Earl's taking… a long time to come."

"He won't be long," replied Edwin.

"You're an intelligent… sod, tell me… I wonder what… it's like?"

"What," replied Edwin.

"Death, Heaven… Valhalla. What do you think… happens to us?"

"Don't rightly know, Os. Many years ago I met someone who, when he was asked that same question, said it was probably like either falling asleep for ever or we wake up to a fantastic adventure in Valhalla."

"Either way… sounds better… than this."

"Well Osgar my friend," said the Earl, "I see they got you spiked in the neck this time."

Osgar tried to move.

"No! No! let me help you," said the Earl, putting his arm around Osgar's head, lifting him slightly, enough to place a rolled length of material beneath to cushion it. He wiped Osgar's sweating brow.

"My lord," Osgar whispered, his gasps for breath becoming increasing difficult, "I really... fucked up… this time!"

"It happens." Earl Harold paused and briefly looked at Edwin. "I hear you want Edwin to give you an honourable death."

Osgar nodded.

"Do you want me to say a prayer for you?"

"Yes… my lord… of the old religion…the religion of my fathers."

"Very good."

Osgar's eyes glanced at Edwin and gave him a half smile.

Edwin unsheathed his seax as the Earl began a short prayer.

"Hail Woden! Receive this bold warrior Osgar in Asgaard, heavenly realm of the Gods and slain heroes, where the dead shall rise again and live for ever."

Edwin leaned forward and kissed his friend's forehead.

"Farewell my ol' friend and good hunting." The knife blade plunged in between his Osgar's ribs and into his heart. It was quick. No sound. Not even a flicker of an eye. Edwin felt sure his friend's spirit had risen to that far away place.

"Move out!" shouted Edwin. The order was repeated by commanders throughout Harold's army. They had been given their instructions. To march north east keeping away from the mountainous area. They were to meet up with Tostig, and his mounted force, who were attacking from the north, and trap the Wealhasc in between.

"That would be a fine thing," said Edwin, "to catch Gruffydd ap Llywellyn with his pants down."

"Doubt we will." replied the man marching next to Edwin, with a shake of the head. "He's a slippery bastard. We won't catch him unprepared."

Edwin thought he recognised the man but from where? He had a weathered face with penetrating blue eyes, a mop of long, tightly curled, russet hair, his moustache and beard neatly trimmed. He was about the same height as himself and probably was in his mid-thirties

"Haven't I seen you before."

He nodded, "It was ten years ago, at Earl Godwin's Easter Court. I was sitting next to your wife. Gwynedd, isn't it?"

"You have a good memory."

"For some things," he laughed. "My name's Berthun but you can call me Thune if you like. Listen Edwin…"

"Call me Ed."

"Whatever…this mess we're in now is partly because of our King. He's been giving away Wealhasc land that ain't his, to these Northmen."

"I know! Listen Thune my friend, these Wealhasc bastards have just killed a good friend of mine! And that makes me angry! Now, Earl Harold has been given orders by the King to kill any Wealhascmen who can carry and use a bow or sword. If that is the King's order, then so fucking be it! I'm pissed off with everything right now, and when Edwin is pissed off the Wealhasc had better run for the hills!"

"Afan! What do you think you are doing?" screeched Beti his mother.

"Getting the bow, that father gave me."

"You silly boy. You're not going to fight the Englisc…are you?"

"Yes I am! Father's away fighting with Gruffydd's men, so that leave just us boys to protect our village! If you want me, I'm off to the woodshed to stock up with arrows."

"Don't be stupid! You're only ten years old and you think you can fight these beasts? These are professional killers. I've seen them in action. They'll scythe you down like wheat. We haven't much time. Come with me into the woods and hide until they're gone."

"No! It's up to us to defend our village, anyway I want to kill the Englisc!"

"For God's sake Afan, come with us, please! I'm taking your sister Bronwen and Grandma here into the woods before we all get killed. Quick! I can hear them coming. It's not too late. Come!"

"No!"

Beti, taking her daughter and her mother, hurried away muttering to herself, "What will his father say… what will the neighbours say? Oooh Beti my girl, nothing good is going to come of this, I mark you."

"Fire!" signalled Afan.

A volley of missiles homed into a small group of Englisc warriors, as they began their advance into the village. One of the men was hit in the leg. His companions, holding their shields up for cover dragged the injured man back out of range.

Afan grinned at the young companions by his side.

"Yea! That stopped them," he said, signalling to his other companions. "Load up Cadog before they come again!" Groups of boys had hidden themselves in buildings on both sides of the track and now they were ready and waiting for the next attack.

"What was that!" whispered Afan to Cadog. "Aaaah!"

The searing pain that wracked his small body was too much for him to bear and was getting worse. Slowly moving his head, he could see he was covered in blood, his friend lying next to him was headless and had no left arm, "Oooh Cadog," he mouthed to himself, "What have they done to you…I didn't want this…."

Screams echoed around the village as the Englisc closed in from behind the boys, their battleswords and axes hacking and shredding all before them.

"This one's still alive, what shall we do with it," grunted a housecarl standing over Afan.

"If it can bear arms, kill it! King's orders," said another.

Afan lay watching helplessly as the huge blade was raised above him and………..

"Look at these callused blood soaked hands."

"What about them, Ed," replied Thune.

Edwin stare at his hands.

"They have so much anger and hate in them," he paused for a moment, then looked up at Thune. "Do you think there's a likelihood of us just lusting after blood?"

Thune grabbed hold of Edwin's tunic with both hands. Lifting him up bodily he jammed his face into Edwin's.

"No chance! And we're not possessed by the devil either! Listen and listen well my friend! I know why you're morose. It's about yer dead friend and the carving up of those kids. Nobody likes killing youngsters but orders are orders and those kids can fire arrows just like their fathers, as was proven the other day. So get yourself together man before the Earl gets to hear, or he'll think you're going soft."

"But I have kids of my own and I keep thinking…"

"Don't think," whispered Thune. "You're a good commander and soldier, there's none better but for all our sakes, just carry out the royal commands. Your job is to obey, let the Earl and the King worry about the rest."

"Tostig's approaching!"

Edwin was glad they had joined up with Harold's brother but he continued to agonize over the royal order.

'It is still the murder of children,' he thought, kicking his shield. 'I've made up my mind. I must speak to Earl Harold, and now!'

He walked across to where the Earls had pitched their tents, their two pennants flying side by side; Harold's red dragon of Wessex and Tostig's red and gold stripes of Northymbria, somehow gave Edwin courage.

"My lord Harold, I crave a private audience."

Earl Harold looked away from his brother and nodded, "Edwin, I'll send for you shortly."

"Thank you my lord."

Edwin and Harold walked away from the camp in the company of a guard of dozen men. At a signal from the Earl, the guard formed a wide circle, enough distance away to be out of hearing.

"What do want to see me about?" asked Harold.

"My lord..." said Edwin hesitantly, looking hard at him in the half light, "I can only describe it as an inner conflict of conscience. The King's order to kill all Wealhasc boys who are old enough to carry arms!"

"And you find that order difficult to carry out?"

"Yes my lord."

"Edwin, I know you well enough to respect you. I will tell you plainly. The King deliberated over this plan of action for many days before we left Lunden. The Wealhasc, under Gruffydd ap Llywelyn, have again started making attacks into the border country and even more serious incursions into Mercia since the death of Earl Ælfgar, killing un-armed Englisc farmers and burning their crops. As you well know, this hasn't been the only time Llywelyn has broken treaties and attacked Englaland. Now it has to stop!"

"But my lord, the King has been giving his Northmandisc friends Wealhasc lands. As an old friend once said, with every action there is a reaction and I think those Wealhasc attacks are Llywellyn's reaction."

"So! What do we have here…Edwin the politician?" Harold smiled.

"No my lord, it's just what I hear."

"Are you saying the King is wrong?"

"I don't know my lord… but these attacks by Llywellyn, as I said, could be his reaction to land that has been stolen from him."

"Does every man here think as you do?"

"Not as far as I know, my lord," replied Edwin, kicking the earth in nervousness but not letting his eyes leave Earl Harold's. "The men will follow you anywhere, they love you as do I. But battles between men is one thing, killing boys of eleven and younger is another."

"You have raised an issue which others would deem a grave offence against your King. I could have you executed for treason!"

Edwin looked intently at the Earl.

"I reasoned you wouldn't harm me for airing my private thoughts to a great leader of men, above all a leader who believes in justice and honour."

"Don't give me your silken words, Edwin of Upper Barnstæd! I dare say, if I lopped your head off, I would probably have a rebellion on my hands. I know the men admire you. Listen Edwin, politics are not easy to understand, but when the King issues a command to me, I have to see it's carried out…I will say no more on this. Be ready to march at first light!"

Edwin watched the Earl and his guards as they walk away. He drew a nervous breath, knowing he had risked all but also knowing Harold thought as he did.

Edwin, Thune and a dozen men made their way slowly through woodland towards Snowy Hills. Harold had sent several groups on foot to penetrate the countryside unseen, attack the unsuspecting

Wealhasc and create panic among Llywellyn's troops and his people.

"Thune! You and the others wait for me. Need to relieve myself!"

"The others have gone on me ol' mate. I'll wait a just little while but we can't hang around for long," replied Thune. "Those bastard Northymbrians you're in command of, have fucked off! Even Tostig has trouble keeping them in line. They hate sutherners, especially the Godwinsons of Wessex. Did you see Tostig grinning when he off-loaded them onto us?"

"Yes! Alright you catch them up, I'll join you in a bit."

"Where are they?" Edwin said to himself as he strode out following the path the others had taken. 'What a liability that northerne lot are, a total liability! And I can hardly understand their Norvegian accent! What's that?' He fell to the ground as a woman's scream came from somewhere to the left of him.

'It's coming from that copse.' He cautiously checked out the lie of the land. The main group's tracks headed straight on but there were other tracks veering off to the left, towards where the noise came from.

Moving slowly, taking cover where he could, Edwin approached the edge of a clearing without being seen.

Three Northymbrians were gathered around a semi-naked girl, laughing. He thought they were more Norvegian than anything else. They were typical of their breed, didn't give a shit and didn't seem to have any thought of danger from the marauding Wealhasc.

Edwin looked nervously about and thought the girl's screams would certainly have been heard by her countrymen. He carefully checked to make sure there were no armed Wealhasc in the vicinity before making his move.

It seemed to him, the men were deciding the girl's fate.

'The bastards are drawing straws.' He lightly touched the pommel of his battlesword then took hold of its leather strapped grip. Withdrawing the weapon, he balanced the heavy double edged blade on his right shoulder and moved silently forward.

"Leave her alone!" he shouted, "otherwise I'll take you all on!"

"Look who we have here! Our brave little Mercian leader, friend of the Godwin clan!" said the housecarl who seemed to have the biggest mouth, growing out of the mass of ginger matted hair which hid most of his ruddy face. He was a hand shorter than Edwin and had hair that hung down in curls below his massive shoulders.

"No! He's not a Mercian, he's a sutherner!" grunted another one. He had dishevelled blond hair, was barrel-chested, tall with gangly, mottled skinned arms. Edwin had had words with him only hours before.

"What's a Wessex boy doin here? You're either very brave or stupid disturbing men at play," said the ginger haired man with a cackling laugh, reminiscent of wild night animals. Edwin eyed the third man, who stood slightly apart, his arms folded saying nothing.

'He is their leader, I know it. I've seen him before and he is staying calm and quiet. I'll manoeuvre myself near. If I have to strike I'll go for him first.'

"I'll say this one more time!" said Edwin, edging ever closer. "Leave the girl alone. Go on your way and no one will be harmed!"

"I hate sutherners don't you?" said Ginger, without looking at Edwin. "Piss off, if you don't want to get yer arse kicked!"

Edwin, with one smooth movement brought his blade down on their leader's neck. The man's head leaped into the air. Without changing rhythm he had the blade at the ginger man's neck.

"One more move Blondy, and I'll split Ginger here, from arsehole to breakfast time!"

Ginger, breathed heavily and shook his head signalling to the other man, who raised his chin and dropped his axe to the ground.

"What now? What about him?" queried Blondy.

"First you bury him and if you're thinking of making a pyre, forget it. I don't want to bring the Wealhasc here. Over there are plenty of loose rocks, bury him there. When you've done that, piss off and rejoin the others and no more will be said!"

Once they had buried their dead companion, Edwin allowed them to pick up their weapons and march away out of the wood. He took one last look at the mound of stones then looked at the young woman who was still crouching on the ground. She looked to be about sixteen years of age.

"Are you hurt girl?"

"No!" She curled up tighter than a cat ready to pounce.

"I mean you no harm. Where's your village?"

"Why do you want to know?"

"I'm trying to help you, girl, by taking you out of harm's way."

"But you're Englisc! You hate us!"

"I don't hate you or anyone but we do need to get away from here!" he said pulling her up, without waiting for her to answer. "Where is your village?" he asked again.

"Through there," she replied, pointing to a track which disappeared into the dense weald.

'I should leave her where she is to make her own way to her people,' he thought. 'The lilt of her language is so attractive; much like Gwynedd's. It's very seductive when spoken by a woman. Was it that, that first attracted me to Gwynedd? I don't know. Which reminds me I should have gone with the others, I know it. So why am I doing this? The simple fact is, I feel in some way compelled to take her away from here, to safety.'

"What's your name?"

"Blodeuwedd."

"Your Englisc is very good," said Edwin.

"We all speak your language. We're not forest animals!"

"Sorry I meant no offence," replied Edwin, holding up his hands. "What does your name mean?"

"It means, beautiful as a bunch of flowers," she said, with a smile that seemed to light up her whole being. "Look, suppose you gathered together all sorts of beautiful flowers, of different colours, you would see then how pleasing it is to the eye. That's what my name means."

Edwin smiled in response. He hadn't need a further explanation but she obviously liked talking. Her lilt kept reminding him of Gwynedd, which irked him. 'Why! Why am I feeling guilty? Is it because of the silent pleasure of arousal by another woman? Yes, it must be.' He looked casually towards Blodeuwedd. Her dress was untied and she was walking hurriedly. Her firm, small breasts jiggled at each step, one of her nipples perked shamelessly in full view the other, though concealed, impressed itself through the thin fabric.

"Can we stop? My leg hurts," said Blodeuwedd, flinging herself onto the ground. She pulled up her skirt and began rubbing her left thigh.

"I thought it was your leg that was hurt and anyway I need to get back to my own people!"

She ignored his remark but looked seductively at him, her long, dark brown hair hanging loosely across her face in tight, curled rivulets, partly masking her deep brown eyes.

"You saved my life."

"I don't like women being mistreated, especially by those animals!"

"But you saved my life!"

"I know and that's the second time you've said it.

"There were three of them. Weren't you scared?"

"No!" Edwin replied, looking away. He was smiling.

"I must have twisted my leg when they threw me to the ground. I hope I haven't broke anything, not that you're interested."

Edwin turned and looked down at her. She gave him another imploring look.

"Look, I can't move my leg. Please, couldn't you help me? I need you to feel if something is broken. Here, right here," she pleaded pointing to her left thigh and anyway I need to rest here a while, otherwise I will never be able to walk at all."

'There's nothing wrong with her!' He looked around expecting her Wealhasc friends to leap out from behind every tree at any moment but he couldn't see or hear anybody.

By the time he returned his gaze, she had pulled her skirt further up revealing the top of her legs. He couldn't help but notice her flawless skin. 'It's as smooth as a baby's, surely this is the sight which makes grown men lose their reason.' Edwin's eyes rested on the dark triangle of hair between her thighs. His heart pounded under his heavy jerkin. 'This woman's dangerous, she's trying to manipulating me. Bitch!' He momentarily closed his eyes, 'I must remain calm and standing! If I sit or lay next to her, I'm done for.'

"Please... don't just stand there, come and sit next to me."

"Alright but only for a little while." 'Oh shit! What am I doing, I'll shall fall like a young idiot at his first sight of a woman's body! For the love of the Gods why didn't I remain standing? Why didn't I leave? Now her hand is on my knee, I can hear her panting or is that me? Odin! Help me! I can feel the swell of desire! I'm as stiff as a rock, if I give in now and sink between her young, dark, delicious thighs, it will be the end for me. I've got to get away!'

As if sensing his hesitancy she tightened her grip. Leaning towards him she whispered. "Please! I've never seen any man as strong as you. I want your child."

"What!"

"I know a place where we won't be discovered. Please, I want your child!"

"Aaah!" Jumping to his feet, he drew his sword and struck the nearest tree... "No! No! Get fucked by one of your own!"

Edwin strode away, his arms flailing, striking out, as if wiping away an invisible web.

"But I don't know your name!" she called after him.

"Tough!" he shouted back without turning his head. He felt a weight had been lifted from his shoulders. He was now almost euphoric. It seemed he had broken a spell, a web of something that had enfolded him and now he was free. He took another swipe at a tree. "To think, I nearly fell for that sex starved bitch. She knew every trick. What has happened to me? My brain must be addled! Get a grip Edwin lad. Let's find my ragged arsed troop!"

"You were gone a long time," said Thune.

"It's a long story. You lot move quickly," replied Edwin.

"Had to, the only way to catch up with the Wealhasc. They have stopped their usual tactics and have run; probably up into those hills," said Thune, pointing to the west.

"Thune, you see those two Northymbrians?"

Thune nodded.

"Watch them carefully, they're trouble. I'll explain later."

"We must rejoin the main force. Give us a leg up. I'll climb this tree and see if I can see anything of interest."

"I've got more cuts and scratches climbing this tree than anything else. Look," he showed Edwin his torn leggings, ripped between his thighs.

Edwin laughed.

"It's alright for you! Any closer I would've been talking with a squeaky voice," said Thune, brushing twigs and leaves from his tunic. "It's your turn next time."

"Well, never mind that, what did you see?"

"I think our boys are over there." He pointed eastward, "I saw a pall of smoke."

Edwin turned to his men.

"Come on lads grab your stuff. How much smoke?" he asked Thune.

"A lot! Probably a whole village has gone up in flames."

"This village is devastated." Edwin said to Thune. "Is there no end to it? Bodies everywhere and not one grown man among them, nor any women come to that. All I can see are more dead kids!"

"The men are probably up in the hills."

"Come on let's get out of here," shouted Edwin, "we've still some way to go. Where did you say the smoke was coming from?"

"Over there in that direction!" replied Thune pointing towards a black smudge above the forested skyline. "Look at those magnificent beasts," he exclaimed.

Edwin was taken aback and shook his head.

"Magnificent what? Where?"

"Oaks man. Oaks! They produce the finest timber for shipbuilding. I'll have my own yard one day; take over from my father."

"Shipbuilding? I didn't know your family were in that line of business but then again why not. So where do you come from?"

"Fefresham on the north coast of Cent."

"Cent. Now that's an ancient name. Now it's part of Wessex."

"I know, but we Centisc folk still hang on to our old traditions, we're traders, shipbuilders and sæfarers."

"And warriors!"

"Yes, that as well. We're a tough, versatile and talented race." Thune came close to Edwin, "And we're still Centisc no matter what others might say," he said with a laugh.

"So, if I want a boat, I know where to come."

"It'll cost yer."

"What happened to our friendship?"

"If you want a boat, I'll get my father to make you a special deal but of course my brother Kæfrid is also a ship builder. I'm sure *he* would construct one to your liking," replied Thune.

"I'll hold you to that." Edwin brought his men to a halt. "There's movement ahead. Positions!"

*September, 1063*
**- Upper Barnstæd -**

"Shush! Quiet!" said Gwynedd, "your father's sleeping."

"Is he ill?" enquired Wulfnoth.

"No. He's just tired. Isn't it time for your morning's training?"

Wulfnoth looked around.

"Yes, when I find my brother. He was here a moment ago."

Gwynedd watched Wulfnoth amble away out of the main hall.

'They're fourteen, soon they will be old enough to go to war.' The very thought of losing them frightened her. She walked to the far corner of the hall. Making herself comfortable on a bench seat, she uncovered her harp and began to play. In times of stress she found the very act of plucking the strings, making music, soothing. The moment of anxiety gradually began to pass. Feeling tired, she put her feet up, covered herself with a rug, leant back and slept.

All she wanted was to stay asleep, to indulge herself for the first time in weeks in that delicious luxury. Half opening her eyes she was aware of a figure standing over her.

"Gwynedd." Edwin bent down and kissed her forehead and whispered, "Gwynedd it's me Edwin."

"Aah, you're back from the dead. You came home trudging into the bedroom at some godforsaken time this morning, not even a kiss, and collapsed on the bed. Now, with a soft kiss, you expect me to spoil you!"

"I was tired! I'd been riding for three days and you….."

"Come here…"

Edwin broke away catching his breath.

"You *are* hungry."

Gwynedd smiled at him and rubbed her nose against his.

"You're still my hairy hunk of a man."

"Never mind all that, I'm not letting you sleep away the day in a darkened corner of the hall."

He lifted her, carried her into the bedroom and put her gently down on the bed. Suddenly, a vision crossed his mind. He fought to support himself by holding onto the bed. He closed his eyes; faces, bloodstained boys. He was aware of Gwynedd looking at him.

"What's the matter? Are you ill?"

Edwin began weeping.

She put her arms around him.

"Last night I looked in at our boys sleeping peacefully in their beds…and I felt ashamed. I have never felt ashamed before. Never in all my years as a soldier. Fighting for the Earl and the King I have had to carry out the killing of boys. Boys the same age as ours and some younger. So many," his voice dropped to a whisper, "so many." He held onto his wife tightly, burying his head into the nape of her neck then down against her breasts as if trying to erase those memories from his mind.

"Where was this? You haven't told me."

He didn't want to answer her questions. How could he tell her about what happened in Wealh! The children! Osgar! And Edmund!

He began to tremble violently.

Gwynedd held him closer.

"We found Edmund," he said through the tears which were now coursing down his cheeks. "He was standing over a woman, about to hack her to pieces. The girl in our village, he murdered her. He'd been hacking women to pieces and leaving a trail of 'em everywhere he'd been."

"Oh my God! Not Edmund,"

"Yes, Edmund."

"How many?" Gwynedd said, deeply shocked.

"God knows. Now I have to tell his father. I think I should I say he was killed in battle. At least that would protect Egbert from shame. He is such a good man. He doesn't deserve this or the disgrace it would bring on him and his wife…" Edwin looked at her, "For now, we'll keep this between ourselves."

Gwynedd agreed.

"Where is Egbert?"

"He's away."

"Who's training the boys?"

"Alric. Egbert's friend from the old days," replied Gwynedd.

"I think I know of him," Edwin took a deep breath to calm himself and thought for a moment. "Does he come from Wicford?"

"I believe so."

"Of course. He was also a friend of my father. Where are the boys now?"

"Over by the barn."

On approaching the barn, Edwin and Gwynedd could see the boys walking towards them.

"Has Alric been hard on you?" Edwin asked.

Edric smiled, turning to his brother. "Sort of but he's good and quick for an old man."

"He is as cunning as a fox," added Wulfnoth.

Alric, a tall, bullnecked muscular man, dressed in dark leather, was inspecting a sword, weighing and checking it for balance. He looked up and peered from under his wide brimmed leather hat, tipping it in greeting as Edwin approached. Squinting his bright blue eyes, Alric took in everything. He had a faceful of white hair, apart from his bushy eyebrows which were dark brown. His overgrown white drooping moustache merged with his long beard which was platted into four braids swaying at his every movement. The skin on his face, difficult to see through the hair, was pitted as though he had suffered at some distant time from the pox.

"You knew my father?" Edwin was smiling for the first time in days.

It was as if Alric had brought a spirit of light; lifting the darkness which had lain heavily on Edwin's shoulders. "You look like a wizard," continued Edwin.

"No." Alric gave a low chuckle. "Your wife's more wizard than me. I just help when and where I can." He looked towards Wulfnoth and Edric, as they disappeared from sight, with their mother. "Your boys are doing well. They're almost ready."

"Their mother won't like that."

"What mother does," replied Alric.

"Any sign of Egbert?"

"Turn around, our friend is here."

The figure on horseback coming towards them was slumped forward. After their brief greeting Egbert asked of the whereabouts of his son.

"I have bad news, my friend," replied Edwin gently. "He was killed soon after we landed at Nedd. Sorry Egbert, I wish I had better news."

Tears began streaming down Egbert's face. Ushering them into the barn, he sat down and began wringing his hands and thumping a bale of straw in front of him.

"If only," he closed his eyes, "if only that were all. I would be a happier father had he fallen in battle, with honour."

"What do you mean?" enquired Edwin.

"I've just come back from Stoneford."

'He knows,' Edwin thought.

"He's dead you say?" continued Egbert. "Just as well otherwise I would've had to killed him myself."

"Why?" said Edwin, feigning surprise.

Alric remained silent.

"My son was about to chop a girl in pieces with an axe. She was only fifteen."

"She's still alive?" asked Edwin.

"Locals heard her screaming and stopped him just in time."

"How did he escape them?" asked Edwin.

"All I know is, they saved the girl but feared for their own lives when he went berserk, wielding his battle-axe, so they let him go." Egbert began sobbing, something Edwin had never seen him do before.

Pulling himself together he closed his eyes.

"My son was the one who butchered our local girl and probably the other one over in Wintancæster." He stood up and edged away from his friends, without looking at them. "Edwin, my wife and I will leave tomorrow morning!"

"You're *not* leaving. You're staying put. I need you here!" replied Edwin.

"Look, you and your father have been good friends to me and my family but… but this business. I have blood on my hands. I have to take full responsibility for what he did…I'M HIS FATHER!" he shouted. "and when the rest of the village knows of it, my wife and I will be finished."

"It was not your fault, Egbert! Bad seeds can be born into any family."

Alric put his hand on Egbert's shoulder.

"Remember Æthelwalh back in the old days, you couldn't have ask for a better companion. A fearsome swine in battle especially with his skeggy. He had balls, scared of nobody… But his greased, slobbering bastard of a son Coenred was another matter. We had to put *him* down. It was the only way. The butcher of Anglia they called him."

"I remember," said Egbert, trying to stem his tears.

"So you see, you can't leave, you can't be held responsible. You're a good man. The lad's dead. Out of the way! He can't hurt anyone else nor bring disgrace on your family any more! Move on and say nothing about it to anyone."

They watched as Egbert trudged off to his home in the village. Alric gave Edwin a sideward glance as they turned to walk back to the hall.

"What?" said Edwin.

"What else happened?"

Edwin thought for a moment. "It's a long story and I don't want to go back over it, at least not now," he replied.

Alric lifted his hat, scratched his head then, putting his hat on again, nodded.

"I can respect that. I'll be with you later," he said as he walked away.

Gwynedd was waiting at the entrance of the hall.

"How did he take it?"

"He knew. He knew what his son had done. I told him Edmund had died in battle and that's the end of it," he replied.

She nodded, "I thought as much." They walked in silence into the hall.

"I'm coming up to forty five, my warrior years are nearly over. It's a job for younger men. I'm thinking of giving it up…for good," he said at last, taking his seat at the long table.

"What's brought this on?"

Edwin looked around the hall and beckoned Gwynedd to come closer.

"First I had to…" he paused, "we had to get rid of Edmund and later after landing off the west coast of Wealh, Osgar got himself spiked. The poor bastard was paralysed, nothing worked below his shoulders. He would have been crippled for life. He begged me to kill him."

"And you did?"

"Had to. He knew he was finished. It was kindest thing to do. Look! I'm pissed off! I'm either killing kids, executing murderers or killing friends to put them out of their misery."

"You need a good rest."

"You can say that again."

# CHAPTER XIII

*April, 1064*

- **The Royal Palace at West Minster** -

"Sire, Duke William has had in his charge, for the last thirteen years, Lady Ælfgifu's son Hakon and also my brother Wulfnoth," said Earl Harold. "Those boys have done no wrong, surely he must concede to a request for their release?"

"What do you want me to do exactly?" replied King Edward.

"Sire, make a formal request for their release, of course!"

Lady Ælfgifu, fought back her tears.

"My son was only five years of age! A mere child when he was taken into *your* care and protection and then torn from my arms by that uncivilised beast, Jumièges."

"Lady Ælfgifu! How dare you! He is a man of God and my Archbishop!"

"*Was* your Archbishop!" replied Lady Ælfgifu, now fighting hard to keep her rage in check. "Sire, you know what he did to me, I was left bleeding and unconscious, by his hand alone. All the while his only concern was for himself. And now? How will my son look upon me now, after all these years? He will not be able to speak his mother tongue and will barely recognise me. It is as if… I have lost him forever!"

"Lady Ælfgifu," the King replied, in a conciliatory voice. "You know very well I could do nothing to stop that tragedy from happening."

"And my brother?" interrupted the Earl Harold. "What of him?

He is probably lost to me for ever too, by the hand of Jumièges! Wulfnoth was not even given the courtesy of being allowed home to help bury our father! So much for your Northmandisc friends."

"Sire," said Lady Ælfgifu, who's hands were gripped together in anger, her nails digging into her flesh almost drawing blood. "Eight years ago, almost to the day," she paused to gather her composure, "Duke William visited you within these very walls when you, by all accounts, made him your heir, without consulting the Witan and without any mention of my child being released from his prison."

King Edward, shaken by the ferocity of their pleas, took hold of his walking stick, barely able to rise. Slowly, he prised himself out of his seat. Without saying a word he moved away from them with, what appeared to be, an exaggerated hobble, leaned against the wall and closed his eyes.

Harold, not moved by the King's performance, judging it as pure invention, felt nothing but contempt. Aware of Ælfgifu shaking with frustration and anger, he took hold of her arm to reassure her. An idea, a plan was forming. He knew the King's half closed eyes were focused on him. He didn't much care how rapidly Edward had aged over the last two months; his stooped body and sallowness of face. All Harold had was an overwhelming feeling of distrust and anger.

The King eased himself away from the wall and paused. Harold could almost hear the cogs and wheels turning in his head.

"Guards! Leave the room!" he commanded, with renewed energy, as if he had suddenly come to life.

They were now alone with Edward who avoided eye contact with Harold.

"Archbishop Jumièges, had to flee for his life."

"He had no reason to fear for his life. But he would probably have had to appear before the Witan. Anyway, an archbishop has no business to abscond with two children, like a raider in the night!"

The King stood still and leant heavily on his stick as if gathering his thoughts. At long last his head inclined, his watery blue eyes, peering through his overlong eyebrows, focused on Harold. He replied softly and deliberately.

"I think, Earl Harold, you should go to Duke William yourself to plead both your cases. If that is agreeable to you, I'll have a letter drawn up in the morning stating as much and... I think you should take Lady Ælfgifu with you as he may well listen sympathetically to a mother's plea."

"My lord, I will appeal to no-one, least of all to a bastard duke. He has no business holding these two innocent boys prisoner!"

"Earl Harold! Hold your tongue! Your language is unfitting within my court! Duke William is a good man and has been a loyal and true friend to me, to my dear departed mother and to Englaland. He is to be treated with respect. How dare you speak so, to me your sovereign!"

'Forgive me, Sire," replied Harold, "but the responsibility for those children was yours and yours alone. And now you want *me* to plead to their gaoler who may well make us his prisoners too?"

"I am getting on in years and not in the best of health and the last thing I want is to see is a mother bereft of her only child and you, Earl Harold, vexed over the absence of your younger brother. I will draft a letter demanding, I repeat, demanding their release, which you will hand personally to Duke William. I am sure he will then accede to my demands. Does that meet with your approval?"

Harold, keeping his own council, replied, "Yes Sire, thank you."

*Early morning*
**- Bosham harbour, Wessex -**
Bosham, West Sussex


Edwin stepped aboard the Karve, a smaller version of the usual single masted longship, ideal for commercial shipping and shallow coastal waters. He gave a nod of greeting to a man he didn't recognise, who was sitting at the stern. As far as Edwin could judge he was one of the crew, of middle years, a touch younger than himself but with a headful of ruffled black hair, short clipped beard and a bushy moustache which gave emphasis to the man's bulbous nose. Edwin wondered why he was just sitting there and not working with rest of the crew, who were loading supplies onto the ship.

Edwin asked where the captain was.

"Who wants to know?"

"I do!" he replied, "Look! Let's stop this shit and talk plainly. I'm Edwin of Upper Barnstæd. Who …"

"I know who you are! What is the matter with you, get out of bed the wrong side or something? Anyway I've seen you around. You're a friend of Earl Harold."

Edwin gave a nod.

"I've been on campaigns with him and have always given him my loyal support, if that's what you mean."

"I'm Horsa, captain and steersman of this ship. Who did yer think I was?"

"Alright then *Captain Horsa*. Or should I just call you captain?"

He stared at Edwin for some moments before breaking out into a guttural laugh.

"You can call me Horsa. What can I do for yer?"

"Do you know where we're supposed to be going?"

"Do yer want a long or a short answer?"

"Just give me the short answer."

"Not sure! The Governor hasn't told me yet. He just said, make this ship ready. But I suspect it's somewhere along the Northmandisc coast."

"The Governor?"

"That's right. It's what I've always called him. I picked up the name up from a French sæ captain. Many a time I called ol' Godwin, Governor, and now I call his son the same. Anyway, are yer going to be crewing or are yer a going to be a lazy bastard, cos I could always do with an extra pair of hands."

Edwin smiled to himself and thought, 'Perhaps I'm wrong about him.' He looked sæwards, beyond the calm water of the harbour.

"I'm not crewing this time unless you're short of an oarsman. I'm just a passenger. What's the weather forecast?"

"Not sure." Horsa sniffed the air. "Trouble is, this time of the year it's changeable. We could hit a storm and then maybe not."

"Let's hope we don't then," replied Edwin, "I'd like the impossible. A nice quiet, calm sæ. But between you, me and your steering oar, I prefer solid ground under my feet."

"I'll tell yer what… I'll have a little chat with Ægir perhaps he'll make the sæ nice and calm for yer," chuckled Horsa.

"You shouldn't make fun of the Gods! This isn't exactly a big boat in which to do battle with a storm."

"Listen friend, small it maybe but it's a ship and a good'n."

"Sorry, a small ship then!"

"Mmm. I'm sure Ægir wouldn't take offence. Anyway, wherever we're going, can't be too far because the Governor's taking a couple of women, a couple of hounds and his pet hawk, so I expect he'll be going hunting."

"Mind if I sit here in the stern?"

"You can sit where you like, mi ol' shipmate."

"Captain!" shouted Earl Harold. "Let's get under way!" The Earl leading his hounds and his young steward, carrying his hawk, picked his way amidships, followed by the tall Lady Ælfgifu, wearing a long, heavy cloak. With her was a lady companion.

"Where are we going, Governor," shouted Horsa.

"Just get us out of here and onto the open sæ," returned the Earl.

Horsa gave the order and his crew maneuvered the ship slowly away from the dockside.

"Strike!" shouted Horsa, in a booming voice.

Edwin could see the pleasure of being in charge, written all over Horsa's face, as he gripped hold of the steering oar, raising himself ever so slightly from his seat as he gave each command.

Edwin felt the familiar surge of the ship, at every pull of the oarsmen.

Horsa continued his commands.

"Strike…and…strike…and…strike." until they had picked up pace and settled into an even tempo. He nodded with satisfaction, sniffed the air and renewed his grip on the steering oar as the ship cut through the now turbulent open sæ.

"I know that face. How did *he* get on board without me knowing it,"

"Who are you talking about?" queried Horsa.

"I just saw an old mate of mine." Edwin maneuvered himself forward and stopped by one of the oarsman.

"Thune! Where did you come from?"

Thune looked up and smiled.

"Do you mind… you're spoiling my… rhythm… met up …with Horsa…the other day… and he needed… another oarsman…. Let's face it… it beats… fighting the Wealhasc! "

"No talking! Put your backs into it, lads," shouted Horsa.

"Talk… later Ed!"

Bosham harbour, the village and church had passed out of sight when Horsa gave the command to raise the sail. The headland was now behind them partly lost in the low-lying morning mist. The Earl approached and, without saying a word, took hold of the sternpost watching all the time without blinking an eye, it seemed to Edwin, the far retreating blur of the Wessex coastline.

'What is he looking for?' he thought.

Then as if in answer, Earl Harold turned to Horsa.

"Maintain this course until I give you the order, then we'll steer to port but wait for my command!"

"East Governor?… You mean, we're sailing to Flanders and up the Yser?"

"Yes captain. We're going to Flanders." The Earl came close, "In front of your crew address me as my lord, is that clear?"

"Right you are gov…sorry… my lord."

"Good man." Harold turned to Edwin, "Come with me."

Edwin and the Earl moved amidships to the port side. Earl Harold leaned over the side letting the salt spray whip across his face. By now the wind was getting up, blowing spray across Edwin's face as well. He licked the salt from his lips and looked at the deep green swell of the sæ, its white tipped waves, feeling the rocking motion of the ship. 'I shouldn't be doing this, it's churning my stomach.'

"Edwin, Edwin!"

"Yes! my lord!"

"I shall out fox the old sod yet!"

"Who's that, my lord?"

"The King, you fool!"

"I didn't wish to presume, my lord?" smiled Edwin.

Not answering Edwin directly, Harold began talking as though he were speaking his thoughts aloud.

"I shall talk to Count Baldwin."

Edwin was now having difficulty hearing, because of the increased sound of the wind, which was swirling through their hair. He raised his hood to hold back the strands of hair which had been whip-lashing across his eyes and face.

"I heard a rumour." Edwin wasn't sure the Earl could hear him and repeated, "I heard a rumour…"

"Yes I can hear you!"

"…that we were going to Rouen."

"Wrong!" Harold took out a scroll from his jerkin and poked Edwin in the chest with it. Edwin could see that its royal seal had been broken.

"Edwin! The King has *deceived me*! He is a lying, sod! Look! This…! This was supposed to demand the release of my brother and nephew but instead, it commands me to take an oath! Oath of fealty to that…!" He shook his head. "Look! Look man!" and opening the scroll, showed Edwin its contents.

Edwin leaned closer and began reading the beautifully crafted, inked words which were now dissolving in the sæ spray. He couldn't quite make out the beginning but managed to read most of it, at least as much of the letter as he could:

> *'William II, Duke of ..rthmandig, gr..tings,*
> *...*arl *Harold Godwinson is commanded in all good faith*
> *to hereby employ all means to assist my noble Duke, William II of*
> *Northmandig,*
> *my nominee as heir, to the throne of Englaland on the event of my*
> *death.*
> *As such...yo...to fac......... oath o... feal...*
> *f..........t......so.......*
>
> *Edward III by ..... ..... of God, King of Engla....d.*
> *Da..... day, 20<sup>th</sup> April 1064'*

Edwin had read enough. He handed the scroll back.

With lowered voice so that only Edwin could hear, although it would have been impossible for anybody else to hear their conversation even five feet away, Harold said, "Well it doesn't take a genius to work out his intentions, but without the backing of the Witan he hasn't got a chance. So, our saintly King, as he likes to be thought of, is trying to trick me and Lady Ælfgifu into going into the 'Bastard's' lair to be used as his pawns. He is insane, to disregard the Witan and the boy ætheling, Edgar, who is the *real and live* heir. Thank God Edgar hasn't ended up like his father, that poor wretch, King Edmund's son, Edward who I brought back from Hungary only for him to be poisoned. And I know who did it!... Edwin, I have no intention of going to Northmandig. Even the Norvegians have more claim than that bastard. The King has lied to my face. I hate that devious swine. I can still hear him saying, and I don't know how many time he repeated it, "When we were exiled in Northmandig, I was like a father to that young Duke. He was the son I was not blessed with." Just the sound of those winging words makes me sick. Listen Edwin and hear me well my friend... never ever repeat any of what I have just said to anyone else... not even to your wife, you understand me?"

"Yes my lord."

"And believe me when I say we would have sailed into a well organised Northmandisc trap, with that bastard waiting at the dockside."

Edwin nodded, trying as best he could to hear, despite the increased howling of the wind.

Harold, slapping Edwin on the shoulder continued, "So, instead I shall speak to my brother's father-in-law, Count Baldwin. He should have some clout. After all, he is the bastard's father-in-law too. He should be able to put pressure on him, to release Lady Ælfgifu's son, Hakon and my brother Wulfnoth." He moved even closer, their salt sæ dripping faces almost touching. "Edwin, I will need your wise council."

"But my lord, surely there are more learned and much wiser men at your court than I?"

"That's what I'm afraid of, that's why I needed you here, *you Edwin.* You're a man who has intuition, not bound by politics and religion, you are someone I can trust with my life! You're not afraid of speaking your mind, that's why I chose you."

Edwin swallowed. 'I don't like politics,' he thought.

"It is truly an honour to be so trusted, my lord, but this honour is a heavy burden as well. Of course I will do my best to deserve your trust."

"Good man. We'll speak some more later."

Harold turned and moved forward to rejoin Lady Ælfgifu.

Edwin watched the Earl in animated conversation with Lady Ælfgifu and her lady companion both of whom, it seemed, had some influence with him. Then, to his amazement, Harold tore up the royal document and threw it overboard.

He took a deep breath, 'I wish he hadn't picked me for this trip. Some bloody honour. He knows I'm not too keen on the sæ and this tub isn't exactly large as ships go. All I want is a quiet life at home and not be summoned to Bosham, at will, for the Earl's adventures. I'm an old warrior and wise or not, I've been there and done it all.

Now I'm ready to put my feet up and enjoy blissful retirement but he won't let me! My hair's grey *and* I'm going bald! At least that's what I told him yesterday. He wouldn't listen. He took me aside, "We're going on a short trip," he says," he didn't tell me it would be to Flanders and that country isn't exactly around the corner. "Where to?" I had asked him. "Never you mind *where,* lad, I want you with me!" "Why?" I replied. "You're the man I want. A man of wisdom and experience." I didn't like it then and still don't like the sound of it. Now that I know for certain where we're going, I have even less liking for it. Especially going east to the wild Northerne Sæ or, at least, to the suth of it!'

Wihtland was now far behind, and the Englisc coastline a mere shadow as they continued suth into the Englisc Sæ.

By mid-day the Earl had given Horsa the signal to turn to port. The wind was stronger now, filling the sail to near breaking point and, as far as Edwin could see, putting a tremendous strain on the rigging, hurling their ship through the waves at a surprising rate.

"Will this rigging hold together?" shouted Edwin.

"Yea!" shouted back Horsa, "I've had that sail billowing out so much, this ship was skimming across the waves, hardly getting its arse wet and my steering oar here was barely touching the water."

"You mean, like *I* can walk on water," Edwin laughed.

"Alright, alright, laugh as much as you like but she's a fast, tough ol' ship with rigging to match and with this wind, we'll be off the coast of Flanders by tomorrow morning."

"What's that ship over there?" Edwin shielded his eyes to get a better view.

"That's a longship and I think it's flying the King's White Dragon pennant. If that's true, that won't please the Governor."

"Not much we can do about it now," replied Edwin. "Believe it or not I'm enjoying this trip. And there was me, thinking of storms and being wrecked and smashed on some desolate rock."

"Early days mate! Early days! There's plenty of time for storms yet," laughed Horsa, his large stomach bouncing up and down. "Yer take the weather as it comes and before yer know it, you'll be wanting a ship of your own and if that's yer business, you're talking to the right lad here and he's standing next to yer. He'll get yer one built."

"You must have read my mind," said Edwin. He turned to face Thune. "You remember a while ago you mentioned about building me something. Not as big as this but a smaller version."

"Tell you what, Ed. When we get back I'll talk to my brother," replied Thune, "but it won't be for quite some time yet because we're building a new house and this time it's away from our yard. Do you know what?"

"No, tell me," replied Edwin.

"Well, the other day I took possession of three wagon loads of oak timber from a client who couldn't pay his bill," laughed Thune, "I shouldn't laugh because the builder, who was supposed to do the work, turned out to be a prick-an-a-half, he didn't know one end of a chisel from the other, as I said not only a prick but a limp one."

"So who's going to build your house now?"

"Me and my brother…the trouble is Ed, you can't trust builders these days and as for fitting window shutters! Yer don't want to go there."

"Thune! You like playing with boats," said Horsa. "Take a turn at the steering oar, I need to piss and catch up on some shut-eye."

"I think I'll get some too, as there's not much else to do."

Edwin sat near Thune. He was more tired than he cared to admit. He draped his cloak around himself and soon fell into a deep sleep.

Horsa nudged Edwin awake.

"Looks like we're heading into a storm, you had better get yourself prepared for a nasty one!"

Edwin shivered. He ached all over.

"Heading for it! We're in it yer numb scull!"

Horsa was already asleep again, snoring under his fur cloak.

"Thanks for nothing! You should have left me in the land of nod."

Edwin muttered turning to Thune. "I can't believe I was sleeping through this stuff, with the ship tossing about as it is. Anyway, where do you think we are now, anywhere near the coast of Flanders? I can't see land at all, just this… mountainous sæ and a lot of rain!"

"Dunno Ed! We'll keep on this course till dawn, which should be soon. Horsa seems dead to the world but he ain't. This weather doesn't worry him. I've seen it before, he catnaps with one eye open. I don't know how he does it. He's a good captain and steersman and a handy man to have around if there's trouble."

"What trouble?"

"Damaged rigging, broken steering oar, you know, the usual stuff you get when you've been battling through a storm."

"You think it will be that bad?"

"We'll see. I'm going to leave you here me ol' mate so grab onto that steering oar because I want to go for a piss. Back soon."

The high wind, shrieking through the rigging, made Edwin somewhat nervous. Though he was used to lightning, this was something else. Immediately overhead a brilliant flash illuminated the whole sæscape.

CRACK! The sound of an exploding clap of thunder shook every bone in his body. Blackness descended once more.

"Ed! Ed! You alright!" shouted Thune.

"Can't hear you." He shook his head. "That's better. Yer! I'm alive. That was deafening."

"That lightning was right above you… thought you were a gonna."

"It put the fear of the Gods into me that's for sure." The lightening had been so close he had feared its brilliance would blind him.

"I'll take over the steering," said Thune.

Edwin moved aside but now his stomach was really beginning to churn as the deep, heavy swell worsened. Huge crested waves came crashing over the ship, momentarily obliterating the bow from view.

He tried to stem the dread that was beginning to take hold of him.

"What have you two done? You've stirred up a shit-full of weather!" shouted Horsa, rubbing his eyes. "Has there been any thunder or lightning?"

"Hear that Ed! I told yer! He's a deaf ol' bastard and can sleep through anything."

"Give me back my steering oar," shouted Horsa, "before you roll my ship over."

Though the thunder had moved away the winds were increasing. Edwin swore again as an almighty gust caught him off balance. The ship lurched to port, propelling him to the side. He stopped himself from somersaulting overboard by grasping hold of part of the rigging. Real fear seized him as he imagined himself being thrown overboard into the cold, dark green rearing sæ. He saw himself descending out of sight, without hope, down, down into the murky depths. Mesmerized by his own fear, he couldn't take his eyes and mind away from that vision of horror.

Loud laughter brought him back to his senses. He turned towards Horsa and Thune who were still laughing.

"You bastards! It's not funny," he shouted. 'I won't give them the pleasure of seeing how scared I am.' He gave them both a hard look before making a leap for the ship's crutche and felt Thune's helping hand, grasp his arm.

"Thanks, I have it! If this crutche is strong enough to hold the mast when it's lowered, it's strong enough to hold and keep me from being thrown overboard." He wrapped his arms firmly about it, and thanked Thune again.

Although it was now easier to ride with the movement of the vessel, he kept wondering why he was here and longed for his quiet life at home! Ignoring his friends, he glanced amidships where the two heavily hooded women were seated. Harold had secured the women with ropes to the mast. 'I wonder what Lady Ælfgifu is going through right now? Her son has been a prisoner for thirteen years. She must be agonizing over him. How does she hold herself together? She's obviously made of stern stuff. As a father, how would I react to having one of my sons taken from me and kept prisoner for that length of time? I'd be more than pissed off *that's* for sure! I wonder who the other woman is, obviously a member of the family, I should have asked.'

A jarring thud reverberated throughout the ship's timbers, momentarily knocking Edwin of balance, forcing him to tighten his grip ever more firmly around the crutche. 'That was a near one. I shall be a physical wreck by the end of this voyage. And that clap of thunder and lightning was too close for comfort. It left a strange sort of burning smell I've never encountered before.'

The screeching wind whipping spray across his face, made him feel he was being attacked, by clawing eagles. Maintaining his grip on the crutche, he felt secure for the moment. 'I need to be roped to this thing.' He looked nervously at the billowing sail, which was at full stretch and marvelled that it was still in one piece. 'I can see what Horsa meant about this being a tough old ship but… this storm is something else!' His thoughts turned once more to Lady Ælfgifu.

'What was the story I heard? Oh yes, Lady Ælfgifu was once the Abbess of Leofminstre, until Harold's brother Swegen did what he wasn't supposed to do. Coming back from fighting in Wealh, being without you-know-what for so long and, being so bloody horny he couldn't help himself. Stopped by, so the story goes, to see his old sweetheart Ælfgifu and before you know it he'd kidnapped her. Kept her his prisoner for a year they say.' Edwin shook his head and changed his grip on the crutche. 'A whole year! Until the King made him set her free. Too late my ol' sanctimonious sovereign, who can't or won't, which is more to the point, get it up and do the necessary with his wife.' Edwin smiled to himself. 'Swegen made her pregnant! Nine months later, out pops Hakon and bye-bye Swegen. Then the Witan banished him and declared him, 'Nithing'. Actually I liked him. His dad, Earl Godwin, loved him so he couldn't have been all bad, just rough around the edges, a bit out of control. Still the King and the Witan threw him out of the country. Then they sent me to bring him back from dear ol' Flanders, the family bolt hole. Getting his leg over an abbess, what a thing to do, eh! Can you imagine it!' Edwin took the risk of letting go and stretching one arm then the other before taking hold of the crutch again.

The ship was still pitching and tossing alarmingly. Another huge wave broke over the bow, leaving the ship awash, everybody holding on for dear life. Horsa completely disappeared under another deluge only to re-appear still holding on to his steering oar, shaking his head and grinning. His surprisingly full head of white teeth, gleamed through the darkness.

"Don't yer like it, Ed?" he shouted.

"You gotta be out of yer fucking mind to like this stuff!"

"Half sail!" came the command.

"A bit fucking late," shouted Edwin to Horsa.

"Fuck you!" shouted back Horsa. "Now the land-lubber knows more than me about sailing this ship."

"Let it be captain," shouted Thune, "he meant no harm."

Edwin let go of the crutch and scrambled to grab hold of the rigging again as yet another wave came crashing in, hurling the vessel to steorbord, before pitching through one more giant wave.

Edwin, Thune and some of the crew managed to lower the sail and secure the ropes. Edwin, clawing at anything he could, moved hand over hand back to the stern and, with a spare rope, secured himself once more to the crutch. Again, to keep his mind off the storm, he thought about the previous day, in the Earl's great hall at Bosham.

It now seemed an age ago since he had first seen Ælfgifu at the high table, he had glanced towards her whilst he was spooning the last dregs of his stew. He just hadn't been able to keep his eyes off her. Slim as a willow reed, her pale fine skinned face almost elfin in shape, she had come in with the Earl's wife, Eadgyth and the other woman. He had to say, Lady Ælfgifu did look…how could he describe her, quietly dignified, stunning? Yes that was about it and yet her dress had been quite simple. A fine white linen smock with light blue edging over a dark blue undergarment, with tight fitting sleeves. She had worn very little in the way of adornments he recalled, save for a necklace of coloured beads. Her head had been covered with a white wimple held in place about her forehead by a blue ribbon. Her long braided copper red hair could be seen hanging down her back below her wimple. He could see why Swegen had been smitten, but…that was no excuse to go raping her; or had it been rape? Even this salt sodden, shrieking wind and thick hooded cloak, couldn't disguise the fact that she was a fine looking woman and the other one wasn't bad looking either, they could be sisters, perhaps they were.

"Shit!" shouted Edwin, almost losing his grip. "Thank the Gods for this rope." He renewed his grip, fingernails torn and bloody, holding on desperately, not wanting to rely completely on the rope. "I'm soaked to the fucking skin and am fucking cold!"

"Ha, ha, ha," laughed Horsa, as the stern of the ship plunged down. "There'll be plenty more where that came from."

"Horsa! You certainly know how to wear out friendships. Look at you. You're enjoying it. You've got a death wish!"

The wind was still whipping across his face partially blinding him as another jarring thud threw Edwin's head forward hard against the very crutche he was trying to hang on to. The rope had loosened. Dazed, he felt the ship at this moment was somehow suspended, as if held up by a giant hand. The next moment it plunged. The bow from where he was standing disappeared only to rise up again. It was as if he were riding a bucking half crazed unbroken horse.

As the dim light of dawn approached the wind lost its ferocity though the storm persisted with heavy rain and mountainous waves, making it almost impossible to bail out the waterlogged ship with any noticeable effect. It was a frustrating and forlorn experience, especially when looking at the wind battered sail and rigging, now flapping in tatters.

"I think I can see land!" shouted a voice, from the bow.

"Ye Gods!" shouted Horsa. "Need help! Steering oar's broken!"

"Where are we captain Horsa!" called Earl Harold. He had taken his boots and stocking off and was splashing towards them through the waterlogged ship.

"I'm not sure, my lord. If I don't fix this steering oar, we'll be done for!"

"What do you need?"

"A leather strap, my lord. Thune! That box you're sitting on. Open it and bring me one of those straps!"

"I've had this happen before," said the Earl. "It shouldn't take too long."

"I'll do the best I can, my lord," replied Horsa, taking hold of the strap. "Thune! Grab hold of my legs and don't let go!"

With no raised sail and nothing to steer by, the ship wallowed in the sæ; pitching and rolling from side to side, taking on more water as the waves cascaded over it.

Thune, with his arms wrapped around Horsa's legs, acting as a counterweight, managed to manoeuver the captain precariously over the side. Thune's legs were stretched out, his feet up against the side preventing him from being pulled overboard.

Edwin admired Horsa. Undaunted by the conditions; his head disappearing and reappearing from beneath the surface as wave after wave broke over him. At a signal of desperately waving arms, Horsa was pulled back on board to continue the repair, all the time shaking the sæ from his hair and laughing.

"Salt has got in my eyes, I can't see a fucking thing. Edwin! It's your turn on the steering oar, just maintain the course while I go forward. And don't break the oar again!"

"Me!" shouted back Edwin, "I didn't break it, it was you!" He untied himself, let go of the crutche and leapt to the side of Horsa. "You broke that fucking oar not me ol' son!"

"Just grab hold of it and don't argue." Horsa moved amidships shouting, "All hands! Raise the sail to half."

"Get bailing!" commanded the Earl.

"There's more water in here than in that there sæ," moaned

Thune, taking off his own sodden boots. "Aah! That's better, now I can flex my toes."

"I don't know why we didn't think of it before," replied Edwin. "Earl Harold took his off a while ago. Not much fun walking about in squelching boots."

"You need help with the steering?" asked Thune.

"Might do. It's heavy going and I don't like the way the ship's rolling. We've taken on too much water, we're likely to topple over if that sail is not lowered to quarter sail."

"I think you're right Ed, I'll get… I think Horsa's read our minds."

With only half the men rowing and the rest bailing, the danger of the vessel turning over had passed.

"Where are we captain?" asked Harold.

"I think we're somewhere off Ponthieu."

"Can you get us as far as the Yser?"

"I doubt it, my lord. The storm has torn the sail to shreds, we're waterlogged and with this raging sæ, it's difficult to bail sufficient water out of her. If we leave the shelter of the coast, we'll be back in rougher sæ and it will be impossible to get past Wissant, that is if we make it that far."

'Come with me."

"Edwin! Stay with the steering oar, I'm going forward with Earl Harold."

Horsa, following Harold, pushed the two hounds aside and stood next to him. He looked down at his stinking feet. "What a mess. Sorry my lord, I've trodden in some dog shit."

"Steward!" shouted the Earl, clean that dog mess up!"

Putting his arm on Horsa's shoulder, urging him a little forward, Harold said, "My steward is young and is no sæfarer. Now to business. Do you recognize this bit of the coast?"

Horsa cleared his eyes of spray and peered at the nearing coastline.

"I think we're approaching the Canche! I had hoped we'd be

further along, my lord."

"Me too. If that's the Canche, we're in trouble. To the east are Eustace's lands. Over there! Look! A couple of lookouts. They must be Eustace's men and he has no love for us. On this side to the west is Ponthieu and I'm not sure where Count Guy's sympathies lie but we'll have to chance it and hope we can do the repairs before Guy's men know we're here."

"Yes, my lord," replied Horsa, signalling to Edwin to steer ahead.

"They must have been watching us since first light."

"There's only one of them now. One other thing, my lord, I meant to tell you yesterday. Soon after we turned east, I'm pretty sure I saw a ship flying the King's pennant, bound for Bosham."

"I saw it too," said Harold. "Once we beach, captain Horsa, get to work double quick, make whatever repairs necessary and then we'll be on our way."

"A little to steorbord, Ed!" shouted Horsa.

"That spot over there!" said Harold pointing.

"I'd better get back and relieve Edwin, my lord."

"Do that!"

Horsa took over the steering again.

"Thanks Ed, the Governor doesn't want us landing over there to the east of the bourne, Count Eustace and his merry men will be waiting for us and let's hope he doesn't tell Guy."

"I know all about Eustace and what happened at Dofra."

"Too right! We Centish folk have long memories," said Thune.

"He'll have his men posted all along that bit of coast, looking out for easy pickings," mused Horsa.

"Hey up lads the Earl's coming back," joked Edwin.

"Just in case Count Guy's men *are* about we'd better be prepared, weapons at hand when we beach and remember, Captain, I want this ship ready and back out to sæ as fast as possible before they get news we're here!"

"Yes, my lord."

"Do you think we're that much safer on this beach?" asked

Edwin.

"I wouldn't bet on it!" returned the Earl, "Count Guy, like his neighbour Eustace, is a plundering swine and as I recall he is a friend of Duke William and that makes him dangerous."

"So Count Guy is that much of a threat?"

"Yes! Both he and his neighbour Eustace. They regard any vessel landing on their beaches without permission as fair game; to rob and hold to ransom."

They watched Earl Harold splash his way amidships to talk to lady Ælfgifu then splash his way back again.

"My God!" he shouted. "It's like wading through a lake!"

Edwin could hear him cursing under his breath.

"That bastard Eustace has always been a pain in the arse. Landing over there would be the end of us."

"Did you say something, my lord," shouted Horsa.

"Nothing, Horsa. I'm praying this ship stays afloat long enough for us to reach this beach ahead. You rowers, put some effort into it!"

Edwin, like everyone else not rowing, continued to bail until he felt the keel touch the beach."

"We can't get any further up this beach my lord, the tide's going out," said Horsa, trying to straighten his back.

"What's wrong with your back?"

"I felt a click when I was putting my shoulder against the sternpost."

"Mmm! You had better rest awhile."

"If I sit down, I won't be able to get up," Horsa replied, standing somewhat stiffly. Wincing in pain he continued, "I've got to be doing something, my lord."

"Alright, then help me organise the men."

Harold strode off towards the prow of the ship, kicking up the sand with his bare feet, Horsa following him at a slow pace. "Move everything out of the ship. With the state of the tide, we should soon be clear of the water. In the meantime, I want lookouts posted."

After careful examination the ship seemed to be intact. No damage could be found as far as Horsa and Thune could see.

A movement beyond the ridge caught Edwin's attention. He nudged Thune.

"Looks like we have company."

"Where?"

"Can't see him now, but he'll be back!"

The vessel, now empty of water, was righted.

"It's too heavy to move," shouted Horsa, "stop what you're doing!" Turning to the Earl he said, "It'll break everybody's back at this rate. We'll have to wait for the incoming tide to refloat her, which shouldn't be too long."

"I agree," said Earl Harold. "I want the women and the dogs on board the moment the stern is afloat."

"Two horsemen beyond the sand dunes, my lord," shouted a lookout.

Edwin moved alongside Earl Harold and pointed out the intruders.

"They're half hidden among that nearby clump of trees."

In the blink of an eye the figures vanished.

"My lord," asked Edwin, "What do we do if there are more of them?"

"Have your weapons ready. In the meantime, we'll maintain a constant watch and hope we can get away in time."

"My men have patched up the sail as best they can," said Horsa. "The storm seems to have passed. Once at sæ, we could make the Yser in half a day."

"Good man," said Earl Harold. "After the women, get everything back on board."

"Shouldn't be too long now, my lord. The tide's turned. The water will soon be lapping against the stern."

"The Yser is only half a day, you say?"

"Well, more like a day with this wind."

"Right captain, enough talking. Let's get this ship in the water."

"You sure we're in Ponthieu?" asked Edwin, lifting the first of the supplies on board.

"Yer, I should know the place by now," replied Horsa, "I've been sailing off this coast and shipping stuff up the Canche to Montreuil for years. Look at this," Horsa said patting his ship with pride. "All along here and the same the other side, solid as a rock. Nothing wrong with the hull at all."

"I know," Edwin nodded, "I've examined it too. Shame about the sail though. Now she's almost ready, all we need to do is wait for the tide to do its work."

"Enough talking Captain!" commanded Earl Harold. "Once the stern's afloat I want all hands to push this ship out!"

"My lads will have their shoulders to it, " replied Horsa.

"What do we do about the sail?" asked Edwin."

"Let's just hope it stays together," laughed Thune. "We can renew it once we're in Flanders."

Horsa in the meantime was keeping his eyes on the incoming tide.

A tap on Edwin's shoulder brought him around to face Horsa who was smiling. The water was now lapping against the stern of the ship.

They put their shoulders to the hull and began pushing at the Earl's command.

Edwin took a momentary rest, stood erect, flexed his muscles and began pushing again at the next command. He could clearly see that the ship had moved about five paces. Another three or four to go and with incoming tide she would be free of the beach and floating.

"Weapons!" shouted Earl Harold. "Steward! Get Lady Ælfgifu and my sister on board quickly!"

"What about the hounds, my lord?"

"Them as well."

"Hey ho, the local militia," grumbled Edwin, reaching for his sword.

"Fuck!" responded Thune.

They took hold of their shields, most of the others grabbing for their battleaxes.

"Shield wall!"

Taking up their positions around and in front of the prow of their ship they faced, what seemed from a distance, to be locals on horse and foot.

"Mmm," said Edwin, nudging Thune. "I think I saw a glint of something. They don't look friendly. What do you think, did they know we were coming?"

"It does make you wonder," replied Thune, spitting on the ground.

The armed locals had moved forward again, stopping just beyond the sand dunes. Making no sound, they looked on as if waiting for the order to attack.

"What are they waiting for?" said Edwin, taking a firmer grip on his sword. "Hold on, they're wearing leathers and chainmail. Now they're donning their helmets. This ain't a rag-bag outfit of locals, Thune, they're trained militia… and if I'm not mistaken, they've got greed written all over them. We could set the Earl's hounds on them, if they weren't so stupid. Throw 'em a bone and they'll be anybody's."

"Pity is, Ed, we only have two of them. Why not let loose his hawk on them as well."

"Piss off, you silly sod! Still a pack of thirty hounds would be fun to watch."

"If we can hold them off a bit longer," said Earl Harold, manoeuvring himself next to Edwin, "the tide will be high enough to refloat our ship, then we can be on our way. How say you Captain."

"Yes my lord," replied Horsa, who had moved between Thune and Edwin. "The stern's already afloat. It won't take much to get her under sail."

"Let's hope that's all they're waiting for. Perhaps they could give us a hand," said Thune, sarcastically.

A few men behind them began to chuckle. The laughter subsided when the militia started to advance. Edwin could feel the Earl's nervousness.

"The stern is definitely afloat, my lord, I can feel the movement even from leaning on the prow," said Edwin.

The militia moved forward again, stopping fifty paces away. Some of their ranks now began to part, letting a horseman, wearing a highly burnished helmet and full body armour, come through. Raising his sword he twisted it to catch the sun's rays. Focusing it, he directed the powerful light at Earl Harold. Edwin, standing next to him, also caught the glare, dipping his head slightly and half shutting his eyes.

"He's a bright spark!" he quipped. "He wants to blind us with his magnificence no doubt, I wish I had my bow, I could easily bring the bastard down."

"That man is Count Guy of Ponthieu and I don't want him to recognize me. Keep calm men, with any luck they will let us go," said Harold.

"Stand your men down and sheath your weapons!" shouted Count Guy.

"We come in peace," replied Harold, breaking ranks and stepping a little forward. His dark grey cloak had its hood up, covering his head, obscuring his features.

"Identify yourselves!"

"We are pilgrims beached by the storm," lied Harold.

"Ahh! That's the Wessex pennant on your masthead, no?"

Edwin heard the Earl swear under his breath.

"Pilgrims from Wessex are you?"

Earl Harold ignored the man's sarcasm.

"We are just pilgrims on our way to Ghent?"

"And I'm the Pope!" replied Count Guy.

Laughter issued from his foot soldiers.

"We find ourselves beached," replied Harold, "God's storm has thrown us here but we have made all necessary repairs and wish to refloat our ship and continue on our way."

"But your sail is in tatters. Your ship is in no fit state to continue."

"God will keep us safe on our journey," replied Harold.

"I know who you are! Show your face and stand your men down. Your pretence is futile."

"We just want to be left in peace and to continue on our journey."

"Your ship won't get you far in this weather."

"God will protect us."

"Look man! I want to be of assistance. My men will aid yours to get the ship refloated."

"I thank you, my lord, but we have made all necessary repairs. The storm has abated and we shall be on our way with the incoming tide."

"Archers! Take aim," commanded Count Guy.

"We mean you no harm!" shouted Earl Harold.

"Then identify yourself!" retorted the Count.

Earl Harold stepped back behind the shield wall formation.

"Men! I can't play with the Count any longer, he's not to be fooled and I don't want a bloodbath. We are too few and they are too many. I can see more men joining them." He looked to Edwin for agreement.

"My lord, we would need our entire force to refloat this ship. That would mean leaving our backs exposed with little or no protection from attack."

"Count Guy!" shouted Earl Harold. "Stand your men down and come forward so we can speak terms!"

The Count's men lowered their bows as Guy dismounted and strode forward half way, stopped and dug his sword in the sand before him.

"Wish me luck men," whispered Harold walking forward, his head now uncovered, to meet Count Guy.

Guy had a triumphant smile on his face.

"How long could you have kept up this pretence?"

Harold scratched his forehead and thought for a moment.

"Our shield wall is very effective and we would have taken out a good number of your men."

"Admit to me now, that you are Earl Harold of Wessex."

"Of course I am. We came in peace, forced to beach here to make repairs before continuing our journey."

"I cannot let you go that easily."

"And why not?"

"I wish you to accompany me to Montreuil and there I will entertain you and… and the ladies I see you with."

"Mmm… nothing escapes you, my dear Count. One is Lady Ælfgifu of Leofminstre who wishes to be re-united with her son and is under my protection."

"And the other woman?"

"My younger sister, her name is also Ælfgifu."

"Ah" replied the Count, with raised eyebrows.

"You seem surprised Count."

He shook his head. "No, I suppose your sister is Lady Ælfgifu's companion?"

"Yes."

"Well, I can promise, no harm will come to any of you, if you agree to my terms."

"Permit me to introduce Lady Ælfgifu and… my sister," said Harold formally, bringing them forward.

"Ladies, allow me the honour of entertaining you and Earl Harold until such time as your ship is sæworthy. After which you may continue your journey."

"I appreciate your assistance Count, but we must be on our way as soon as possible," insisted Harold.

"What can be more important my lord Harold, than the blossoming of new friendships? Did you know I knew your father?"

"Yes, I believe so. He travelled a lot."

"He was a forceful man," replied the Count.

"He knew what he wanted. There were no sides to him, he was

straightforward in all his dealings."

"Look!" said the Count, pointing at Harold's ship. "I insist my men help yours and you will have a new sail when we reach Montreuil."

"I regret I must still refuse. My mission is an urgent one. The incoming tide is already partially floating my ship and once it's refloated, we will be able to continue on our way without causing you any more inconvenience."

"My lord Harold! It is no inconvenience! Not at all but I cannot let you leave." The Count said, adamantly. "Not just yet. You will attend me at Montreuil."

Harold looked at the growing number of the count's ranks.

'Even if we make a stand,' he thought, 'and fight it out using the ship's hull as a defensive barrier, with just twenty three men we would be overrun and cut down before we have any chance of launching the ship. It would be suicide and I have to think of the safety of Lady Ælfgifu and my sister. However I must push him one last time.'

"I am sorry my dear Count, I must refuse, my place is with my men."

There was a pause. Harold met Guy's eyes. 'There's something in his eyes, something he's not telling me,' he thought.

"Lord Harold, I applaud your sentiments towards your men but you do offend me! My only thought is to help you and for you, in turn, to accept my offer of friendship. I await your reply," said Count Guy.

Harold turned and rejoined his men.

Throwing off his cloak, he said, "We have no choice but to accept this over-stuffed wool merchant's offer." He looked at Edwin, "What do *you* make of him?"

"I'm not sure, my lord. I didn't hear the conversation. It's difficult to judge but I think it's a trap. I believe he's trying to separate you from us!"

"I know! We have two choices; make a stand and fight or accept his terms, God help us!" Earl Harold looked around at his men.

Horsa came forward, "The men are willing to stand and make a fight of it but if you accept his terms they will think nothing less of you, my lord."

Count Guy, making a slight bow towards Lady Ælfgifu and Harold's sister, returned his attention to the Earl. "Do you accept my terms of friendship?"

Earl Harold glanced at the ladies who were standing next to him.

"Yes, we accept your friendship and… the terms for allowing us to continue on our journey by tomorrow," he replied.

"Good! I am pleased. I'll leave what men I can spare. Your ship and its crew will be ready for you at Montreuil."

He gave, as though it had been pre-arranged, a signal. Twelve heavily armed men dismounted and stepped forward to join the ship's crew.

"My dear Count, as well as Lady Ælfgifu and my sister, I will also bring along two stewards."

"*Two* stewards, surely just the one is normal."

"No, I always have two," replied Harold.

Guy thought for a moment, "No matter then, two it is."

Harold beckoned Edwin and Thune to join them.

"Now, Lord Harold, take these horses and let us leave your crew and my people to do their work. Follow me!"

Harold drew along-side the Count.

"I am keeping you to your word! Tomorrow we continue on our journey."

"Of course, of course!" Guy replied, somewhat flustered. "Arrangements will be made for your stay and for your journey tomorrow."

Harold took a mental note of their armed escort. He felt vulnerable being separated from his men. The thought of being held hostage was paramount in his mind. Count Guy noted his discomfort.

"My lord, I can see by the worried expression on your face, that you do not believe me. If that is so, you offend me. I only wish to be of service to you after your disastrous and hard sæ journey. You and your men must be tired and the two ladies too no doubt. As I said, it will be my pleasure and *honour* to entertain you. Once your sail is renewed, you will be in Flanders in no time at all. There you have it." Guy raised his hands, palms upwards, as if to open his heart and beg forgiveness.

"Excuse me Count, I didn't say anything about sailing to Flanders, just Ghent. Lady Ælfgifu wishes to consult the Bishop of St Braco!"

"Oh! My apologies. I had thought, where else would you be going, but to the court of your father's old friend and your brother Tostig's father-in-law, Count Baldwin… but these things are unimportant."

"True, Lady Ælfgifu may wish to consult with Count Baldwin to help her be reunited with her son."

"And you with *your* young brother," replied the Count.

"I am more concerned with Lady Ælfgifu and her son."

"Yes, of course! Absolutely! Let's go!" shouted the Count, smiling.

"We stay until tomorrow," repeated Harold.

He dropped back to the side of Lady Ælfgifu and his sister. Leaning close, he whispered, "He's a crafty, lying swine, I don't trust him."

"Harold, we should never have journeyed, least of all to here," said his sister, nervously.

Harold didn't reply but gripped his reins ever tighter.

Lady Ælfgifu gave him a dark look.

"We must hope and pray he is not what you suspect he is. That he is a truly, honourable man."

# CHAPTER XIV

### - Upper Barnstæd –

"The King's messenger is here, my lady," announced Ælffled, he's asking for the master." Ælffled, a local girl, had been taken on to help around house while Egbert and his wife were away.

"Bring him in then, don't let him stand outside in the rain."

"He's already the hall, drying himself by the fire. He's left a trail of water everywhere and I have only just cleaned the floor."

"I wouldn't worry about it, girl. There's going to be a lot of mess this morning." Gwynedd followed her out of the kitchen and into the hall.

"Messenger! What do you want with my husband?" she said drying her hands on her smock.

The young man turned around and faced Gwynedd. He was bare headed and looked so drenched from the rain he resembled a drowned rat, even down to his sodden shoes. His long, tangled fair hair, now darkened with water, hung down in rivulets over his pale, immature, stubbly face, making him a pitiable sight.

"Have you just ridden from Lunden?" she asked.

"Yes, my lady."

"What do you want of my husband?"

"The King com-m-mmanded me, m-my lady, to ride here as r-rapidly as p-possible to demand, Edwin, Th- th –thegn of Upper B-Barnstæd appear at court by the m-morrow," stuttered the messenger, remembering the King's exact words.

"The King demands does he? Well, young… what is your name?"

"R-r-ricbert m-my lady."

"Well then Ricbert…" Gwynedd looked closer and smiled inwardly. He was standing in a pool of water and shivering. "Do you normally suffer from chattering teeth when you speak to a lady?"

"N,n,n,no m,my lady."

"My husband, for your information is not here. He has business with Earl Harold at Bosham. But more importantly, you're in need of dry clothes. I advise you to change them otherwise you will die of fever. Come with me!" She led him to Edric's room and found some suitable clothes. "Catch hold of these and change in that room, then give Ælffled your wet things."

Ælffled, took his wet clothes and hung them in front of the hall fire to dry.

He nervously walked back into the hall and stood by the fire.

"W,what am I t,to do now?"

"If I were you, I would wait for your clothes to dry! In the meantime, amuse yourself. I'll be back shortly,"

Gwynedd went back to the kitchen to finish making a potion. Having strained a herb mixture through a cloth, two or three times, carefully making sure it was clear, she bottled it for a local fisherman who was suffering from aching knee joints.

"Well, it might give him some relief," she said to herself, "though Alric should stop wading in cold water and let his son do more of the work."

She had built up a large circle of patients and, in agreement with the local priest, her home had become a regular meeting place for the village people.

Gwynedd could sense one of her sons standing behind her.

"Edric what are you looking for"

"How did you know it was me?"

"Because I have eyes in the back of my head. What do you want?"

"Something to eat. By the way who's that odd looking creature in the hall, wearing my clothes?"

"The King's messenger," she replied, in a hushed voice. "He

wants to know where your father is. I think he's been sent here to snoop around. Take him to one of the out-buildings and find out what you can, but be careful he may not be as dumb as he looks. If it's the oat cakes you're after, they're over there."

Edric began munching on one of the cakes, putting another four in his pouch.

When she had tidied the kitchen and put her precious herbs away, Gwynedd and Edric returned to the hall.

"Tell me what does the King really want with my husband?"

"I don't know, my lady."

"Surely you must know. The King's most trusted Earl, commands my husband to join him at Bosham and the King doesn't know about it? This is very odd."

"My lady," interrupted Ælffled, "the young man's clothes are dry."

Gwynedd watched Ricbert leave the hall to dress. 'What is the King so nervous about,' she thought, 'well my boys will soon loosen this messenger's tongue.'

"That rain sounds like a waterfall" joked Wulfnoth, raising the exercise log for the twelfth time before putting it back into its rest. "Thanks for the cake Ed…and you suffered all that rain for me?"

Edwin leant against the barn door post and swallowed the last bit of his cake.

"You're right. The things I do for you in this pissing weather!" He craned his neck and looked outside.

"It looks to be setting in for the day. Hey up Wulf, the royal spy is about to rejoin us."

"Do you think he *is* a spy?" said Wulfnoth, munching on another cake.

"Probably," replied Edric. "The King must have known about Earl Harold's letter to Father and sent this squirt to find out what was in it. Here he is again, act normal."

"What's normal… shall I hang him up by his balls from the

rafters?"

"No! Kiss him and wash his arse. We'll do a mulberry on him, that should loosen his tongue."

Wulfnoth raised the log out of its cradle again and carried on with his exercises.

"Sorry about that," said Ricbert, looking at Wulfnoth, "I was caught short. It must be this cold, wet weather,"

"Mmm…" replied Edric, trying not to laugh."

"Do you know why your father has gone to Bosham?"

"I think he's gone fishing with Earl Harold," said Wulfnoth, who had just completed another twelve lifts before putting the log back into its cradle. He began brushing the cake crumbs from his chest.

'I've never seen exercises done like that before. How many times can you lift that log?"

"On a hot dry day, a hundred and fifty but on a wet day like this, only twenty cos the logs are heavier with damp," replied Wulfnoth, grinning.

Ricbert took off his leather jerkin.

"Could I have a go?"

Wulfnoth arched his back and sprang onto his feet.

"Lay down there as I did."

"Then all I have to do is just lift this log out of its cradle and raise it up and down?"

"Mmm," murmured Wulfnoth.

"That sounds easy," said Ricbert, feeling the log in its rest.

Edric had to go outside in the rain for laughing. Ricbert strained his thin arms which shook as he tried to lift the log out of its cradle, but couldn't.

"Don't you do any training at all?" asked Wulfnoth, incredulously.

"None, except for riding and hunting."

"So you couldn't hold a battle sword, shield or a skeggox?"

Ricbert looked embarrassed.

"Not in battle."

He struggled to his feet, brushed the straw off his tunic and put his jerkin back on.

"I lost my father some years ago and was brought up by my mother who is the Queen's maid. My mother forbad me from taking up arms and did her best to educate me for royal service."

"Doing what exactly," asked Edric, returning into the barn.

"Working with the exchequer."

"You mean you're a pen pusher and a future tax collector, instead of becoming a warrior?"

"I've never trained in anything other than learning to write and mathematics."

"We can write, so do many of us. But mathematics, that's something else. Are you any good at carpentry or stone carving?" asked Wulfnoth.

"No, but I'm good at drawing landscapes and buildings."

"There you see, Wulf. Just because he's got no muscles and can't do much with his hands, doesn't mean he couldn't draw up plans for buildings, like those Northman engineers you see prancing around at construction sites carrying rolls of parchment, rulers and those long pointed compasses; telling everybody else what to do but can't do it themselves."

"I definitely think you're right, Ed. Our friend here needs a change of occupation. With his knowledge he should approach one of the King's engineers."

Wulfnoth turned towards Ricbert, "Then your future would soar like an eagle."

"Do you think so?"

"I know it!" replied Wulfnoth.

"The fact is," said Ricbert hesitantly, in a hushed voice, 'Do you promise not to tell anybody else?"

"We will give you a housecarl's honour," returned Wulfnoth and Edric, holding their right hands to their chests. "We won't tell a living soul."

"Well, the King is angry," whispered Ricbert, licking his lips, all the while glancing at the open door. "He knows that Earl Harold has taken his sister and Lady Ælgifu and, instead of sailing to meet Duke William, has sailed somewhere else, probably over to the east, towards Flanders."

"Nooo! I don't believe it! Do you, Ed? And you were trying to find out if we knew where they were sailing to!"

Ricbert nodded.

"You seem a nice person Ric, you don't mind me calling you Ric do you?"

"No, not at all."

"The thing is Ric, we wish we could give you more information but we have no more idea than you," said Wulfnoth, putting his arm around him like a big brother. "The fact is, we didn't even know he was going sailing, just that he had to be in Bosham. Look! The rain has stopped. You had better get back to Lunden and the King before it begins to get dark."

"I've really enjoyed myself here with you and I will think seriously about what you advise me to do, thank you both so much. We must meet again."

They watched Ricbert mount up and ride out of the village.

"A milksop. Father was right. The King is surrounding himself with creatures like him."

"He seemed harmless enough but what is it with the King and Duke William?" queried Edric.

Wulfnoth raised his eyebrows, "You don't want to go there. It'll be like looking up a horses arse."

### - Fortress, Montreuil, Ponthieu -
Fortress, Montreuil, Picardy, France

To Edwin, this great hall was quite small considering the height of the building, which was made of stone. From his brief look on his approach to the citadel he had estimated four floors in total. Yet it did have an overawing effect on him, possibly because he had never been into or seen such a large stone building before, except for West Minster, which still wasn't finished.

He sat quietly in thought, attentive in case he heard anything resembling his own language.

'If the imported wool trade is as important as it is, I should be able to find someone who speaks Englisc.' He felt alone and vulnerable even with Thune by his side; almost naked without his sword. Thankfully he had been able to hide his seax under his jerkin. He grinned, 'They weren't very professional at all, didn't give me a thorough search. But I do want my sword, my ol' 'Head Biter' back!'

He continued to survey the hall and noticed the Count hadn't stopped talking to Earl Harold's sister and Lady Ælfgifu. 'He is nervous. He keeps glancing towards the main entrance. What's he waiting for. Something's afoot, I know it!'

The log fire in the centre of the floor was giving off a great deal of smoke and the fumes were making Edwin's eyes water. He glanced at Thune. The same thing was happening to him and everyone else nearby.

"The Count is certainly trying his best to entertain us. Or is he trying to blind us?"

"We're being lulled, mate," replied Thune.

Apart from this stone prison of a place, Edwin thought he could be almost anywhere in his own country; the familiar hounds fed from scraps thrown from the tables. 'Come to think of it, I wonder where the Earl's hounds and hawk are. Still on the ship I suppose.'

Count Guy's hounds were of different breed. Preferring the warmth of the fire, they were obviously not affected by the fumes and stayed sprawled on the tiled floor around it.

"He's serving plenty of pork meat and wine, especially the wine. Here's somebody with another platter of meat. I wouldn't have minded having another helping but the one I had was over cooked. What do you say?" he asked Thune, who was being unusually silent and thoughtful.

"A bit like biting into soft wood, and there's no gravy," he said at last.

Edwin beckoned a steward over, dug around and found some moist tender pieces and a slice of crackling.

"Don't you want any more, Thune?"

"No. Too much on my mind to relax."

"Well, these pieces shows promise." He dug his knife into a slice and flicked it into his mouth. "Miracles will never cease," he said, knifing another piece. "Now this is good and very tasty."

"Is food all you think about, Ed?"

"Not one 'bite' of it, my ol' chum. I'm trying to look as if I'm enjoying myself." He shook his head, refusing a second cup of wine. "There's too much of that stuff being served. I'm certain the Count's trying to get us all pissed."

"Hey, look Ed, Horsa's just arrived." Edwin stood up, waved and beckoned for his friend to come over.

"What a place this is. I was escorted here by guards. They took my skeggy and that's not nice," whispered Horsa.

"They took our weapons too. What do you think; a formidable place isn't it?" said Edwin. "Even got a stone wall all around the town and another one around this place. It's a stone prison the like of which I haven't seen in Englaland."

"You're right. I've been to the local port and seen it from the outside loads of times, shipping wool and stuff," whispered Horsa, "but I've never been up here and into this place before." Leaning closer he continued, "How do we get out in a hurry, if you see what I mean?"

"I don't know. I would think it would be difficult but not impossible. Stay here and talk to Thune. I'm going for a walk."

"Before you go, let me try and find the buyer I usually do business with, he might be here."

"Do you think he could get us out of this place?"

"I don't know," replied Horsa, "It's worth a try. Let's face it, he's one of the wealthiest men around here." Leaning closer to Edwin and

Thune, he whispered, "He could probably buy out the Count several times over."

"I tell you what," said Thune, "there's a small door down there, at the end of the hall, could be a way out."

"I'll go and have a look." Edwin slowly looked around and without letting his eyes settle on any particular area, casually moved away and walked down to the end of the hall to the partially hidden, curtain covered, doorway.

'Shit! It's locked.'

"Can I help you?" said a guard, in broken Englisc, taking the curtain out of Edwin's hand and adjusting it back into position.

'They do speak our language,' he thought.

"I'm feeling a bit off colour. I think it's the smoke and fumes from the fire and I need to find some fresh air."

"You won't find any in there. That's a private apartment. You'd better try that door over there, to the left of the high table, then take the stairs up to the roof gallery."

'This is nice. A cool breeze and a tremendous view of the town and river.' Edwin could see their ship. They were already working on the sail. That was a good sign. He leaned out further from one of the stone embrasures and looked towards the west, his eyes following the bourne meandering like a snake towards the coast. He wondered what was happening at home. Thoughts of his wife and two boys were always on his mind. 'They're not boys now,' he said to himself. 'Grown men and as fit as I was at their age. Gwynedd has every right to be fearful. They are battle ready.' He thought about what he would do, when he returned home. 'Only the god's know when that will be. The Count did say, he would let us go on our way by tomorrow. Let's hope he's a man of honour and keeps his word. But I don't trust the bastard.' From gazing at the distance his attention was taken by a movement nearing the castle. "Hello! I wonder who that is?" he said under his breath. "A troop of knights on horse. I wonder who's leading them. Must get down to the hall and warn the Earl, although what use that would be is anybody's guess. I'll tell him anyway."

Rushing back, Edwin gained the hall before the visitors, and approached Earl Harold.

"My lord, may I have a word in your ear?"

"What is it?" replied the Earl, recognising the urgency in Edwin's voice.

"I've been up on the roof gallery," whispered Edwin, "and saw a troop of armed knights approaching. Thought I had better tell you," he added, looking about and around him. "Not that we can do much about it, being under lock and key, unarmed and somewhat outnumbered."

Above the din Edwin heard the unmistakable sound of marching feet coming from the main entrance to the hall. An over large balding man appeared. He abruptly signalled for his troop to halt. Edwin had seen Eustace before and thought he looked old for his forty odd years. His few remaining wisps of greying hair had fallen forward and down over his left eye. Others might think he looked comical but Edwin knew it belied his real character.

"My dear Count," greeted the newly arrived guest.

"My God! It's that bastard, Eustace of Boulogne,' Earl Harold hissed.

"Eustace! Good to see you," said Count Guy. "Let me introduce to you, my guests, Earl Harold of Wessex, his sister Ælfgifu and Lady Ælfgifu of Leofminstre."

Edwin had remained standing against the wall close to Earl Harold. The visitor ignored him as if he were just a piece of decorative drapery.

"Ladies, Earl Harold, I think I've…err yes! Your father and I go back a long way," Eustace said. He leaned towards Count Guy, "Guy, a word with you in private!"

They left the hall, giving Edwin enough time to return to his seat, re-entering moments later with a troop of Guy's heavily armed guards, most of whom lined up around the hall especially around the exits. Count Guy looked embarrassed, almost imploringly towards Harold, while Eustace stood himself a distance away and, it seemed to Edwin, was smirking. Eustace and the Count turned away and left the hall again as four of count's heavily armed guards took hold of Earl Harold, his sister and Lady Ælfgifu and led them out of the hall. A further two guards took Edwin, Thune and Horsa, forcing them also out of the building. Horsa was led away to his ship while Edwin and Thune joined the Earl and the two ladies in another waiting ship.

Edwin reached for his sword but grasped only its empty sheath. There was nothing he could do but join the others and sit in the bow.

"Where are they taking us, my lord," he whispered.

"I think I heard one of the guards mention, Belrem."

"Where's that?"

He shook his head, "We'll soon find out," he replied.

In the fading evening light, Edwin watched helplessly as the vessel was eased from its moorings. The oarsmen struck the water, sending the ship further along the Canche.

"My lord," he whispered, "I have my seax hidden in my jerkin."

The Earl shook his head.

"We'll play it out, see what happens because I have an inkling of Count Guy's plans."

### - Chateau Belrem, Ponthieau -
Beaurain Castle, Picardy, France

After a short time they came to a pier, where they disembarked. They were led in the semi-darkness along a winding track, to a stone twin towered, fortified geathouse.

Their captors shouted to a guard above to open the geat. After passing through the arched entrance they stopped. Before them was a large courtyard which looked, to Edwin, like an assembly area with a half dozen huts close to the perimeter wall. At the far side was a huge mound which they called a motte, on top of which stood a timbered tower, similar to the ones Edwin had seen in Wealh built by King Edward's Northman friends.

Edwin had expected to see both Lady Ælfgifu and the Earl's sister crying, or even distraught, but there were no tears, none of it.

'They're tougher than I thought,' he mused.

Immediately they had entered the tower, both the women began to organize the room which the five of them were now going to share. The earthen floor was covered in straw, the furniture was primitive; the five beds seemed comfortable with their fur covers, a table, eight chairs, a barrel presumably full of water, a large bowl for washing and at the far side, to the right of the door, a curtained area for a privy.

'Why eight chairs?' Edwin thought.

After a short time the door opened and a bundle was thrown inside containing their boots, shoes, socks and a pile of heavy cloaks, three of which were familiar, all dried and cleaned.

"I thought for a moment they'd thrown in our weapons," said Edwin, trying to break the silence.

Ignoring Edwin's quip, Earl Harold began prowling about the room. Then after a while, he sat at the table, seemingly lost in thought, gazing down at the table top as if he were examining the grain in the wood. He lifted his head and faced everyone in the room.

"I'm sorry, I am very sorry I've brought us to this but there was nothing else I could have done. After having opened and read the King's document, intended for Duke William, of which you know the contents, I had no alternative but to go to Count Baldwin of Flanders, Duke William's father-in-law. And now here we are, having not made any threat to anyone, nor to any country, at the mercy of this two-timing bastard, Count Guy,"

"My lord, I think Eustace is to blame for our present situation. He obviously has some sort of hold over Guy."

"I agree. Because of it, whatever it is, we are now here in this tower and Guy will, no doubt, either try to ransom me or inform his friend, Duke William and we'll be in the same bloody hole as we would have been had we sailed directly to Rouen. I dare say the King has already surmised my intentions." He focused his eyes on Edwin. "You have a calculating look on your face, Edwin, what's on your mind?"

Edwin, knowing what he knew so far, felt their lives were not at risk and was assessing the possibility of their escape. He was about to speak, then hunched his shoulders and decided otherwise.

"Come on man! It's what I brought you here for, to see beyond… these timbered walls!"

"Harold! It's not fair of you, to tangle this man in our politics," broke in his sister, who had hardly said a word since their arrival.

"Edwin can speak for himself," Harold said, pointing his finger at him. "He is the only one, out of all our lordly noblemen including the bishops, I can truly trust. Go on Edwin."

'It's a pity we couldn't have sailed from Dofras,' Edwin thought, 'but we didn't and it might have made a difference. We might have missed the storm but our destination would have been obvious.'

"My lord," he said at last, "I agree. Guy will try to ransom you because you are too valuable to kill. He needs you alive! Your high station has kept us all from being killed, at least so far. The question is, for how long?"

"Guy promised to release the crew and give the ship a new sail into the bargain."

"Having reneged on his promise to you, how can you possibly trust him now, my lord?"

"I did trust him until Eustace arrived." The Earl moved over to where the women were sitting. "Best to put a brave face on it and see what happens, tomorrow."

They agreed and without undressing, retired for the night, falling asleep almost immediately.

Harold, making sure they were properly covered, told Edwin and Thune to get some sleep too.

Edwin couldn't sleep, his arms and hands seeming always to be in the way, not matter how he lay. The more he tried to sleep, the more his mind raced, turning the past day's events over and over in his head, devising any and all kinds of permutations for escape. He did not fear for his own life but for that of the Earl, his sister and Lady Ælfgifu. Whatever could have gone wrong with this trip had, by the boatload. He decided to get up and sit at the table. He gazed into the flame of the oil lamp hoping for some inspiration. A movement across the room, caught his eye, it was Earl Harold who quietly came over to join him.

"You too?" he whispered.

Edwin nodded.

"There's nothing we can do but play for time."

"So what did Count Eustace want?" said Edwin searching Harold's face for some logical explanation.

"Making trouble, that's for sure. Convinced Guy to ransom me off to Duke William. Eustace has never got over, what happened at Dofras."

"How do you know?"

"It's the only thing that makes any sense. To lock us up here."

"Then, how long do you think Guy will hold us here?"

Harold tapped his foot, rocking backwards and forwards. At last he whispered, "Two or three days, difficult to tell."

"You mean, the time it takes for messengers to inform whoever?"

"That's about it," replied the Earl.

"There's something else that has been bothering me, in fact for the past seven years, my lord."

"And that is?" responded the Earl, leaning closer.

"What happened to Edward the Ætheling?"

"As I've told you, he was poisoned," Harold replied, leaning back in his chair and raising his hands. "No more, no less."

"But who. Who was behind it... Duke William?"

Harold sat thoughtfully in the dim light for quite some time. "Why do you want to know?"

"Because... it has been on my mind. If he were alive today, it would make Duke William's claim baseless."

"You're well informed for a country Thegn."

Edwin leaned close to him and whispered, "I have heard all the rumours but I also happen to have heard Prince Edward, as he was then, making a promise to the young Duke William, back in forty-three, that he would be heir to the Englisc throne."

"How so?"

"I and others, including Bishop Ælfwine were sent to Rouen with King Harthacnut's warrant summoning Edward to his court as heir. I happened to be listening at the door. That's when I heard his pledge."

"Does anyone else know of this?"

Edwin knew the answer was yes, two of them had heard the pledge but he hadn't seen his friend Wilfred for twenty-three years and assumed he was dead, although it was dangerous to assume anything. Nevertheless he answered. "No, my lord."

Harold shook his head. "You must not get involved or speak of this pledge to anyone." He looked down at the open palms of his hands, spread out on the table.

"The Witan, it was the Witan that discovered that Edmund's son Edward was still alive.... no wonder they called Edmund, 'Ironside', he had been a brave King. Brave as a lion by all accounts, as opposed to his father, Æthelred. Anyway, his son, Edward the Ætheling, was alive and well in Hungary. I made two attempts to bring him back to Englaland. On the second attempt, I was successful. We docked at Dofras on the seventeenth of April. When we arrived in Lunden, our gracious King, refused to meet him or to have him and his three children at court. Two days later Edward, this healthy, forthright forty-one year old heir to the Englisc throne, was dead!"

"Who could have done it?"

"You tell me!"

Edwin looked at Harold and whispered, "The King?"

"He tried to blame the murder on me."

"Blame you, my lord? After bringing the Ætheling and his family all the way back from Hungary? That doesn't make sense."

"He had tried to blame his brother's death on my father! Why not blame me for Edward's death. After all, I am a Godwinson."

There was an owl outside hooting to its mate, it broke the Earl's sombre mood.

"If only I was as free as that owl. Its only worries are finding a mate and the next meal of mice or whatever."

"What was this Edward like?"

"He was rugged and strong, would have made a fine King. His seven year-old son, Edgar, had to suffer two bossy sisters, especially the eldest, Margaret. Poor youngster, I didn't envy him."

The door opened letting a bright shaft of sunlight into the cramped and somewhat stuffy room.

An armed knight with a hairless, ruddy face stepped inside, looking around as if expecting to be attacked.

"My lord, the Count Guy wants you all back at Montreuil, so bring your possessions."

"As you can see," answered Earl Harold, "we have none. They were taken from us for safe keeping."

"Come my lord!" ordered the soldier. "The Count is waiting."

'He's held us for two nights surely he can wait a little longer,' thought Edwin, gathering his clothes.

"How about you Thune, are you ready? We're on our way back to Montreuil."

Thune nodded, his eyes looking heavy with sleep.

### - A ride west -

Now, feeling somewhat less like prisoners, Edwin and the others, had departed the fortress of Montreuil well fed, watered and rested. Had Count Guy had an epiphany? Edwin thought otherwise and was convinced Guy wanted to impress Duke William in some way but still the very thought of such a ruse made him smile. It certainly didn't blind Earl Harold to Count Guy's antics; bringing them back to Montreuil to be entertained, each given a splendid cloak and the return of their weapons. Guy had also given them back their boots, cleaned and waxed, together with their stockings washed and dried.

Up ahead, riding with dignity, was Earl Harold, with his hawk and his two hounds, which had been returned to him, running freely at his side.

Edwin nudged Thune who was riding next to him and whispered, "What's with the new gear?"

"I don't particularly care, Ed. I'm armed, warm, had a good time last night and I'm wearing clean stuff. My worry is, if we end up as Duke William's prisoners, as I suspect we will, how are we going to get out alive?"

"Good question."

"Anyway, where are we making for, exactly?"

"A place called Eu," replied Edwin.

"You're late!" said Duke William in a deep guttural voice.

"It's before mid-day as arranged my dear Duke."

"Don't play with me Count Guy, it's late and you know it. Here is your money," he shouted, throwing a bag to one of the Count's men.

'So we're only worth a bag of coins,' thought Earl Harold, 'I hope it was gold, if not, Guy, you bastard, you're easily bought. No wonder he had a conscience back at Montreuil. Amazingly he kept his mouth shut.'

"Earl Harold, I hope you are well and your sister and Lady Ælfgivu?"

"My name is pronounced Ælgi*fu*, but thank you I am well my lord," she replied.

Edwin could see the Duke was annoyed at being corrected.

"We'll waste no more time, if we are to get to Rouen before nightfall. Come!"

As they left Eu and the bourne they call the Bresle, more of the Duke's mounted troops, who had been hidden out of sight behind a mill, joined them.

Edwin watched Duke William in animated conversation with Earl Harold. He had seen and heard all he needed. It had been twenty-three years since he had last seen the Duke. In that time he had grown from being a warm and dedicated youth into a bully of a man; insulting those whom he thought were not his equal. He also saw a darkness in him. Seldom did he fear anyone. But this Duke he did.

At a signal they started to gallop at a good pace.

"How far is it to Rouen?" said Edwin, to the rider next to him. The man returned a puzzled look, indicating he didn't speak Englisc.

# CHAPTER XV

*May, 1064*

### - Rouen, Northmandig -
Rouen, Normandy

On entering Rouen's fortified, east geat, Edwin drew back so that he was abreast of Thune. They rode along a partially cobbled roadway towards the stone citadel. He had never seen such crowds in a city before. What also struck Edwin was the contrast between the tranquil countryside, immediately outside the geat, and the frenzied atmosphere inside the city. Hundreds of people were milling around; peddlers, their stalls piled high with goods of every conceivable type, dogs running underneath, between the legs of their horses.

"Before we leave here, Ed, I wouldn't mind buying… Good God! What's that smell?"

"Smells like last month's shit to me… put a rag over yer nose."

Having passed the smell, they saw the crowds had now thinned out and soon they were passing through the geat of the citadel.

"Thune," Edwin whispered, "you can keep Rouen, give me Lunden any day. It has certainly changed since I was here last. I hardly recognise the place."

Lying back on his bed, Edwin watched Thune carefully and painstakingly sharpen the double-edged blade of his sword with a small stone. It was the familiar, almost tuneful rasping sound that he knew so well, especially before a battle. He moved his gaze to the ceiling.

"I wonder what's in store for us tomorrow?"

Thune leaned over, shook his head and whispered, "How would I know? This gemæd lot, with religion stuffed up their arses; anything can happen."

"Well, it can't get any worse than what's happened to us over the past few days, or can it?"

Edwin remembered the rumpus in Duke William's great hall the previous night.

Everyone had been seated for the evening meal, except for Lady Ælfgifu who was late in arriving. She had been given permission to see her son Hakon. Emerging from an entrance, behind the high table accompanied by him, she was set upon by the Archbishop of Rouen's clerk.

"What right have you," he began shouting and waving his finger at her, "to come here, claiming your son. A disgraced and fallen Abbess of the Church of Christ, sunk in the abyss of fornication with the known lecher, Earl Swegen Godwinson, a person of low moral character, who was declared 'Nithing' by his peers. Now you walk in here, into my Lord Duke's house, calling yourself a Lady!......" Stepping forward he had slapped her hard across the face. "Whore!" he had shouted, "Whore!" Edwin had been stunned, he couldn't believe, what he was seeing or hearing.

"Thune," he said.

"Mmm."

"When that clerk slapped lady Ælfgifu across the face and kept calling her a whore, her son seemed to be rooted to the floor. He didn't defend her or say a word. How old is he, eighteen?"

"I don't care how old he is. He was probably in shock as we all were," replied Thune.

"If it happened to my mother, I would have shut him up immediately and kicked him in the bollocks, if he had any!"

"Maybe he was too scared of what might happen to him and his mother, Ed."

"It has to be said though, once Hakon did move he bundled that weasel of a clerk outside rapidly, no messing," Edwin, puffing up his makeshift pillow, changed his position, his arms folded behind his head. "That weasel, was about to give her another slap, did you see that?"

"Yes, I did," replied Thune.

"Well, from where we were seated across the hall, it looked as if the Earl was about to completely lose it, almost overturning the table from the dais. But what puzzles me, considering the Duke has us in the palm of his hand is why was he so apologetic to Earl Harold and Lady Ælfgifu. I couldn't believe it. It looked as if Duke William was grief stricken. Didn't that seem odd to you?"

"Yes, I've been laying here puzzling over it," replied Thune.

"Me too."

Thune turned on his side and faced Edwin.

"All I know is, we're here in Rouen and can't leave until Duky-boy allows us to. So what is his game? Not knowing pisses me off!"

"Same here but we're still alive and living well. I don't think you and I are in any danger but here in Northmandig, they do have their religious lunatics," laughed Edwin. "Whipping themselves, I hear, for getting a hard on. I suppose that story about Lady Ælfgifu, being an Abbess, jumping into bed with her old boyfriend Swegen, must have pissed these religious nuts off. Either because they can't get any, or they remember with embarrassment, what the Duke's father got up to with a local tart. Up skirts and at her and …out pops our present Duky-boy. They're a gemæd, insane bunch of sanctimonious sods, it's a wonder they have any pleasure in life."

### A little excitement in Brittany

"Wake up! Wake up!"

Edwin looked over at Thune. They stared at each other through bleary eyes.

"What now, it's not even sun up?" said Thune.

"Dress for battle," shouted the guard in bad Englisc.

"Your Earl wants you with him. We go and fight!"

"I'm all for that. How about you, Thune?" Edwin swung his legs out of the bed.

"It's about time we severed a few arms and legs," replied Thune, with a grin.

"Where are we going and who are supposed to be fighting?" enquired Edwin.

"Dol, to fight The Duke's enemy."

"And he is?"

"Duke Conan of Brittany."

Edwin and Thune looked at each other and shrugged.

"Never heard of him," said Edwin who thought, 'Any enemy of the Duke is a friend of ours. Shame we've got to fight him.'

After dressing and buckling up his sword belt, Edwin picked out a frayed ended twig from his pouch and cleaned his teeth, rinsed his mouth with water and spat it out, after which he cleaned his ears. All the while the Northman guard looked on stupefied.

Edwin felt his hair and beard, to make sure his braids were tidy.

"How do I look?" he said turning to his friend.

"You look just right, Ed," Thune answered.

"You Englisc pretty boys, are like our women," laughed the guard.

Edwin had his sword at the guard's throat in the blink of an eye.

"Pretty boys? Listen, idiot! We Englisc are a civilised people and proud of our good looks, as opposed to you lot, who can't read or write and are un-civilised. So, you say that again Northman and I'll do my very best to improve your Northmandisc short back and sides and leave you with a face to remember!"

The mounted troops were gathered in the bailey, immediately outside the towered fortress.

"Keep close," said Earl Harold, riding nearby.

"How far is Dol?" enquired Edwin.

"You know?"

Edwin nodded.

"Three days ride to the west, my Anglian friend. We are to relieve the Duke's forces in Dol. Duke Conan of Brittany has attacked the town and put it under siege."

The Duke's standard bearer was holding aloft William's banner, which bore a gold lion on a crimson background. Earl Harold moved forward and joined the Duke.

Next to the Earl was Roger de Montgomery, Vicomte d'Hiemois, a senior advisor to Duke William. Someone had pointed him out to Edwin yesterday. Edwin couldn't help smiling at his title. "That's a mouthful," he had said.

The Vicomte's wife, Lady Mabile de Bellême and his young son Robert, were waving to him as they left the citadel. Edwin looked back at the mother and son, he didn't know why, maybe it was the way the mother stood. Though she was quite small, petite as the Northmen say, yet he detected something powerful in her bearing.

Late evening on the second day, not far from the approach to the bourne Couesnon, Edwin spotted a group of riders who seemed to be following them.

"Thune, do you see what I see?"

"Umm, I wonder if anyone else has seen them."

"I don't know. I'll ride up ahead and find out."

"I'll ride with you," replied Thune.

They edged their way to the vanguard, immediately behind Earl Harold.

"My lord," said Edwin in a hushed voice, "I think we have some unwanted company to the left of us."

"I know. We're waiting for them to make the first move."

"They've gone. Disappeared behind those trees."

"Allons-y! Attaquer!!" shouted the Roger de Montgomery.

"Look! They'll never catch 'em," said Edwin.

"You game, Ed?"

"Gets dark quickly here. I wonder where they are?"

"Thune! Over there... something's wrong, look, I can see a horse but no rider."

"What's that?"

"Quick, Thune, Someone's in trouble."

"Aidez-moi! Je me noie!"

"I can see him. Shit! He's in a bog. Get me my blanket!"

Edwin took hold of the blanket and threw it out in front of him.

"Whatever you do, Thune, don't let go of my feet!"

Edwin began sliding himself out to the struggling man. Grabbing hold of his hands, he shouted, "Thune! Start pulling me out. Now what! What the fuck are you doing?"

"Do you want to be pulled out or not?"

"Get on with it!"

"Right, I've roped yer feet and I'm just going to...."

"Well come on! Start pulling! We're sinking in this shit!"

"Just hang on! I'm trying to tie this rope to the horse."

"Be quick about it... tie it around the pommel, the saddle or something," shouted Edwin, desperately trying to stop himself and the man from sinking further into the mire.

"Oh yes! With your weight, it'll tear the fucking saddle apart."

"Never mind your precious saddle, we're sinking! Get us out of here and stop pissing about!"

"Here we go," shouted back Thune. He had tied the other end of the rope around the saddle and neck of the horse and began backing it up.

"Thanks mate! Look! I'm covered all over in this stinking mud!"

"Merci mes amis, thank you for saving my life."

"My lord Roger. I didn't recognise you," said Edwin, sitting down beside the Vicomte.

"I'll go and let the others know you're safe," said Thune, mounting his horse. "Don't go away!"

"A few moments ago, I thought I was a dead man," said Roger de Montgomery in surprisingly good Englisc. He was covered from head to foot in mud. "My horse has more sense than me. It stopped abruptly but I carried on over him.... and landed in that…" he laughed. "Who are you and where in Englaland do you come from?"

"I am Edwin, Thegn of Upper Barnstæd, in the earldom of East Anglia," he replied, picking out the mud and weeds from his beard and hair. "I have a wife and two sons. If you don't mind me saying so, my lord, your Englisc is very good."

"I know a little of it. Your hair? Do all you Englisc grow your hair so long and in braids as yours is?"

Edwin nodded, "Mostly. We take great pride in our hair and groom it daily, my lord. I couldn't help noticing, back in Rouen, was that your wife and small boy, waving to you when we left?"

"Yes. That was my wife, Mabile de Bellême and my seven-year-old son, Robert. Now, because of you, he still has a father and my wife, a husband. You saved me from a certain and horrible death."

Roger de Montgomery took a metal cross, attached to a leather cord from around his neck.

"When you go into battle who do you pray to?"

I suppose, Woden. Yes it would be to Woden, the God of my fathers but I've never given it much thought before."

"Here," Roger de Montgomery put the cord and the cross around Edwin's neck. "Here is a Christian cross and I pray that it keeps you from harm as it has protected me."

"Thank you, Vicomte."

"Tell me Edwin. What kind of man is Earl Harold?"

"A fair man. He is resolute; a true leader of men."

"What of honour?"

"Earl Harold has the respect of all his men, my lord. I have heard the word honour used in many quarters and for some it is just a word but for me, life without honour is life without meaning."

Roger de Montgomery thought for a while. He was about to say more but was prevented by the sound of men approaching.

## - Rouen, Northmandig -
Rouen, Normandy

It was more than a parade, more than just a ride to the cathedral. Duke William was showing off his prize; Harold Godwinson, Earl of Wessex.

Edwin and Thune had been kept apart from the Earl and Lady Ælfgifu and left to languish in their unlocked room. Although they were restricted as to where they could move within the citadel, they could at least stroll about the grounds, though they were closely watched. However they did manage, singly, to reach the Earl's room at night unobserved. As Edwin's father, Wulfric, used to say, "Where there's a personal strength of will, there's always a way."

The stink of the city occasionally permeated into the citadel, depending which way the wind was blowing. It was beginning to make Edwin feel bilious. The Northmen, it seemed, didn't notice the stench. He tried to shut it out of his mind.

On the second night in Rouen, since their return from Dol, Edwin, after listening to the intriguing political games Duke William was playing, came to the conclusion that this Duke would use any excuse to expand his borders. Recently he had subdued the Bretons. Their Duke Conan, who had by all accounts got fed up with being Duke William's vassal had rebelled and had started to take back what was his by right, the town of Dol.

'Of course, he hadn't been a match for William,' remembered Edwin. 'When they saw us coming they rode away like scared rabbits. As my father used to say, "If you want to hang on to your land be prepared to defend it to the death," which they clearly had not been prepared to do.'

The smell was getting less. 'Thank...' he felt the cross... 'God? who knows, can't do any harm. What was it Earl Harold had said to him last night?'

"William has me by the balls! Tomorrow, I have to make a pledge of fealty to him and be his man. Do you know what that means,

Edwin?"

"Yes, I think so, my lord. To be his puppet, to do what he tells you to do!" he had replied.

"Exactly, I couldn't have put it better myself. What William wants me to do, on the death of King Edward, is to force the Witan to accept him as heir to the Englisc throne. Clear the way for him to be made King, otherwise you, me, everyone of our party including the boys will never reach Englaland alive!"

"That would be an oath taken under duress, my lord." I had said. "Therefore that oath would not be accepted by the Witan nor in any other court."

"Well put Edwin… you would make a fine Earl. But back to my present predicament. I shall take the oath, which of course will be witnessed in the cathedral by his barons, so that we can all go home, alive!"

"What happens if the Witan goes against those demands and choses Edgar, Edmund Irionside's grandson, as King?" I asked him.

"I shall not make any demands of the Witan on the Duke's behalf. And regarding young Edgar, again that's up to the Witan itself. We'll have to wait and see, won't we? Oh, and by the way, in order to *solidify*, if I can use that word, my friendship with Duke William," Earl Harold had given a mocking laugh, "he is going to dub me, make me one of his heroic knights. I believe they call it, 'Giving me my Spurs.' Edwin, I can't believe the arrogance of the man. Me! The Earl of Wessex, the most powerful Earl in Englaland. The outrageous audacity! On top of which, he has offered me his eight-year old daughter, Adeliza in marriage, as well half of Englaland as my prize when he becomes King!"

Edwin remembered laughing at that and saying, "But she's only a child!"

"I know. I told the Duke as much. I don't want to baby sit a child bride and anyway I'm already married. However that didn't seem to bother him."

"I don't like the sound of it, my lord. This northmandisc knight thing and offering you his child in marriage and *half of Englaland*? Never! That bastard would never part with any of it, he's far, far too greedy for power and control."

"And I'm not a traitor, Edwin."

"I know that, my lord."

"I would never sell myself, or my country, to that bastard. If he takes me for a fool, be it on his own head. I'll take the pledge and get us out of here."

## *May, 1065*
## - The Pledge, Rouen Cathedral -

The next day, Edwin and Thune were ushered forward, together with the Duke William's leading barons, to take part and witness the proceedings. There were not many people in the cathedral nor, for that matter, were there many involved in the actual ceremony. Though to Edwin, it was an unreal, melodramatic event.

First came the dubbing ceremony, the Duke placing his sword on the shoulders of the kneeling Earl Harold. Then the highlight of the proceedings, the oath taking. Two heavily covered cabinets were brought in and placed each side of the Earl. He then had to lay a hand on each one. After he had taken the oath, the cabinets were uncovered revealing in each one a reliquary, containing the sacred bones of two martyred Englisc missionaries.

A dark thought came over Edwin.

'This is not the everyday oath taking that I first envisaged. Their Church and Bishops are involved in this sham, as well as the Barons and of course, Thune and myself as witnesses. It has been deliberately made to look as if Earl Harold is not under any sort of threat.

Another, a darker thought occurred to Edwin, 'Why was there this heavy emphases of religious ceremony? Was it for the Pope's benefit? I bet it's going to get back to... where is it? Rome? The Earl's on a hiding for nothing here. William is a bastard in more ways than one and is going to try and use this to beat Harold over the head, with the Pope's blessing.'

## - Bellême -

"So, what of this Earl Harold?" asked Mabile de Bellême, who had ridden out to meet her husband, as he approached their home at Bellême.

"He seems..." Vicomte Roger looked thoughtful for a moment. "You saw him at Rouen. He's like most Englisc men, long blond hair worn in a single plait, but has a neatly trimmed moustache."

"A plait and that silly silly moustache! He doesn't look like a real man," she said dismissively, dismounting her horse and walking into the main hall of their castle, ahead of her husband.

"Far from it," he said catching up with her, ruffling his son Robert's hair. "He and his men are tougher than you may think. Resourceful fighters.

"Primitive fighters!"

"And they carry great axes, I saw," interrupted Robert.

"Meat cleavers you mean," laughed Mabile.

"No! Let's stop this," said Roger. He looked at Robert. "Stay here while I take your mother for a walk. I need to stretch my legs after riding from Rouen."

"Why can't I come too?"

"Because I have some serious business to attend to with your mother."

Young Robert stomped out of the hall and slammed the door in temper.

Roger stepped back outside. Holding his wife's hand they crossed the bailey, out through the main geat and stood by the moat.

"What's on your mind?" asked Mabile. "What's so important that you can't talk inside, behind closed doors."

"I don't want anyone to hear, especially young Robert. Look I'll be plain. I'm not sure William is doing the right thing in lusting after the Englisc crown."

Mabile gave him a quizzical look.

"Yes! Lusting after the Englisc crown! He's obsessed by it."

"Well, you know Edward promised it to William on more than one occasion, to my knowledge. And don't forget," Mabile said, waving her finger at her husband's chest, "the pledge that Earl Harold took."

"That pledge was taken under duress, and doesn't really count in law."

Roger looked nervously about, "There is only one legitimate heir after Edward and that is Edgar, they call the Atheling, grandson of King Edmund who was murdered I believe by King Cnute's men."

"What goes on over there or in Norveg and Danemark, are of no concern of mine. The only thing I do know, I didn't like Edward's mother Emma. A controlling bitch! When she was bustling about over here all those years ago, I didn't trust her."

"How could you have known her? You were only a child," answered Roger.

"I knew her alright. I was nine years of age when Edward left for England. I was not a child!"

"It doesn't change anything." He came closer to his wife and whispered, "You know as well I that William was born out of wedlock to that… tanner's daughter. His only blood connection to Edward is on his father, Duke Robert's side and through to Emma. To my reckoning, that blood line connection is so thin, it's is not even in contention. Yet he's building all those ships, ready for an invasion in case Earl Harold does not make good his pledge."

"Why are you worrying about it now?" said Mabile, with a slight shiver, feeling the cool evening air.

"Because my dear, the risks are too high, that's what! If we do try to invade and are either destroyed by a storm at sæ or defeated on the Englisc beaches, that will be the end of us and Northmandig."

"You think the Englisc are that strong?"

"From information I have gleaned and what I saw of the Earl and his Thegn Edwin, who saved my life, yes. The Englisc will be a force to be reckoned with."

*May, 1065*
### - Quayside, Rouen -

Touching the unfamiliar cross that hung around his neck, Edwin looked among the Duke's entourage for Vicomte Roger but there was no sign of him.

He wondered, who the boy standing next to Duke William was. He had never seen him before. He looked to be about...ten or eleven years of age. 'He's looking over towards me, perhaps he senses my interest,' he thought. 'He's coming over here.'

"I do not know who you are but could you tell me where the Vicomte is?" asked Edwin.

"I am Prince Robert, Duke William is my father. The Vicomte has returned to Bellême."

"Where's that?"

"To the suth of the country near Alençon," he answered.

"You seem to be well informed."

"Yes, I am! I know everything about my father's closest allies, and Robert de Bellême is my best friend.

"I apologise for asking so many questions."

"No matter. You are Edwin, Thegn of Upper Barnstæd who rescued the Vicomte, aren't you?"

"Yes, the very same."

"You Englisc seem to make a habit of it. Your Earl Harold saved two knights from drowning in the same river. I believe you call it a bourne in your language."

"Yes. It is a bourne. You speak very good Englisc."

"One needs to speak the language of the people, my father will be King of."

'Ooops!' Edwin thought.

"It was nice to have met you," he said, with a smile at the boy.

"Everybody is boarding, I must leave you."

Prince Robert stood staring after Edwin for a while, then turned and rejoined his father.

"Papa," said Adeliza, "Earl Harold is a very tall and handsome man. When I am married to him will I have to leave you and Mama and Robert?"

"Marry him! Never, child!" replied Duke William.

"But Papa you promised! You held both our hands together when you made the pledge!"

"In your dreams girl. I'd rather you had married Alphonso the Spaniard but your mother defied me. Now you've gone gooey eyed over that blond, long haired thing. Never!"

"But Papa!"

"Shut up child and join Curthose."

Adeliza became frightened. She hated her father when he lost his temper, especially when he called her brother that name in that horrible way! Mama didn't say that, she was always gentle, full of love and warm comforting hugs. Adeliza couldn't help thinking of the Engliscman. 'He has a kind face. Would he give me lots of warm hugs? Strange, that Papa has changed his mind. Why is he annoyed with me.' She moved away from her brother to the dockside, sat down, and let her legs dangle over the edge. She looked down into the clear water. Fish, in gathered shoals, were swimming about and around the ships' hulls, momentarily breaking the surface of the water as they poked their heads up. 'They look so happy,' she thought. She bent over to try and touch them.

Prince Robert seethed in silent anger. 'Why does he always try to make a fool of me in public by calling me short pants? I can write, I can speak three languages to his one, and yet he treats me like a fool!'

"Where's your baby sister!" shouted the Duke.

I don't know Father!"

"Then find her!"

A shout, echoed around the dock!

"My lord! Your daughter!"

A man was struggling in the water, trying as best he could to hold aloft the bedraggled body of Adeliza.

"Help that man!" shouted the Duke pointing. "Rescue my child! Don't just stand there gawping!"

A scramble of people on the dockside lifted the body onto the quayside. A monk pushed his way forward, turned the child onto her chest and began pressing down on her back.

"Out of my way!"

The Duke pushed his way through and knelt by the monk.

"What are you doing?"

"Pushing the water out of her, my lord. There is a chance I may be able to revive her." After some moments he stopped, shook his head. "Your daughter is with God now."

The Duke turning to one of his aides said, "Do you think the Englisc Earl saw this?"

"I don't think so my lord."

"Good."

### - Homeward bound -

Now that they were underway, Edwin began to breathe more easily. Not only because they had left Northmandig and its dark oppressiveness, but also because of the sense of freedom in this, their homeward bound ship. Looking towards the stern, he could see Horsa sitting at the steering oar, grinning through the hair on his face at Earl Harold.

"Glad to see yer back, Governor. That's a good horse you have there."

"A present from the Duke," said Earl Harold, wryly.

"Hope there ain't any strings attached, Governor."

"As much as I'm glad to see you again Horsa, keep your eyes on the sail and not on that bloody horse, it has had too big a price. Just get us home as rapidly as possible."

"Will do Gov… my lord."

"So am I Horsa! Glad, to see you again," said Edwin, clasping his old friend. "Now that you have a new sail, can you manage to steer us back to Bosham without losing the Governor's horse?"

"Piss off and make yourself useful for a change."

"I will after I've seen the Earl." He turned around and made his way forward.

Earl Harold was standing at the prow, lost in thought.

"My lord," said Edwin, "I'm sorry your brother isn't with us."

"Yes…so am I. He will never be released and returned home now. I suppose I should be grateful the Duke released Hakon."

"Were you able to see your brother?"

"Yes," he replied, almost in tears. "Despite trying to hang on to his Engliscness, he has become more Northmandisc than Englisc now, at least in speech!"

"Duke William made such an elaborate production at the cathedral, nobody would have known you were under duress."

"That's what worries me, Edwin. Word will get back to the Pope that I willingly took the oath."

"I had thought of that, my lord. Would that be a big problem?"

"It could be. The Pope's influence is very powerful."

"Not in my household, my lord."

"But that's just you, not the rest of the country. Tell me, how old are your boys?"

"Wulfnoth and Edric are in their fifteenth year."

"Are they ready?"

"They've been ready since last year, although their mother would rather they weren't."

The Earl gave Edwin a shallow smile.

"You had better get back to your friends. I need time to myself."

# CHAPTER XVI

### - Upper Barnstæd -

Having flung himself onto the bed, Edwin leaned his head back into the hollow he had made for himself in the pillow. Closing his eyes, he luxuriated in its welcoming comfort.

"That's better, I am so glad to be home." Pausing for his brain to catch up to his familiar surroundings, he said, "Gwynedd, you have no idea what I've been through for our lord and master."

Lying next to him, she began asking her husband where he had been, what had taken him so long and what was so terrible about a fishing trip, but he was already asleep. Leaning on her elbow, she noticed the metal cross hanging from his neck.

'I haven't seen that before. Perhaps he's found religion... I hope not!' She shook her head, got out of bed, removed her husband's boots being careful not to disturb him and left the room.

"Where's Father?" asked Wulfnoth.

"Asleep," replied his mother. "Now go and see what your father's friend Thune wants."

Thune was nowhere to be seen. His horse, a bay mare was hitched securely and munching happily on a bundle of fresh hay.

Edric brought his hand up to shield his eyes from the late afternoon sun and noticed, emerging from a block of elongated shadows, a distant figure walking through the village.

"There, just past the church. Come on Wulf, let's see what he's up to."

"Mmm, do we have to, he's probably just gone for an evening

stroll. I'd rather wait here until he gets back."

"Come on Wulf," said Edric, bounding away.

"Alright," he replied, easing himself away from the side of the building.

Thune continued to amble along, in what would seem to be his usual manner, through the village and on towards the Tames. He didn't turn around, even though he could feel the presence of someone following.

Mounting the landing stage, he walked the length of it, leant over and took note of the depth of the water, judging it was now about low tide.

'I reckon you could easily dock a fifty footer here,' he thought. Looking along near the bank, left and right of the jetty, he noticed the soft oozing mud. 'Difficult for anybody to land either side, along this bank.' He stood for a while and after making a mental note, slid down, his back firmly against the end docking post. Leaning back he closed his eyes and waited for his expected visitors. He felt the vibrations of his followers mounting the jetty.

"It took you long enough!"

"Are you Thune?" said Wulfnoth, thinking the man was half asleep.

"Who's asking?"

"Wulfnoth, son of Edwin."

"Ah, met you two at long last. You had better come closer as my hearing ain't so good."

Wulfnoth held his brother back.

"I think you're a crafty old fox," he said. Both the boys drew their swords.

"Very good," laughed Thune. "Your ol' man was right, you're a smart pair, and ready."

"Ready for what?" asked Edric, sheathing his sword.

"You want to see some action don't you?" Thune said, leaning forward, "Draw some blood?"

"Probably. How long have you known our father?" asked Edwin, throwing a pebble into the bourne.

"Couple of years. Give me a hand up."

"As long as you keep your hands where I can see them and away from yer knife... there!" Pulling the man to his feet, Wulfnoth was surprised at how light and agile he was. He certainly hadn't needed any help getting up.

"You took a liberty with our feed," said Edric.

"You wouldn't begrudge my horse a fistful of hay would you, because that wouldn't be very friendly?"

"Will you be going now?" asked Wulfnoth.

"I'll be staying just the night, bedding down in the hall and I promise not to snore."

"Where are you from?" asked Wulfnoth.

"Fefresham!"

"Where's that?"

"Well... what year are we in?"

The boys looked at each other in confusion.

"Hold on, hold on, don't tell me... let me guess, if we're in '65, then Fefresham is now officially in Cent. Last year my village was in Wessex. With all these bloody Earls carving up the country for their pieces of land, it's difficult to know where you are, right!"

They nodded.

"Same with us," said Wulfnoth. "This here, used to be in East Anglia now we're in Cent but father still holds loyalty to Earl Harold and not to his brother, Gyrth."

"In the scheme of things does it really matter?" said Thune, smiling. "We Centisc people, born on the piece of land in the suth east corner of the country, remain Centisc no matter what the King or some bloody Earl may call it.

"I suppose not," replied Edric, laughing.

"So what's the latest news? We hear very little tucked away down here, away from Lunden," asked Wulfnoth.

Thune, leaning against the post, pursed his lips. "You ought to ask yer ol' man."

"He's asleep and you're here, talking to us," said Wulfnoth.
"Well, all I can tell you is that there's trouble at Eoforwïc."
"That's not much... tell us the rest," chipped in Edric.

Thune shook his head and looked over to the west at the disappearing sun.

"I'm hungry. Perhaps yer ol' man is awake."
"I wouldn't bet on it," replied Wulfnoth.
"I know him better than you," Thune replied. "He catnaps. Drops off to sleep, just like that, and when he does nothing will rouse him. Then, all of a sudden, he's wide awake. He pisses me off, 'cos to function I need a good night's sleep. But not him."
"How long will it take to ride to Fefresham?"
"Ride? I hope not! If Ed can coax one of your fisherman friends to sail us around the coast to my yard, I'll make it worth his while."

*Early morning, May, 1064*
## - A meeting with the King at West Minster Palace -

Harold waved to his wife Eadgyth, as he departed the family's manor house in Suthweca. The house had a special place in his heart. It had been his father's favourite residence when in Lunden and so it was with Harold. It was as if his father's spirit was still there in every nook and cranny, even its furniture evoked so many memories; not forgetting his father's favourite chair, from where the old Earl had received the news thirteen-years before, of the Witan's damning sentence, branding him and his family, 'Nithing', banishing them from the country. Harold was saddened as he thought about those passing years.

He had been summoned to the palace by the King and had been ordered to come alone. He crossed Lunden Brycg, then on through the city stræts, his mind still dwelling on the recent past, trying to gauge what was to be done; the future was unclear, unsafe, especially with the King becoming ever frailer. Harold envisioned himself in the middle of a frozen lake, the ice cracking all around him, trying to decide the safest route to dry land. His King had lied to him by devising a Northmandisc trap, which he had tried to avoid but had inevitably slid into. Now he was summoned by the King who was probably still yearning for his dominating mother. A woman whose only desire had been to put her countryman, the bastard, Duke William of Northmandig on the Englisc throne, ignoring the proper, legal and hereditary rights of Englaland.

Arriving at Lud Geat and away from the smells and the bustling crowds, he continued along Fleet Stræt and onto the Strand. With the morning sun beating down, he drew in a deep breath and prepared himself for the meeting ahead. The ride through Lunden had cleared his mind. He had a good idea why the King had summoned him but he wasn't going to back away, he would remain firm in his resolve. He remembered, with a smile, his wife Eadgyth saying, "Don't let the old sod get away with his treachery."

Veering off the Strand and onto a rough narrow track, just wide enough for a wagon, his horse gave out a neigh and shook its head. Harold leant forward and patted the animal soothingly.

"Steady boy, steady. Perhaps you know something I don't. Well, we'll soon see what the old fart wants, won't we."

The track passed over the Ty Bourne and onto Thorney Igland via a wooden brygc that had seen better days. The hooves of Harold's horse clanked dully across its planks giving him a slight feeling of anxiety.

'One day someone crossing these rotten planks is going to get a nasty surprise by falling through into the shit below.'

On the firm ground of Thorney Igland, the track bore left, staying close to the Tames. Passing by St Margaret's church, he rode on towards the sound of stonemasons' hammers and the general construction noise of the King's new, West Minster. His prized church.

'Edward must feel his end is nigh and is reserving his place in heaven,' he thought laughingly as he rode on towards the King's palace overlooking the Tames.

"It's one thing being summoned here," Harold muttered to himself, "quite another being kept in the anteroom for hours, the only comfort being a wooden seat, hard enough to numb anyone's arse, not to mention the cacophony of the masons working outside."

He looked up at the high window at the end of the room and judged it was approaching the middle of the day. He sighed. Then out of the corner of his eye he saw the door to the King's chamber begin to open.

"My lord Harold," said a man, holding onto the edge of the door as if to prevent it swinging shut. Harold recognized him as Brihtric Meaw, a member of the King's staff.

"His majesty will see you now."

"Nice to see you Brihtric. You're looking so well," remarked Harold, "how is Gleucestre?"

"Very well, my lord, I can't complain."

"Listen! I met an old acquaintance of yours. She asked after you," Harold lied.

"She? Who?"

"Matilda, Duke William's wife."

Brihtric turned pale but before he could stammer a reply Harold had walked passed him, towards the King, intent on getting down to business.

King Edward, his hands firmly clasping his left knee, looked up.

"Lord Harold, you seem none the worse for wear after your recent sæ trip?"

"No Sire," Harold held himself in check and counted to ten, "I am very well, despite the fickle scales of fortune." He was mindful others might be present and within hearing.

"Your words are barbed, Earl Harold! Say what you mean," said the King loudly. "Now, about your voyage, I hear you were sailing east instead of going to Rouen!"

The small door behind the King's throne, discernibly clicked shut, its heavily woven screen showing a slight movement before becoming still.

'Just as I imagined. We are not truly alone,' Harold thought.

"What I mean to say is, Sire," he noticed, without letting the King realise he could see it, both Edward's left hand and his head had a steady tremble, which he had not observed before, "we encountered a severe storm and were forced to beach in Ponthieu."

"I gave you a sealed letter for my cousin, Duke William of Northmandig which he did not receive, instead you decided to sail somewhere else. You were seen travelling due east. How do you answer?"

'I knew that solitary ship would come back to bite me,' he thought, 'but how did he know the Duke didn't receive that letter.' Harold was not shaken by the King's latest information. He took his time in replying. He felt and urgent desire to savour every word and make them count.

"Sire, in the storm your letter was damaged by sæ water, rendering the seal broken. I read what I could, before it became unreadable, the ink was dissolving before my very eyes. What I did deduce from the letter shook me to the core of my being! You Sire, my King! You had betrayed me! You were leading me, my sister, Lady Ælfgifu and my men into a trap!"

"A trap!" shouted Edward, who had tried to stand but had fallen back into his seat. "You dare think I would do such a thing!"

" I am *not a fool* Sire nor am I *illiterate!* I know what was written!"

"It was a personal letter to Duke William! You should *not* have read it!" The trembling of his hand had become more pronounced.

"Sire! I had no option! The writing, as I said, was dissolving before my eyes. How could I relay your message to the Duke if it were to be unreadable by the time I arrived in Rouen!"

Edward, who tried once again to stand, slumped back into his throne mumbling, knowing he had lost the argument.

Harold glanced around the room. Satisfied they were alone, he continued, "Sire! Was it your idea or did others persuade you to force me into making an unlawful oath? To confirm an illegal promise?"

"You took the oath?"

"How could I not? I had no option! If I hadn't I would not be standing here, speaking to you now. I would either be dead or incarcerated in one of that bastard's prisons where my brother still is, right now."

"How dare you speak of my cousin in such terms."

"Sire, if I may remind you. William is not only a bastard, his unmarried tart of a mother was low born, the daughter of a piss ridden tanner! Also, William is only a very, very distant blood relation, on your mother's side." Harold, keeping himself under control, chose his words carefully. "You promised a letter demanding the release of those two innocent boys, instead your letter to Duke William was a trap. A trap to set me up to make an unlawful oath. Sire! You made me Earl of Wessex, to enforce *just laws*, to lead and fight your battles, to safeguard your realm and yet you connived to lie to me in front of Lady Ælfgifu, to cast me and my family aside like so much chaff thrown on the wind. Are we so loathed by you, that you would happily destroy our lives and freedom, in order to advance that Northman bastard, William?"

The King sat motionless for what seemed an age and then changing tactics, began smiling.

"Harold! You're taking this entirely the wrong way. This is politics! Listen, I owe the Duke and his father my life, they kept us safe for twenty-five years, they are my family."

"I dare say," replied Harold.

"For twenty-five years, Harold, they unsparingly gave me and my mother succour."

"But Sire…"

The King silenced Harold with the wave of his hand.

"I am not blaming your father for the murder of my brother Alfred, that's forgotten and out of the way. No! We have settled all that."

"Oh no you haven't! You still hate my father!"

The King began to shake with sudden rage. "Your father, could have prevented King Harold Harefoot's men from dragging my brother away into the night to be butchered!"

"My father had no part in that and you know it!"

"The trouble is… your father as Earl of Wessex was as thick as thieves with that pagan, Harold Harefoot and of that there is no doubt!" replied the King.

"That is a lie! At the Oxford Witenagamot, my father voted against the crowning of Cnut's son, Harold, as opposed to some, including Earl Leofric of Mercia. My father was an honourable man who loved his family and championed the cause of the Royal Wessex House of Cerdic. He championed *your* royal cause, to King Harthacnute, paving the way for you, Sire, to ascend the Englisc throne! Why would he harm your brother Alfred? It is not to be believed! It was malicious gossip spread by others!"

"But the evidence man, the evidence!" shouted the King, his face flushing with guilt.

"What evidence?" replied Earl Harold, coldly and calmly. "My father made your brother Alfred welcome into his home. King Harold's fully armed troops arrived in the middle of the night, and dragged him away. My father was powerless to resist. Those same royal troops, tied your brother to the underbelly of a horse and thereafter at some place unknown, gouged his eyes out with knives…"

"Alright! Alright! Alright! I know the details! I know what happened to my poor brother!" cried out Edward.

"My father always loved and supported you. Even back in fifty-two, when he could easily have taken your crown. But no! Instead he bent his knee before you, gave you his sword, wanting only fair and proper justice and to be free of the malicious accusations. Sire, you have been ill advised over the years by your Northmandisc friends… and others."

"In exile, it was my Northmandisc friends and family who saved us. If we had stayed in Englaland we would have been butchered and thrown, headless into the fens as your namesake, Harold was twenty-four years ago."

"Sire. A little while ago you used the word politics as if it were an excuse for anything foul. You may well owe the Duke's family your life but the plain fact is how could you make such a promise to William, knowing all along of the existence of your nephew, Edward the Ætheling; of the direct bloodline he had to the royal house of Cerdic? How could you *not* know about Edmund Ironside's son, your rightful heir?"

"I am aware of my Cerdic bloodline and I certainly don't need you, a Godwinson, to give me a history lesson! I shall repeat it again for you, as you seemed to be too deaf to hear the first time. The Witan knew of him but I did not! Is that clear enough! Was it not I, who instructed you to bring Edmund's son and his family back from Hungary!"

Harold saw a chink of light, a glimmer of weakness in the King's lying and now he knew the King knew that they both knew the truth.

Now emboldened he said, "You knew of Edward Ætheling's existence and your mother certainly knew back in fifty-one when Bishop Stigand informed her of it. Yet she still went ahead and invited William here, to your court at West Minster, promising him heirdom to the Englisc throne… over the heads of the Witan!"

"That was my mother's doing… I… I had nothing to do with inviting William over from Northmandig!" replied the King nervously.

"And yet you refused to meet your true heir, Edward, in Lunden on his return from Hungary." The King sat in silence. Harold continued, "Then he was *poisoned* two days later!" He waited for his words to sink in. "Now his son Edgar, is the rightful heir to your throne… unless, of course, he too is mysteriously poisoned!"

"Are you implying I had Edmund's son murdered?"

"Sire," Harold was able to form tears in his eyes, making sure the King saw them. "I do not know what to believe! The truth must speak for itself. And on the subject of my apparent lack of hearing, Sire, I will say it yet again. I did take that oath to Duke William but under an implied threat to my life and liberty. Thankfully my nephew, Hakon was released to his mother but my brother Wulfnoth is still confined in Northmandig."

"I agree, those boys should never have been taken from my custody. That was unforgivable. My heart goes out to your brother. They did no wrong."

Harold could hardly believe the hypocrisy of the King.

"Jumièges was *your* Archbishop. He took those boys from *your* custody in the first place and gave them over to William."

"I am quite aware of that!"

"But you are apparently unaware of the fact that William is a hard, uncouth, calculating swine who would try to extract blood from a stone. You knew him when he was a boy. I know him as the man he is now. I know how his mind works! I was on campaign with him in Brittany. Don't you understand, that while we were in Rouen and under guard, my hands were tied? I had to take that bloody oath."

"Lord Harold, in all this, you lie! Didn't I give you instruction to sail straight to Rouen?"

Harold was taken aback. 'What is the old idiot on about now? Is the old fool losing it or am I,' he thought, 'we've already gone through all of this.'

"Sire! I had no option. Having read your letter to Duke William, there was only one decision I could possibly make, without putting our lives in danger and that was to sail elsewhere. That happened to be Flanders to seek the assistance of Duke William's father-in-law, Count Baldwin and for him to put pressure on the Duke via his daughter, Duchess Matilda, which was… to release… those… two… boys."

"But in the end, you didn't go to Count Baldwin."

"I know!" replied Harold, through clenched teeth, barely able to control his anger. "As I have said, a fierce storm forced us to beach in Ponthieu to make repairs."

"I heard you and… some Thegn… what was his name?"

"Edwin, Sire. Edwin, Thegn of Upper Barnstæd."

"Ah yes, you both saved the lives of three of Williams knights."

"Yes, Sire," replied Harold, beginning to tire of this royal audience, which was getting him absolutely nowhere.

"Look here, about this accession mess. My mother, rest her sainted soul, was a very strong willed and persuasive woman. It was she who invited Duke William, not I."

'Good God! It's not to be believed, he's still on about his damned mother. The man is either a born liar or is off his trembling head. Does he think we don't know what is going on here?'

Harold now knew that the King was seriously confused. Surely he must know he had made promises to William before he left Northmandig and repeated them again in the company of his batty old, Northman mother, Emma and yet again in that letter.'

"She promised him," the King continued, "the crown when I die. Yes! She said it in front of me, true as God is my witness. Even though as you well know, the Witan has to be consulted. But William just laughed, accusing me of being too soft. That I should be telling the Witan what to do, and who should be the next heir, not the other way around. Harold, I'm getting tired of all this but I'm glad we've had this little chat, you know… to straighten this messy business out."

"Just one more thing, Sire," said Harold, now almost beside himself with frustration.

"Oh, if you must," said the King, like a spoilt child.

"I believe you have consented to reorganising the tax system in Northymbria."

"Ah yes! Earl Tostig and I have agreed on a plan to raise the levies."

"But to raise them by fifty per cent? Without the consent of any of Northymbria's leading Thegns? This is asking for trouble!"

"Trouble? What trouble? Who questions the King's Law?"

"It's not about your royal law," replied Harold. "Their taxes are lower than in most of the country I agree, but to raise them so high in one stroke is something else. I thought I had to mention it."

"It has been recognised in the past as a lawless part of the country," said the King, petulantly. "Enforcing order and proper laws is expensive, you should know that Earl Harold."

"But this is not the way to do it, Sire. You must first communicate with your people."

"Enough! Enough, I'm too tired to continue with this… business." The King this time managing to raise himself out of his throne, stretched his arms and legs.

"Harold. How is your wife? Oh I forgot, you have two wives now, silly ol' me. Eadgyth is a lovely woman, is she's well and the children?"

"They're all well, Sire. Eadgyth and I are staying at our hall in Suthweca."

"Ah yes, that was your father's place and your other wife, the one with the raven hær, Ealdgyth, daughter of, Earl Ælfgar how is she?"

"Much the same, she's at Wintancæster, doing what she knows best."

"And that is?"

"Administrating the earldom," answered Harold.

Edward nodding as if he had understood, but Harold didn't know for sure, shuffled to the small door, parted the curtain, opened the door and without turning or uttering another word, disappeared from view, leaving Harold standing in front of the empty throne.

*8 July, 1065*
**- Upper Barnstæd -**

For most of that afternoon the twins had had very little in the way of luck with their fishing, except for the occasional bite and the one small fish, which Wulfnoth had caught with his first cast. Edric thought it was a mullet but wasn't sure. Wulfnoth adjusted the small twig on his line and threw the fish back, while Edric concentrated on his own fishing.

The twig in place would allow the hook to hang a little lower in the water. Wulfnoth threaded the bait onto the hook then, making a tremendous cast, watched the floating twig move slowly down with the tide. Suddenly it disappeared!

"Got one!" Wulfnoth shouted, holding onto the rod with one hand. With the other he grabbed hold of the line and began gradually hauling it in.

Edric moved over to make more room for his brother.

"You're just lucky. What are you using for bait? What's the big secret?"

"Secret?" responded Wulfnoth, with a laugh.

Yer… what do you use?"

"Rotting mussels. They can't resist them," answered Wulfnoth.

"What! You've kept this from me all this time. That's not very brotherly of you, letting me fish for hours with these useless worms. I wondered what that smell was. I thought it was you, farting!"

"Nice one, Ed. Now I'm a smelly bastard. Here! The line is cutting into my hand. Grab hold of it and help me land this fish. Wow! It's a big'un, it's trying to pull me in!" shouted Wulfnoth, quickly taking hold of a handful of long grass to bind around his hands. "That's better! Now, let's land this monster."

Having taken the line back from Edric, he began hauling it in. "It's fighting like mad!"

"Your line's getting tangled," said Edric, standing out of the way.

"Never mind that Ed, you stay here and be ready to clobber it when it comes ashore, I'll move back to haul it up on the bank."

"That's a cod," said Edric, shaking his head in surprise.

"Yes. I think it is."

"Think? Of course it is! It's the biggest fish I've ever seen landed by a line." He bashed the fish's head in with a rock. "Mum's going to be well pleased when she sees it. It'll keep us in food at least a couple of days."

"Not with you around," teased Wulfnoth. "Get the smell of that cooked fish and you'll be carving off lumps and stuffing them in your mouth. The fish will be gone in no time, head and all."

"You speak for yourself, I don't like fish heads except the cheeks."

"Want to carry on fishing?" asked Wulfnoth.

"No, not really, not much point is there, and anyway that monster will start smelling soon, if we don't get it back home."

"Have you heard the news from up north?"

"Yes. It's not good. Listen Wulf, if there's trouble I don't fancy you and I having to fight against our own just because Earl Harold's brother can't control his Northymbrian Thegns."

Wulfnoth had given up trying to coil his line in any sort of order, so he just gathered it together as best he could.

"Dad told us ages ago, the Northymbrians were a tough lot to handle. Tostig had better tread carefully if he wants to head off any real problems. He's not like his older brother, Harold. Tostig's an arrogant bastard, especially now he's rubbing shoulders with the King. If he's not careful, well, you know what I mean."

"I think," replied Edric, thoughtfully, "he's jealous of Harold and wants to be next in line for the crown when Edward coughs his last!"

"Jealous of Harold? No way! Harold doesn't want to be King, how could he. Little Edgar is the next in line."

"Little?" laughed Edric. "He's not so little! He's fourteen years old!"

"Perhaps you're right but from what I hear, he's not exactly kingly material."

"Between you and I, nor is Edward," replied Edric.

"That's dangerous talk, Ed."

"Let's change the subject. What did you think of Thune, his family and his shipyard."

"He seemed alright," said Wulfnoth. "A wily bugger though. I'm glad he's on our side and not against us, if you see what I mean. But I liked his family, they were very friendly especially his wife,

Bregus… was he serious about building us a boat?"

"He sold the idea to Dad last year."

"I know but I'm still somewhat surprised, especially after that storm. You would have thought Dad had had enough of the sæ."

"What did you think of Bregus?" said Edric. "With her muscles, she must be quite a handful. Thune told me she has her own cargo ship and captains her vessel across the Englisc Sæ as far as Flanders and she is handy with a sword. Last year Thune gave her his old battlesword. "

Wulfnoth, who by now, had gathered up his fishing gear and put it on his shoulder, agreed with Edric.

"She certainly looks strong enough to wield it?"

Edric nodded. "She's not very tall but she packs a punch."

"Thune's brother, Kæfrid is very different. He doesn't want anything to do with weapons or anything military, preferring a safe family life and building ships."

"But he is a great dancer, tremendous footwork."

"He'll need to have lovely footwork," replied Wulfnoth, "if Englaland is ever attacked and he wants to protect that beautiful wife of his. What's her name, Mæna? And what about their tear-away son, Garick?"

"I know… we're not all suited to be warriors but did you hear Garick play that stringed instrument, a fair ol' talent they have in that kid."

"That's even more reason to be trained up, to be able to defend your hearth and family. That's what grandfather believed and he was right! But that's their business. I think living here, close to the Tames and close to Lunden is better than being out in the wilds of Cent, where nobody seems to know what's going on."

"Listen Wulf, are you saying you would prefer to live in Lunden?"

"You've got to be joking. Still it's good to be near Lunden, yet not having to suffer those crowds and all that stink."

"This fish looks even more enormous now it's opened out like that," said Edric, eyeing the gutted and butterflied fish, propped up on two skewers in front of the fire. Couldn't you have propped it up whole, on one skewer?"

"We haven't got one strong enough! Blame yer brother, wherever he is, not me!" said their mother, wiping her hands on her apron. "He certainly caught a monster."

"Hey up!" said Edric. "Who's that skinny bastard limping in with Wulf?"

"I'll go and see," said Gwynedd.

Wulfnoth, rolling up his sleeves as he entered the hall, called out, "Right where's my lunch?"

"Who's your friend?"

"Messenger from Lunden but I couldn't get any information out of him. He said he would only speak to mother. So I know no more than you, Ed. Mum looks serious. I don't like it. Where's Dad?"

"He went out early to the creek," replied Edric, beginning to laugh, "to get some… fish!"

"What am I going to do with this lot," said Edwin entering the kitchen, holding out a basketful of freshly caught fish.

"Don't look at me," said Gwynedd pointing to the fire, "your boys caught that!"

"What do you mean… *my boys*, retorted Edwin, "I suppose you had nothing to do with giving birth to them! Ah well, this was a waste of time, I suppose I'll have to throw these fish away in the bourne."

"Alight, alright… I'll make some soup with them. By the way, that sheepish looking person sitting in the corner of the hall, is a messenger for you and I'm not happy about it."

# CHAPTER XVII

*Early morning, 5 July, 1065*
**- Niwe Geat, Lunden -**
Newgate, London

"What are you laughing about," said Edwin, looking around at his two sons who were riding behind him.

"We were joking about the stench," answered Wulfnoth.

"If you want to know what real stench is, you should try the stræts of Rouen. Lunden smells sweet in comparison... believe me," replied Edwin. He was still thinking about Gwynedd and how she had clung to him after he had taken her into their bedroom.

"No, no, no!," she had sobbed.

No matter how Edwin had tried to console her, she didn't want her boys to go off to fight.

"That's what they have been trained for, my love. I shall be with them and keep them both out of trouble," he had promised.

They had ridden along Tames Stræt close to the city wall, turning right at the tower which overlooked the Fleet. After passing by Lud Geat they headed for Niwe Geat. There, Edwin rode on ahead to where Earl Harold was surrounded by his men.

Harold looked surprised at seeing Edwin. After a short while he took him aside, out of hearing of the others.

"I didn't expect to see you," said Harold. "Where are your boys?"

"Over there," replied Edwin, pointing.

"Ah yes!" The Earl took his time before speaking again. "Edwin my friend, I have to tell you, I can't include you in this mission. This is not for you."

"But my lord, you need me!"

Harold shook his head, "Not this time. This is a young man's profession. It's time to put up your sword and skeggox and spend time looking after your wife and homestead."

"Why?" Edwin felt the words choking in his throat, "I'm as fit as any man alive! I can still wield a sword, swing an axe and my brain is not addled!"

"I can see your pain, my friend. This is not easy for me either! Edwin, your sons need experience in the field and if anything should happen... I wouldn't want to lose their father as well. Is that plain enough! Look! I'll take them under my personal care, if it eases your mind."

"But my lord," replied Edwin, "I fought for your father and I have fought for you. I am a warrior! That's what I do! It's what I'm trained for. I am nothing without a sword in my hand and at your side."

"Edwin, you have done more for me than most and... I will still have need of you in the future, believe me."

"Father! Where are you going?" asked Wulfnoth.

"Home! The Earl has other plans for me." Edwin put his long arms around his sons. "You're my boys. It's up to you now. Remember everything you have been taught, make your mother and me proud."

Mounting his horse Edwin, without looking around, waved his hand and rode away through Niwe Geat and along Watling Stræt, with a heavy heart.

"I need a drink," he said to himself.

Riding past St. Paul's, he turned right and down towards Tames Stræt, to the Vintry.

"Gawd bless mi soul!" exclaimed Alfred, the owner of the Grape Vine. "Haven't seen you here in... let me see," he shook his head, "I dunno, at any rate a long while."

He was a jolly rotund man, who was just a touch shorter than

Edwin. He was shaven, unusual for an Engliscman. His round fleshy face especially his chin showed a dark stubble which at times was coated with beer froth. His roughly clipped greased brown hair hung down to his shoulders. Edwin had the impression Alfred's wife had cut it, using a pair of shears and a pudding basin.

"What will, yer have? Ay, what's the matter Ed, you look down in the dumps?"

Edwin gave him a rough idea of what had happened.

"Well Ed, they're big lads now. You would have had to untie the reins and let them loose at some point in time."

"I know! I know all about that," exclaimed Edwin.

"It's not your kids at all, is it?"

"Not exactly," returned Edwin.

"Earl Harold turned yer down, pensioned you off. I'm right, aren't I?"

"Sure I'm pissed, angry, whatever! How would you feel, to be told you are useless at forty-six? I still have a few good fighting years left in me yet!"

"Now, now Ed. I'll get you a cup of my special.... 'allo, here comes an ol' mate of yours, just you wait here. Back in a bit."

A heavy hand clapped Edwin on the shoulder.

"You ol' bastard. Where've you been?'

Edwin turned around and there before him, as large as life was Osbert, the man who invented muscles. Even one handed, this smithy could knock cold an entire troop of warriors, with ease.

"What brings you here, Os?"

"Funny you should be asking." Osbert sat his great frame down next to Edwin, who heard a distinct creak from the sagging bench seat. Catching Alf's eye Osbert called, "A mug of mead me ol' mate! Where was I… Oh thanks Alf."

Alfred had placed their mugs on the table. Picking them up, Os and Ed gave him a toast.

"Here's to your good health and may you always have a strong sword arm!"

"Yes, this is nice stuff... where was I, oh yes. I'm in the middle of a big job." Osbert leaned forward, close to Edwin's ear. "I've got fifty byrnies and helmets to make and I've lost count of how many battleswords and skeggies."

"What's going on then? That's a big order."

"Sh... not so loud, keep this information under yer helmet, so to speak... it's a special order from Earl Harold."

"Yes, I get the idea Os, but why?"

"What do I know! I'm just an armourer. Look. A messenger comes to my workshop with a document, all official like. I read it and sure enough, there's the Earl's seal and mark. He doesn't let me keep the document, saying it's best if it wasn't hanging about the workshop for others to see. So, I'm here taking a break before me and my lad get back to work on this order, which will keep us busy for quite a while and... best of all, it's lucrative."

"Sounds like Harold's expecting trouble from that bastard over the sutherne sæ," replied Edwin.

"Dunno about that! But I do hear a lot of talk, especially Viking talk. King Edward, some might say, is now feeble. Consequently those over in the east are getting ready to pounce."

"You mean the Viking King, Harald Sigyrdssøn?"

Osbert nodded.

"I wouldn't take heed of that. For sure, the King's getting on in years but, as far as I know, he ain't feeble minded." Edwin suddenly caught himself from saying too much, remembering the King's letter. "Take my word for it, he is as crafty and devious as he ever was. Anyway we all know Englaland is surrounded by greedy, envious bastards who want part, if not all, of our country. We must be doing something right if we're such a prize. But believe me, I know where the real danger is from, because I was there. Northmandig. The Bastard Duke won't rest till he gets Edward's crown!"

"This is getting too deep and serious, enough to put me off my tipple. Here! Drink up and I'll get you another one," offered Osbert.

"No thanks. Must get home to Gwynedd, there's something I have to tell her."

*6 July, 1065*
## - Cærtaff, Wealh - mid-morning -
Cardiff, Wales

"Excuse me, my lord," called Wulfnoth, as Earl Harold was passing along the ship. "I thought we were going to be fighting, not rowing and pulling on sheet and ropes!"

The rest of the crew collapsed with laughter. The Earl gripped the mast, turned and shouted, "Quiet! Young Wulfnoth here and his brother want an answer and they shall have one. While you two lads are on board my ship, consider yourselves as buscarls. When we get on dry land, warriors."

The crew began laughing again and broke out in a slow rhythmic song;

"Row, row and row yer boat,
Gently up the bourne,
Merrily, merrily, merrily, merrily,
A buscarl's life is yorn."

Wulfnoth was initially embarrassed, then angry but as much as he tried to keep himself stoically aloof, he couldn't. He shook his head, smiled and joined in with the singing.

Theirs was the lead ship of Harold's hurriedly assembled fleet. There were six ships in all, carrying three-hundred Wessex warriors. They were sailing to rescue merchant shipmen who had been stranded in the tidal waters of the Usk, by the attacking Wealhasc.

"Lower the yard!" shouted the captain. Men rushed to man the halyard, two braces and the sailyards.

"Stow the sail!"

After the yard and sail had been secured on the crutches, the order was given, "Oars!.... Ready!..... Strike!"

Wulfnoth and Edric were in near panic, trying to keep pace with the other thirty-two rowers.

"Did it! I did it in time," shouted Edric in relief. He was sitting alongside Wulfnoth on the steerboard side.

Both of them, being new boys, had found it difficult to master the discipline and speed which they had to employ; gathering one's oar, stowing it when the yard and sail was raised and when lowered, grabbing hold of the oar, opening the oar ports to thread the oar through and begin rowing. Soon, their hands were sore and bleeding from torn blisters. Still they pulled their oars, not showing the other crewmen they were in agony. They had to ignore the pain, even look to be enjoying it. They were involved members of this ship's crew, a tightly knit unit of sixty-five fighting men.

As Wulfnoth struck and heaved with the rest, he could feel the sleek vessel surge forward at every pull.

Passing the Wealhasc headland, Harold's small fleet glided in through the narrow channel which opened up into a wide, naturally formed harbour, surrounded by small timbered, thatch roofed houses which formed the fishing village of Cærtaff.

Mooring unopposed, Harold's men rapidly disembarked and formed up along the dockside.

"I wonder where Rhiryd and his crowd are," muttered a senior officer, behind Wulfnoth.

"Who's he, sir," asked Wulfnoth, not wanting to turn around.

"Rhiryd ab Ifor, is the local Wealhasc supremo who is causing us a bit of trouble hereabouts."

"Move out!" came the command from the front.

They headed east. Wulfnoth turned his head in time to see the fleet set sail and return to sæ with the remaining crews.

Harold's warriors marched through, what seemed to be an empty village and on into the countryside.

"What now?" said Wulfnoth, nudging his brother in the ribs.

"We keep marching until we stop!"

"Very funny. There's nobody about, that makes me nervous. Remember what Dad told us about when he was here last."

"Yea, I know," replied Edric. "Watch out for surprise attacks, especially from the Wealhasc with small bows."

"At least marching with our shields on our backs, gives us some protection…"

"Silence back there!"

"As a matter of interest, sir," queried Wulfnoth, "this Rhiryd ab Ifor, is he someone we should be worried about and… why are we here?"

"You ask a lot of questions," replied the officer. "If you must know, we're marching overland to the Usk, a major bourne for trade. This 'ere local bantam, Rhiryd ab fucking Ifor, is the grandson of King Gruffydd, as he likes be known by everyone. He has taken it into his head to charge double the normal toll fee. Our poor ol' Wessex merchantmen are up in arms about it, and have refused to pay. So Ifor sent in his boys to cut the anchor rope of one of our ships, running off with it… the anchor that is. The crew had to swim for their lives and board one of our other ships. Now we are going to catch those bastards and teach them a lesson they won't forget. Understood?" chuckled the officer.

"Yes, but why did they up the toll charge?"

"I don't know… they probably heard about Tostig upping the taxes in Northymbria and thought, if it's alright for him, it's alright for them, so they did the same. Any more questions?"

"No, but thanks," replied Wulfnoth, somewhat surprised by his lengthy answer.

"Don't mention it," said the officer.

*6 July, 1065*
**- Upper Barnstæd -**

"He didn't want you then?" said Gwynedd, following Edwin into the main hall. "Can I get you a drink?"

"No! No, not at the moment, I need to be doing my job, the job I've trained for all my life. I am a warrior, for God's sake! A housecarl to the Earl." Edwin dropped down hard, on the bench seat "Now I don't know what I am."

"All I'm hearing is about you! What's happened to our boys?"

"The Earl is taking them to Brycgstow and from there on, I don't know. Doesn't what's happened to me mean anything to you?"

She gave him a hard look.

"You mean, you're not going to war against somebody but our boys are! That means they may not come back home in one piece, if at all!"

"The Earl said he would take care of them. Other than that, there's nothing more to tell.... 'It's a young man's profession,' he said. And I am not a young man any more. I'm old and passed it. 'Hang up yer sword and axe,' he said!"

"Well none of us are getting any younger," replied Gwynedd, with a shrug.

"I know... and I feel useless!"

"Oh dear... so you want me to feel sorry for you? Well, I don't! You're my husband. You're here, safe, in one piece and as far as I'm concerned, that is better than fighting on the other side of the country or elsewhere. So get your arse off that bench and see to the roof of this place because it's leaking, and hope that our beautiful boys come home safe and sound!"

Gwynedd started to cry.

Edwin put his arm around her and pulled her close.

"Gwynedd, Gwynedd. They're grown men. They're well trained warriors and I pity anyone who gets on the wrong side of them."

"And can you promise me they'll come home safe?"

"No one can promise that. All we can hope for is that they'll use their skill and intelligence. I have every confidence that they will come home with honour and that Earl Harold will be proud of our lads."

He took a piece of cloth and wiped Gwynedd's eyes.

"Look at me, a blubbering baby."

"Gwynedd, you're not a blubbering anything. You're a mother

who loves her boys."

"And look at you," she replied, looking up at her husband's moist eyes. "Don't you go all teary eyed on me, one person is enough for one day."

"So, what am I going to do now?" said Edwin, wiping his own eyes.

"You'll do what you always do… get on with your life and this time, here!"

"The sun's still shining, let's go for a walk."

*6 July, 1065*
**- Approach to the Usk bourne, Wealh, late morning -**
River Usk, Wales

An arrow glanced off Wulfnoth's helmet, piercing a warrior close by. 'Shit! I heard the noise of it coming,' thought Wulfnoth, 'I should have known better and put my shield up or ducked down at least. No, better the shield because you only end up getting spiked or somebody else does. Why did it take me by surprise, it shouldn't have done? What did father say, always expect the unexpected and remember that it can come from behind any tree or bush and it could split you from arsehole to gullet. Yes, that was certainly a wakeup call, Wulf me lad.'

"Scieldwiath!" shouted Henric, a senior officer.

Harold's men had stopped, grouped into a square, holding their shields so that each overlapped in the fashion of a wall.

"Anyone hurt?"

"One man down, sir," came a voice. "He's wounded in the shoulder."

"Serious?"

"No sir, I'll survive," replied the wounded man, a rank away to the right.

"Another man down!"

Wulfnoth glanced from behind his shield and immediately took cover as several more missiles streaked in, only to thud into the shield wall.

"Where are they?" shouted Earl Harold.

"In the wood a little to the left of that small ash tree."

"Take cover! More missiles coming in!"

The enemy hadn't moved from their position. Wulfnoth saw a glint of metal. 'I know where you are, dummies! You've given your position away.'

"Forward in slow formation!"

They moved steadily ahead, the odd arrow hurtling in, slamming into a shield.

"There can't be many of them," whispered Wulfnoth. "They're keeping pace with us and stupidly too, not very clever at keeping out of sight."

"Keep moving!"

"You know what," said Edric. "I wouldn't mind getting my hands on one of their short bows."

"Do what?"

"Another bow to my... string," he laughed, nudging Wulfnoth in the arm.

"Ha fucking ha... piss off! We've got enough to carry, never mind, bows and fully loaded quivers. How about I hand you a walking stick to keep you upright under the weight?"

"Oy! You Barnstæd boys," warned Henric, you're pissing me off. Shut the fuck up and keep moving!"

The wooded area seemed to be never ending and after about an hour they stopped. Moving amongst the troops were two senior officers, who stood in front of Wulfnoth and Edric, one was Henric. Suddenly he turned on the spot and smiled, if one could call it a smile. Through his black beard, it was more like an evil grin. He handed Edric a short bow and a quiver full of arrows.

"Now, big mouth! See what you can do with these toys."

"I've only fired a long bow, never one of these small things before!' replied Edric.

"Well, now's yer chance to shine and find out all about it… right."

"But…!"

"No fucking buts," commanded Henric. "Get on with it! You're the one who wanted to play with these wood an' string toys!"

Edric turned to Wulfnoth for sympathy.

"Nothing to do with me bro."

"Thanks a lot," replied Edric.

Henric took Wulfnoth by the arm.

"For some peculiar personal and unknown reason, the Earl looks very favourably, if not kindly as to a father on his children, on you two new boys. Don't ask me why 'cos I haven't honestly worked it out as yet…but I will, believe me! As you have very cleverly spotted our enemy, darting like roe deer among the trees yonder, see that your brother doesn't catch cold or do something stupid. Do yer follow me?"

Wulfnoth nodded.

"Right! You other six. I want you all…" said Henric loudly, winking at the men, "to follow young Wulfnoth here, and flush those bastards out of that wood. Bring 'em back here and don't take all day about it!"

'Shit!' thought Wulfnoth, taking charge, shouting his first command.

"Swinfolce!" The troop of eight, rapidly arranged themselves into a phalanx of two abreast, resembling a 'hogs snout', their shields held ready, forming a wall around them. "Prepare to advance, in formation. Abrecaaaan!"

Their charge into the wood brought no return of fire.

"Halt!" commanded Wulfnoth.

They squatted in formation with drawn swords listening in silence for what seemed an eternity.

Wulfnoth, crouching, felt as if his heart was almost pounding out of his chest.

'The whole forest must be able to hear my heart thumping,' he thought. After a little while his pulse calmed. He wiped his forehead with the back of his hand. 'These men are experienced, not like Edric and me. Brilliant! I give a command and it's done. I could really get to like this. Funny how, in a flash, I can remember all those commands Dad and Egbert taught us. Where did the command, 'Swinfolce' come from, I can't recall it? Must have been from Dad but the men knew what it meant, and fell in formation immediately.'

From among the forest sounds of animals, birds and rustling trees, came a muffled, soft choking cough, audible enough for Edric to know the direction the sound came from. He pointed to a large holly bush. Wulfnoth nodded. Edric gripping the bow, nocked an arrow aimed and, steadily pulling back the string, fired.

"Aah!"

"Stand faest!" commanded Wulfnoth.

Edric had already drawn the bow again and fired once more.

His second arrow disappeared into the bush clipping the branches as it went in but no other sound came except for a rustle in the undergrowth.

"Advance with caution!"

On the ground lay a young Wealhascman. He had dark curly hair a stubbly face and small eyes that stared defiantly at Wulfnoth and the men standing nearest to him. It was a steady gaze; the look of a man who expected death. An arrow was sticking out of his bloodied left shoulder and was obviously causing him a great deal of pain but he tried not to show it. Edric stepped forward and was first to speak.

"Where are the rest of your men?" he said in Wealhasc, feeling very grateful to his mother for her lessons in her native tongue.

The man didn't reply but kept his gaze on Wulfnoth, as if he were gauging his next move.

"Right! It's pointless talking any more," said Edric, taking hold of his skeggy and aiming it at the man's stomach. "Wulf, undo his breaches I want the see what he's got down there before I chop it off."

The man responded shaking his head and pointed with his right hand.

"The rest of them are over there!"

"How many?"

He indicated with two fingers.

"There were only three of us, I promise."

Wulfnoth, shifting his gaze from the man, peered in the direction indicated.

"Your man is badly wounded," he shouted. "He will be taken care of. You two had better come out. Now! You will not be harmed."

"We don't believe you, Englisc," came a reply.

"Prepare to attack! Scieldas!" shouted Wulfnoth.

"We're coming out! We're coming out!"

"Well done lads," said Earl Harold. "Just the three of them?"

"Yes, my lord," answered Wulfnoth.

The prisoners were led away and out of sight.

After a short rest, Harold's men were on their way again and crossing a shallow ditch. Wulfnoth and Edric saw, strewn and half hidden amongst the tall grass in the ditch, the bodies of the three Wealhascmen.

Edric looked at Wulfnoth, "That ain't right."

"I know! I gave my word," answered Wulfnoth.

"Shut up!" came Henric's voice behind them. "Taking sides with your Wealhasc friends are you?"

"They're not our friends. We just happen to speak their language. They surrendered to me and I gave my word they would be safe."

"Word of warning, boyo," said Henric. "Let 'em go today and tomorrow those same Wealhasc bastards will cut yer throat!"

Wulfnoth didn't say any more but was beginning to feel angry. 'Am I cut out for this life? If we had spared their lives and released them, would they again have attacked us? Probably. After all, this is their country we're invading. I need to think some more on this. For the time being, I'll keep my own council and discuss it with the lads later.'

The Usk, a waterway, meandered for miles from the Sabrina well into the suthlands of Wealh. A nerve centre for trade, it was normally packed with merchant ships. Now the Usk was deserted as was the toll office, save for the Offa. The ship had been plundered and stripped of its valuable cargo, including its sail and oars. Now it was stuck firmly on the muddy reach.

"They must have seen us coming," said Wulfnoth. "There's no one in sight."

"Don't just stand there like a bunch of pregnant fairies!" shouted Henric. "The ship won't move on its own!"

"You wouldn't think it all that difficult to shift this boat, would you?" said Edric to his brother. They were both up to their ankles in mud.

"And this ain't no fucking boat, as you call it," shouted Henric. "It's a ship!"

"Thanks… for that bit of information, sir," replied Wulfnoth, sarcastically.

"I hope you two aren't going to give me any trouble," said Henric, who seemed bent on pushing the boys.

"But it might be easier if we were to wait for high tide," volunteered Wulfnoth.

Henric was about to walk away, instead, he shook his head, muttering.

"I'll find out about you two. In the meantime, get yer battle gear!"

"Right! I've got another job for you. Fall in here, with that lot," commanded Henric.

"Where are we going, sir?" asked Edric.

"Ee, lads, 'e wants to know where we're going," Henric replied, sarcastically. "Up there to the village of Stow, leastways that's what the locals call it. Yer see that stone church?"

"Yes sir."

"Well that's St Woolos and a little birdie told me our ship's missing anchor might be in there. Now we're going to find out if it's true. Understood?"

"Yes sir," replied Edric

The door of the church crashed open, Harold's troops began searching every corner of the building, tearing away curtains, overturning seats, tipping over any furniture that could possibly hide the stolen anchor.

"What are you doing," protested a short fat priest, from a small doorway, his long, drab looking cassock accentuating both his girth and his thick neck. He also had a red mottled face with a bulbous, pitted nose. Its appearance was probably due to drinking too much wine. He sat down on a bench shaking his head as the men continued their search.

"Well, it ain't by the altar or anywhere," somebody moaned.

"And it ain't here either," grumbled Henric.

"Who are you people?" shouted the priest. "You can't come in here tearing my church apart, this is a sanctified, House of God!"

"Look in here, sir!" shouted one of the men to Henric.

"Well, well, well," said Henric, almost euphoric. "What 'ave we got 'ere."

The main door of the church opened and slammed shut again with a crash as more of Harold's men came inside.

In a back room beyond the high altar, were crates of food, stolen from the Offa but still no anchor and for that matter, at least for the moment, no priest.

A commotion on the far side of the church made Wulfnoth stop as he was about to enter another door, by the side of the altar.

"I'm a man of God!" the priest was shouting, struggling in the arms of one of Harold's men. "You have no business holding me and desecrating my church."

"So what's all this 'ere then," said Henric, pointing to the crates. He uncovered a cheese resting on the nearest crate, "Phew! Cor!

What a smell! We've got a load more smelly ones 'ere. You call this cheese? And were you about to bless it? 'Allo what's this?"

Henric had parted the already unwrapped cheese, to discover it was a blue cheese with a hole in the centre, half filled with red wine. Tasting the wine, he licked his finger.

"Mmm, nice. Nothing like a drop of sweet red wine with yer cheese, eh, priest?"

"That's blood!" cried the priest, his mottled face getting redder. "It's blood! The cheese is bleeding! In the name of our holy father! See what have you done. God's wrath! The blood of Jesus!"

"Shut 'im up someone!" shouted Henric, "or I'll shut him up myself!"

"You'll do nothing of the sort!" ordered Earl Harold, marching down the central aisle. "I'll handle this priest."

"Yes my lord," answered Henric.

Earl Harold was able to placate the priest and had the church put back into order but the anchor was never found.

On the high tide the men had refloated the ship and from the back of the tollhouse, a dozen oars were recovered.

Because of the gentle flow of the tide and the fact there was no wind, they were able to manoeuvre the stranded ship into the centre of the bourne without difficulty, hoisting the Wessex Dragon pennant to the top of the mast.

Approaching from the direction of the Sabrina was Harold's returning fleet, leading two merchant ships.

On arrival they dropped anchor, alongside the Offa

"I want as many hands on this ship as possible," came the command.

Men were ferried out to the Offa. The new sail and yard, which had been brought from Brycgstow, were raised and the ship's rigging was inspected and seen to be intact, as was the steering oar. A spare anchor was brought on board.

By the end of the day the Offa was declared sæworthy and had begun its return to Brycgstow.

"Where are we going now sir," asked Edric.

"We're staying the night here and in the morning, we're marching further east, to a safer place, a spot nearer to the Wessex coast."

"How far will that be?"

"Not far," replied Henric," but you two are not marching with us, you are going to *row yer boat,* in one of the Earl's ships. Nighty, night lads." He sauntered off chuckling in a manner Wulfnoth found provocative. It was as if he wanted an excuse to put them down.

*8 July, 1065*
### - Earl Harold's new fortified base at Porth Ysgewydd, Wealh –
Portskewett, Wales

By the time the boys had arrived with the ships at Porth Ysgewydd, work had already begun on Earl Harold's fortified base. The ground plans, which included his hunting lodge, had been completed. The Earl himself was now making arrangements to leave; the King had called him back to Lunden for urgent talks. Henric had been put in charge, with orders to complete the building project as rapidly as possible.

"I've got both a scary and a sad feeling," said Wulfnoth, seeing the Earl and his ships leave.

"I get a scarier feeling knowing that Henric's in charge. What I can't understand is why does the Earl need to take the rest of the men and ships? I'd feel happier if he had left at least one ship here. With its anchor of course," grinned Edric, "and say a hundred and fifty men, just in case. Instead, there's only seventy of us, twenty of them carpenters and they ain't, by any stretch of the imagination, sword wielding warriors. I shouldn't think they would scare the Wealhasc, waving their hammers and chisels!"

"I suppose not," laughed Wulfnoth. "Maybe Earl Harold feels this place is safe enough, being that it's so close to the border. Especially after the peace treaty with the Wealhasc."

"Safe or not, we are now labourers!" complained Edric, taking another shovelful of earth and throwing it onto the pile above. "Or are we digging our own graves? I want some action!"

They were digging a defensive ditch and a raised earth foundation to put the palisade on.

"Action is it you want?" shouted Henric. "You'd better pray we don't have any. Out yer get! Right! Next detail!"

"About time, I just fancied a rest," said Edric, straightening his aching back.

"Not yet awhile," laughed Henric. "You two wanted action. Join Swefred's logging group, we need timber! Off yer go."

To Wulfnoth and Edric, all this was a new experience. They had never seen, let alone built a burh before, or any fortified base for that matter. Why would they? They had never travelled far from Upper Barnstæd. They had been told about fortified towns and villages but their village hadn't seen the need to have a defensive ditch and wall, so far nobody had ever attacked it. But here in Wealh, close to the Englisc border, King's peace or no, there was a need for protection, if only from raiding Vikings.

Earl Harold, having promised the merchants a safe base, chose to build it at Porth Ysgewydd which would not only be an important port in its own right but would be close to Gleucester and only three miles across the Sabrina to the Englisc coast.

From the forest close by there was plenty of available timber. The building work soon began to take shape and after two and half weeks the timbered palisades and surrounding ditch had been completed, leaving the lookout tower and other buildings, including the Earl's hunting lodge, still to be finished. It was hoped the lodge would be ready in time for the Fat Season.

Standing guard at the main gate, Edric gazed towards the forest.
"I'm tempted to do a bit of hunting," he said. "I saw some red

deer the other day, how about it, Wulf?"

Wulfnoth shook his head.

"Not me! It's not the season and anyway, it'll be just what ol' Henric would be waiting for… an excuse to make an example of us, and put us in bad with Earl Harold."

"He would as well. I wish the Earl had taken Henric with him and dumped the bastard in the middle of the Sabrina. He took a distinct dislike to us, right from the word go." Edric stopped, gazing towards the forest then looked around at the building works. "It's amazing how much work can be done when you have the manpower and the raw materials close by. I was only saying to someone the other day, if we had found the locals, we could have pressed them into doing the hard work, then the place would have been finished by now. Do you know what he said?"

"You're going to tell me they searched high and low, and couldn't find them," replied Wulfnoth, "'cos they had run away. They had seen us coming?"

"That's right, that's what he said but I don't believe it. I know they're around here somewhere, lurking in that forest," said Edric pointing, "I feel it in my bones!"

"You may well be right, Ed, which is even more reason why you shouldn't go hunting…wait a mo… are you seeing, what I'm seeing?" Wulfnoth began scrutinising, not only the forest north of them, but the shrubland in between.

"You're right! I think we may have found them. I told you so. All this time they were hiding nearby, watching us. Now the Earl's gone with the bulk of the army, there are not enough of us left to fight them off," Edric said, slowly shaking his head.

Wulfnoth looked at their small compound; at the soldiers and the carpenters.

"Doesn't look good. I've always thought it would only take few fire sticks thrown into this place for it to go up in flames."

"We had better let Henric know."

By the evening, within their fortified base, the noise of rasping saws and pounding hammers had ceased. The golden hue of the setting sun, which had cast its ever-elongating shadows across the enclosure, had given way to a haunting darkness. Henric's men silently took their positions on the palisades and waited.

"It's as we said," whispered Wulfnoth, "If the enemy fire this place, we'll be trapped."

"And now, I can't see a fucking thing out there and here we are waiting to make a fight of it, that is, when it comes," replied Edric, looking to see where Henric was. "He does love organizing people doesn't he, throwing his weight around but do you know, somehow I'm beginning to like him."

"You worry me sometimes Ed, but I have to say, for the last week or so he hasn't bothered us, in fact I think you could be right, he's become almost human. Doesn't that worry you?"

"Here they come!"

Glints of light from fire sticks could be seen in the shrubland. Suddenly propelled into the air, they fell among the timbered buildings, most falling harmlessly to the ground.

"You lads," said Henric, emerging from the darkness, out of breath. "Are you alright?"

"Yes, at the moment!" replied Wulfnoth.

"Just keep yer heads down until they try to climb over the palisade and keep yer eyes peeled. If yer need me, I'm over by the lookout tower."

They watched Henric race over towards the half-built tower in the northeast corner holding his shield above his head.

"Duck!" shouted Wulfnoth.

CRASH! A siege ladder pounded out of the darkness against the palisade. More followed crashing against the defences where Wulfnoth and Edric were. They could see even more, all along the palisade. Wealhasc troops were screaming, shouting their battle cries as they climbed their ladders.

"They're everywhere! Like fucking ants!" shouted Wulfnoth,

"Back to back, Ed!"

"Never saw that coming! Shit! There's hundreds of them," Edric shouted back, showered in blood from slicing into the first of the enemy who had come within reach. Then chopping at another and another, this time with his long handled skeggy. By now the Wealhasc were pouring over the palisades.

"It's a bloody nightmare!" shouted Wulfnoth.

Self-preservation had kicked in. The brothers, using their immense strength, fought nonstop, wielding their battleswords and skeggies in a frenzied fight to stay alive.

Back to back they protected each other, as in a well-choreographed dance macabre. Let loose for the first time on a battlefield they were a double killing machine, fending off blows with shields, chopping down, slicing and thrusting. Never in a million years could they have imagined such a battle! Stomachs sliced open, the smell of entrails; spouting blood from severed limbs and heads. No matter how hard they had trained, they could never have been prepared for this.

Eliminating the enemy in front of them was their only objective, they had no mind for the other warriors and the tradesmen, nor how they were faring. They were focussed on survival. So they continued to battle against the ever increasing numbers of screaming Wealhasc whose only thought, if thought it was, was to smash and hack the Englisc into oblivion with knives, swords and cudgels.

"There are too many," shouted Wulfnoth. "We can't hold them for much longer. Make for that pile of timber where Henric is."

Heads down and shields up they scrambled down from the palisade and raced for cover.

"Fuck!" shouted Henric. An arrow had pierced his shoulder. "I'm spiked! Get me behind the Lodge!"

Wulfnoth and Edric dragged Henric and propped him up next to a freshly cut, tree trunk.

"Take those boards away!" ordered Henric, pointing to the

ground.

The boards had been covering a carefully dug hole, long and deep enough for a four man grave and it was close to the palisade.

"Get in," ordered Henric, "before they see us!"

"What about you?" replied Wulfnoth.

"Just get in!"

Henric, bleeding from his shoulder wound, began struggling one handed to topple the tree trunk over. Wulfnoth, realising what Henric was trying to do, pushed him away and toppled the trunk onto its side. Sliding down into the hole, pulling Henric with him, he rolled the trunk over, covering them from sight.

"You all right, sir," whispered Wulfnoth.

Wulfnoth felt a hand on his arm, "Thanks."

Wulfnoth knowing Henric, realised it was against his nature to say more. It would make it seem, to them and others, that he was no longer the tough, senior Housecarl, a 'Thingalith' as he was supposed to be. They stayed crouched in their hole and waited.

"Hope the others got away," whispered Edric.

"Doubt it," replied Henric, who was leaning half against and wall and half on Wulfnoth.

"I don't know what the Wealhasc are doing up there but there's a lot of noise, like they're having a party but at least the cries have stopped!"

"Sorry lads, needs must. I've got to have a shit!" whispered Henric.

"I suppose... when yer got to go, yer got to go," replied Wulfnoth.

Edric nudged Wulfnoth who had mockingly put a rag over his nose.

"Actually I've never known Henric to smell any different."

"When I see your father I shall tell him what a couple of shi... stupid bastards you are."

"You don't know our father," replied Wulfnoth. "And what's more, you need us more than we need you, if you want that wound attended to."

"Piss off! What are you now, physicians? 'Ere 'av you got anything I can wipe my arse with, straw or leaves?"

"No! You'll have to stay shitty and smelly," answered Wulfnoth. "And, about your shoulder, we know enough but we can't do much down here in this stinking privy!"

"Yea!" laughed Edric, softly, "I've never been stuck in a privy before, have you, Wulf?"

"Who's idea was this anyway," answered Wulfnoth. "Armed to the fucking teeth with battle swords and stuck in... a shit hole!"

"Shut up! Did you ever hear about how King Edmund Ironside met his end?" said Henric, trying to be friendly.

"Poisoned, wasn't he?" replied Edric.

"Nah, not a bit of it," whispered Henric. "Cnut sent a couple of his men to kill him. They sneaked into the royal chamber, slid down into the royal shit-pit and waited for Edmund to sit on his privy."

"How could they've waited for so long, up to their ankles in that stinking stuff? It could have been hours, or days," sniggered Edric. "But then again, it was top draw shit... royal shit!"

"Shut up!" hissed Henric. "Anyway, when he came to his privy and sat down, the bastards thrust their spears right up his royal arse!"

"Ooh," cringed Edric, feeling his own stomach and arse. "It's too painful to think about. Did he die of constipation?" Edric began to laugh. "Or, please sir, I've got a terrible stomach ache. Never mind lad, we'll soon iron that out... what a way to go." The tears of laughter were now rolling down the cheeks of both the boys.

"And in the call of nature," quipped Wulfnoth.

"You two think you're so fucking clever and funny," snorted Henric. "Wulf, try to control your brother, on second thoughts, you're both as sick as each other."

"Cheer up Henric!" whispered Wulfnoth, close to Henric's ear. "Methinks our late King Edmund died of, a gladio usque ad rectum." He tried in vain, once more, to control his laughter.

"Smart arses! Ha, fucking ha," replied Henric, wincing with pain.

"Where did you learn that monkish stuff?"

"Never you mind," said Wulfnoth, "some of those priests know a thing or two. Listen!"

They craned their heads in silence. To their surprise, all above had gone quiet.

"Either they've heard you two idiots laughing and are waiting up above," whispered Henric, "or they've taken what they want and left."

"What do we do?" asked Edric.

"Wait! And then we wait some more," replied Henric.

Wulfnoth and Edric stretched up and slowly rolled the tree trunk away from the entrance and climbed out, pulling Henric up after them.

The silence which met them was only disturbed by the crackle of glowing embers in what was left of the unfinished buildings and tower. They lay low in the dark for what seemed an age before moving away from the smouldering remains of the hunting lodge. Then they began searching for anyone who was still alive. The compound was littered with corpses; friends, workmen and the few merchants who had stayed behind. Furniture and goods for the lodge had gone or had been burned, as had the merchants' supplies.

"Hey!" whispered Wulfnoth, " I've found what we need!"

"What's that," replied Henric.

"A blacksmith's iron and a spoon. Come over here."

"Oh no!" said Henric.

"Look! If you want to survive that wound, I need to get that arrow-head out of your shoulder and sear the wound before it goes bad. But it's going to be painful."

"I know, I've seen it done before," replied Henric. "Are you sure you can do it?"

"Our mother is a healer and she taught us. That arrow head has got to come out. Now!"

"Then get on with it," said Henric, taking off his jerkin. "If I die,

I'll stick this arrow up your arse and kill yer,"

While Edric held Henric's upper arm steady, Wulfnoth inserted the silver spoon into the wound, manoeuvred it around the arrowhead and withdrew it, in one pull.

"That was neat!" said Henric, examining the barbed arrowhead, "and you just encase the head with the spoon and pull?"

"Yes." replied Wulfnoth. "Now comes the painful bit." Withdrawing the red hot iron from the glowing embers, he seared the wound. Henric made no sound.

"Right! Let's get away from here," said Henric, leaning on Wulfnoth. "Help me strap my shield onto my back."

"Are you up to walking?"

"Of course! I'm just a little faint, that's all. Any more searing with that fucking iron and I'd have had a cooked shoulder. I'll be alright, got to get away from this place an' make for the border."

"Over there," said Edric, who was out in front, pointing along the beach. "A boat!"

All three had drawn their swords and were approaching with care. Nobody seemed to be about. What light there was came from the waxing crescent of the moon. Within the boat were two sets of oars, carefully stowed. It seemed to be a new boat that had been pulled well up above the high tide mark and left for tomorrow's fishing.

Once they had pushed the boat down the shallow beach and into the water, they checked it for leaks. Seeing it was sæworthy, the boys grabbed hold of Henric's legs and heaved him up, toppling him unceremoniously into the boat. Edric was next up, pulling himself aboard.

Shouts of alarm shattered the night! Their theft had been discovered.

Wulfnoth, pushing the boat further out, was up to his waist in water, when an arrow passed close to his head with a whoosh and imbedded itself in the hull. He called for his shield as another and yet another came crashing in against the boat.

## - Upper Barnstæd -

Gwynedd was inconsolable. It was if she felt the pain of every agonising sword striking against the injured and dying in the Wealhasc assault.

On hearing news of the attack, she had ran out of their homestead, screaming for her children, falling on the mudded ground and pounding it in fury with her fists.

"My boys! My boys!" she cried, "I want my boys! I want my boys!... I just want my boys, alive! Safe and sound in mind and body!"

"Gwynedd my love, they were not found at the site. That mean they're not dead but alive!"

Still sobbing, she said, "Why! Why do we have to have these wars? Why can't you all leave the Wealhasc alone! God knows I have more cause to hate them than you!"

Edwin gathered his wife in his arms and hugged her.

"Our boys are well trained. They are smarter and they are stronger in arm than anybody else I know, and they are resourceful. Earl Harold's messenger assured me, Wulfnoth and Edric and their officer were not found amongst the dead... look read, the letter for yourself. The Wealhasc do not take prisoners, so our boys must have escaped."

"So much killing, why?"

"I don't know why, Gwynedd. I questioned the messenger and from what he said it was an unprovoked attack on a new, safe base they were building at Porth Ysgewydd."

"Where is that?"

"In the suth of the country, overlooking the Sabrina."

Gwynedd dried her eyes. "And you think our boys will be home soon?" she rested her aching head on her husband's shoulder.

"Listen my girl, you know you have extraordinary talents... sensory or whatever! Use them! Now, close your eyes, slowly and calmly concentrate and reach deep down into those senses. Feel as to whether our boys are alive."

Several moments passed.

"I can't feel any pain," she whispered. "Anxiety yes… I think they are alive," she wiped her eyes again. Holding Edwin close, she whispered, *"They must be alive."*

"I feel so too."

Gwynedd had no idea what her husband was doing. Since the news of the attack he hadn't been able to sit still. He had become a whirlwind of activity; if he wasn't cleaning his armour, he was arranging repairs to the house or taking stock of the land and fishery. Gwynedd had not been able to focus on anything at all, wanting only to see her boys again. At first she would walk to the to the outskirts of the village waiting until nightfall, straining her eyes into the far distance. One day she saw a smudge on the horizon and thought, 'Is that them, yes it must be!' As the figure came closer she realised it was only a traveller.

She wanted to ask him, "Have you seen my sixteen-year-old sons on the road? Both have reddish hair, good looking and tall?" But she knew the man would only shake his head, "Sorry, no," he would say.

Day after day she waited, watching as the sun set behind the forested land before making her way home, more dejected than the day before.

Then she refused to leave the homestead in case of news. But every day, every hour, her hopes were beginning to fade.

Thump! Thump! Thump!

"Who's banging on our bedroom door," shouted Edwin, grabbing his sword, "Gwynedd, get your seax, we have company."

"Who's there?" he shouted.

"Who'd yer think?"

Gwynedd, flung open the door and threw herself into the arms of both her sons.

"Oh, my boys! My lovely, lovely boys. We near thought you

were dead."

"And what time do you call this. It's past mid-night!" said their father, vainly trying to hide his emotion.

"But did yer miss us, Mum?" asked Edric.

"Well, not really. We've had so much to do here what with your father seeing to the land and the house and everything."

"Oh! Well then," said Edric, looking at Wulfnoth, "If they didn't miss us, we'll go back and fight the Wealhasc again."

"No! No you don't. You are not budging from this place, you're staying right here!" said Gwynedd, leading them back into the main hall. "You must be hungry, I'll rustle up something for you to eat."

She stopped suddenly, pointing at a huddled figure sitting at the table. "Who's this?"

"This is our friend…"

"Bloody hell, as I live and breathe! Henric you old bastard," greeted Edwin.

"'Allo, Ed," he said smiling.

"What brings you here?"

"I took an arrow in the shoulder. Your boys brought me 'ere, for your wife to 'ave a look at the wound. The last thing I want, is to lose the use of my arm."

"Who tended your shoulder?" asked Gwynedd.

"Wulfnoth and Edric. Why is it gone bad?"

"No… the wound is healing. That's a good job boys," she said turning and giving both her boys a tearful kiss.

"Edric 'ere held me down while Wulfnoth did the necessary. Do you know what 'e used?"

"You're going to tell us," replied Edwin, with a grin.

"One of the Earl's silver spoons and he near cooked my shoulder with a red hot poker." He shook his head. "And the worst of it, they were enjoying it."

"You must have given them a hard time then," said Edwin.

"Well….you've got to train 'em up, haven't yer?"

Henric got up and taking Edwin by the sleeve, led him outside.

"You 'ave two smart sons there Ed, and when the going's tough, they're as good as ever I've seen in battle. You've trained them well, I know! I saw them in action… a new one on me though, fighting back to back. They were…" Henric began to laugh, "Fucking devastating!" He then lowered his voice. "Have you heard any more news from Lunden?"

"Just rumours about the King's health," replied Edwin, "and the unease in the north. But I fear that Northman bastard across the sæ. We haven't heard the last of him, I know it!"

They stood together and looked up at the predawn sky.

"If you're right Ed, we'll all be drawn into that fight, retired or not!"

### - A secret summons -

"My lord!" said the messenger dismounting, "an urgent message from, Earl Harold."

Edwin took hold of the document and broke open the seal. 'It doesn't give any reasons other than I should attend him along with my sons at his manor house at Suthweca. Why our presence? Why urgently? Perhaps it's a meeting of the Earl's inner circle. Friends he can trust. What of his family or official advisors? Surely they would be… but I've said that to him in the past. This can only mean the King doesn't know of the meeting. It sounds ominous.'

Edwin had an uncomfortable feeling, 'Is the King dying or dead?' he thought. 'No. It would say so. A rebellion brewing, involving the Earl's brother, Tostig and he wants my advice? Surely not.' He cast his mind back to their sæ journey the previous year and remembered how the Earl had sought his advice then. How he had opened his mind to him and the reasons why. 'But why bring Wulfnoth and Edric? I'd rather not have them involved.' He put the document down and considered the contents. 'Well, if he wants to see the boys, so be it.'

Turning to the messenger he said, "We shall be there tomorrow morning. Oh! By the way, who else will be there?"

"Only you and your sons my lord. Earl Harold wished to stress the meeting is to be kept a secret. Tell no one!"

"A secret? The message itself doesn't say anything about this meeting being in secret."

"He made me promise to tell you that. He was most insistent."

Edwin nodded, "Tomorrow then."

"Thank you, my lord." The messenger mounted his horse and galloped off, back towards Lunden.

Edwin couldn't help grinning to himself.

'My lord, he called me… I hardly think so.' He gazed after the rider who in a few moments was no more than a distant dusty blur, finally disappearing from view. Edwin, looking along the now empty road had a nagging feeling of unease.

The very notion of being urgently needed and in secret, sounded more than just trouble. What could it possibly be, he wondered.

"What did *he* want?" asked Gwynedd, from the doorway. "I hate messengers, they never bring good news."

"It seems Earl Harold now needs me and the boys! We are to attend him at Suthweca but it's to be kept secret. Where are the boys?"

"Secret?"

"Yes, secret!"

"So, I heard nothing and I saw nothing?" she replied.

"What are the boys doing?"

"What they are always doing," she said, shaking her head. "Wielding those bloody blades for hours and hours on end."

# CHAPTER XVIII

*October, 1065*

**- A meeting at Suthweca, Lunden –**
Southwark, London

"My lord!"

"My dear Edwin!" exclaimed Earl Harold. "come inside, into the dry."

"Thank you, my lord," replied Edwin, leading his sons through an open doorway, handing their sodden cloaks to a waiting steward.

They followed Earl Harold into the hall.

"I've heard good reports about you two." The Earl looked from one to the other. "You're Wulfnoth and you're…"

"Edric, my lord."

"Yes, of course," Harold said, nodding his head. "The steward will take you to your room. It used to be my room back in the old days. Now, I wish to talk to your father, alone."

When the twins had gone, Harold offered Edwin a seat near to him, close to the fire. On a table next to them was a platter of cold meats, a jug of mead and a collection of odd sized goblets.

He poured them some mead, then proposed a toast.

"Here's to your health, my friend and that of your sons who have gained much honour. And to our wives."

Harold bending forward raked the fire. Looking up he asked, "And how is your wife, is she well?"

"Yes, my lord, although it is a worrying time for her."

"Yes, I can well understand that… Gwynedd isn't it?"

"Yes, my lord."

'Surely he hasn't requested us to come all this way just to make small talk?' Edwin thought. 'He's nervous. He wants to make an important decision but is not sure what to do. I'll take a chance by asking him outright.'

Holding his goblet, clasping it around the bowl with both hands, he asked, "You summoned us here on an urgent matter?" Edwin looked steadily at the Earl, waiting for him to respond.

Harold looked away, screwed up his eyes and gazed into the fire, his face reflecting the flickering light of its flames. as if he were seeing into the future. Finally he broke the silence.

"My brother Tostig is in serious trouble. He has spent far too much time out of his earldom in the company of the King, especially in the last twelve months. He should have spent more time attending to the business in hand and now I fear it is too late. He has lost touch with the people of Northymbria, in particular his leading thegns. During the ten years since becoming Earl, he should have tried to gain respect and support. Instead he has employed heavy-handed methods to get rid of the lawlessness in the earldom. Though successful, it was attained at a price. Last year he increased the land tax." He paused for a few moments and looked at Edwin. "Raised it by fifty per cent!"

"Why so high?" asked Edwin, shocked.

"Because, and I believe this to be true, Edward advised him to do so. Wrongly in my view. It was to put the tax in line with the rest of the country. Northymbria's tax, I have to agree, was somewhat lower but it was low for various reasons, many of which were good However, if you're going to raise the tax, especially by that amount, you have to negotiate with your thegns first, to keep them on your side. But of course, he didn't. Now he has a rebellion on his hands or at least it's brewing, from what people tell me, and could flare up into a full blown conflict at any moment. I warned him of the possible consequences of this tax but he wouldn't listen. Instead he acts as if he is God almighty and is untouchable."

Edwin had expected something serious but not this. He had heard the rumours but this latest news was making him nervous. This was so highly confidential; the Earl was treating him as his friend, as his intimate friend! On the one hand he felt privileged but on the other he wasn't sure he wanted to hear Harold's secret outpourings.

"My lord! This is heavy political and private information, not for the ears of a retired warrior like myself, living out his final years in the countryside, mucking out his barns and seeing to his fisheries."

"My friend, you underestimate yourself. You are unique, totally trustworthy. I can tell you these things knowing they will go no further and knowing I will get an honest, unbiased, rational opinion. In the coming days I shall be needing your wise council."

Edwin thought for some time turning over in his mind all that he had heard and what he thought could possibly happen. Because of it, he felt reluctant to voice his views.

"Come on man, what do you think is going on? Surely my brother is not so stupid as to act as he has apparently done."

"It's just… I hesitate to answer, my lord."

"Why?"

"Because I fear the possible consequences."

"What consequences?" asked Harold.

"Because my words could be construed as treasonable. Therefore I would fear for the life of my wife, my boys and my friends, as well as myself."

"You have nothing to fear from me, Edwin. I promise you."

Edwin drew his chair closer to Harold and whispered, "I fear that your brother is being duped by the King."

"Duped? For what reason?"

"To bring about a Northymbrian rebellion."

Harold remained silent.

"What if the King's intention is to bring about civil war; a war between the north and suth."

"A war! For what reason?"

"What if the King wants to weaken the country? Weaken it

enough to make it easy for Duke William to take the crown? After all, Edward's dearest wish is to *give* him the crown. The only real barrier to that is yourself and the power of your family. United."

"You believe the King would do such a thing? But what kind of inducement would turn Tosti's head?"

"I don't know, my lord. Promises made for his future perhaps; a false promise to make him heir."

Harold, as if talking to himself, said, "And here was I thinking I was being paranoid; thinking of a similar conspiracy."

"The signs, I believe, have been there all along: the murder of Edward the Ætheling, the rumoured promise, as heir to the throne to William in fifty-two, when you and your family were in exile. The letter you showed me and, of course, the conversation I overheard all those years ago in forty-one."

"About that conversation. Can you remember any of it?"

"It was a long time ago, my lord," Edwin paused. Strangely, he had been thinking about that same dialogue on his way to Suthweca. "What I can recall was, Edward loved William more than a son and that he said he would have no children and guaranteed that William would be his heir… and that Englaland and Northmandig would be joined under one Kingship. I hadn't thought much of it until now. It seemed irrelevant at the time."

"The cunning old sod. Is it possible Edward has been planning this all these years? Even if I thought this was true, it would never be believed by the Witan and I'm not sure whether my brothers, Leofwine or Gyrth would believe it either."

"It is the truth, my lord. With this knowledge how will you go forward and how can you stop this rebellion?"

Harold drank the remains of the mead and put his goblet aside. Standing, he turned resolutely to Edwin.

"The Witan has been called and I am to attend. You will be part of my personal guard my 'Thingalith', to use an old expression and your boys will come too but rest assured Edwin, nobody will know of our conversation here tonight."

Edwin laughed nervously.

"Well… how can I refuse. Yes the my lord, I agree."

"Prepare yourself. We will have to make an early start tomorrow for Searoburh and then to Britons Ford. Good night Edwin."

"Good night, my lord."

Edwin watched Harold make his way slowly across the hall with, it seemed to him, all the burdens of the world on his shoulders, before disappearing into his room.

'I hadn't realised how bad the situation was. How could I have known? This is a weighty problem and beyond my experience.'

He rose slowly from his seat and made his way over to the room where the boys were. They were fast asleep.

'Just as well, my lads. Tomorrow will be a big day.'

*16 October, 1065*
**- Britons Ford, Wessex -**
Britford, Wiltshire

Edwin stood immediately behind Earl Harold's chair, still wondering why he was there. The Earl hadn't convinced him that his presence was necessary. He would just have to keep his mouth shut and listen.

A soft cough brought his attention to the man standing next to him. He hadn't even noticed who it was. Henric turned his head and gave a wry smile.

'Where has that ol' bastard's been in the last few months?' Edwin wondered. 'Suddenly appearing at Upper Barnstæd then disappearing just as quickly and never saying where he's been. Now here he is standing next to me as large as life.' He shook his head. 'I had better concentrate on what's going on here.'

Sitting opposite Harold at the table were Earls Gyrth, Leofwine and Tostig. Next to them sat Archbishop Stigand of Cantwareburh and three other senior churchmen who Edwin didn't recognise.

A royal steward called for all to rise as King Edward and Queen

Edyth entered. The King motioned for his nobles to sit.

'I hate all this ceremonial stuff,' Edwin thought. ''Allo, I knew *he* looked familiar, I haven't seen him in years. Brihtric Meaw, as I live and breathe. You've done well for yourself.'

The Witan having discussed all other matters, the King invited Earl Tostig to speak on the main topic of the meeting.

The Earl rose, leant forward, shaking with suppressed rage, looked at each and every one of his peers in turn.

"I see, Sire, that Earl Edwin of Mercia is absent! No matter. I have… terrible news! While I have been away, in peaceful pursuits in the company of Your Majesty, enemies of our land, criminal Thegns of my own earldom, have risen up against me! Attacked! Seized! And ransacked, my capital, Eoforwïc!"

Tostig, a broad shouldered, thirty-eight year old, with a powerful personality, much like his father, dominated the shocked Witan.

"My wife… my two sons… barely escaped alive!" He took a deep breath. "My housecarls were murdered, trying to protect my home!"

'Harold was more than right,' thought Edwin, 'this is leading to war!'

"Now," continued Tostig, "the rebels are marching suth as we speak!" He looking directly at the King, "I need not tell you, Sire, the country must confront these rebels and crush them before they wreak more damage in our land. I am reliably informed the rebels have reached Northumtun!"

"My Lord Tostig," replied the King calmly, "your wife, Judith and your sons, are they safe and well?"

"Yes Sire, they are as well as can be expected."

"Thank the Almighty for that," said the King, giving Tostig a sympathetic look. "We must confront these rebels as quickly as possible and find out what they want. We should seek a peaceful solution before we embark on any sort of military action but I feel sure it will not come to that, and that these rebels will come to their senses."

The King looked towards Harold.

"Lord Harold! Go to Northumtun and meet with them. My lords! We will meet again in twelve days' time, at Oxenaforda." Rising from his chair, King Edward turned to Harold, "And then, we can proceed from there: we don't want to be hasty."

Edwin followed Earl Harold and his brothers out of the room. Tostig, who was, by now, close to Harold, suddenly gripped his sleeve.

"Harold! You've got to help me!"

"I will, I promise Tosti, I'll do whatever it takes! Let's go somewhere more private." Harold took his brother aside.

"Harold," Tostig began, when they were out of hearing, "I've just heard your brother-in-law Morkere is involved. He has taken my title and land!"

"Well, you have more information than I do. I only knew there was trouble. If Morkere is involved his brother Eadwyn is too. We both know Eadwyn doesn't take chances, like Morkere, and that he will see sense... he must!"

"For God's sake Hal, I hope you're right because if something is not done to stop this madness... I will lose everything..." Tostig put his arm around his brother's shoulders. "The King appointed me Earl... it was something I always wanted... it hasn't been easy cleaning up that land. Old Siward left it in a mess and totally lawless. Just when I thought I had it all straightened out... it's crumbling back into chaos. Hal... I want my earldom back and I don't care what it costs... cancel the fucking tax, give 'em back their money, anything but I must have my earldom... Hal, just do it!" He had tears in his eyes.

Harold was now convinced, Edwin had been correct about the King's motives but couldn't say anything, at least not now.

"Tosti! Get yourself together. I'll do whatever I can. I know what you're going through and what you fear, and I'm sure they'll see sense, they must do! At Northumtun I'll assess the situation and see what's to be done, I promise."

"Here's me blubbering like a woman. Let's get back to the others. This is a black day Hal, very black. Now it's up to you. I'm... we're all in your hands now."

"This is a black day for us all, Tosti," Harold replied. "As I've said, I'll do all I can, believe me."

*20 October, 1065*
**- Northumtun, Mercia -**
Northampton, Northamptonshire

"I didn't think I'd ever see *you* again," said a voice.

Edwin closed his eyes momentarily and grinned.

"I know that voice," he turned around and there in front of him was Hengist, the Mercian. It was years since he had seen him. His hair was grey and longer but his eyes, from under his bushy eyebrows, were as bright blue as ever. He still had a few teeth left, despite complaining, as Edwin remembered him doing, that he only had one tooth in his head.

"The Earl's come to negotiate and the rest of us are here to protect his back."

"The Earl and you will be alright. Who are these two young warriors?"

"Meet my sons, Wulfnoth and Edric."

Hengist greeted them with a slight nod of approval.

"You look as if you can handle yourselves. Want to join us? I can guarantee plenty of action."

"We've got enough action down suth," replied Wulfnoth, with a grin.

"You will always be welcome. Ed, my sutherne friend, there won't be much negotiating here, I can promise you. The Northymbrian lads have made up their minds. Morkere is in charge now. Harold's brother Tostig is out. Enough said. See yer later, I've been called."

"Who was that?" asked Wulfnoth.

"Hengist, an old Mercian friend of mine from way back. Your mother once saved his life."

"What's he like?" asked Edric.

"Better to have him on your side than against you. He turned out to be a man to be trusted and, in times of trouble, that is more valuable than gold. Yes, he is as good as the best of men when you get to know him but, with this business… well, he is a Mercian, who knows!"

"What happens now?" asked Wulfnoth.

"Come close," Edwin whispered. "There's going to be a meeting but from then on, it's in the hands of the Gods. Do as we planned. Go and mix with the people. Anywhere where men are drinking. That's when their tongues are loose. Access the general mood; their opinions. Find out what's been happening up in the north but do it subtly… and above all, be friendly."

"We're always friendly," replied Edric, jokingly. "We're certainly not going to make any trouble with this scary lot."

Edwin watched his sons move among the troops, picking up proffered mugs of beer. Wulfnoth, leaning over to grab some food, laughed at someone's joke.

A hand on Edwin's shoulder brought him face to face with Earl Harold.

"Follow me."

Edwin turned to take a last look at his boys but they were nowhere to be seen.


"These are our terms," said Morkere, the newly elected Earl of Northymbria, looking around and noting the approval of his men in the packed hall. He pushed across the table to Harold, an unsealed scroll.

Harold took his time unrolling the document and spreading it out flat, pinning it down on the table with a wooden blotter and a mug. Only then did he begin to read it. After a few moments he lifted his head, looked at Morkere, scratched the back of his neck and continued reading.

He looked up again.

"I can't take these proposals back to the King," said Harold. "You can't just oust Earl Tostig without the King's permission! Without holding a Witenagemot! What's this? 'Nithing'! You've sentenced my brother, 'Nithing'! To be outlawed? This is an outrage!"

"Read the rest of it," said Morkere.

"Did you not ask for Earl Tostig to appear before this… meeting, to answer whatever charges you have against him?" Harold quickly scanned the room. "No, clearly you did not! This document is totally unlawful!"

"Not unlawful, brother-in-law. Up here we *are* the law. The Thegns of Northymbria have voted," answered Morkere, looking stoney faced at Harold. "It makes no difference whether you or the King like it or not. The vote was unanimous. It's very simple; I'm in, Tostig's out, and sentenced. Everything else is on the table."

"Morkere, you know very well Tostig was appointed by the King with the Witan's consent," countered Harold, "and as such, you will have to put your proposals to both the King and the Witan."

"Don't talk to us about the Witan!" laughed Morkere. "We have our own council of wise men up here, and real justice for once. Something which we didn't have while your brother was Earl? He was lucky to be out of Northymbria, otherwise he would have been strung up, with the rest of his murdering bastards! The men of Northymbria have made their choice! I'm their Earl now. All King Edward has to do, is ratify it."

"Just one moment Morkere! What about my brother's wife and children! They barely escaped with their lives from Eoforwic! Was that justice? Was that your doing?"

"No! That happened before I was summoned to Eoforwic by the Northymbrian people."

"By God, I hope you're telling the truth," replied Harold, "because they're my flesh and blood and that would be a very black hole for you to fall into."

"You are in no position to threaten me, Harold, and for the second time, I wasn't there. I had no part in that!"

"I accept what you say, Morkere. I know what this unrest is about… it's this bloody land tax, isn't it? Isn't it? You realise, it was not *all* my brother's fault! The King was partly to blame. The King sanctioned this land tax. No one could possible know it would bring about such hardships. The last thing my brother and the King wanted was for people to be starving and destitute! I can tell you, Tostig is as distressed about this as anyone can be. Look, Morkere, if only you would see reason and accept my brother back, I can guarantee the King will put back the taxes, as they were in the days of Earl Siward… but first, you must cease this… turmoil!"

The whole room broke out in laughter.

"Turmoil! Is that what you call it?" shouted a voice.

"Oh yer!" shouted another. "Siward was a good Earl, not like your brother. Send Tostig back to us and we'll give 'im a real Northymbrian welcome. You obviously 'ave no idea what 'e was up to. Last winter was an 'ard one and Tostig knew it; livestock frozen where they stood, people dying of cold, then we 'ad the worst 'arvest on record and 'e still wanted the flesh off our bones. 'E went an' raised the land tax by fifty per cent, and you want us to take 'im back? On yer 'orse. All that bastard ever did, in all 'is finery, was traipse off to the Pope or ponce about huntin' with the King, while 'e sent paid Danisc mercenaries about the land, picking us off one by one 'cos we couldn't pay his bloody taxes! 'Ave 'im back? Don't make me laugh!"

"Yer!" added another voice from amongst the crowd. "We've 'ad over ten fucking years of 'im. We know what 'e's like. We'll never take 'im back! We know what 'is hired Danisc special's do… we have the marks and the dead to prove it!"

"If he had any regard for his people," shouted a tall man, pushing his way to the front, "why didn't he ever listen to us? There's many a man who can't pay his taxes and 'ave gone starving!"

Morkere, stood up and commanded silence. Nodding with approval at the general mood, he began.

"Harold, brother-in-law, I can guess what pressures you are under, coming here bravely, without a military force, to talk peace. Peace is what we want too. You have heard our complaints and… our decision, which, believe me, the Northymbrian people have thought long and hard about and do not take lightly. We have no complaint against you, Earl Harold, or of your two other brothers, just Tostig, who the people will not have back at any price. Because of his past actions against the people of Northymbria, he has been sentenced, 'Nithing'! So I ask you Harold, to respect our position and our decisions by taking our demands back to the King."

Earl Eadwyn of Mercia, Morkere's older brother, spoke up.

"Harold, we have known each other for a long time and I respect you and I hope we can remain friends but on this there will be no further negotiation. The King has to accept my brother as the new Earl of Northymbria."

"Then, my lord Eadwyn, you give me no choice," replied Harold.

Earl Eadwyn slowly shook his head.

"What's been done, is done. Tostig's rule has brought about nothing but violence and burning hatred from every corner of Northymbrian society, especially from those he should have listen to. Now the people have spoken."

"My lords, I am speaking for the King and he is most passionate about the rule of Cnut's laws. This rebellion is against those very laws, against the King and the King's appointed Earl. This situation can only lead to war; a war that would bring this country to its knees and bring about a terrible loss of life. Englaland would be so weakened it would only benefit our enemies from across the sæ!"

"We are adamant and we are prepared for war if war it is. Our troops are gathering in ever increasing numbers," replied Earl Eadwyn.

"Then there is nothing more I can do to change your minds?"

"No, Earl Harold, just convey our demands and proposals back to the King. Take with you two of our trusted Northymbrian Thegns, Gamelbearn and Glonieorn. They will also put their case, to the King. I must ask you Harold, to make a pledge for their safety; to keep them from arrest and guarantee their safe return."

"My Lord Eadwyn, you have my promise. They will be returned unharmed."

*28 October, 1065*
**- Oxenaforda, Mercia, Witenagemot -**
Oxford, Oxfordshire

Before the dawn sun could break through the heavy cloud cover, the late October weather was boasting its usual cold, dank mist, which hung like a grey smear over the landscape.

They had made a wide berth of the flooded banks of the Nen and were heading suth, away from the bourne and the cold low-lying, shrouded grasslands.

Edwin, peered from beneath a dew covered hood.

"I didn't see you last night, how bad is the mood?" he pulled his cloak even tighter around him.

"As bad as it bloody well can be," reported Wulfnoth. "After mingling and moving around, as you told us, we eventually joined a bunch men from Cair Daun, whose families have been hit hard by Earl Tostig's rule. But it is the new land taxes that have brought things to a head. So bad has the effect been, whole villages have upped and left, moving further suth to make a better life. I'll give you an example; if the taxes weren't paid on time, Danisc mercenaries would come crashing into their homes, taking what valuables they could and raping the women. God forbid, anyone should defend their women folk, they would be cut down. Dad, there is so much hatred for Tostig, raw hatred, you cannot believe it!"

"I heard as much at the meeting," replied Edwin.

"Earl Tostig is never going to be allowed back into Northumbria, unless by force of arms," concluded Edric, "Wulf and I, moved around the camp and no matter where we went last night, it was the same story… Earl Tostig is finished!"

Harold signalled for Edwin to drop back and leave his sons to ride up in front, next to the two Thegns from Northymbria.

"So, Edwin, what further information did your sons glean."

"As you know, my lord, they spent the evening among the troops."

"And?"

"Very much the same as we heard at the meeting. There's a tremendous amount of ill feeling directed towards your brother."

"I want specifics, Edwin. Never mind how personal it is. I need the truth man!"

"Alright!" answered Edwin, changing his grip on the reins, "A typical example, a family can't pay their monthly tax. Tostig's Danisc mercenaries arrive, break down their door…"

After Edwin had concluded his son's account, Earl Harold remained silent.

"They will never have him back, under any conditions, unless the King makes war and defeats the northerne armies."

"You mean the rebel army, surely," replied Harold, searching Edwin's face.

"No, my lord, the northerne armies. The Northymbrian, Mercian and Wealhasc armies! You saw for yourself how many they have under arms. These are no longer a bunch of disorganised rebels but a full blown army led by Morkere and Earl Eadwyn."

"So, what would you suggest I say to the King?"

"To avoid a war against the north, persuade him to accept Morkere's terms."

"You know what you're advising me to do?"

Edwin nodded. "What other option is there? The situation has gone on far too long. I can't see any way the damage can be undone."

Earl Harold slowly nodded and lightly tapped Edwin's arm.

"My brother won't like this! Let's see, what the King has to say."

For the rest of the four-hour journey, Harold rode ahead, alone, not speaking to anyone. Edwin riding behind, watched his sons in animated conversation with the Northymbrians.

Earl Harold had the onerous task of reading the rebels report to the King, to a subdued room full of men. When at last he had finished, he handed the document to the King's steward and sat down to an ominous silence.

Earl Tostig remained unusually quiet, not looking at his three brothers or anyone else, staring with eyes unfocussed down at the long, heavily built table in front of him, grinding his teeth all the while.

King Edward, as frail as he was, tried to stand, assisted by the Queen. He brushed aside the scrolled document.

"I sanctioned those taxes so that Northymbria would be in line with the rest of the country. So why should they have special privileges, are they not part of my realm? You there! What is your name?"

"Sire...?"

"Stand up, when you speak to me!"

"Sire!" The man replied, "My name is Glonieorn, son of Heardwulf, Thegn of Cair Daum."

"You're a long way from your home, Glonieorn son of Heardwulf. What is your complaint against Earl Tostig?"

"I have many, Sire."

"Many? This man has the audacity to charge Lord Tostig with *many* complaints?"

"Sire!" said Harold, with due respect. "We must hear what this Thegn has to say."

"Yes! Well, get on with it!" replied the King, testily.

The man swallowed nervously but continued, "Sire! The land taxes are too high, especially so, after the hard winter and the disastrous harvest. Families in the last two years have been left destitute, not able to pay these taxes. Then, because of this, Earl Tostig sent his Danisc mercenaries to rob those very same people, stealing anything of value. These mercenaries even rape our women folk!"

"That's a lie!" shouted Tostig, "Sire, it's all lies! Tell me what farmer doesn't complain; it's either too wet, not wet enough or it rained the wrong time of year or… it's too cold or too hot and now this, outrageous accusation!"

There was a general snigger of laughter.

Tostig turned to Glonieorn.

"And what of the city of Eoforwïc? You ransacked my home! My wife, who had no way of defending herself and our children, had to run for their lives, just managing to escape. And what of my friends, Amund and Ravenswart? Men you know very well. You dragged them outside the city walls and butchered them like dogs. Would the fate of my family, have been the same. Butchered?" Tostig waited for his words to take effect. "And what of the people, suth of the city who too were defenceless, what of them? Again, butchered by these ravening dogs! Sire, my lords, over two hundred of my friends and their families were put to the sword."

"Sit down, Lord Tostig. This is indeed terrible news and I can well understand your anger but let these…rebels tell us, all they know. You there, the other one, what is your name?"

"Gamelbearn, Sire."

"What have you to say for yourself?"

"Sire," he replied, in a soft northerne accent, "We are not rebels or ravening dogs. We're proud Northymbrians. We are not rising up against you, Sire. All this… this chaos, didn't happen overnight. We tried to negotiate, to put our case to Earl Tostig but it was always the same; he either turned a deaf ear or sent his men out to murder us."

"These are all lies," shouted Tostig.

"My Lord Tostig! Enough!" The King turned back to the Thegn. "Continue."

"Sire," Gamelbearn pleaded, "this rebellion was the only way left open to us, to stop his brutal attacks upon the people of Northymbria." He pointed at Earl Tostig. "He is a murderer and a tyrant! The people of Northymbria will not have him back! We have had ten years of his brutal rule, and enough is enough. He has lost the respect of the people!"

"How dare you tell me, you will *not* have him back! You are rebels!" shouted the King, "Gamelbearn, and you Glonieorn, son of Heardwulf are both rebels and deserve to be cut down where you stand, along with the rest of your rabble! You have risen up not only against your lawfully elected Earl but also against your King. If you had had any complaints, they should have been brought to the Witan and dealt with accordingly, not like this." The King began trembling. "This murder and chaos! You have brought disgrace on the people of Northymbria, and on the rebellious Mercians, who support you in your madness. Where is Earl Eadwyn of Mercia?"

"Not here, Sire," replied Archbishop Stigand. "He failed to come to this Witan. He is still in Northumtun with the rebels."

'What's up with the King?' thought Edwin, 'He knows Earl Eadwyn is in Northumtun. Why doesn't he…? he's forgotten every word of Earl Harold's report. His mind is going. Yes, I've seen it before, a man becoming confused with age.' He looked around the table, 'I don't see Harold's brothers saying much, in fact nothing at all, I wonder what Leofwine and Gyrth are thinking. Perhaps they're just content to sit and wait and listen like the others. Let's hope they see sense. I know what I would do.'

"Lord Tostig! What say you to all these serious charges laid against you!"

"Sire, since the death of Lord Siward, and I stress I do not wish to tarnish his name, but as everyone here knows, Northymbria had been a lawless land for many years. Taxes were the lowest in the country; the wealth was in the hands of local Thegns, in order to keep them happy no doubt. When I became Earl of Northymbria I found it impossible to raise an army from the local Thegns, to police the country, in order to maintain its freedom from crime. I had no choice but to employ foreign mercenaries, yes, Danisc mercenaries, and at some cost to myself. Now these rebels have undone all my good work. From a land of relative order, it has once again descended into chaos and barbarism!"

"Sire! That's a lie!" shouted Glonieorn, banging his fist on the table. "The barbarism is all Earl Tostig's doing; he and his paid savage mercenaries! We tried to put our case to him. We sent, Gamal and Orm to see him but he butchered them, in his own home! Their only crime was to complain! But he doesn't want to listen."

"Again Sire! These are all lies!" shouted Tostig.

"Sire," said the Bishop of Searoburh, "I would like to put a question to Lord Tostig."

"Ask your question my Lord Bishop."

"My Lord Tostig, *how* did these two thegns, Gamel and Orm, come to be killed?"

"They came to my apartments to put their case to me."

"Yes, Lord Tostig we understand that, but how come they were killed?"

"They demanded I reduce the land tax. When I said no, we got into an argument and when they drew their seaxes, I killed them!" Tostig looked around the table. "There was no other way, they attacked me. It was either me or them."

"They drew their knives you say and you killed them?" interrupted, Ealdred, Archbishop of Eoforwïc. "Two of them against just you or did you have your guards close by?"

"Sire! I'm being cross examined as if *I* were a criminal?"

"No, no, my Lord Tostig," answered the Archbishop "Sire, I just wanted to know, to have that particular point cleared up."

"When they saw I wouldn't give them what they wanted, they drew their weapons so I called my guards; and yes, my guards were close by, Sire. These rebels were sent into my home with hidden knives to kill me. It was the same with that other murdering pig, Gospatric Uhtredson at your Christmas court, in sixty-four, he also planned to kill me, Sire. My sister, your Queen will bear this out."

"Liar!" shouted Gamelbearn.

"Sire," pleaded Tostig, "surely we have heard enough from these two lying, murdering rebels."

"Remove these men," ordered the King, "and hold them under guard."

"Sire," said one of the other churchmen, putting up his hand to be noticed, "May I make a suggestion."

"My dear Archbishop of Lunden, speak."

"I think we should all spend a few moments in prayer, in order for our Lord Jesus to give us wisdom and strength in this confusion, and then confront these... rebels with open arms and love. Thereby they will see the error of their ways and seek God's peace, and the reinstatement of Lord Tostig."

A spell of silent disbelief and puzzlement descended on the room.

Tostig was the first to break the silence.

"Sire, this is war!" he shouted. "It's the only language they will understand! War! We'll raise a fyrd and crush the lot of them!"

"No! No!" replied Harold, "Sire, I made my report to you, and whether we like it or not, the north is in rebellion, against my brother Tostig…"

"Earl! Earl Tostig! I do have a title," screamed Tostig, glaring at his brother. "War, we have to make war on these rebels."

"I meant no offence, Earl Tostig! We are brothers! Both of us from the same beloved father and mother. I have always held you in high regard," said Harold, trying to pacify him. "Tosti, believe me, I saw their numbers and they are growing more numerous day by day. We are not dealing with a band of undisciplined, ragged rebels that we can put down easily. What I saw was an army. An army of hundreds, probably thousands by now. We can't have a war, it would tear the country apart. There has to be another way!"

"Sire! My brother has become weak as a woman! We must make war on them! Let them see our numbers from behind the royal, Dragon Standard. They will back down when they see the might of our King!"

"And if they don't back down? What then: a bloody civil war, suth against the north? I tell you, it would destroy the nation. We would be weakened militarily, unable to defend ourselves from enemies across the sæ. It would be a tragedy of unimaginable magnitude, far greater than the Roman invasion of our land, back in the distant past."

"Appeaser! Traitor!" growled Tostig, his voice becoming louder. "My brother… is… a… traitor! He gave me his word, he would make these rebels yield."

"I made you no promise other than I would do my best to make the rebels see sense. What they have done is illegal and is against the King and Cnut's laws."

"Rubbish! He is a traitor and has made a deal with his brother-in-law, Morkere, the ring leader of the rebels! You," he pointed towards Harold, "You were behind this rebellion from the very start!"

"This is madness!" answered Harold, thumping his fist on the table. "Sire! I swear it! I had no part in this rebellion. All I want is to see peace, not a bloody disastrous civil war."

"Sire! My brother! My own flesh and blood has turned against me, and his King!"

"Not true. I am always loyal," answered Harold.

"He lies! He's part of the rebellion!" retorted Tostig.

"I am innocent of all charges laid against me, by my brother, Earl Tostig."

"I am bound to say, Lord Harold, I accept your assurance that you had no part in this uprising."

"Thank you, Sire!"

"Now!" said the King, looking around the table, "What I have heard so far, leads me to only one conclusion and that is, we must make war on these rebels. They have violated our laws. They have rampaged and destroyed vast amounts of property, killed hundreds of innocent people, and have defied their Sovereign. If we do nothing, this realm of Englaland will be in chaos. My lords, I call on you to follow me and make war on these rebels?"

Harold shook his head and looked towards his other two brothers, as if pleading for their support. Their help for peace.

The only hand raised in answer to the King's call for war, was Tostig's.

"Clear the hall!" The King shouted, angrily pointing at all the Thegns lining the room. "Clear the hall of none essentials!"

'So, we are none essential. We are so none essential that the King wouldn't last more than a day without us Thegns,' Edwin moaned to himself, shuffling, with the rest, to the door, waiting outside the building with his sons.

"Dad... so, what happened?" asked Wulfnoth, looking briefly beyond their father, as the hall door slammed shut with a loud crash.

"Well," replied their father, momentarily hunching his shoulders, "it's bloody; things being said that shouldn't be said. We'll be lucky if we don't have a civil war on our hands!"

"Do you think it likely?" asked Edric who, admiring someone's plaited beard, had started to stroke the little bit of hair on his own chin.

"Who knows."

The noise of shouting and crashing from inside the hall had suddenly stopped. After a lull, the Archbishop and the other bishops emerged, followed by Earls Walthrolf, Leofwine and Gyrth and moments later Earl Harold, who beckoned Edwin to join him. Just then Earl Tostig thrust open the door and made for his brother Harold, grabbing him by the shoulders. He was about to reach for his seax, when he was stopped by Edwin.

"My lord Tostig, I think that would be very unwise if you want to live."

Shaking his arm free of Edwin, Tostig stepped back from his brother.

"You made a deal with Morkere. Your precious Morkere! His sister, whispering in your ear for favours was she? Or was it..., fucking jealously! You couldn't stand the thought of me spending so much time in the King's company. Edward loved me like a son, did you know that? Now you have turned him against me. Forced him to accept the rebel's demands, and ruined me, your brother, your own flesh and blood!"

"You're mad! I made no such deal with Morkere! But you should have listened to me. You should have seen this coming a long time ago; I was shocked at what I heard! Before you and the King slapped that land tax on them, you should have communicated with the people! You should have listen to them! Not butchered them into submission! Now they hate you. I tell you another thing, Tosti, without the people behind us, we're all nothing! At Northumtun I tried to make them accept you back. Not even the King in person could have done more. I even warned them we would to go to war, a civil war, which would destroy this country. They still said, no! Now I have to go back to Northumtun, with my tail between my legs, and give them what they want... unless of course, you would like to go in my place?"

Tostig sucked spittle within his mouth and spat it out at his brother.

"I've lost everything because of you! You promised me support. We could have gathered such a force, even the King of Norveg would have trembled before us. But no, you had to have your own way, like the coward you are! Now I have nothing but hatred for you!"

"Reconsider man! Reconsider!" pleaded Harold.

"Ballocks! After I've gathered together my family and our possessions, I shall leave this land. But be warned! I shall return and take revenge on the lot of you!"

Earl Harold and Edwin watched Tostig furiously kick his horse into action and ride away.

"Where do you think he will go now?" asked Edwin.

"To Flanders, to his father-in-law, Count Baldwin. Perhaps by then he will have calmed down and seen the sense in what we did, for all our sakes. Edwin, you and your sons get ready; we're about to stop a civil war."

After Morkere had been officially made Earl of Northymbria, though resentfully by the King, and indorsed by the Witan, the King's health began to fail. It was as if he had lost the will to live. Some thought Tostig had been like the son the King never had, which made Tostig's banishment by the Witan all the more painful for the him.

After an emotional farewell meeting with King Edward, Tostig had set sail from Dofra with his wife, two sons and a group of supporting warriors, bound for Flanders.

# CHAPTER XIX

*December, 1065*

- The King's Palace, West Minster -

The Christmas festivities were somewhat muted. Though King Edward did take part he had to be assisted and by the following afternoon, had retired to his chamber, feeling unwell. The court was not only gripped with uncertainty over the King's health but was rife with rumours.

Earl Harold was surprised therefore to see the King looking so well and walking in the palace gardens, assisted by his physician, Baldwin.

"My Lord Harold, are you here to gloat over the state of my health?" said the King.

"Sire, no such thing," answered Harold, noting that Baldwin had turned away in embarrassment at the King's hostility. "Like all your subjects, I am concerned for my King."

"Thank you. No need for your concern, I feel much better today. Have you heard from your dear brother, Earl Tostig?"

'What is he talking about? My brother is no longer an Earl.'

"My lord, regarding my brother, I am so sorry all this has come about."

"You should be!" replied the King, bending down to inspect a yellow flower.

"Sire. I still love Tostig. The Witan's decision to banish him, no matter how painful to both of us, was the only possible course, without going to war."

Harold thought to himself, 'I cannot tell him that I believe he duped my brother, making it look as if Tosti was the instigator of his own destruction. Besides the King is still unwell no matter how much he seems to have recovered today.'

"Are you trying to justify yourself to me," replied the King, trying to pull up a weed.

"I don't know… I suppose I am. It has left me irrevocably torn; Tosti believing I was behind his downfall. Yet how could I have supported a war that would have destroyed this country."

"Aaaah!"

"My Lord Harold," begged Baldwin, "help me get the King back to his chamber."

*5 January, 1066*
**- The King's chamber -**

Archbishop Stigand ushered Harold into a side room.

"My Lord Harold, I have terrible news. I have spoken to the King's physician and he is of the opinion the King will not last the day."

"And?" Harold replied.

"We must revive him… get him to make a will, because nothing has been settled as yet. Are you up for the job!"

"Up for what job? What do you mean exactly?"

Stigand stared straight at Harold.

"Come on man, stop playing games with me. You're the only one acceptable, the only one who could wear the Crown!"

"I couldn't," replied Harold, stunned by the Archbishop's suggestion. "What about Edgar? He's of the royal house of Cerdic."

"No," he replied. "That would only bring about chaos and I'll tell you why. As you well know, years ago, when Edward the Martyr was thirteen years of age, he was made King. He was young, inexperienced and weak, like our young Edgar. When his protector was away on campaign others influenced the young King's mind for their own ends, bringing about civil chaos and we don't want that"

"Leaving aside Edward's Northmandisc friends, who in the King's court would attempt to influence Edgar?"

"You'd be surprised, Harold. Especially now," answered the Archbishop.

"If I accept, what of those who would scurry over to Duke William, saying I had snatched the crown, when it had been promised to him."

"You were with the King just before his relapse," said the Archbishop. "Did he say anything to you, to indicate he wanted Duke William as his heir?"

"No," replied Harold.

"There you are then."

Harold came closer to the Archbishop.

"But I believe Edward made some sort of unsubstantiated promise to Duke William some years ago before he became King and also, as you well know, back in fifty-one when William came over. Then, of course, there was that business two years ago when I was coerced into taking that bloody pledge."

"Yes but everyone knows you were intimidated, and that makes it illegal," replied Stigand.

"Yes, but I still have doubts."

"Well, doubts or not Harold, let me tell you this, you have to act now, while there's still time. I've already briefed Archbishop Ealdred and he is more than willing to conduct the coronation ceremony."

"I see," replied Harold. "I know you, Archbishop, can't because you haven't received the pallium from the Pope but Ealdred has."

"Exactly."

"Archbishop, as I said, I cannot be seen making the first move. Tongues will wag and that will precipitate a war with Duke William, or even King Harald of Norvig and King Sweyn of Danemark!"

"Forget Sweyn. We don't know what the Norvegians are doing, or are about to do, but you know as well as I, William is already building his invasion fleet. And let me tell you plainly, none of us want that Northmandisc bastard as our King. So I suggest we stay close to Edward's side when his physician Baldwin and the steward fitzWimarch, wake him up and we'll go from there."

"Agreed," replied Harold, reluctantly.

"Sire," whispered Baldwin, shaking the King. "Your subjects are here and wish for you to be fully awake."

The King stirred, mumbling, "What do you want with me."

"Your subjects await you Sire; to wish you well," said Archbishop Stigand in a loud voice, intruding his great frame between Baldwin and the King.

King Edward blinked and moved a little trying to adjust himself into a comfortable position. Seeing his chance, fitzWimarch adjusted the King's head by adding another pillow.

The King blinked his eyes again and focused on the people around him.

"Where are my servants, my royal staff? I want them here!"

FitzWimarch beckoned Brihtric Meaw over. "Get everyone here, quickly man.

Edwin, taking the opportunity, followed Brihtric and the others into the King's chamber.

'I'll stay where I am, at the back. Ah, I can see the King, or just about, they are all crowding around his bed. Somebody is pushing me, can't help but move further in. I didn't expect to be in here. Looks as if they're giving the King his last rites. Difficult to see exactly. I wonder what Gwynedd is doing? I left her with Eadgyth at Earl Harold's place at Suthweca, she's probably getting grandiose ideas on how to furnish our manor. The trouble is, we don't have that sort of wealth. I didn't like the idea of leaving the boys outside. I shouldn't worry about them, they're more capable than I know. They'll probably go back to the Vintry. I didn't think much of the King's Christmas Day festivities, very formal. The banquet in the evening was alright, though I shouldn't have had so much mead." Edwin shut his eyes at the thought of it. 'That was powerful stuff. I don't mind having a few cupsful, now and then, but that evening and the following morning really got to me. Shit, I had one hell of a head, couldn't think or see straight for hours. I must be getting too old for this lark. I was wasted, I have never felt so bad in all my life, and to top it all, Gwynedd kicked me out of bed for snoring! And then said I stunk like a winery! It wasn't entirely my fault. I was trying to be sociable, that's all.'

The King was still for several moments gathering his thoughts. He looked down at his wife, who had his cold feet in her lap, trying to keep them warm by massaging them. He scanned the crowded room and was moved to see so many people crying.

"I ask you all, do not weep but pray to God for my soul. I know… I am aware that I have not much time left in this world but give me leave to go to him."

At that, the Queen broke down, weeping loudly, even her lady-in-waiting could not comfort her.

"Edyth! Please! You must not be in fear! By God's mercy I could get well again," he said, managing a slight smile. Clearing his throat he seemed to gather his strength.

"May God repay my wife for her loving and dutiful service."

The King, lifting his hand, took hold of Harold's arm firmly.

"My dear Harold, listen to me closely. I commend my Queen, your dear sister and all the kingdom to your protection. Do not take away from her any honour that I have granted her. Remember she is your Lady. Serve her faithfully and honour her as such for all the days of her life. Harold, my foreign vassals and servants, please look after them by giving them employment but for those who decline and wish to return home, give them safe conduct with all they have acquired in royal service."

By now the King had loosened his grip on Harold's arm and was tugging Harold's coat.

"Have my grave prepared in the Minster, in the place that will be shown you. When… and it will be soon, when my death comes, have it announced throughout the realm so that all the faithful can beseech almighty God to have mercy on me, a sinner."

Looking around him, he lifted his hands, gently touched those who were within reach and closed his eyes. "I am tired, so very tired…"

FitzWimarch and the King's physician were aside, out of hearing, in earnest conversation. Harold looked to where his two brothers were standing as they comforted their sister Edyth,

He turned to Archbishop Stigand.

"As a family we've had enough grief, one way and another. We must stay here. That's the least we can do for Edward, and our sister needs us. For her sake we should remain. And I don't want those Northmen fitzWimarch and Baldwin running to William with tales of usurpation of the Crown."

Folding his arms, looking straight at the Archbishop, he continued in a voice which could clearly be heard,

"I wasn't mistaken, was I? The King did offer me the Crown?"

"Most certainly, Lord Harold, he commended the Queen, your sister and all the kingdom to be under your protection."

Moving close to Archbishop Stigand, Harold whispered, "It's not quite the same thing is it, as asking me to be his heir?"

"My lord Harold, when his Majesty dies, which I feel will be very soon, we must call a special Witenagemot. I am certain that you will carry the support of the majority for your succession to the Crown."

"I don't doubt it. Nevertheless, I feel uneasy."

"Archbishop. Abbot Baldwin," called Earl Harold. "The King seems to be choking and is being sick!"

"Edward! My darling," wept Edyth, holding a cloth, trying to wipe spittle and vomit from her husband's mouth and chest. "What is it, what are you trying to say?"

The King was moving his head violently from side to side,

mumbling unintelligible words from the side of his mouth. His body suddenly arched, his mouth and eyes opened wide. Then he fell back and remained still.

The physician closed Edward's eyes and looked up at Harold. "The King is dead!"

The Vintry, on a wintery Friday night, was usually crowded but tonight the place was bursting at the seams. Outside, Lunden was freezing over. Sleet and globules of ice were raining down with such force men had no choice but to wear their helmets. It didn't stop the people braving the weather, wanting only to know the result of the Witan's vote.

"Who wants to be out in this stuff, Ed?" said Wulfnoth, shutting the door, pushing back his hood and shaking his cloak. "Look at my boots, covered in ice and muck. How can anyone live a decent life, ankle deep in this stuff?"

"We must be out of our minds, Wulf," replied Edric, "leaving our lovely home fire."

Pushing their way through the masses they grabbed a corner table just as it was being vacated. They sat and waited to be served.

Charging his way, in practiced fashion, through the crowded room was Alf, the owner.

"What'll yer 'ave boys?"

"A couple of jugs of your best mead, Alf," said Wulfnoth.

"So what's wrong with my wine, bought at great expense, not good enough for yer?"

"Too much French in it," laughed Edric.

"Ha fucking ha," replied Alf. "Here, what's the latest from your ol' man at the palace?"

"Not much. Apparently, it's the biggest Witan in years. Over sixty noble lords and bishops taking part. Other than that, haven't seen him all day," said Wulfnoth. "We were hoping you had some news, being this is the fount of all knowledge and leaked information."

"I don't know about that, young warriors," replied Alf, "'cos there ain't anyone 'ere who knows what's going on down the road. But last night… we 'ad some shifty, short back an' sides Frenchies in 'ere, trying to squeeze information out of us."

"What about," enquired Wulfnoth.

"About the Witan. Who they were going to vote for. So I says, I don't know, nobody knows. The Witan discuss it, then they vote on it. What they were really after, was info on the Godwin brothers, especially Harold."

"Seen them since?" said Wulfnoth.

"No, they knew I was on to them and they soon went… I'll have your drinks in a mo," he charged his way through to the other side of the room and disappeared, reappearing moments later. "There you are. Must dash."

From where they were sitting they could command the whole room. They looked at one another, supped their drinks and waited for their father.

There was a sudden draft of icy air as the door of the Vintry opened. Edwin pushed through the crowds, as others were doing, proclaiming, "The Witan has voted! Harold for King!"

"That's it then?" said Wulfnoth.

"Yes. There were four possible candidates. Harold, fifteen year-old Edgar, the Norwegian King and Duke the Bastard. The last two nobody wanted to consider. They had had enough of Vikings and Northmen. Quite a number, in fact wanted Edgar, and let's face it he has the strongest claim, being of the Cerdic bloodline and all, but the Witan thought he was too young. Bearing in mind the problems of the past with so called royal advisors, and the intensions of those from over the sæ, they unanimously chose Harold. Alf! Pour me a drink… make it a large one." Turning to the boys he said, "We need to have an early night, we have a big day tomorrow!"

On a raised dais in the centre of the main hall of the Palace, the prepared, aromatic body of King Edward, wrapped in woollen bindings, lay in state, with crown and sceptre.

His uncovered face had been slightly made up to look blushed. His pale, delicate fingered hands, partially obscured by his flowing white beard, had been positioned across his chest as though invoking some mystical power.

Archbishop Ealdred, after giving his blessing, signalled for the eight pallbearers to come forward. They lifted the King's, now shrouded body and placed it on the open bær, which had been covered with a richly embroidered pall. At a further signal the eight pallbearers, Earls Leofwine, Gyrth, Eadwyn, Morkere and Waltherof, with Robert fitzWimarch and Harold's thegn, Edwin, lifted the poles onto their shoulders and slowly, in step, carried the bær out of the palace. An acolyte walked on either side each ringing a bell. The procession, led by Archbishop Ealdred, walked the short distance to the newly consecrated West Minster. Following were clergymen, four of whom were choristers singing the anthem, Earl Harold, consoling his sister the Queen and behind them, a great crowd of mourners.

After the funeral service, the body of King Edward was completely wrapped in the pall and placed in a stone sarcophagus, which was then packed with an abundance of sweet smelling herbs. The pallbearers closed the sarcophagus and using the hide straps which had been placed under it, lowered it into the open pavement in front of the high altar. Then a large slab of paving was placed on top, sealing it.

Edwin, not having anything more to do, moved to the side of the Minster. He hadn't known the King personally and was now feeling somewhat guilty of the thoughts he had had about him and felt grieved to tears, seeing the emotional state the Queen was in.

After a lull of some time, Edwin noticed he had a new companion by his side. The Northman, Robert fitzWimarch.

"You are not an Earl or anyone of importance?" queried fitzWimarch, full of his own importance.

"I am a Thegn," replied Edwin, not wanting to volunteer too much information.

"Why were you a pallbearer if you are just a Thegn?"

"Because, I am a distant kinsman of the King," lied Edwin.

FitzWimarch came closer and whispered, "Really! Why weren't you one of the ones to be chosen by the Witan? Why didn't they choose Prince Edgar?"

"Because," Edwin whispered in reply, very quietly in fitzWimarch's ear, "Edgar is too young and I'm a bastard, born on the wrong side of the bed."

There was a pause in which Edwin's companion was taking time to think.

"I believe," said fitzWimarch, "the absence of Duke William is astonishing, downright insulting! He should have been invited. He should have been at the Witan. After all, he is the rightful heir. King Edward promised the crown to him you know and…" fitzWimarch came closer, "Earl Harold made a pledge to have Duke William crowned! What do you think of that?"

"I don't know anything about that, my friend, I keep out of politics."

"That's the trouble with you Englisc. There are too many primitive warriors, unsavoury churchmen and shopkeepers and not enough leaders championing civilised behaviour. Look what happened with Godwin's eldest son, Swegen, or whatever his name was, and what of the unsavoury character of Godwin himself?"

"Excuse me, my friend I can see my sons, it has been interesting talking to you." Edwin moved further away and out of sight of the Northman.

Gwynedd tapped Edwin on the shoulder.

"How did you find me?" he said.

"I looked for the tallest, most handsome man with wonderful braids."

"I don't know about the most handsome. Am I that noticeable?"

"Just a bit… they're starting," said Gwynedd, balancing on her tiptoes, trying to see above and around the other people.

"Can you see what's happening?" said Edwin.

"Yes… sort of... I can just about see Earl Harold, dressed in a red robe but I can't hear what's being said."

Edwin could see the Archbishop, flanked by the other bishops. They were singing an antiphon. Then they began the litany with Harold responding. He lost sight of Harold when he was prostrating himself before the altar.

The ceremony had previously been explained to Edwin especially the 'Third Ordo' an addition which Archbishop Ealdred had recently composed and which Edwin found bizarre and mystifying. Apparently this 'Third Ordo' caused the King to become 'divine'. God's representative on earth. He wondered what Harold made of it.

Now the Archbishop was announcing, in a loud voice, "Sirs, I present unto you, Harold, your undoubted King. Wherefore all of you, who have come here this day to do homage and service, are you willing to do so?"

A great shout from within the Minster went up.

"Long live the King! Long live the King! Long live the King!"

Facing the assembly, Harold declared aloud, the threefold promise.

"I solemnly swear to keep the peace."

"I solemnly swear to prohibit all rapaciousness and iniquities."

"I solemnly swear to maintain just laws as well as any King before me has done."

After these promises the Archbishop began anointing Harold, with scented holy oil, on his hands, his bared chest and lastly on his head.

"I can't quite see," Gwynedd whispered in Edwin's ear, "what's happening?"

"Our King has just been made divine," he whispered in reply. "I can understand Harold being made our King, no problem. But this new thing, making him God's representative on Earth? Divine? All because of being anointed with oil. The prostrating and the hymn singing?"

They looked at each other. Edwin drew a deep breath, shook his head, half smiling, and carried on watching in fascination.

By now, Harold was seated and had received the regalia of his office; Orb, floriated sceptre and as the Archbishop placed the crown on Harold's head, a great shout went up again.

"Long live the King! Long live the King! Long live the King!"

*May, 1066*
**- Upper Barnstæd -**

Seeing Edwin lying on the floor close to the fire, Gwynedd ask what he was doing there.

"I've been outside in the rain. I'm wet, have a pain in my back and am feeling bloody miserable and lying down is the only way I can think of to get dry and relieve my back at the same time," he replied.

"So what's wrong with your back?" asked Gwynedd.

"I don't know but it gives me a nasty twinge every time I try to lift something or bend down. Somebody once told me that lying on flat ground, keeps your back straight and lessens the tension."

"Well, why don't you go to bed?"

"Because I like to be here with you and the boys."

"Well I can't stand here all day talking, I have things to do."

"Can't you stay and talk a while?" said Edwin, feeling his clothes to see whether they were getting dry.

"All right," said Gwynedd, pulling up a chair.

"I've been lying here thinking."

She pulled a face, "That could be dangerous."

Edwin ignored the remark, "You know, I'm not so sure Harold should be King."

"Why do you say that?"

Edwin told her what he had overheard when he had gone to

Northmandig with the Bishop of Wintancæster to fetch Prince Edward home.

"Why haven't you told me that before?" asked Gwynedd. "Still, he wasn't married then, so how could he have made such a promise. He could have had any amount of children by now."

"What's more," Edwin said, "Brihtric, one of the King's stewards told me, when Edward was on his deathbed, he didn't actually offer the crown to Harold at all but said, 'I commend the Queen, and all the kingdom to your protection.' That is not making Harold his heir."

"If you're right," replied Gwynedd, "Edward's statement was somewhat ambiguous."

"Ambiguous… I like that. That sums Edward up. Anyway, it was the will of sixty lords of the Witan that Harold should be crowned. Nevertheless it does worry me. Now, from what I hear, Duke William is building an enormous fleet, and that can only confirm what we already fear…"

"You mean an invasion from Northmandig. What's that noise?" Gwynedd said, hurrying outside.

"Warning bell! An attack!" shouted Edwin after her. Getting up from the floor with some difficulty he struggled to put his clothes in order. "Can it be? Who would want to attack this village?"

"Yes, it's an attack." confirmed Gwynedd, returning.

"It's the first time I've heard that church bell ring a warning in all my years." Edwin grabbed his sword and shield. "Where are the boys?" he called as he left the hall.

"In the barn."

"Raiders! Raiders!" shouted Wulfnoth, running towards his father.

"Where's your brother?" answered Edwin.

"Getting his weapons together."

"This is no time to piss about, getting!" replied Edwin, "Gwynedd!"

She emerged from the house with sword and shield.

"Stay inside!" he ordered.

"Never!" She gave her husband one of her looks and held up her battle sword and shield. " I've been training for this for a long time. Do you expect me to sit at home knitting?"

"I've no time to argue," replied Edwin, running towards the church.

By now most of the villagers had joined them, falling in behind Edwin, Egbert and Henric. Edwin shook his head from side to side in disbelief on seeing Henric.

"Where did you spring from? Don't answer, we need every able-bodied person. Where's Edric?"

"Ready with some of the others, out of sight," replied Wulfnoth, "but keeping pace with us."

"So who was ringing the bell?"

As if in answer, the body of the priest crashed down in front of them from the bell tower.

"Shields!" shouted Edwin, turning to Egbert. "Does anyone know how many there are?"

"From here, I can only see the mast of one ship. There could be twenty to thirty raiders."

"Let's hope there are no more than that," replied Edwin, thinking of ways to flush out the Priest's killers from inside the church.

Several moments passed. Then there were shouts from the left side of the village. Edwin's men stood ready and waited in an arc.

A dozen raiders ran into the stræt in front of them, followed by Edric with a small band of villagers firing a salvo of arrows which the raiders struggled to fend off with their shields. One fell to the ground with an arrow in his throat.

Charging forward, Edwin's men struck into the rest who retreated into the church followed by another storm of arrows. The door slammed shut.

"That won't get them far," said Edwin.

"Easy," said Edric. "All we have to do is smoke 'em out."

"Are there any more?" asked Henric, wiping his blade.

"Don't think so," Edric replied.

"For a shipload of men, that doesn't seem enough," said Henric.

Edwin looked at him, "Let's send some lads to the barn for straw and smoke this lot out."

"You do that," said Henric. "I'll take Egbert and six lads and fire their ship."

"They've escaped," shouted a villager, suddenly appearing from the door of the church. "They've cut their way out through the rear wall!"

"So much for wattle and daub," grumbled Edwin. "I should have known they would do the unexpected. Let's get inside the church and make sure they've gone."

They only found one of the raiders. He had been seriously wounded. An arrow was poking out of the side of his chest. Propped up against the altar and hardly able to raise his sword he shouted, "Come and get me!"

Edwin threw the man to the ground and put his sword to his throat, demanding, "Who are you people?"

"We only came for supplies. We would have been gone before the priest rang that bell."

"You're not Viking, you're Englisc, Northymbrian by the sound of you?"

"You can't kill me, I'm one of Earl Tostig's men."

"How many of you are there?" demanded Edwin.

"Twenty. The rest are either on the ship or near it somewheres."

The ship was well ablaze by the time Edwin and the rest of the villagers reached the pier. Henric, Egbert and the others had boxed the raiders in, stopping them from breaking out into the surrounding countryside.

"Shields ready! Abrecaaan!" shouted Edwin.

The battle lasted only a short while. Edwin's men had left no survivors. The villagers threw the remaining sixteen bodies onto the burning ship, cut its mooring line and watching the ship float out to mid-stream and sink.

On their return to the village, Edwin came close to two bodies lying in front of the church one of them with an arrow through the neck. He leaned over him but unbeknown to Edwin the man was not dead. Still clutching his sword, he suddenly raised himself and made a swiping blow, catching Edwin in the abdomen.

Gwynedd caught Edwin in her arms, pulling him away from the attacker. The man had lost balance and had fallen back, onto his side. Then with a hideous look he regained his feet and as if in defiance of death itself, broke the arrow and pulled it out of his neck with his free hand. He gave Gwynedd a sickly leer, goading her to come nearer. Shaking with terror and hatred, Gwynedd raised her sword, came forward and in a double circular movement, brought it down hard on his blade, sending it clattering to the side, and again down severing his sword arm.

Strangely he never made a sound but she could see the pain and terror that was now in his eyes. As she stood over him she raised her sword once again, plunging it into his mouth and out through the back of his neck.

"That's put paid to you, whoever you were!"

"I would hate to get on the wrong side of you," laughed Henric, walking towards her.

"Who was he?"

"He was one of Tostig's men. That's why I came here. To warn you Tostig's fleet has been raiding all along the suth coast for supplies, pressing men into service. That ship was probably a straggler. How is Ed?"

Gwynedd began cleaning Edwin's wound, which was long and severe. The tip of the blade had only nicked his lower stomach but had cut deep into his upper left thigh.

"I'm done for." Edwin grimaced, as his wife finished sewing up the wounds.

"No you're not, so stop feeling sorry for yourself," she replied.

"Oh yes I am… I know it! Do you remember last month, when

we watched, night after night for a whole week, that bright shining star with a strange tail?"

Gwynedd nodded and squeezed his hands.

"Well, some people said it foretold doom for somebody and I reckon that somebody is me."

"Shut up and take another swig," she said, pouring him some more mead.

'I know he fears the worst, thought Gwynedd, 'and I do too because that wound is deep and has pierced the bone but thank goodness the blade didn't penetrate his stomach. She looked up after bandaging the wounds and saw he had drifted off into a drunken sleep.

"Rest my love," she whispered. "I've done my best and with any luck you won't be leaving me yet awhile. But there's one thing for sure, they'll be no more battling your enemies for now boyo, or for that matter, for a very long time. Now sleep awhile, sleep and let the wound heal."

# CHAPTER XX

*15 September, 1066*

**- The Vintry -**

Wulfnoth and Edric were seated outside, leaning their backs against the wall, their feet up on the table, supping their beer in the late morning sun.

"Osbert didn't stay very long," said Edric.

"He has a lot of work on. When he hasn't time for a drink, you know he's under pressure."

"Well," replied Edric, "I hope he doesn't forget to forge me a decent sword with the design I gave him. I have to say, it was good of him to offer me this one, at such short notice. I wonder where they're going to send us next." He was watching an elegant looking young woman, walking slowly on the opposite side of the stræt with an elderly couple who stumbled along next to her. "Poor ol' Thune and Kefrid, fancy them being stuck in Wihtland with the royal fleet, waiting for the Duke's lot." He continued to watch the girl who every now and then stooped to help the man he believed to be her father. They were soon lost in the crowds. "The thing is, will the Bastard Duke attack and if so, when?"

"What did you say?" replied Wulfnoth.

"Your mind is still back home and worried about Dad."

Wulfnoth nodded, "I am. One day he seemed to be getting better and the next… his spark, his energy seems to have gone. Mum is doing her best but it doesn't seem enough."

"And I feel responsible," replied Edric, forgetting the girl. "My arrow should have killed that sod outright. Instead, it only pierced the side of his neck. Now, Dad's wounded and we can't do sod all about it."

"It wasn't your fault."

"Who is that entering the Vintry? I think I've seen him before," said Edric.

The man had entered in a rush, his cloak flowing after him. A few moments later he reappeared, looking left and right until his eyes settled on Wulfnoth and Edric.

"Are you Edwin's boys?"

"Who wants to know?" asked Wulfnoth.

"Your King does, numb heads!"

"Who are you?" asked Edric, calmly supping his drink and ignoring the insult. "Have I seen you before?"

The man shook his head, "Not me you 'aven't."

He came close, close enough for Wulfnoth to notice through his unkempt dark hairy face, his pockmarked, leathery brown skin.

"My name's Horsa…" he whispered, "Captain Horsa to you. You two have been chosen, yes chosen, though I don't know why, to save your King and country." Coming even closer, he put his arms about their shoulders as to a huddled coven. " Tostig's allied himself with the Northmandisc Duke and the Norvegians."

"If you're going to tell us something, tell us something new," answered Wulfnoth.

"For your information," replied Horsa, tapping his nose, "The Norvegians have amassed an enormous fleet."

"How do you know that?" asked Wulfnoth.

"Because I've got friends over the other side and they tell me everything so you had better get your arses out of here and over to the palace fast, because Archbishop Stigand is urgently waiting for you!"

In a small room at the far end of the palace sat Archbishop Stigand at his desk; the only light, a large thick candle in its holder against the wall.

The Archbishop, looking up his face in half shadow, turned to his newly arrived visitors.

"Thank you captain Horsa, you may go." He peered at the boys as if inspecting a document. "Has Horsa told you anything about your mission?"

"Er, no, Your Grace," replied Wulfnoth.

"Then listen to me carefully. You have been chosen by the King to take this message, urgently, and I mean urgently to Tamaweord and deliver it in person to Earl Eadwyn of Mercia. Do you understand?"

"So far, Your Grace," replied Wulfnoth.

"Good." The Archbishop leant forward in his chair and spoke softly, with urgency in his voice.

"The Norvegian King, Harald Sigyrdssøn is about to attack the north. He has brought together over three hundred longships, far more than we had ever supposed. They are waiting to sail and join up with Tostig."

"Excuse me Your Grace," interrupted Edric, "Tostig? Can you be certain of this?"

The Archbishop raised his sparse looking eyebrows.

"Edric, great-grandson of Ædric Amlethussøn, I know *everything!* The King, in his wisdom, has chosen you two for this mission. So again I say, the Norvegians are about to attack the north of the country but have been held up because of the bad weather. Hopefully it will give our Earls in the north time to prepare. This is why your mission is so important. Ride to Tamaweord and give this message to Earl Eadwyn. He has been called upon to join with Earl Morkere and his Northymbrian troops to stop this attack. Is that understood?"

"Suppose the Earl is not there, Your Grace," said Wulfnoth.

Archbishop Stigand stood up. "Then you will have to find him, won't you and find him you must! It is imperative you hand this letter to him!"

"Yes, Your Grace," they replied.

"The fate of this land is in your hands. God speed."

*17 September, 1066*
**- Tamaweord, Mercia -**
Tamworth, Staffordshire

"The water is running fast and that's a rickety old brycg we've crossed," said Edric to his disinterested brother.

"Never mind that, let's find some shelter. The only part of me that is not soaked is my hair."

"Your hair and braids, are they all you care about?"

"No!" answered Wulfnoth. "We're soaked and I don't mind telling you my arse is sore, I'm hungry and I'm surprised our horses are still going."

As they rode along the muddy stræt through the centre of Tamaweord they were struck by the silence of the place. It was nearly empty of people, especially of young men.

"Excuse me," Wulfnoth called out to a group of women, "I'm looking for Earl Eadwyn. Could you tell me where he is?"

"The Earl's gone!" shouted back the tallest of the women.

"Gone where?"

"Up north to join up with Morkere to fight the Norvegians."

"When did they leave?"

"Day before yesterday."

Wulfnoth looked at his brother.

"Shit! The weather must have improved. So much for the Earl giving the Norvegians a surprise reception. Don't know about you Ed, I'm about to fall off this horse after two and a half days of pointless riding."

"Me too. Looks as though the Archbishop and Horsa didn't know as much they thought they did."

"So much for the early warning," replied Wulfnoth, patting the leather pannier.

"What shall we do now?" asked Edric.

"Rest the horses otherwise they'll die under us, have some food, find a place to put our heads down and make our way north in the morning. Just think, we could end up returning to King Harold with some good news."

*Evening, 20 September, 1066*
**- Suthwest of Fulford, Northymbria -**
Southwest of Fulford, Yorkshire

"Movement in the far distance," said Edric, pointing. "Look, down there, further along the road!"

"Difficult to see in this light," replied Wulfnoth, leaning forward. "Aah yes, I see what you mean but it's just a dark smudge. Let's keep going." They continued watching as if mesmerized by the silhouetted group which became more discernible as they neared.

Wulfnoth dismounted and led his horse off the road and into the trees on the edge of the forest.

"Where do you think you're off to?" said Edric, still keeping his eyes on the distant figures.

"Needs must, bro," returned Wulfnoth, disappearing from view.

"Oh, I see. And while you're squatting, you're leaving me to defend your naked arse. I'm wondering Wulf, why are we following Earl Eadwyn's troops when, it seems, he obviously knew all about the Norvegian's imminent attack, long before Horsa's warning?"

"We don't know he did. I reckon Morkere was surprised, panicked and shouted for help. Now, do you mind leaving me in peace for a moment or two?"

The group of men they had been watching were now closer. Wulfnoth and Edric remained off the road, among the trees and waited.

"After we've seen who it is, we still have to deliver the King's message. Anyway I want to have a look at the village where Dad came from," Wulfnoth said.

"You mean, Suthford?"

"Yes, that's the place! It's just east of here. Shouldn't be too difficult to find." Patting his horse, he whispered, "Quiet. They're here."

Thirty or so warriors, were hobbling along the road, four pulling a makeshift bær which had a familiar figure, half lying on it, shouting instructions.

"I know him. That's Hengist," said Wulfnoth, spurring his horse out of the trees in front of the group.

The men immediately took up defensive positions.

"We're friends," shouted Wulfnoth. "Is that Hengist on that bær?"

"What the hell happened to you lot?" asked Edric.

"Fucking Hardrada. A right name for 'im. Harald the 'ard Bastard. And the King's brother Tostig, was with 'im. That's what!"

"Ed, let's rest up and hear what they have to say."

"There were thousands of 'em," said Hengist. "At least six to every one of ours."

"I don't understand. Are you telling us you lot are all that's left of Eadwyn and Morkere's army?" queried Wulfnoth in amazement.

"Not exactly, what's left of us have split up into groups and escaped across the countryside."

Wulfnoth surveyed the injured and battle-scarred group.

"Here," said Hengist, "prop me up. Thanks. The Earl had an urgent call from Morkere and we rushed up north to join him. Didn't 'ave time to get a proper fyrd and full strength together."

"That's what we thought must have happened. What's wrong with you?" asked Edric, looking at the blood soaked blanket covering Hengist.

"That's what's fucking wrong!" swore Hengist, wincing with pain as he peeled the blanket away, revealing his left arm wrapped in bandages. "What are you two going to do now?" he asked.

"I'm going to see what we can do for you," said Wulfnoth.

"Why! Are you telling me you can fix this?"

"Yes. That is quite a wound," said Edric, watching his brother unwind the bandage. Hengist's arm had taken a severe blow and, from what Wulfnoth could see, a blade had nearly sheared off the skin below his elbow, leaving a flap of flesh that someone had put back into position.

"Did you have this wound cleaned?" enquired Wulfnoth.

Hengist nodded. "The physician we had got himself killed."

"I just hope for your sake, the blade didn't cut into the bone."

"It didn't."

"Good! Ed, get that twine and needle from my saddle bag."

"Well, that's the best I can do. Anything else while we're here?" said Wulfnoth, wiping the blood from his hands.

"Yes! My left leg," called a man, who had been watching them.

"Ed! We'll need a fire and an iron to fix this wound."

They had patched up the rest of the wounded as best they could by nightfall. By the light of a fire, Hengist told them the rest of what had happened at the battle.

"Earl Morkere had sent for help. Did you know Eadwyn and 'im were brothers?"

Wulfnoth and Edric nodded, "You already told us that," said Wulfnoth.

"Sorry, my head is muddled. Well, when we left Mercia there were about fifteen hundred of us, a third of whom were local levies, and by the time we met up with Morkere at Eoforwic I suppose, all in all, there were about five thousand of us. If we had had more time, we could have mobilised every able-bodied man in Mercia. Anyway, after spending the night outside the city, I tell yer it was quite a party." Hengist started to cough. When his coughing had subsided, he continued. "We made an early start before dawn 'cos we heard the Norvegians were on the move. We marched a few miles suth to a place called Fulfordegade. We had to stop Hardrada from getting to Eoforwic or anywhere else. So there we were, waiting for them, with this tidal bourne Germany Bæce, in full flood in front of us, stretching from the Ouse on our right, wending its way east through the marsh lands to our left.

"So where were Morkere's troops?" asked Wulfnoth.

"Oh, they were lined up to our right and on the other side of the main road and, like us, in front of the Bæce.

After about an hour the Norvegians arrived… there were thousands and thousands of 'em, all professional warriors! I know the levies can be good fighters and earlier today they proved it but they can't beat housecarls and that lot had at least three to our one! Somebody said they came in three hundred longships, well, all I can say is they must have been big fucking ships!"

Edric stirred the embers of the fire and threw on some more wood, watching the flames rear up in waves.

"There they were all along the other side of the Bæce shouting at us, banging their heavy round shields with swords and axe heads. As the floodwaters receded so they attacked. We pushed and carved and chopped 'em right back cross the Bæce," he continued with a grin. "I think Morkere's boys were doing alright as well until, out of nowhere, came hundreds of the sods, attacking our rear, to the left. They must have crossed the marshes on an ancient roadway and got around the back of us. There we were, lured over to the other side and now we had the Bæce behind us. We were almost encircled, fighting to get back to our original lines. That's when I caught this lot. I was downed by an arrow in the leg. Now that was a new one on me. I didn't know the Norvegians had any archers."

"It might have been one of Tostig's men," interrupted Edric.

"Whatever. So there was I on the ground when this bastard wields his fucking axe and slices my arm but I got 'im, clean in the stomach with my 'Eabæ'," he said, patting his battle sword. "I don't remember much else other than waking up some time later, being dragged along this road. Sebbi here, saved my life and got a crack on the head for his pains. Do you know what pisses me off?"

"What's that?" asked Wulfnoth.

"Being chopped by one of my own."

"Norvegian?"

"That's right. I was born and bred in Norveg."

"Tell us more," said Edric.

He shook his head, "You don't want to know."

"Well, so what! Our great grandfather was Norvegian," replied Edric.

"No he wasn't," interrupted Wulfnoth. "He was Danisc and his name was Amlethussøn.

"Still a Viking," Hengist joked, then winced in pain. "Anyway, join the family."

"Where are the others?" queried Wulfnoth.

"Some of those who got away are behind the city walls of Eoforwic, at least that's where we're told Morkere and Eadwyn are."

"We have to ride back to Lunden and tell the King."

"No need! Earl Eadwyn has already sent two riders to Lunden. Look Wulf," Hengist said. "Do me a favour… go to the battle field and see if you can find a mate of mine."

"What's his name?" asked Wulfnoth.

"Glonieorn. You might have seen 'im at the Witan last year."

"Aah yes. Didn't he speak against Tostig?" said Edric.

"Yer. If you find 'im and he's dead, not much you can do but if he's alive, do what you can for 'im or anyone else."

Wulfnoth nodded.

"I'm tired." Hengist pulled the blanket over himself. "And if you're gone before I wake up, thanks for everything."

*21 September, 1066*
## - Fulfordegade wælstow, Northymbria -
Fulford Gate battlefield, Yorkshire

"Look at this one," said Wulfnoth, feeling he was about to throw up, "his throat's cut. Shit! No! His head's almost hacked in half as well, look at the rest of 'im, butchered beyond belief. As far as I can see, he has at least dozen sword and axe wounds, it's a wonder his body is still hanging together in one piece."

"Whoever did this, did it with real hatred!" said Edric.

"No, no, this is not hatred," replied Wulfnoth.

"Not hatred? What is it then?"

Wulfnoth stood back and studied the body… "Retribution more likely! Look at his dress and armour. He's not your ordinary Thegn but a senior Northhymbrian. I bet this was the work of Tostig. Probably singled him out for special treatment! Hey, Ed what are you doing?"

"Searching him," replied Edric, "what do yer think I'm doing. I'm trying to find out who he is. What's this?" He took a piece of a parchment from the dead man's helmet which lay by his side. "It's a letter from his wife, her name is Hilda… I know who this is, it's that Northhymbrian, Gamelbearn who spoke at the Witan. I wouldn't have recognised him."

"Hang on, the one next to him, turn him over."

"I know *that* face," said Edric, "That's the other one, Glonieorn, Hengist's friend, remember? We rode with them from Northumtun."

"Wait a mo!" said Wulfnoth, putting his ear to Glonieorn's chest. "He's still alive!"

Wulfnoth began thinking about what they could do for him, at the same time scanning the battlefield and beyond to see whether the enemy were about. He started taking the man's body armour off.

"He was lucky, he only has a nasty gash in his side. Lucky to be alive. Tostig, or whoever it was, must have been disturbed, didn't finish him off."

"Here, I have some water for him," said Edric, handing his brother a leather bottle.

"I don't understand it."

"What don't you understand?"

"Why he's still unconscious," replied Wulfnoth. "He must have taken a blow to the head." He lifted the man's head. "Ah, no wonder." Wulfnoth's hands were covered in blood.

Edric held up a dented helmet he had found close by Glonieorn.

"He must have been poleaxed!"

"Let's get away from here to somewhere safer then we can fix him up," said Wulfnoth, taking a last look at the piles of dead bodies. "There must be over a thousand here and Glonieorn is the only one left alive."

"With all Dad's training, nothing could have prepared us for this and just think, we'll be in the thick of it as well as these poor bastards were when the King arrives," replied Edric. "Wulf, while it's still light, let's make one last effort to find anyone else alive."

Wulfnoth tried to imagine what it had been like just hours before, fighting with such ferocity. Looking again over the field of slaughter, he felt in himself a sense of insignificance and uselessness. 'To be cut down in the prime of life… is there any point to life at all?' he thought, noticing one particular body with a woman's scarf around his neck. 'Men, good men, ordinary men, men with wives and children, men of honour, young men, with hardly any hair on their faces, cut down and so mutilated, their mothers and wives would find it hard to recognise them.'

The day was drawing to a close and, as they continued to search among the piles of bodies, a movement on the road ahead alarmed them. Dark shapes of people were coming from the direction of Eoforwic, in search of their loved ones.

With Glonieorn lying unconscious on a makeshift bær, Wulfnoth and Edric started to move away from the carnage and were passed by a couple of women searching among the dead, when the older one of the two looked up.

"If you're taking him to Eoforwic, forget it. They've surrounded the city."

"We need to fix his wound, is there a forge nearby," said Wulfnoth.

The old woman came over and took one look at the man.

"Where did you find him?"

"Over there," replied Edric.

"Take us there," said the old woman.

Wulfnoth caught her by the arm, "Who exactly are you looking for?"

"Gamelbearn," she replied. "My son. I must see him."

Edric led her to the dead warrior.

"Don't look too closely," said Wulfnoth, hanging on to her.

Pulling herself away from Wulfnoth, she bent down, immediately recognising her son. Her screams were made worse when she tried to hold him.

"Aah! No! What have they done! My son!"

Wulfnoth and Edric stood back, allowing the two women to pour out their grief.

The old woman eventually looked up, while the younger one continued wailing, rocking backwards and forwards, cradling the bloody remains.

"He was her husband."

Wulfnoth gave her the letter he had found in Gamelbearn's helmet, and left the two women cradling the body.

Overtaken by the sheer grief the women had poured out, both Wulfnoth and Edric couldn't help themselves. They wept as they left. Eventually moving suth, away from the ground of horror, they followed the course of the Ouse.

"I think," said Edric, wiping his eyes with his sleeve, "I saw a forge before we came here, back along the road."

## - Suthford -

"Well, if this was where their bakery was," said Edric, clambering over what remained of an oven, "We're lucky to find it at all. Look!" He kicked at the brickwork. Part of the oven roof began to crumble and fall away. "Give or take another twelve months, it'll all be gone, leaving no more than a mole hill amongst the undergrowth to show where it was."

"Be careful where you're treading, Ed, that oven could collapse at any moment."

Edric stood, unsteadily, his arms outstretched to balance himself.

"Wulf."

"Yes."

Between our great-grandparents, Ædric Amlethussøn and Hildegard… who was the baker?"

"I think it was Ædric," replied Wulfnoth.

"So we had a Danisc baker in the family," Edric laughed. "Shit!" Some of the oven brickwork started to collapse again. Changing his foothold he looked down at the broken tiled floor, which was mostly hidden by roof debris and brambles where there would have been either a workroom or parlour. "This was a big building Wulf; it must have been quite important. I bet he was more than a baker, look!" He pointed. "That's a large area, that must have been a storeroom. They must have had a good business."

He carried on inspecting the ruin from his elevated but precarious position. New life had sprung up from the debris in the shape of an ash tree, its roots firmly entrenched underneath the broken flooring.

Jumping off the oven, Edric took his bow and pulled the string back as if he were about to shoot.

"Perhaps we'll have a chance to use these."

"Why not indeed," replied Wulfnoth. "I think we should leave this place soon."

Edric slung his bow over his shoulder, kicked at some blackened timber and called to his brother, "You can still see charred wood. What was it, thirty years ago when they left?"

"More than that," returned Wulfnoth, despondently.

The whole scene had taken over Wulfnoth's mind. Remembering what his father had told him about that night, he shut his eyes and tried to imagine the fire, the panic, Grandmother screaming for her youngest child lost somewhere amongst the flames, the raiders taking them prisoners bound and dragged towards their ships with the rest of the villagers. Then rescued by Mercian troops. And their escape across the marsh lands. Their trek to Lunden. 'How could our grandparents possibly live or want to live in an area like this, it is as flat as flat can be, bordering on marshlands. The flies and swarms of mosquitoes must have played havoc with them in the hot weather. Ah well,' he thought, 'each to their own, I suppose.' Wulfnoth continued to muse, trying to imagine what the village and his grandfather's bakery would have been like. He had a good imagination but even so, it was difficult to visualise among these crumbling ruins what the scene that night would have been. The place haunted him, forcing him to sit with tears in his eyes. He continued scanning the ruins, realising it was all reverting back to the natural landscape, and soon there would be no mark at all of their ancestry, no building to point to and say, 'Here was where our great-grand parents built their bakery, where Grandfather and Father were born. Now... Nothing.'

"If Hengist is correct," said Wulfnoth, taking a piece of the charred wood out of his bag and sniffing it, "the King would have gathered together his army and be on his way by now."

"What's that?"

"Part of a burnt doorpost, I guess it has seen better days," he replied.

"Wulf, I have never seen you as being the sentimental type but you are. You're an old sentimentalist."

"Sentimental or not, we should be seeing the King's army on this road soon."

"Let me see, where are we now?" said Edric, calculating where King Harold would be. "Well, by my reckoning, we should be approaching Ceaster. So, any time now."

As the road began to drop away, they could see a fair distance.

"Hey! What's that?" Edric said, pointing. "I told you so."

"That has to be the King and his army," exclaimed Wulfnoth. "Look! It stretches right back to the horizon."

"What a vision. It is not to be believed," replied Edric. "That is one big, big army."

"They don't seem to be moving very fast," replied Wulfnoth. "But it does look impressive. Let's hope the enemy haven't spotted them yet."

A lone rider left the main force and galloped towards them. Wulfnoth and Edric stopped and watched him approach. It was one of the King's outriders.

He scrutinised them. "Are you Wulfnoth and Edric?"

Wulfnoth pushed his hood back, "Yes."

"Come. The King wants to see you."

They spurred their horses and, on reaching the main force, stopped in front of King Harold.

"What kept you?" asked the King.

"Sire, Earl Eadwyn had already sent two riders informing you of the battle, so we went to rescue any that were injured at Fulfordegade."

"And what did you find?"

Wulfnoth and Edric gave the King a full account.

King Harold, turning in his saddle, looked back along the road and at the sky. Rubbing his chin he turned to his two brothers.

"We'll make camp here. You know the road," he said to Wulfnoth and Edric, "I want you to act as scouts."

"Yes, Sire," they replied.

Looking from one to the other, Harold continued, "We are going to surprise the enemy. I don't want you going off on any other enterprise. Hide your helmets and weapons… look ordinary, simple folk. Do what you have to do but I don't want the Norvegians finding out about us until it's too late and I have the Viking Hardrada in my sights. Is that clear?"

"Yes, Sire!"

"Find yourselves some food and water back there and then be gone."

## - An unexpected encounter near Tadas Caester -
Tadcaster, North Yorkshire

The brothers had ridden through Tadas Ceaster. Not a half a dozen miles further along the road towards Eoforwic, they came to a crossroads. There, sheltering under a tree on the edge of a wood with their packhorse, was a couple of indeterminate age, with a child. They appeared to be in some form of distress.

Casting their eyes over the countryside and seeing there was no sign of the enemy, the boys nudged their horses towards them.

"Have you ever seen a sadder or sorrier sight?" remarked Edric.

Wulfnoth had moved his horse closer in. The bedraggled man detached himself from his wife and child.

"Please don't harm us, we are not armed."

"We won't harm you," returned Wulfnoth. "Have you seen anything of the Viking army?"

The man just blinked as if he didn't know what he had been asked.

"You heard about a great battle a few days ago?" asked Wulfnoth.

The man nodded repeatedly, in a state of terror.

"Have you seen anything of the enemy soldiers?" Wulfnoth said again.

He nodded once more.

"Have you heard anything of Earls Eadwyn and Morkere?" queried Wulfnoth.

"I don't know for sure. I've heard stories."

"And they are?" enquired Edric, trying to be patient.

"Last we heard, they left Eoforwic a couple of days ago. Now the Norvegians occupy the city."

"Do you know where the bulk of the Viking army is?" said Edric.

"Somebody told me they were northeast of the city."

"Have you seen any more of them on the road?" asked Wulfnoth.

"Yes. We were robbed by 'em."

The boys dismounted and joined the man's family under the tree.

"Sir, I'm a tooth puller and physician. My wife and I were making our way to Featherstone but were stopped and robbed not one mile from here." He pointed back along the road towards Eoforwic. "There were two of them. One was a big feller, biggest I've ever seen and Norvegian by the sound of 'im. They were hiding in the last of a row of old ruined cottages to the left of road, over the hilltop, just beyond that wood. The big'n had a great sword and spear and was going to kill us. Edyth here threw a jar of lime at 'im but not before they had stolen our money belt. We barely escaped with our lives. We always carry two or three jars of lime for cauterizing wounds. As I said, if it wasn't for Edyth throwing that stuff into their faces, I don't know what would've happened."

The man had begun coughing, almost unable to catch his breath. His wife unpacked something from their saddlebag, came back to him, with the child in her arms, and passed him a phial of liquid to drink. After a few moments he stopped coughing, spat on the grass and continued.

"I must have breathed in some of that stuff. Anyway, as I said, the thieves took our money belt, all the money we had. We are now ruined! Those two villains may still be there," he said looking at the brothers, expectantly.

Glancing along the road, Wulfnoth knew what had to be done. He had decided in his own mind the best plan of action.

"We skirt around the wood and catch them from behind?"

Edric nodded in agreement. It was an easy decision. To the right of the road there were just open fields with no cover. Wulfnoth was the first to mount and taking hold of the reins, spurred his horse and rode off.

Edric leaning forward in the saddle, said in a cheery voice, "Stay where you are, we'll be back with your money." Following his brother, he leapt over a stream bordering the wood, eager for the chase.

Wulfnoth dismounted and secured his horse before approaching the cottages. Unsheathing his sword, he moved silently among the ruins, stopping momentarily from time to time, to listen.

A groan came from a tall building at one end of what had been a village. He judged it would have the best view of the road's sutherne approach. A horse, tied by the doorway, gave a snicker of alarm at seeing Wulfnoth. Cursing himself for being careless, he ducked out of sight. In an instant, leaping out from the shadow of the doorway, was the largest man he had ever seen. He waved his sword about his head as though he were clearing clouds from the dank air. Wulfnoth kept very still trying to calculate how to get the better of the man and his reach.

The huge warrior spotted him and, tilting his head back, bellowed in a foreign tongue, looking down at Wulfnoth as if he were some small prey to be played with. He began grinning from ear to ear, his hairy mouth appearing to split his lime blotched face in half. Though the makeshift patch covering his left eye impaired his sight, he was still dangerous and Wulfnoth felt a knot of apprehension. Taking the initiative he lunged forward only to be met by a clash of steel.

'Shit! quicker than I thought.'

At that moment a shining metal object whistled through the air and crashed into the man's forehead, embedding its lethal spikes between his eyes. Not missing a chance, Wulfnoth lunged, sliced his sword into the man's neck and, with some relief, watched him crumple to the ground.

"Where's the other one?" he called to his brother.

"Eating one of my arrows!" laughed Edric. "Got him straight in the mouth. By the way, here's the old couple's money belt."

"Well, that's that then... easy!" said Wulfnoth, sheathing his sword and rubbing his hands. "That should make them happy. Let's hope there's no more of those bastards hiding out in these ruins. By the way, what was that spiky thing you threw?"

"Something I picked up at Fulfordegade. It's called a caltrop. I thought it might come in useful."

"Oh yes," replied Wulfnoth, "I've heard about them. They've

been around for years but I've never seen or used one."

It was only a few miles to Eoforwic. Wulfnoth and Edric thought it wise to stay where they were and wait for Harold's army to arrive.

They returned the money belt then searched the rest of the buildings but they were empty. Edric went back to the other body and retrieved his arrow.

"Salvage all you can. That's what I say and anyway, it takes time to make these."

"We should have buried them," said Wulfnoth.

"Nar, let 'em rot."

"I wish we had because by tomorrow the stench will be too much for my sensitivity."

"Ha fucking ha," replied Edric, combing his fingers through his long hair and counting his arrows.

"Do you know what Earl Leofwine said to me before we left?" Wulfnoth said, looking at his brother's long shaggy locks.

"As I'm not a mind reader, you'd better tell me," replied Edric.

"He said, with long hair you either cut it off or plait it before a battle."

"Well I ain't going to look like a Northman at any price. Wulf, do yer have any string?"

"Yes… here."

"Tie this lot back for me will yer."

The weather was hot, made worse by the lack of wind. Knowing they could do nothing more, they lay back in comfort, in the shade of a wall and waited.

"Don't get too comfortable, or you'll be falling asleep as the King arrives."

"Piss off, Wulf. You don't have to worry about me… see to yourself. By the way, I've been thinking."

"Oh, yes? Am I going to like this?"

"Earl Eadwyn, like his brother Morkere, suffered severe losses against those Norvegians, right? And we're about to take them on now, without the northerne Earls. Look, I've been doing some calculations."

"What's your point, Ed?"

"Even if we're successful up here, what happens if Duke the Bastard lands in the suth?"

"From what I hear, the sæ is too rough for his fleet to cross so probably they won't invade till the calmer weather next spring," replied Wulfnoth.

"You don't know that for sure. The Norvegians crossed the Northerne Sæ and that gets a lot rougher than the Englisc Sæ, they say."

"It depends which direction the winds are blowing… I don't honestly know, Ed."

"As I said, we have in our army, by my reckoning, including the levies, twelve to fourteen thousand troops. Then if we defeat the Norvegians, which I'm sure we will, given the law of averages we should take at least two thousand casualties. If William should land, there will be a long march back down to Lunden, and then, wherever! By the time we attack him, even if we only suffer minimal casualties, we'll be half dead with exhaustion."

"Your casualties are based on what exactly?" said Wulfnoth, now feeling more than a little depressed.

"Based on what I heard some time ago when Father was discussing battle strategies with Egbert."

Wulfnoth raised his eyebrows, "And if the battle is lost?"

"Well," replied Edric, "in that case, you double or treble your casualties."

"Let's hope we win here and Duky can't make the crossing, otherwise we could be in deep shit."

"It was just a thought," replied Edric, untying his hair, combing it and, for the first time in Wulfnoth's memory, making a rough braid. "Satisfied?"

Wulfnoth nodded, "Not bad. What will you do with your beard?"

"Just leave it to me, you're not the only one with hair. Give it a few years and it will be good and long. A mirror. Look," said Edric, holding out a shiny piece of metal so that his brother could see his own reflexion.

"Where did you get it?" Wulfnoth asked.

"From the one I shot in the mouth. He had a whole bunch of stuff." Edric opened a bag and let the contents tumble out. "Here! Take yer pick, there's a comb in there somewhere. We have to look our best when the King arrives."

"Hey up Ed, they're coming!"

Meeting the column as the early dawn was breaking, Wulfnoth and Edric addressed the King, assuring him that there were now no enemy scouting parties in the vicinity.

Since well before dawn King Harold's army of fourteen thousand had been marching in order to relieve Eoforwic as soon as possible and to find the Norvegians.

When the city came into sight, King Harold sent forward mounted troops to cut off any Norvegians making their escape. News was brought back that the enemy were about seven miles further on, to the east of Eoforwic, at a place called Stoneford Brycg.

Stopping only briefly to ensure the freedom of the city, they carried on, through the wood, keeping the great Derva, a fast running bourne, below them to their right.

Wulfnoth looked at Edric. "Don't forget, we fight using our very own technique?"

Edric nodded, pointing, "What's left of Eadwyn and Morkere's lot have joined us."

Wulfnoth lent towards his brother. "Never mind that. We are not going to be part of those casualties you talked about, right? We're going to win and earn some glory."

As they emerged from the wood, they could see, slightly below them, a line of Norvegian troops marching by the side of the Derva in the direction of Eoforwic.

"Abrecaaaan!" came the command.

At the sight of the advancing Englisc, the Norvegian troops retreated back to the timbered brycg. In front of it, they formed a half circle line of defence.

Harold's mounted troops, having thrown their spears in their first attack, withdrew and dismounted. By this time the main bulk of his army had arrived. A detachment forming a shield wall moved forward to gain the brycg.

Wulfnoth, using his long reach, thrust his sword forward catching his opponents in the body and legs. Pulling back his sword he knew he had scored by its blooded blade and yet he had felt very little resistance to the blade's sharp point. The housecarl to his left, swung his axe down on enemy shields with devastating effect. They were now moving further forward, treading on bodies as they inched closer, with each blow and thrust, to the entrance of the brycg.

Suddenly, the Norvegians turned and ran across the brycg, leaving, standing alone in the middle of the brycg, a giant of a warrior. He was armed with a full head and facial helmet which had two slots to see out of, chain-mail, front of leg armour, shield and a great axe.

The narrow brycg allowed only two abreast and as fast as the giant warrior was attacked, so he cut them down. In no time at all, a pile of Englisc bodies was blocking the brycg.

"Ed! See our horn blower feller?"

"Yer."

"Take him to the left of the brycg and get him to make as much noise as possible."

"Why, where are you going?"

"I'm going to get under that brycg and stick a spear up that giant's arse."

Wulfnoth waded into the flowing bourne, up to his waist. He had spotted a wooden barrel and used it to float himself gently down to the brycg. He couldn't hear the battle horn, with all the screaming and shouting going on, but hoped his deviation plan was working. Once under the brycg and in position he could see daylight between the planking revealing the figure above.

"Shit!" he said to himself, "It's deeper than I thought."

Carefully treading water he found a large rock underfoot. Balancing against the flow of the bourne, he took aim, shoved his spear blade between the rotted planks and, with all his might, pushed the spear up managing to thrust it into the giant's left leg.

He smiled to himself as he heard the man roar in pain. He gave another thrust. The warrior collapsed to a huge cheer, followed by a surge of Englisc troops as they crossed the brycg, trampling over the body of the fallen giant. A moment later, the huge body was pushed over the side, splashing down next to Wulfnoth.

"Mind where you're dumping rubbish," he shouted, clawing his way up the banking. "You ungrateful bastards!"

Edric grabbed his hand and pulled him clear. "Did yer see us?"

"See what?" replied Wulfnoth.

"I was on the bankside, jumping up and down exposing my arse, while Osred here, was blowing his horn. And you saw nothing?"

"No, not a thing."

"Well, for your information, I drew that iron clad axeman's attention away to my arse, just so you could spike him. See… team work, and you didn't see my performance?" said Edric, incredulously.

"No! Not even a wink! Hey, we're being left behind, let's get across the brycg and get stuck in," said Wulfnoth, scrambling to his feet.

After crossing they tried to push their way forward.

"Fuck off! At the back you two," shouted someone.

"What do yer have to do to get to the front. Buy a ticket?" said Edric.

"This way," shouted Wulfnoth, punching a way through.

"'Ere! Where do yer think you're going," shouted another, as the twins crashed past him.

"To the front line!" Wulfnoth shouted back.

"Let them through!" ordered the King, spotting the disturbance in the ranks. "You two, stop giving me trouble. Get yourselves positioned there in the second rank."

They were drawn up in five columns, in a square formation. King Harold held the centre, Leofwine and Gyrth to his left and on the King's right wing were Eadwyn and Morkere.

Ahead were six to seven thousand Norvegians behind their shield-wall, spread out from left to right in one solid phalanx. Behind them were several rows of men, shouting, banging their shields and thrusting their swords and axes in the air. Amid all this spine chilling show of bravado, the Norvegian King's Black Raven banner, 'Landwaster' was held high.

"I haven't seen that banner before," said Edric, over the noise.

"It's meant to make us quake at the knees," said someone behind them.

"What a load of bollocks!" returned Edric. "Whoever's holding that bird banner, I'm going to have him and hang that banner on my wall."

"Yer, but you'll have to get it first," laughed Wulfnoth.

Harold raised his hand in greeting. The banging and shouting on both sides died away; the place became silent.

He walked forward. As he did so Sigurdssøn, the Norvegian King, the man known to all as Hardrada, and Tostig did the same, stopping equidistant from their respective lines.

For a moment, the three men looked at each other in silence.

"Enough blood has been spilled," said King Harold, breaking the silence. "Surrender now and I promise you, you can leave here in safety to sail back from wherever you came."

Not receiving any reply from the Norvegian King, other than a smirk, Harold addressed his renegade brother, Tostig, who had taken another step forward.

"Tosti, for the sake of the family. For peace. You and your men, come with me."

"What do I get in exchange," replied Tostig.

Harold answered, looking him steadily in the eye, "I'll reinstate you as Earl of Northymbria as long as you swear fealty to me as your legitimate King."

"What about Morkere and his brother Eadwyn, aren't you afraid of them starting a north suth war?"

"With what? You know as well I, their armies are a spent force," replied Harold.

"And what will be your gift to King Harald Sigurdssøn who, as opposed to you, has a legitimate claim to the Englisc throne."

"The Witan elected me King, and that's *Englisc* law."

"It won't do," replied Tostig bitterly, shaking his head. "It definitely won't do! The Norvegian King is a direct descendant of King Canute. That makes his claim legitimate!"

"Look behind you man! I've caught the lot of you by surprise. Most of your men are without their helmets, byrnies or heavy armour. You're outnumbered two to one. But you are still my brother! I am trying to save your fucking life!"

Tostig, turning became engaged in a long animated conversation with the Norvegian King.

"The King advises me," said Tostig, "for peace, if peace is what you want, he is prepared to accept the gift of the north-eastern part of Englaland; in other words, half of Northymbria."

Harold looked incredulously first at his brother then at Harald Sigurdssøn.

"What's wrong with him, can't he speak for himself?"

"I'm his spokesman," replied Tostig, "and I have to inform you, he has now changed his mind and is quite willing to accept your surrender. If you will give up your usurped crown and accept him as your sovereign lord."

"What! Have you lost your mind? I have double your army, still fully armed and equipped. Are you telling me your meagre, half-dressed force is a match for my army! You are insane! Open your eyes man!"

Tostig stood still and, for a moment, Harold could detect his brother's nervousness.

He gave the Norvegian King a quick glance.

"Your last chance, Tosti. Come with me, man. Please!"

Tostig slowly shook his head.

"Tell me then," said Harold, "does he take me for a fool? Look, I'm still willing to speak peace, if you will lay down your arms and return to your ships."

Tostig went to consult the Norvegian King. After a few moments he returned.

"We will not budge. Our original offer still stands. If you will give up the crown."

"Well tell him this," said Harold calmly, to his brother. "The Englisc crown he will never have; if he wants a piece of Englaland so very much, I'll willingly give him a piece of it. Let us say, six by two by five feet to lay in. No! Why should my gift be so modest," he looked the Norvegian up and down. "Due to his great size, I'll give him seven feet."

Turning promptly Harold marched back to the Englisc lines, angrily clenching his fists as he went.

"Abrecaaaan!" commanded Harold.

The crash of shields jarred every bone in their heavily muscled bodies as the leading housecarls charged, penetrating deep into the centre of the Norvegian shield wall in a Swinfolce formation, splitting up the enemy's front ranks.

"Change!"

Wulfnoth's rank came forward, taking up the pressure. With heels dug in they pushed, shoved and struck out.

"OUT! OUT! OUT! Came another command, producing an even greater surge of Englisc shields pushing forward.

"Watch it Wulf," shouted Edric, as an axe sought his brother's head, only for the handle to be chopped off mid-stroke.

Wulfnoth rammed his sword home, between the shields, withdrawing the blood covered blade as another axe went wild again. His sword sliced once more between the shields. They were moving forward, feet trampling over slippery bodies. The stench of guts was everywhere.

"Change!"

Wulfnoth's rank fell back as another rank took its place. Time and life meant nothing amid the shouting and the screaming; only the forward movement, the killing and the conquering.

Wulfnoth looked up briefly realising they had been fighting for at least three hours, judging by the sun.

Edric nudged his brother's elbow.

"That big bastard up there, he's mine." He took aim. "Shit! Someone's spiked him before me."

The Norvegian King held the arrow that was protruding out of his neck. He slowly slumped down out of sight. The crush became less as the enemy fell back. Edric let loose an arrow bringing down the banner holder. "That's mine!" he shouted.

Fighting became more intense, as they moved ever forward at an increasing rate; axes swinging down on bare heads and bodies, swords and spears slicing through unprotected flesh.

"Stoppian!" came a shout.

For Wulfnoth, the sudden halt in the fighting seemed unreal after so much slaughter. The silence seemed noisier than the battle.

"You! Wulfnoth, hold aloft our banner and follow me!" commanded King Harold.

The Englisc had advanced about fifty yards and were in close order with locked shields. Wulfnoth followed the King to within ten yards of the enemy, who were gathered around their Raven banner.

Limping out from behind their shieldwall, came Tostig, covered in blood.

"Tosti! Enough is enough!" called out Harold, to his brother. "Your leader is dead, I've slaughtered half of your army. Surrender now while you're still alive and go safely back to your ships."

"I can't!" replied Tostig.

"Why not?"

"For me, this is all or nothing. Eystein Orre is now our leader."

"Do you mean Olaf, the King's son?" asked Harold.

"Yes!" replied Tostig, struggling to breath.

"What is he, sixteen?" said Harold. "And what of those two Earls, Paul and Erlend Thorfinnsson from the Orkneys, do you want them to die in this blood bath?"

"Don't concern yourself with Olaf, or the others. I'm surprised you even know their names," retorted Tostig. "This is the end! You should have thought more about me, your own brother, when you had the chance. Instead you listened to that piece of shit, Morkere! If you ever get within my reach, I'll take you with me!" Tostig began raising his battle-axe.

"Tosti, Tosti, don't!" shouted Harold.

As Tostig brought his axe down, so Harold side stepped and swung his battle-sword, sending Tostig's head tumbling to the ground.

"Why? Tosti, why?" cried Harold, falling onto his knees, looking at his brother's lifeless body.

"Wulf! What the fuck happened?" said Edric.

Wulfnoth couldn't reply after what he had just witnessed... he didn't know what to say. The moment was unreal. He tried to understand how it could be. Harold had killed his own brother in the blink of an eye. Had Tostig committed an extraordinary form of suicide? With the Norvegian King gone, he had had nothing to live for.

Wulfnoth had heard that Tostig had been to see the Northmandisc Duke first before going to the Norvegian King. The plain fact was, Tostig had been a traitor who had lost the battle. Wulfnoth shook his head. He was exhausted and up to his elbows in blood from the killing; the unbelievable killing. This battle had been something else and he was finding it difficult to come to terms with what had happened.

"Wulf! Wulf, are you alright?"

"Yes," he replied slowly.

"Look over there! I swear the Norvegians have increased in number," said Edric.

"They've probably called up reserves from their ships or from wherever," Wulfnoth replied, hardly believing this was not yet over.

"By the looks of them, this lot are fully armed. Here! What are we waiting for?"

As if in answer, there was a call for action…

"Abrecaaaan!"

"OUT! OUT! OUT!" chanted the Englisc as they went forward.

Wulfnoth's shield took a bone crunching shock as the two sides clashed once again. Their shields locked together, heels dug in, he and the others pushed and shoved forward, dodging axe blades and swinging their own axes down into flesh and bone, thrusting swords into as many bodies as they could reach. He no longer thought of the slaughter they had witnessed at Fulfordegade. There was no time to think; think of anything, not even the carnage they were causing, only the cold, matter of fact shoving, shield against shield, wielding axes and thrusting swords, pushing the enemy back, back and back until they were no more.

"Healt!" came the King's command.

Edric had found his way back to the side of his brother. They were both leaning on their swords, covered in blood and gore, panting, ready to drop with exhaustion.

"This… has… been… a… slaughterhouse," gasped Wulfnoth. He waited before continuing. "This is not what I thought it would be."

"What and how did you think it would be?" replied Edric, still trying to catch his own breath.

"Dunno," said Wulfnoth. "It's… a meat grinder for sure. Look!" He held up his hands one at a time. "I can hardly hold my sword It's so fucking slippery with blood."

Edric nodded. "Same here," he looked towards a column of their men chasing a detachment of Norvegians. "Where are they running to?"

"I expect," replied Wulfnoth, "They're chasing them back to their ships to see what they can find."

"They're welcome to it… I'm all done in. I don't think I could lift my dick never mind anything else."

"Well, this is what we've been trained for. It's all in a day's work, I suppose," said Wulfnoth, "protecting our King and country. If there is a hell, we must have passed through it."

"It's over! They've surrendered!"

Wulfnoth and Edric looked at one another, cleared a space between the dead bodies and collapsed on the ground.

Edric, sitting upright, leaning forward on his shield with his sword stuck in the ground next to him, looked down towards the bourne.

"I just want to jump into that water, lay there and let it wash this shit from my body."

"You'll be lucky to find enough strength to stand up, never mind walking down there," said Wulfnoth, "unless I roll you down. We still have to lug our equipment over the bourne and back to base and pick up our horses. That is if they're still there." He looked up to check the sun's position. "Do you know, Ed, It's late afternoon and we've been battling all fucking day, I'm all done in."

Evening, 25 September, 1066<br>
- Eoforwic, Northymbria -<br>
York, Yorkshire

They rode, with the rest of the men in their squadron, back along the old roman road to Eoforwic.

"I'm right glad to see the walls of this place again," said Wulfnoth.

Out in front leading his army was King Harold, victor and saviour of the Englisc, on his grey warhorse the highly prized, part Percheron part Arab steed, which had been a gift from Duke William.

The King looked the part, tall and muscular, his blond hair

flowing in the light breeze. His brothers Leofwine and Gyrth and the two northerne Earls, Eadwyn and Morkere followed, riding next to a wagon carrying the bodies of Harold's brother Tostig, King Harald Sigyrdssøn and Eystein Orre, who were to be buried with honour at Eoforwic Minster.

They passed through the great creaking North Geat and into the city, scouring the cold faces lining the stræts.

"You would have thought these people would be cheering," said Edric, "and basking in the glow of sweet revenge, after what happened at Fulfordegade."

"I wouldn't make too much of it Ed,… these are mostly women who have lost their men folk, young and old. How would you react? Just because we won, doesn't bring their dead back to life."

"I'd give my axe for a mug of beer," said Edric, changing the subject, but his brother remained silent. Edric shifted his grip on the reins and winced as he felt the pain in his left arm. Wulfnoth, his face expressionless through his blood matted beard, just grunted and continued looking ahead, his mind elsewhere. He knew their victory was a hollow one, bought at a heavy price. This shadow of an army, which had marched with pride in such great numbers past the city, only hours before, was now in tatters.

Edric very gently prodded his tired horse forward to keep up with his brother and the rest, their shields slung at their backs. Still the crowds lining the route looked on and remained silent.

"It's such a shame these people have lost so many," said Edric.

"I'm wondering how many of them are, in fact, Norvegian and where their sympathies really lie?" Wulfnoth replied. "The sooner we get through here the better."

The day was drawing to a close and with the now grey sky no shadows were cast. Passing through the Suth Geat, a lush green meadow opened out before them where the Fosse and Ouse joined. Here they made camp for the night, sprawled along the side of the Foss. From the centre of the camp, two dragon pennants, the White Dragon of Englaland and the Gold of Wessex fluttering almost carelessly in the light breeze seemed to mock the day's human loss.

The following morning Harold and his brothers returned from the funeral held in Eoforwic Minster. Harold and his brothers were so affected by the loss of Tostig, they wished to be left alone in their grief.

Edric roused himself and looked out, holding back the tent flap. The morning mist had lifted but still left remnants of a carpet of sparkling dew. He shivered with cold and reached out for another fur skin, wincing with pain from the previous day's battle.

He could see a red headed girl going around the camp with a leg of ham on her shoulder. His eyes followed her as she stopped to cut slices of meat for the groups of soldiers who were beginning to rouse themselves from their sleep. With a quick movement of her left hand she caught a coin in payment.

Untangling himself from his shield and furs he felt the old longing in his body, his juices were beginning to flow again. Forgetting his injured left arm he made a sudden movement and regretted it; the pain stopped him in his tracks. Memory of the battle the previous day came flooding back. He had made a slicing swing with his sword when a Norvegian whacked him with a broken shaft, near paralysing his arm for the remainder of the battle. He hadn't mentioned it to his brother because it was his own fault, he had made a stupid move.

By now Wulfnoth was awake.

"What's wrong?" he said with sarcasm, hearing a groan from Edric. "Are you whinging about your arm?"

"How do you know about my arm?"

"I know everything," replied Wulfnoth.

The bruising damage, which seemed to cover most of Edric's arm, made Wulfnoth regret his remark.

Edric twirled his cloak away with his right hand, revealing the rest of the damage.

"It will soon heal," said Wulfnoth, playing down the alarm which his brother's injuries had aroused.

Edric began attempting to pull his chainmail off.

"It's no use Wulf," he said, wincing with pain. "I need your help."

Manoeuvring Edric's injured arm out of the metal ringed byrnie, Wulfnoth grabbed hold of the top of the garment, heaved it off and cast it to one side in a single swift movement. Edric cursed with pain.

Wulfnoth sat down, leaning up against a pile of weapons and began rubbing his eyes as if wiping cobwebs from his brain. Staring bleakly in the vague direction of his brother he took a deep breath and exhaled limply, thinking of the previous night when someone had offered him some wine from Wessex. Poison would have tasted better. It was the roughest drink he had ever had. He attempted to say something, but decided against any further mental or physical effort and remained still.

"You look rough," said Edric, "There's only one way to get you back to land of the living." He nodded playfully in the direction of the girl.

"You must be joking," Wulf replied, "I feel too tired, I couldn't raise a sword arm, never mind anything else."

"I've seen her face before. We know her! Isn't she… what's her name? Hilda! That's it Hilda. Remember that letter at Fulfordegade, the two women, one was the daughter, well that's her."

"Yes, I think you're right," replied Wulfnoth, turning away from the girl, "I'm hungry." They dug into their bags for some scraps of food gathered from among the pickings at Stoneford Brycg. After a short while, they fell into a further bout of troubled sleep.

"Wake up!" A man shook Wulfnoth. "Wake up!" He kicked Edric, "and you, yer bastard."

"Who the fuck… Glonieorn!" shouted Wulfnoth. "Well, as I live and breathe. I didn't expect to see you up and about so soon. Last time I saw you… was in that rundown forge, with Edric over there, pumping the bellows, and me sealing you up with a red hot poker…

"And you enjoyed every searing, fucking poke of that iron,"

laughed Glonieorn. "But it worked. It still gives me a lot of pain but I'll survive. Never really had time to thank you two."

"We did what we could, and any friend of Hengist is a friend of ours," said Edric, rubbing his eyes. "So, we finished at Stoneford Brycg what you at Fulfordegade had started."

"Bollocks! We took the brunt of them, all you had to do was mop up the rest of those bastards."

"What now for you?" asked Wulfnoth.

"Don't know… I was very close to Gamelbearn and his wife's family, now all the men in their family have been rubbed out."

"I saw her, his wife a little while ago," said Edric.

"You mean, Hilda?"

"Yes, she had a ham on her shoulder, feeding the troops."

"Where?" replied Glonieorn.

"Over there somewhere," said Edric pointing.

"If I don't see you again," he hesitated, "look after yourselves and tell Hengist… I'll see him soon."

Wulfnoth looked at his brother, "I think he's about to find himself a wife, don't you?"

"Mmm," he muttered.

# CHAPTER XXI

*30 September, 1066*

**- Bad news from the suth -**

It had been only five days since their victorious battle yet the exultation, if any, had already evaporated. Gone were the prospects of going home, glowing with success, with stories and plenty of good pickings.

The King's messenger from Lunden had put paid to all of that. He had arrived, bringing the dreaded news that the 'Bastard' Northmandisc Duke, with his armies, had landed and was invading and destroying the King's earldom of Wessex. William was threatening to take the crown of Englaland.

At sunrise the next morning, horns sounded for the army to break camp. Gathering together their possessions and weapons, they mounted their horses, ready to ride out.

Messengers were sent to all parts of the country, carrying orders to the shires commanding every Thegn and freeman to rally to the King in Lunden, for the great mobilisation against the Northmen.

As they made their way suth, every available cart was commandeered from the surrounding countryside, mounted housecarls harnessing their horses to them in an effort to carry as many foot soldiers as quickly as possible, using the ancient road network suth to Lunden.

As the troops passed by the bloody battlefield of Fulfordegarde each man made a sign, some a cross, and uttered a silent prayer for the dead. Wulfnoth and Edric were also moved, remembering when they had found Hengist's friend alive.

"Wilfred told me," said a voice behind, "Alf and his brother Darth and his three sons, fell here."

"They were good axe and bowmen," said another, who lived just north of Eoforwic.

Crossing the Humbre by ferry was a welcome relief. The horses, too tired to struggle, had allowed themselves to be herded onto some of the ships which had been abandoned by the retreating Norvegians. On one of the sand banks two more ships could be seen, stuck fast and deserted except for the dead bodies of soldiers who had tried to escape the slaughter.

"Somebody was sharp with a bow," said Edric, with a chuckle, "'cos they nearly made it."

Once landed on the other side of the Humbre, the army encamped and made preparations for a dawn start the following day.

The five days which followed were just one long painful memory for men and horses as, mile after weary mile, they made their way through the rugged countryside along the broken road suth. Some men fell by the wayside through physical exhaustion, others were pulled onto overloaded carts. But still the King rode on regardless; he was a man possessed, determined to reach Lunden, not only to rest his army but to raise an even greater army than before.

By the sixth day, they were on familiar territory.

"Just a few more miles to go and you can rest for a week," the King shouted.

To the right of the road, as they approached the capital in darkness, there could be heard the rushing, swirling waters of the flooded Walbrook. Then out of the blackness appeared the welcome sight of Lunden's Bishops Geat. The lantern above the geat burned like a beacon; a beacon of safety, welcoming the lost souls of the night.

"You two! Wulfnoth and Edric! You are the King's heralds!" Earl Gyrth thrust the King's banners into their hands and they rode forward. Guards appeared above the geat. Words of greeting were exchanged and after a few moments the huge doors swung open. The banners were taken from them; the King and his two brothers disappeared inside. Once the doors were closed, the army made camp outside the walls.

"What was that about? Why did we have to hold the banners?" exclaimed Edric.

"No idea!"

It was two hours after sunrise when Wulfnoth and Edric, leaving their horses outside, made their way through the open Bishops Geat. Pushing through the mass of people and leaping out of the path of horses and wagons, they arrived at the end of the stræt where the traffic was even heavier. Merchants were taking their goods, freshly loaded from the docks, towards the city geats and out into the countryside.

Turning right into Corn Hill they made their way along Tames Stræt until they came to the 'The Grape Vine'. There, as large as life was their old friend, Osbert the armourer, a boasting connoisseur of fine wines, leaning against the wall. The bench seat he was sitting on, though sagging under his weight, was tilted back onto two of its four legs, his feet resting upon a trestle table. He held a silver goblet, which seemed miniature in his oversized leathery hand. The goblet was the price paid for work done. He was sipping the wine, as he usually did, as if it were nectar from the Gods, which he assured every one within listening distance, it was. He looked contented, enjoying the morning sun and the bustle of the Saturday crowds. He was also an attentive listener and a great debater of things political. He waved in welcome to Wulfnoth and Edric, moving the weight of his body forward on the seat and his feet from the table and immediately ordered more wine.

"Just down from Eoforwic lads? I bet that was a battle and a half you lot got mixed up in."

"Yes, I suppose you could say that," Wulfnoth, said dryly.

Turning to Edric, Osbert continued, "I've got your sword ready. It's worked out just fine, with the rose motif running down both seams of the blade. A keener and stronger double edged blade you'll not find in the whole kingdom, just as you asked."

"I hope so," said Edric, "because that bloody thing you lent me, before we went north, was bending like a willow reed, every time I crossed a blade. I spent more time straightening it under my foot than battling with it."

"Liar," whispered Wulfnoth in Edric's ear.

"Well, you'll be all right now," said their friend, draping his big arm around Edric's shoulder.

They talked well into the morning and at mid-day, set off for Osbert's smithy.

Moving north, away from the Tames they passed through West Cheap, then turned left near the Jewry where they caught sight of small crowd of Jews leaving their Temple, their shawls covering their heads, hurrying along the stræt to their homes.

"Ain't they supposed to be rich, with bags of gold under their beds," said Edric, wiping his nose with the corner of his cloak.

"Nah," said Osbert, quickening his pace, "they're no richer or poorer than anyone else in this world and they don't drink the blood of kids either, a load of bollocks put out by the church." He guided them into Milk Stræt where they entered an alleyway and in no time at all were at the smithy. It was the only stone building amongst the surrounding timbered houses.

Opening the familiar, thick wooden door, he beckoned his friends in. Bending low, they entered into what at first, seemed a hot black emptiness. Edric and Wulfnoth stood still for a few moments so that their eyes could become accustomed to the darkness. Moving forward they could now see the interior of the armourer's workshop. It was a large room, the light source being four small arched windows built high up just below the roof beams. Three burning torches set at an angle in their metal holders, protruded from the walls.

The room always gave the illusion of being much larger than the actual building. At the far end of the room a great fire spitting forge dominated. The charcoal embers glowed red, throwing out an immense heat. The bellows were being pumped by an apprentice, a youth who was putting the finishing touches to a coat of chain mail with a reinforced chest piece.

"Your son?" asked Wulfnoth.

"No, although he could be," he said with a wink. "His name's Jon and despite his lean frame, is as strong as an ox."

"I see business is good, Os," said Edric, looking around the workshop in wonder. He never ceased to be amazed at the paraphernalia that hung and stood about him. Suspended from wooden beams above him, resembling rows of washing hanging out to dry, were newly wrought coats of mail.

Standing on the shelves were row upon row of helmets and on the floor, in a score of buckets of various sizes, were hundreds of arrow heads, lance heads and the fearsome, heavy caltraps, the size of a man's hand, a weapon shaped like a ball, covered in long spikes for piercing horses hooves.

"I used a weapon similar to this up north a little while ago," said Edric, feeling the weight of it.

"This is my version based on an old idea," said Oswald. "It's weighty so you can also throw it a fair distance."

All this was nothing, compared to the evocative smell of the workshop with its blaze of charcoal and the sound of hammer beating on glowing ironwork.

"Remember when you made this blade for me in sixty-four?" said Wulfnoth, unsheathing his sword and sniffing the air. "We came here with Dad."

"Yes I remember. How is your father?" asked Oswald, lifting a large sword and scabbard from a hook on the wall. "Here you are Edric and for God's sake don't lose it, especially to the fucking Northmen."

"Not well, he's still suffering from his wounds. Our village was attacked by Tostig's men."

"Talking about Tostig," enquired Oswald, "I hear he's dead,

topped by his brother, they tell me."

Wulfnoth glanced at Edric and then at their friend.

"You heard correctly. You could call it a form of suicide."

"How's that," replied Oswald.

"Tostig threatened Harold by raising his axe and taking a swing at him. Harold side stepped and struck him with his blade. Tostig was so slow with the swing… it seemed to me, he hadn't anything to live for. He had lost his earldom, turned traitor; make a deal with Duke William and then with that tall, mad Norvegian bastard, Hardrada."

"Sad times, sad times indeed," said Oswald.

"You heard anything more about the invasion in the suth?" asked Wulfnoth.

"Well I do hear a lot of talk. Hordes of Northmandisc horsemen, carrying a gold on red, Lion pennant, charging across Wessex, putting to the torch, towns and villages and doing their best I believe, to rape every female they come across."

Picking up one of the spiked iron caltraps, Edric felt the familiar weight of it in the palm of his hand and taking from his pocket a leather sling put the prickly weapon into its pouch, whirled the loaded sling above his head, took aim and hurled the projectile across the room with devastating accuracy, embedding it into the oaken door, with a loud thump.

Harold crossed Lunden Brycg, with his rested, rearmed, refreshed but depleted army of nine thousand men, the bulk of whom were levies. Men plucked from their homesteads, old retired fighting men brought back into action after seeing better days.

The King's appeal for fighting men from the shires, especially those in the west and from those left in Mercia and Northymbria, hadn't been responded to as he had hoped. Nevertheless, those who had come, marched with purpose, armed with their pitch forks, rusty old weapons and light armour. They showed no sign of fear, wanting only the blood of the Northmandisc invaders.

The massed column passed along the narrow road through

Suthweca, leaving the walled city of Lunden far behind. The road wound its way into the open countryside, through small coppices, which gave them little or no shelter from the driving rain now sweeping over the land. Manoeuvring their new kite shields against the wind for shelter, Wulfnoth and Edric pulled the hoods of their fur capes over their heads.

The King ordered a scouting party. Wulfnoth and Edric galloped forward and accepted the honour.

"Aah, my young warriors, my standard bearers who did so well for us in the north. Take care," said the King, "the Northmen are a different breed altogether. They will be on the watch for us with all manner of cunning. See to it, as you did at Stoneford Brycg, they get no sight of us."

The King waved his hand for their departure. They wheeled their mounts around and sped off in the direction of Hrofescester.

After riding for about four hours, Hrofescester, city of the Caesars', could be seen through the mist, silhouetted against the foreboding sky. The bourne took on a strangely blushed incandescence as it snaked its beckoning skin past the many turreted city walls, as if offering a fiery Viking farewell before flowing away to the far off Cent Sæ, which the locals called, Meduma and which divides Cent, east and west.

'I don't know why,' thought Wulfnoth, 'but the colour of that bourne disturbs me a little.'

Wulfnoth and Edric reduced their pace to a slow trot and, trying to look relaxed and none military, bared their heads, their long braided hair hanging disciplined in the wind, their long fur cloaks covering their shields, helmets and armour.

"Ed, I don't know about you but I have a feeling of unease. A nasty feeling, we're being followed."

"I know. I've felt it ever since we left the main force. How shall we deal with it?"

"Lead them by the nose," replied Wulfnoth with a grin. "Act

normal."

"You? Act normal? Impossible!" laughed Edric.

"Shut up. Anyway, we'll wait until we are past Hrofescester and are deep into the Weald, then we'll decide what to do."

"I'll tell you what Wulf, I don't know how many there are but if it's one or more, they're good. When we stopped a while back to let that family with the three kids pass, I had a good chance to look back but saw absolutely nothing. No riders. Nothing."

"The King did warn us. They were behind us all the time and not in front. If he is who we think he is, a Northmandisc scout, he already knows too much and that worries me. The trick is Ed, as he doesn't know we know, let him know we *don't* know and then we can lead him astray and let him get to know my 'Head Biter'," said Wulfnoth.

"Your what! That's what Dad calls his blade."

"Alright then, if it makes you feel better, I'll call my blade, 'Head Nibbler'," Wulfnoth returned.

"Whatever. Let's hope there is only one of them."

They could hear the cathedral noon bell toll, calling the Augustine brethren from their labours.

Feeling hungry they opened their saddlebags and looked for some scraps of food. Their provisions were meagre and after sharing out the portions of dry bread and cheese, they continued their slow journey, passing houses lying empty along the way.

The highway in the immediate vicinity of the city was busy. Swarms of people, families old and young, with their animals and carts loaded with their life's possessions, wound endlessly away; fleeing for their lives north before the anticipated Northmandisc hordes and their brutality.

The weather was beginning to close in again, reducing everything to a wet and muddy slime. Half turning in their saddles, they looked all about in the gloom.

"So many people!" Edric remarked. It seemed that the only people heading suth were themselves.

They had reached the outskirts of the wild Weald lands and there was still no sign of whoever was following them.

"I know he's there, Ed, and it's pissing me off because it's going against my instinct not to turn around and seek out the bastard."

"Steady on Wulf, it won't be too long. Let's settle it along that track."

There was a forester's track through the Weald. They rode until they came to a small clearing where they dismounted, covered their horses' eyes to calm them and separated to either side of the track. There they strung their bows and waited.

At last they heard the noise of a single horse.

"Arrêtez mon ami!" commanded Edric.

The rider spurred his horse to escape, only to fall with a cry to Edric's arrow.

"Gotcha!" he said, under his breath.

"Where did you learn to say that?" said Wulfnoth in surprise.

"There's a lot you don't know about me bro. Let's roll him over, take his hood off and see what have."

"Look out, Ed!" shouted his brother.

They scrambled aside just in time to take aim and fire at the passing horseman who had thundered in upon them.

Wulfnoth mounted his horse and gave chase.

"Oh deary, deary me," he laughed, bringing his horse to a stop. There in front of him, on the track, sprawled out and blooded was the other rider.

Wulfnoth turned around and smiled. He went up to a battered low branch and kissed it.

"Thank you my friend, you may have saved the day."

Pulling back the man's hood, he nodded. "Short back and sides!" he said to himself.

Satisfied the man was dead, he turned towards the direction the Northman's horse had galloped, shook his head and rode back to where he had left Edric.

"Shame I fancied one of those horses."

"Put it out of your mind, Wulf."

"It's just… their horses are so much better than ours. Faster and, I don't know, almost noble if you see what I mean."

"Well, we may find them later. In the meantime, let's rest up here, in case there are any more following us."

Wulfnoth tried to put the Northmandisc horses out of his mind but couldn't help being pissed off at not capturing them.

As before, they stood each side of the track, their bows at the ready.

After some time, no further riders approached. They waited for King Harold's army to arrive.

## - March to Hæstingas, Wessex -
### Hastings, East Sussex

Wulfnoth, leaned out of his saddle and chopped at another low branch, which was pulled clear by men on foot. They were forcing their way through the long, winding, neglected and overgrown track in the vast Weald Forest, which separated the North and Suth Downs. It was the shortest route between Lunden and the invaders base, at the port of Hæstingas.

"Edric, this axe blade is getting blunt. Do you have that stone in your saddlebag?"

"Ay, I'll look for it when we get clear of this lot," his brother replied.

Wulfnoth, putting his hand on the pommel of his saddle, turned around. Twenty-five yards behind them the King, riding his grey warhorse, his cloak tightly drawn around him, looked ahead impassively.

"Duck your head, Wulf," shouted his brother.

Wulfnoth gave a wry smile as he lowered his head to avoid an overhanging branch.

The blustery wind, which brushed their faces, warning them of the open downland ahead, brought mixed feelings. The Weald had meant safe sanctuary as opposed to the uncertainty and vulnerability of the open land before them.

In the late evening, King Harold and his army emerged from the Weald forest, ending their long march from Lunden. They made camp astride the Lunden road at a place known as the Hoary Apple Tree, situated on the downland ridge. Here the King had a commanding view of the open land below, which would expose the enemy to full view should the Northmen choose to attack.

Harold moved to the edge of the ridge, alone. Leaning forward he patted his horse's neck.

"Mmm, what of your old Normandisc master," he said softly. "Do you think we have surprised him?" The horse shook its head. "You think he knows?" The horse gave a big nod. "You understand my every word. I won't ask you whose head the crown should be on." He took a deep breath. "If William knows we're here, he'll be on the march before dawn and if he doesn't, we'll attack him at his base as dawn breaks. In any event I'll send those two eager young warriors out to scout before then."

Turning in his saddle, Harold called out, "Gyrth, Leo! This is what we'll do...."

Wulfnoth left his brother asleep, snoring under his shield, and climbed down into the valley, inspecting the ground immediately in front of the camp.

He felt restless, hoped and prayed that the Northmen were unaware of their presence.

'I'm sure those scouts knew of our movements as soon as we crossed Lunden Brycge,' he thought. 'Fortunately we were ahead of them but there may have been others and they could have been in front of us. That could be another thing entirely. Let's hope there weren't and that William doesn't know we're here!'

He remembered his father saying, "Whenever you pitch camp, inspect the lie of the land. See where the enemy can best strike at you."

Although the ground sloped away, it did not fall away steeply. He climbed further down the hill and looked back towards the ridge above.

'A position like this'll need a lot of defending. A steeper drop would've been more to my liking.'

The Santlache stream ran along the bottom and he found himself stepping into a bog. Swearing in the half-light, he pulled himself free from the mud and scraped his boots clean in the long grass. Sensing something to his right, he drew his sword. Someone had been watching him not twenty feet away.

On a nearby hillock was King Harold, standing alone.

"Put your sword away young Wulfnoth," said the King, moving towards him. "What are you doing down there?"

Wulfnoth explained his father's advice, to always survey the land after pitching camp.

"I see your father has taught you well. Now get some sleep my young warrior. We march on Hæstingas at first light and we'll need all your strength."

He watched his King disappear into the shadows, then climbed back up the ridge to Edric, who was now awake.

"I just spoke to the King," Wulfnoth whispered to his brother. "He says we march tomorrow but I can't see us moving anywhere if we don't have the rest of our troops."

Edric waved a hand, "Get your head down Wulf. You worry and think too much." He shut his eyes and turned over.

When the alarm came that morning, Wulfnoth and Edric had only to slip on their armour and seize their weapons before presenting themselves to the King.

King Harold appeared from his tent buckling up his sword belt. He was met by Gyrth and Leofwine.

"Have you had word from Morkere or Eadwyn?"

"No, nothing," replied Leofwine.

"And you, Gyrth?"

"No. The only arrivals from the north have been a hundred or so militiamen."

"And what of our numbers?"

"Approximately nine thousand. Two thousand housecarls, twenty five local archers and one crossbowman. The rest are militia from all over, who are swelling our ranks even as we speak."

"I expected Morkere and Eadwyn to be here," said the King, rubbing his head. He looked towards the suth. Drawing his sword, he began marking out the ground with its tip.

"I've just had word from a local thegn, William's on the move. Clearly the element of surprise is not with us." He thrust the weapon hard into the ground, the sword quivering as if to emphasise his statement. "We'll make our stand here and defend this ridge. I'll stop the 'Bastard' in his tracks. The Housecarls will take up the usual shield wall formation, to exhaust and wear down his troops. Then we attack on my signal, driving him back as we did the Norvegians at Stoneford Brycge. Gyrth, you take the left flank, Leo, the right. I'll be in the centre. Any questions?"

King Harold's shield wall of Housecarls spanned some eight hundred yards, just below the summit, left and right. Crowded in behind and twelve ranks deep were the nine thousand troops armed with swords, spears, axes and clubs. Among them were a sprinkling of newly arrived bowmen. They waited in formation covering the ridge, watching for the Northmen. The silence was broken only by the stiffening wind, rustling through the trees of the Weald behind them.

Downland animals scrambled around unconcernedly, looking for food. Birds sang their ritual songs before departing from the Englisc shores on their migration suth to warmer lands. Then in the distance the glitter of Northmandisc armour shimmered in the sunlight, like thousands of flickering fireflies cascading down the hillside, flooding across the valley floor in three great winding columns.

The Englisc looked on as the slowly advancing Northmandisc war machine came to a stop, four arrow shots from Harold's front line of shields.

Duke William, adorned with sacred objects about his neck, the Papal and the Lion pennants held aloft, rode up and down in front of his troops inciting them to fight with valour. Then, at a wave of his sword, the Northmandisc war horns sounded the attack.

The End

Books in the Bellême series:

**Book two; 'BELLÊME The Norman Warrior'**
*This book continues with,
'The Battle of Hastings' and the life
of the Norman baron, Robert de Bellême
a titan of his age.*

**Book three; 'NEMESIS In Pursuit of Justice'**
*Isabella the renegade, bastard daughter
of King Henry 1st and
second wife to Robert de Bellême
seeks justice for her husband and
the safety of her children.*

These books available in paperback and digital Kindle editions from Amazon websites worldwide.

Printed in Poland
by Amazon Fulfillment
Poland Sp. z o.o., Wrocław